THE WITHERED ROOT

PARTHIAN

LIBRARY OF WALES

Rhys Davies (1901–1978) was one of the most prolific and unusual writers to emerge from the Welsh industrial valleys in the twentieth century. Born in Clydach Vale, a tributary valley of the Rhondda arising from Tonypandy, he was the fourth child of a small grocer and an uncertified schoolteacher. He spurned conventional education and left the valley, which was to be the basis of much of his work, at the age of nineteen, settling in London, which was to remain his base until he died.

Early in his literary career, he travelled to the south of France where he was befriended by D. H. Lawrence, who remained an influence in his writing. Though sex remained, for Davies, the primary determinant of human relations, he differed radically from Lawrence in that he saw the struggle for power rather than love, either sexual or emotional, as the crucial factor.

Though the bulk of his work was in the novel he achieved his greatest distinction in the field of the short story. Having few predecessors, Welsh or English, he drew his inspiration and models from continental European and Russian masters; Chekhov and Maupassant, Tolstoy and Flaubert. His view of humanity was Classical in that he saw people as being identically motivated whether in biblical Israel, Ancient Greece or the Rhondda valley. Much of his output was concerned with women, who would almost invariably emerge triumphant from any conflict.

He was a gay man at a time when it was difficult to live openly with his sexuality. He lived alone for most of his life and avoided relationships which seemed to betoken commitment on his part. His closest friendships were with women. He avoided literary coteries and groups, though he might have joined several, and held no discernible religious or political convictions. He lived, to an intense degree, for his art.

THE WITHERED ROOT

RHYS DAVIES

PARTHIAN

LIBRARY OF WALES

Parthian
The Old Surgery
Napier Street
Cardigan
SA43 1ED
www.parthianbooks.co.uk

The Library of Wales is a Welsh Assembly Government initiative
which highlights and celebrates Wales' literary heritage in the
English language.

The publisher acknowledges the financial support of the Welsh
Books Council

The Library of Wales publishing project is based at
Trinity College, Carmarthen, SA31 3EP
www.libraryofwales.org

Series Editor: Dai Smith

First published in 1927
© Rhys Davies Trust
Library of Wales edition published 2007
Foreword © Lewis Davies
Author biography by David Callard
Author picture courtesy of the Rhys Davies Trust
All Rights Reserved

ISBN 978-1-905762-47-7
Cover painting *Pilgrim* by Tony Goble
Cover design by Lucy Llewellyn

Typeset by logodædaly
Printed and bound by Gwasg Gomer, Llandysul, Wales

British Library Cataloguing in Publication Data

A cataloguing record for this book is available from the British
Library.

LIBRARY OF WALES

FOREWORD

It is early February. A blue cold sky but out of the wind the sun is warm. There is a promise in it – of almond flowers and cypresses. Rhys Davies knew he was living a dream when he caught the night train from Gare d'Austerlitz to Marseille in the autumn of 1927. His first novel was a success. It had been published, reviewed, talked about and bought. In the tight literary coterie of London he was a young man to watch. On the slim royalties of the first and an ambitious advance on a second from a group of Oxford graduates trying to start a publishing company he found he had enough to live on for a winter. He had created a currency out of his youth – the Rhondda was beginning to pay.

The Withered Root had put a young man, living with only his ideas and some ambition on the road to a life of writing.

It is a novel of its time. The story of the last great Welsh Revival – a religious thrust of feeling – chapels and coal mines, righteous fervour and fertile, febrile carousal which swept across Wales in the year of the Lord 1904. The Revival was led by a Calvinistic lay preacher Evan Roberts who in *The Withered Root* becomes Reuben Daniel but both share the characteristics of being young, charismatic, Welsh-speaking colliers.

Reuben is a man absorbed – driven – to expound the gospel, seek out the devil, wherever or whoever that may be from the land in a pilgrimage of conversion. He is a young man full of life and its desires but still unsure of its meaning. He progresses from village pulpit at the head of a small band of followers called the Corinthians to Valley's saviour, and beyond in a few hectic months of sermons, pilgrimage and passion.

Rhys Davies didn't make the classic mistake of putting everything of his life into a first novel. Reuben Daniel is a fully formed character based on the true story of the last great revival but he is used by Davies to explore the tensions of a spiritual and physical life in the Valleys.

Beginning in a valleys' town, depicted as a den of iniquity in the classic mode of Victorian moral outrage, the revival takes the lives and souls of the valley as a battleground – pubs serving miners and chapels serving miners, with strays between both heightening the tension – drink was a way out – temperance another passion. The revival spread quickly reaching communities in north Wales and Liverpool but within a year the fever had passed and its architect Reuben Daniels, wrecked by the stresses, mentally and physically exhausted, withdraws from public and chapel life.

By the time Rhys Davies was writing *The Withered Root* – in the mid 1920s – he had already escaped to a smoky London paved with stories. An escape from an education he had grown out of. The regime of school at Porth County had held little attraction for him. It was a long walk and a bus journey away. He usually arrived soaked from the rain. He simply gave up on formal education at seventeen and it too seemed easily to let go of him.

Rhys was an outsider then and he knew it. An observer of life – a mystery to his father but indulged by his mother and sisters – loving this strange, reserved older brother. In his memoir *Print of a Hare's Foot*, Rhys Davies recalls offering to visit the corpse of a recently killed school acquaintance who was laid out in the best front room before burial – a popular custom in a valley always looking for diversions.

He was an astute chronicler of the Rhondda that he had left and would periodically return to in the hard years of the Twenties when funds from his writing ran from a trickle to a drought.

It was a world he would return to in his fiction all his life, with over forty books published including essays, novels and short stories. He did use London and the south of France as settings for his fiction but it was the Rhondda which continued to fascinate him and which became the setting for much of his best work. It was a place he had only really lived in as a boy and young man and he knew it could be a restrictive place to someone who was at heart an outsider. He knew he could get sent to prison for being part of what he was. To be a gay man in 1920s Rhondda was not easy but London offered an escape. Rhys was fortunate enough to make a way out, becoming part of the Welsh diaspora in London in the first decades of the twentieth century. He supported himself with a string of odd menial jobs, while observing and writing, and he found early success with a string of short stories in small magazines. He was fortunate to meet the Soho bookseller and publisher Charles Lahr who encouraged his work and even helped him to type the manuscript of *The Withered Root*.

Rhys Davies was strongly influenced by the major writer of his time – D. H. Lawrence – with whom he shared a mining background. They also both had mothers who had been teachers and who had harboured intellectual aspirations for their sons. Lawrence seeps into *The Withered Root* in the form of the hero, the descriptions of striving for a life in the blood and the search for something beyond the industrial capitalist society enveloping them.

Although searching for a fusion of the spiritual and the physical – the sex is missing from *The Withered Root* – Rhys shies away from any physical descriptions, content to talk on the margins of frustration which were perhaps his experience of being a young man in the Rhondda. Sex of the mind.

But London gave him more freedom and by the time he had enough money to embark on the second step of escape into the warm winter of the Cote d'Azur – the *cambio* was good to English pounds – he is already anticipating further freedoms which he chronicled in his playful memoir *Print of a Hare's Foot*. A freedom of catching crabs in the brothels of Marseille and living with a new manuscript and new lovers.

It was at Nice that a letter arrived from D. H. Lawrence, who was also wintering on the Cote d'Azur. Lawrence had read *The Withered Root* and enjoyed it. He saw the disciple in Rhys and always wanting guests to help smooth the passage of his marriage he invited Rhys to stay with him. 'Would you care to come here and be my guest at this small and inexpensive hotel for a few days? Bandol is on the Marseille side of Toulon. My wife and I would both be pleased if you come.' Rhys caught the train.

It is raining heavily now. A news stand offers *La Provence* across a street running with water. I listen to music in a bar of words and smoke while watching the street above the

Vieux port. A couple of men talk across a table, eyes flirting with each other, blowing smoke and words into the air. Bandol is only a short train journey east. Nice a bit further on.

Lewis Davies

THE WITHERED ROOT

RHYS DAVIES

BOOK ONE

CHAPTER I

Hugh Daniels at last got married, and immediately after the ceremony in Pisgah Chapel, Martha and he settled down to life in the little cottage that was part of Martha's legacy from her deceased father – a dwelling in one of those naked rows, chiefly occupied by colliers, that rise, shrouded in grey coal-dust, on the Valley hills.

At this time the Valley was a community to itself, its squat rock-crowned hills imprisoned hardly any but the native Welsh, and in their bleak isolation the people lived their lives with all the primitive force of the Welsh – a natural life of toil, lust, and worship. Existence was not yet vitiated; the schools were disliked; each man worked long without question, and each woman lived to fulfil, without quavers, the function of her sex. The men obeyed the ancient law of the labourer, and the pits gave forth coal rhythmically and generously; the women nurtured their children in the old bare way. These people toiled and died and the world knew little of them. Only in Heaven could be realized the complete bliss they sometimes dreamed of, a Heaven that was to be an everlasting eisteddfod – all singing and recitals and organ-playing. Pieces of earth, they sank back into the earth in that hope.

Hugh had lived in the same part of the Valley all his life; he had been a collier there, and his brothers, colliers also, were scattered in various parts of its mine-torn ramifications. He knew no other place, he had never once ventured over the hills: the local pits, the public-houses and the chapels were a satisfactory world – all beyond was an alien unknown that he had no desire to penetrate. One of the old colliers – reared so satisfactorily – unknown to rancour or despair, satisfied with his day in the earth's interior, to be followed, according to his temper, with a booze in the pub, or a little meeting in the chapel.

He was forty when he married Martha. He had been almost content with his state, a bachelor, having the chapel for wife and beer for servant, and perhaps he would never have really troubled himself about marriage had not Martha herself proposed to him, revealing also her fortune of two hundred pounds, beside the long lease of her home. Martha was thirty and had kept a widowed father going until a fall of roof in the pit killed him. Then she began to look around with increased energy for a husband, buying herself new clothes and perfumes and cultivating attractive manners as she went about. She met Hugh one gloomy night as he was returning, almost drunk, to his lodgings. In a little lane that runs between two rows of cottages, where there are a few rickety, blackened trees and, at night, always clasped couples. When Martha and Hugh emerged from the lane they were holding each other's hand and laughing together.

Hugh saw that she had a strong body and, after a few enquiries, found out that she was honest and that her father never had occasion to complain about his food and house. There was, however, a rumour that she was sometimes fond of a little drink. But to Hugh that was a virtue then – for he courted her during one of his prolonged inebriated periods. 'More attractive is a female with a bit of spirit inside her,' he had said.

For though Hugh feared and respected God and paid regularly for a pew in chapel, alas, he loved the drink too well. He wavered continually from a state of grace to sottish behaviour and was in despair of Pisgah, the chapel that had fostered his religious boyhood. But though he had long spells of drink, and the little woman living alone in her house of sin near the cemetery was not unknown to him, Pisgah had the greater part of his love. In true contrition and shame Hugh never failed to return to the old chapel after his drunken bouts, hanging his head before the fierce glances of the deacons, but proudly asserting his repentance by singing the hymns louder than anyone else. And he would attend every service, Sunday and week-days, for two or three months, until his disgusting thirst came upon him again and he would creep back to his scandalous other love. He believed that God would always forgive him. Also, he intended becoming the most religious man in the Valley – later on.

Faith burned in him as clearly and simply as love in a child, and even when drunk he was always aware of God and could sing all the verses of a Welsh hymn without a mistake and with deep emotion. (He was often asked, in the pub, to give this performance.) God, he felt sure, in spite of the minister, always winked an eye if one intended to return, faithful and contrite, to his worship.

So Hugh, when he married Martha on August Bank Holiday, said to her after they had entered their home:

'Now let our lives be sweet-scented in the nostrils of God, Mrs Daniels. Kneel you down with me and speak a little prayer.'

And as it was the wedding-day Martha humoured him, but said: 'Speak you for us both, Daniels. A suitable way you have got for such speeches.'

The house was neat and bright, with many brass candle-sticks, painted tea-pots, large pictures, and shining lamps; the fireplace in the living-room as imposing as any to be seen in a Welsh collier's house – brilliant and black, with brass gleaming here and there, two brass-handled kettles and strips of brass nailed round the mantelpiece. A large piece of Welsh bacon hung from a hook in the ceiling and a stout tabby-cat usually sat between the two andirons on the hearth.

'Cosy, this is,' Hugh remarked, looking round the living-room. 'There's nice and fat that bacon is. How much a pound paid you for it?'

From the back of the house, beyond the strip of garden, the mountain curved up steeply, a greyish green. In winter the winds swept down fiercely from the wide uplands, and the snow drifted, half-burying the back of the Row. A single railroad track, leading to the pit, was cut on the breast of the mountain and, about half-a-mile from the Row, the pit sprawled, an amorphous collection of dim sheds and structures coated thickly with black dust, the tall chimney stacks rising up barrenly, smoke issuing from them slowly like black thin banners of submission.

'A little home of my own at last,' murmured Hugh in the bedroom. 'Dear me, empty my life has been before, without a woman and all.'

Martha wound the clock.

'Say what o'clock you want to get up,' she said, a little peevishly. 'A change it will be for me, to get up so early. Working on the night-shift was father.'

Hugh did not offer to get up alone and prepare his breakfast himself. And Martha supposed she would have to see him off to the pit for the present, as they're only just married.

'Not a lady's life, is it, being married to a collier,' she grumbled, getting into bed.

They lived without mishap for a year or two. Martha was indeed a good housewife, and Hugh worked regularly, dimly conscious, as he sweated in the pit, of the hearth, the food, the warm atmosphere of Martha's presence at home. He became quite fond of her, in the Welsh collier's bleak fashion, and on his way back from the pit he would sometimes buy for her one or two sticks of barley-toffee, of which she could never eat enough. She would rise to light the lamp as evening darkened the living-room.

'Leave the lamp alone, Mrs Daniels,' he would ask.

7

'Nice it is to sit by the fire like this.'

But she was no sentimentalist.

'Go on with you: cheap enough is oil. Miserable it is without a bit of light. And dress yourself, man. Lazy you are getting.' She lit the lamp.

For, like all married colliers, Hugh loved, after he had eaten and bathed, to sit in his shirt at the side of the fireplace and feel the heat on his naked legs.

'Down the pit you ought to work for a day. Lazy you'd be in the evening then.'

Perhaps she would prod him in the ribs and say:

'Well, do as you like then. Just going out I am for a little walk with Mrs Williams.'

'Where to now?' he asked suspiciously.

'Mind your own business, Hugh Daniels,' she would tell him. 'Ach, man, don't interfere in a woman's little pleasure. Go you and talk to the men in the Club.'

He did not like this friendship with Mrs Williams, who was an abundant woman with hefty arms and a habit of glowering at a man and denouncing him in her strident voice as a beast only suitable for woman's utmost contempt. Her husband was one of the best-known drunkards in the district, and late on a Saturday night it was a privilege to listen to the couple displaying their reward for each other in no uncertain language.

'An unnatural woman is that Mrs Williams,' Hugh complained. 'Thoughtless of me you are, to go out with her. The people from the chapel will say this and that.'

'Yes, indeed,' Martha observed sarcastically. 'Very holy they are.'

Hugh sighed.

'There's a lot I would give to see you join Pisgah,' he said. 'Happy my life would be then.' He had not entered the pub for two months.

'Ho!' she said, tittering, 'time it is you had a spell from there yourself.' And she went out humming a little tune happily.

Hugh sat for a little time looking into the fire. The lamplight shone on the washed ivory of his thin face. He twisted his beard in a nervous fashion, opening and closing his mouth restlessly. Should he go down to the pub, or not? The two months without a glass of beer had seemed very long, and the sermons of Mr Hughes-Williams, he was sure, were getting poor lately.

He stood up and began to pull on his black trousers. Yes, the chapel was getting richer, but the fire in the sermons was dwindling. Putting strips of carpet in the pews and rugs in the Big Seat! Ach, Pisgah was beginning to stink of money as bad as a Methodist chapel.

Wrinkling his nose and pushing out his lower lip aggressively, he went down to the Angel. Martha was gratified when he returned home, late.

'Ha,' she laughed enjoyably, 'funny are your little ways!'

He looked at her with hostility; he was not quite drunk.

'Woman,' he said darkly, 'dragging me down to your old fleshpots you are.'

She clapped her hands in delight.

'Ho, ho, Hugh Daniels, a funny old thing you are.'

Her plump cheeks and small childish nose glowed warmly and she danced happily about, getting the supper.

She had only just come in herself, and to please him, though she had intended keeping it for her breakfast the next day, she went to get a flagon of stout she had hidden in the umbrella-stand – a sewer-pipe, painted dark green, that stood in the passage.

So Daniels wavered from the Bright Courts of Pisgah to the pubs, and back again. Martha would wake up early some morning and find him on his knees, praying mournfully for forgiveness. And she would turn over and go to sleep again, grunting and muttering at this disturbance of her rest.

'Lead my wife Martha, too, out of her piggish ways,' she sometimes heard drowsily.

Thus their married life proceeded.

If only she would not drink so much! And if only she kept to beer and ale! For to his horror and indignation, he discovered she liked spirits best – whisky especially. She had a little cupboard in the kitchen, which was always locked, the key usually hidden about her garments. But one evening when she was out, he saw the key lying on the floor of the bedroom. And in the cupboard were four bottles of whisky and gin.

When he chided her she flared up hot like a flame and declared it was her own money she was spending.

'Not the money is it I am thinking of, Martha fach,' he admonished, 'it's the sot you will become I am worrying about. And when you have drunk your two hundred pounds, too costly you will become for my wages.'

'Hark at the old hypocrite!' she cried with disgust. 'You old owl, ashamed I'd be to preach at others.'

'Complaining I am of the expensive taste you have,' he pointed out. 'Whisky and gin ladies always drink,' she answered. 'Vulgar is beer.'

Hugh did not know how to battle triumphantly with women, and after a few vacillating attempts to reform Martha he shut his eyes to the addiction of the female, though in his religious moods he prayed for extra long periods about her.

And he read the Bible far into the night for comfort.

Sometimes, when he sat up late thus, Martha would come out on the landing upstairs and in her warm woman's voice shout to him:

'Hugh Daniels, come you up to bed now. Burning dear oil all night! Put away the Bible, Hugh bach, and come you up to me. Asleep I want to be.'

Then he would put out the lamp and go slowly up to bed, sighing and sorrowful, but his large religious eyes shining with peace. He liked her to talk to him caressively.

And the drink never interfered with her energy as a housewife. His dinner, tasty and generous, was always ready the moment he came in from the pit, the water for his bath always plentiful and hot enough, fire bright, his evening shirt and stockings hanging from the brass rod under the mantelpiece. She made cakes and tarts and baked her own bread, she pickled onions and red cabbage and there was always a piece of bacon hanging and a sack of potatoes in the kitchen.

She was not extravagant, never going into debt in the shops, and spoke of loose girls with the contempt and disgust of the respectably married woman.

'There's an example among women you'd be if control you'd use when you was thirsty,' Hugh said.

'Then in the third year of their marriage Martha found herself with child. She told Hugh the news one evening, a few days after her discovery, as she scrubbed the coal-dirt from his back. He was kneeling over the tub of water washing his face.

'Well, well, say it you do as if telling me a bladder of lard you had bought,' he said when he had dried himself. 'Careful you'll have to be now. Rest, and have a girl in to do the floors and the washing.'

'Hugh Daniels,' she said, 'mind your own business. No girl shall do my washing; sluttish is their work. And when I am confined, take you care no neighbour looks here and there in my home.'

Later in the evening she went off to meet Mrs Williams in the little room reserved for ladies at the back of the Royal. And as he had been on the booze himself lately, Hugh made his way meditatively to the Angel and celebrated the news with glasses of bitter.

Martha did not mention the subject to Hugh again; she considered it unsuitable for discussion with a male. When Hugh made one or two tentative efforts to tell her of his satisfaction, she looked at him ominously and cried:

'Go on, Hugh Daniels, don't you interfere in these women's affairs.'

And she went apart from him and treated him as a lodger in the house. But Mrs Williams (mother of seven) called often, and the two would remain closeted for hours in the parlour.

She did not drink much during the period of waiting, and Hugh prayed that the coming of the child would destroy her disgusting and expensive habit. When he came back from the pit one July afternoon he found the child arrived and Martha sitting up in bed, pale and serious as a preacher.

'What is it?' he asked excitedly.

'A female I wanted,' she replied in her usual pointed fashion, 'but a boy it is. Glad I am for his sake though and glad you ought to be, Daniels, that not a woman you are.'

His soul was proud with holy joy as he went downstairs. Laughing to himself, he ate the dinner that had been prepared for him by Mrs Williams. And as he bathed he chanted a Psalm.

Afterwards he walked a long way to the house of a man who cultivated roses. Roses are rare in the Valley: few flowers bloom in that arid soil and dusty air.

'Say how much the roses are, Davy Evans,' he asked.

'A penny each. A hard job I've had to raise them this year.'

'Dear they are. But a shillingsworth I'll have if you'll give me sixteen.'

He took them with an almost frightened air, into Martha's bedroom, the red and white bunch thrust into a jug. 'There's extravagance!' she exclaimed. 'And he always peevish because I spend a bit on liquor. But had them for nothing you did, perhaps?'

'No, indeed now. One-and-four's worth there is here,' he said. 'Just cut they are, and look you, the dew from the evening is on the petals.' He laid the jug on the table by the bed. 'Say you like them?' he asked anxiously.

13

'Ach, go away,' she said, smiling at him. 'Willie Morgans will be waiting for you in the Angel.'

'Staying away from there from now on I am,' he answered resentfully.

'Go you and call Mrs Williams for me then. A little chat I want to have with her.'

'A little chat with me you ought to have,' he grumbled, going off.

She took the child up, shook him gently, and held him before the bunch of perfumed flowers. He opened his eyes vaguely for a few moments, looked at the red and white with a grave scrutiny, then slipped into sleep again.

CHAPTER II

They called him Reuben. And he was a passionate and troublesome child to rear.

As a baby his kicking lusty body seemed to quiver with a young devil that looked out in hostility from his big black restless eyes, and when his mother fed him, his vicious gums often made her cry out with pain. Sometimes his tight fist would land her a sharp blow on her face or breast, and in those moods he would utter short animal noises, like the anger of a little savage, and his ugly face, wrinkled like a shrivelled brown leaf, assumed an expression of indignant disgust.

But he could be oddly tranquil too, especially when Martha sang to him the old Welsh lullabies and hymns – then he lay and stared at her with fascination like a trance in his eyes and remain appeased for several hours.

Hugh made for him a rocking cradle, painting it a dark

green, with yellow flowers here and there. And when he was four and nearly died of a cold, God heard the father's prayer and the child remained in this world of weeping and pale joys.

Hugh was very fond of the boy and always resented Martha's habit of smacking the noisy little beast's bottom. He never failed to take home every Saturday night, when the boy was older, a packet of pear-drops or black-and-white mints, giving the sweets to him on Sunday morning, to eat in chapel. Thus and in many other ways he displayed his love for his only child.

Martha, too, was fond of the child, in her off-hand rasping manner. She, however, did not believe in surrounding a child with the sickly heat of pronounced affection. Let the brats grow themselves and feel themselves alone as much as possible – so much better for them later. So she ignored Reuben as much as possible and looked at him with harsh eyes. When he was irritable and screamed with a peculiar intensity, she would fly into a fury and screech back at him, her voice brutal with threats. And after he was breeched – with puce velvet knickers and a silk blouse to match – she left off singing to him at nights, and the distance between them widened. So now when he climbed to her lap and put his arms round her neck she thrust him away in mocking derision and called him a little girl.

When she mocked him he hated her violently and desired to inflict upon her some of the pain and rage her derision created in his heart. Once he spat at her, his eyes lit with yellow lights of anger, his voice shrieking murderously. Often he would sit on his stool by the side of the fire and with clear inscrutable eyes watch her doing this and that, watch silently, his face never betraying the thoughts behind. Yet for all their animosity, their brawls, their scorn, each was always keenly aware of the other, aware with a kind of unacknowledged pain.

As he got older a sullen cruelty seemed to be his chief idiosyncrasy.

He liked to drown kittens and slit open their bodies, examining the organs with minute precision, and once he brought in a live toad and threw it in the kitchen fire, watching it burn with gleaming eyes vacant of joy or pity. Another time, when alone in the house, he got hold of a mouse and cooked it alive in the oven. He loved to linger near the slaughter-house of the butcher and listen to the noises of beasts being killed. To inflict torture on living creatures, to know they were being destroyed, gave his bowels a peculiar emotion, an emotion that seemed to soothe and soften the tense nerves of his being.

But, growing, he wearied of these pleasures and became almost gentle and affectionate, secretly longing for his mother's touch, her kind words, the comfortable feminine atmosphere about her. Only occasionally he gave vent to the feverish temper hoarded somewhere within him. And to his father, whom hitherto he treated with indifference, he turned with a bright gentle appeal also.

Hugh took him for long walks, speaking to him during them as though the boy were fully grown. Up over the grey hills and along the railroad track to the colliery, which Reuben, listening to his father's grave explaining voice, would survey silently, thinking of the time when he too

17

would wear long moleskin trousers and go in a cage down to the inside of the earth. He thought of that time with a kind of chill foreboding.

And since he could walk Reuben always accompanied his father to chapel, Sundays and other days. At first, unless he had sufficient pear-drops to keep him occupied through the service, he used to drop off to sleep – but eight of the sweets, if sucked slowly, usually lasted through the sermon. But as he grew he became more attentive and he would watch with steady examining eyes the writhings and fervour of the Rev. Hughes-Williams during the sermon. Hugh noticed his interest and asked on the way home:

'Liked you the sermon tonight, Reuben bach?'

Reuben thought he did and exclaimed, 'There's awful red Mr Williams' face went, and the vein on his forehead stood out, I thought it was going to burst. Excited he becomes when he preaches. Why does he go like that?'

'Given him a strong power has God,' Hugh answered. 'Known all over the Valley for his preaching is Mr Williams. Better than the Old Testament his words are sometimes. And there's fire for you, there's inspiration! At the Big Meetings blaze like a furnace he does.'

Reuben pondered for some time. Then he said:

'I would like to be a preacher.'

His father sighed. 'Costly that would be, bachgen,' he replied sadly, 'and poor we are.'

'But if I could preach!' continued the boy.

'A local preacher you could become. But thankless is that task.'

Nothing was dearer to Hugh's heart than to think of his

son as a minister. But he knew the dream could never be realized. Little was saved from his wages, and Martha's small fortune, he was sure, had gone long ago. How could the boy become a minister with his mother a drunkard! Hugh's heart burned with anger as he thought of it. And he resolved to pray harder and longer for the salvation of his wife. God would surely interfere soon.

Almost nightly, now, she went, after Reuben had been put to bed, down to the Royal to drink and meditate with her friends. But usually she would come back cheerful, in her brassy way, and with her little rush-bag containing a piece of fried fish or sliced corned beef for 'my old preacher's supper'. Regularly at about half past ten she arrived back home, snorting vehemently, for it was a stiff long climb up the stony hill.

'Duw, Duw,' she would exclaim, sinking into a chair, 'short my breath is becoming. Spiteful and mad was the one who built houses up here and an old idiot was my father to buy one of them.'

Hugh would look up from the Bible, sniff down his long nose and resume his reading. But Martha went on chattering and would noisily get the supper and put before Hugh the dainty she had bought for him alone.

He seldom had drinking bouts now, though he sorely missed the tranquil joy of mixing with men in public-houses and smoking his long clay-pipe over the huge "commercial-room" fire. But his desire to sit in the Big Seat at Pisgah kept him steadfast in sacrifice and the chapel had begun to look upon him as finally 'saved' at last. In the Sunday evening service his reverent voice would often

19

begin to repeat the last verse of the hymn, when everybody was preparing to sit down again, and the congregation would follow in a swelling chorus. So his reputation with the Pisgah people improved and they would say to each other, 'There's religious Hugh Daniels is now! Pity he is burdened with such a slut of a wife.'

She looked with disfavour on Hugh's habit of discussing religion with Reuben.

'Daniels,' she said, 'idiotic you are with that child. Left alone he ought to be. Make an old man of him you will, talking to him about the sermon! Clear out, you silly sheep. Dear me, glad I'll be when you go on the drink again.'

'Enough it is for one in the house to be – ' began Hugh with sudden heat.

'Now then, now then,' she finished, her voice rising, 'grudge me a little pleasure, would you! Not enough is it to make my back crooked, working in this house for you, cooking your old food, washing filthy clothes and bringing up that little bag of mischief. A nigger you ought to have for a wife, you cruel slave-driver.'

Hugh slowly shook his head in despair. How he wished he had the courage to take and beat the woman, as Will Jones boasted of doing to his wife. He tugged at his beard hopelessly and longed to be a bachelor again.

CHAPTER III

Reuben grew into a tall good-looking boy full of a vigour that seemed to hold itself tight within him. His mouth was strong and fleshy: and under the dark brows his eyes were naked with a strange gleam of unhappiness. Some thought seemed to be forever brooding in sombre meditation behind those eyes. But he did not give utterance to that thought; indeed, after the age of twelve, he had very little to say for himself. The hitherto noisy, bawling child became so austere and silent that Martha thought there was something organically wrong with him. Ignoring him before, she now bought him cod-liver oil and various medicines. But there was nothing physically wrong with Reuben: cod-liver oil and emulsions could never interfere with his malady. He was brooding about God.

God lived behind the sky and he never showed himself to anybody. All people went down on their knees and worshipped God, every human being. God demanded that, insisted upon it, and everyone obeyed because they lived in fear of God. God could blast the eyes out of them: without appearing for one moment this side of the sky, God could destroy the earth into a handful of ashes and array everyone in awful judgment before him in Heaven. The power of God was terrible, and no one on earth had ever seen him, no one knew what he was like, though all said he was great and terrible, the owner of the whole world and everyone in it, their Master.

Reuben had learned that from the Rev. Hughes-Williams' sermons. And he was afraid. The thought of God behind the sky, constantly watching with his dreadful eyes that never missed anything, watching the smallest action of his life and always condemning, condemning. At night he was afraid to look at the stars because he thought they let through the glance of God: when there was thunder and lightning his being crouched within him because God was angrier than usual and meditated destroying the world. But why should God be always angry?

Reuben listened attentively to the Rev. Williams' sermons, and he found that all creatures born on the earth are evil, that each is burdened with a load of sin that can never be shaken off while living on the earth, and that God bore a grudge against us for this mysterious inescapable sin which, however, would be forgiven in the next world if one's life in this had been stainless.

'What are you thinking of, boy?' Daniels demanded, one Sunday evening after chapel as they sat in the living-room, the father reading the Bible as usual.

Reuben looked at his father with sombre eyes.

'Will I go to hell when I die?' he muttered.

'For why you ask that?' Hugh replied in astonishment.

'I don't want to burn in the fire,' the boy said fearfully. 'There's awful is the hell Mr Williams preached of tonight. What can I do not to go there?'

'For why should you go to hell?' asked Hugh seriously.

'Born in sin we are,' Reuben repeated from the sermon. 'Unclean is our lives and the body is a sink of iniquity.'

'Tut, tut, boy bach, not understand these things do you. Time enough is there later for you to use your head about them.' And Hugh returned to the Bible.

But presently, after a further meditation, Reuben said: 'Jesus Christ I like better than Moses.'

Hugh twisted his beard nervously.

'Why, boy bach?'

Reuben shook his head. 'I don't know,' he said slowly, his eyes darkened. And he leaned over to his father with a sudden beseeching gesture. 'More I want to know about Jesus. Tell me about him.'

Hugh sighed. 'No preacher am I, Reuben.' He turned the pages of the Bible lovingly. 'But read you about his life from Saint Matthew I will, if you like.'

He moved the lamp a little nearer, settled his spectacles and, his finger following the words, began:

' *"Now the birth of Jesus Christ was on this wise..."* '

Reuben listened to the simple words, followed that life of sorrow and wonder as his father selected the suitable verses, listened with dropped brows and far-gazing eyes to the vivid tale unfolded in the calm of St. Matthew and the love of his father's voice. How beautiful it was, he thought. And how different to the sermons of Mr Williams!

He saw Jesus calling the little child to him, caressing its hair while he spoke to the disciples of the kingdom of heaven. A sweetness flowed within Reuben: he would like to have been that child and feel the hands of Jesus upon his head.

' *"And Jesus came and spake unto them, saying, All Power is given unto me in heaven and in earth. Go ye, therefore, amid teach all nations, baptizing them in the name of the father, and of the Son, and of the Holy Ghost. Teaching them to observe all things whatsoever I have commanded you: and, lo, I am with you always, even until the end of the world."* '

Hugh closed the book and, his hand over his eyes, remained silent for some time. Reuben gazed into the fire. His being glowed with an inner ecstasy that seemed to quiver with pain... A desire to serve and worship as no other had served and worshipped the man who had suffered and died in agony for the world gathered dimly in the boy's breast. How beautiful it would be to serve, suffer, and die for Christ. Yes, he would gladly die for him; he too could bear the nails in his hands, in his feet...

And father and son remained silent in their meditations, both feeling the mystic harmony of the religion that is the glory of the Welsh.

Until Martha came in. She had been spending the evening with a kindred neighbour and there had not been quite enough to drink.

'Jesus Mawr,' she cried shrilly, 'there's a pair of wooden

donkeys you are. Where's the supper? Waiting for the old slave to come in, to be sure. And the fire nearly out. Daniels, a lunatic you are getting with your Bible. Out of my way.' And she swept the Bible from the table to the floor.

Reuben darted to it with a cry.

'Don't you throw the Bible down like that,' he cried angrily, gazing at his mother with fierce eyes.

'Ho!' she exclaimed, hands on hips, leaning towards him ominously, 'who are you then, my lord, talking to me like that?'

Reuben clasped the Bible and stared at her with burning eyes. She suddenly grasped him and shook him violently. He began to cry – his peculiar dull scream of rage, that greatly irritated Martha. Hugh stood up and began to protest feebly. But the woman had worked herself into a fury that darted like arrows from her eyes and mouth.

'Teach him to hold his snotty tongue I will. Looking at me like murder! An insulting little devil he is. But beat it out of him I will.'

And the emotion that lay buried in mother and son, that each was dimly conscious of and that bound them, sprang into being. Violently she began to slap his bare legs. But Reuben, a curious snarl escaping his lips, suddenly wriggled round and buried his teeth in his mother's wrist. She screamed shrilly, let him go, and hopped about the room.

'Bit me he has, bit me he has,' she cried in pain.

Hugh stood still in horror, seeing the blood on his wife's wrist. 'The little b—,' she screamed, weeping.

Reuben crouched on the floor against a leg of the table. His mother's cries of pain made him shudder. He looked at her fearfully as, still howling, she collapsed into a chair. And when he too saw the blood he hung his head and began to cry softly.

Then his father took him into the kitchen and beat him soundly. He accepted his punishment without further cries, his face white and mournful as the stick descended on his body.

Later he crept up to bed, silent and ashamed. He was sorry, he was sorry. The tears burst forth again in a flood. And as he lay weeping in the darkness his father came up with a lamp and the Bible.

'A wicked ruffian you were, to bite your mother, Reuben,' Hugh said sorrowfully. 'Not worthy of Jesus Christ are you.'

Reuben sobbed.

'Shut you up crying now,' continued his father, 'and we will pray together, for forgiveness. Come you and kneel with me.'

And afterwards he read to his son a few psalms.

The next morning Reuben went downstairs in fear. His father, working on the day-shift, had long ago departed to the pit. He would have to face his mother alone. He entered the living-room with sullen eyes, scowling.

'Come on, wolf,' his mother sang. 'Little wolf, come to your food then.'

He saw that her wrist was bandaged, and he wanted to weep. He sat down at the table without a word, his eyes still sullen. If only she said something kind and gentle! He drank his tea and ate his food, silent. And suddenly she said: 'Tell me sorry you are for biting me last night.'

He looked at her in misery. And he seemed to see her face differently. It was older, almost pitiful, with puffy cheeks and a sad mouth. A feeling of strength and protection came into his heart. He bowed his head on the table and began to cry.

'All right, all right,' she murmured soothingly, stroking his head, 'forget it we will.'

'I didn't mean to bite you,' he wept. The caresses, rare and unexpected from her, made his heart burst with grief. He turned and clasped her round the waist.

But she thrust him away.

'Now then, baby,' she cried mockingly, 'get off to school.'

His suffering eyes looked at her beseechingly. He wanted her love so much. But, singing briskly, she went into the kitchen with some dishes and he knew she would ignore him as before.

But as he walked to school he carried preciously in his soul the memory of her caress.

It was decided to send him to the pit. Hugh talked with Martha on the possibility of making him a minister, or, failing that, putting him in a draper's shop. But Martha swept away these suggestions.

'No brains has he to become a minister,' she said, 'and not crafty enough is he to make success in a draper's. Strong and healthy enough for the pit he is. Goodness me, Daniels, what a toad you are, to scorn your own work. A manly living it is.'

'Indeed now,' he answered, 'different to most boys he is. Delicate seems his mind.'

'What rubbish,' she cried. 'And where is the money for his schooling?'

'Some of yours is left now?' he suggested, half afraid.

Martha resented her husband's prying into her affairs. From the first she had treated her marriage as a business transaction. Hugh laboured and brought money for the upkeep of the house, she gave her services in return, and because it was the fashion since the days of the Bible she gave herself also as a woman to him. But anything else in her life was her own private affair.

'Mind your business,' she said ominously. 'My father left me the money I had when I married you. For my own comfort it is. Enough I want to leave for my own funeral, and if any is left over, Reuben must have it for himself. But none have I got to waste on schooling.'

'All right,' he sighed. 'But no imagination have you, Mrs Daniels.'

And so, like nearly all the boys in the Valley, after his fourteenth birthday Reuben went to work in the colliery. He set out one June morning with his father, his new moleskin trousers white and spotless, and proud enough of his food-tin and the 'jack' of cold tea in his pocket. Everything was thrilling; the swift descent in the cage down the shaft, down through the round black hole into the earth, the eerie journey through the workings below to the gallery where he and his boss were to work. He had left his father about a mile from the shaft and continued his journey with the man who was to employ him. And following the collier through the twisted narrow tunnels he thought fearfully of the awful weight of earth above them.

If there were a fall of roof and they were shut in! This silence and darkness was different to any he had experienced before. He listened to the drip, drip of some water, and the sound seemed peculiar, a dead, shrouded sound. This was another world, a dead world of stale and heavy silence, where the darkness never lifted and where he might die. It was strange, to think of himself wandering about in these caves inside the earth – it was as though it made him another being, as though a light had been darkened within him. However, presently they passed some stables and groups of colliers already at work, and the men hailed them in cheerful and worldly language that made the place seem more human.

They stopped at a certain clearing and the boss took off his coat, shirt and vest, and told Reuben to do like-wise. Hopkin Watts looked at Reuben's well-made body approvingly.

'Strong you look,' he said. 'The last boy I had was no good for this work.'

'Gone back on top has he?' Reuben asked.

'No. Underground he is for good now. Consumption he had. Mad were his people to put him in the pit. Only two months was he down here.'

And Watts, setting his little lamp on a ledge, began to attack the face of coal in the crumbling earth at the side of the clearing.

The hours passed and Reuben became very tired. It was hot work lifting and shovelling the coal into the trams. The sweat oozed from his bare body and ran down over his legs; soon he was covered with black, like a real collier-boy.

Watts was a silent man to work with, and in the heavy warmth of that dim, buried space he and the boy plodded on like mechanical beings of some subterranean race.

When the pause for food came Reuben sank exhausted upon a piece of timber, inserted the neck of his 'jack' into his mouth and drank thirstily. Never was cold tea more beautiful.

'Here,' his boss interrupted him, 'keep you some for the afternoon. Spread it out you must.'

'Dry I was.'

'And drier you'll be later.'

Hopkin Watts was a dour middle-aged man with a large family and a grim and weary face. He had been a miner for thirty years, and his body was covered with the blue bruises of his kind. He was often heard saying he wished he could live always below and never return to the top.

'Think you'll like being a collier?' he asked Reuben, as they sat eating their bread and cheese.

'Hard work it is.'

Watts wrinkled up his nose and thrust out his chin.

'Peace one has down here,' he said. 'No women or anything.' He was silent for some time, munching his food slowly and methodically, like an animal. And when he took up his pick to resume work again he seemed like a god, a god of the underworld, complete in his supremacy and strength. Here, below, he was at peace with the earth. He was one of those colliers who became alien to the sun.

At the end of the day Reuben was thoroughly exhausted. All he could think of was the hot dinner that was waiting for him, and his nice clean bed. He put on his clothes and trudged back through the endless tunnels with his silent boss, splashing heedlessly through pools of muddy water and even disregarding the mice that scurried out now and again from behind the timber. He hoped there would be a good thick broth, with plenty of potatoes, for dinner.

His father was waiting for him at the top.

'Well, Reuben bach, how liked you it?'

'Fine!'

Father and son trudged home wearily together. And even Martha, when they arrived home, was proud of her blackened son. He devoured his dinner silently and intensely, already in the collier's fashion, and after his bath sat before the fire for an hour or so in his shirt, just as the colliers do, letting the warmth caress his refreshed limbs.

'There now,' said Martha to her husband, 'take to the life like a baby to milk, he does. A minister indeed! True colliers' blood runs in his veins.'

From that time Reuben began to think of himself as a man. But some odd streak in his nature prevented him from being intimate with the other youths of the district; the few times he had accompanied the boys of the street in their horse-play or amorous expeditions he had been a silent and brooding witness always apart. And when they gathered under the lamp-post at the corner to tell dirty stories, he listened furtively and laughed with forced enjoyment at the proper time. He knew there was something wrong with him, that he was not as they.

Girls he looked upon as aloof creatures dwelling in a secret sphere of their own, a world he felt he would never know. When a girl spoke to him – their eyes malicious and calculating, for he was attractive – he was tongue-tied and surly and imagined he was despised. He never thought he could ever use them in the way described in the dirty stories he heard.

Now, in the evenings after his day in the pit, either he sat reading the Bible or went alone for a walk up the mountain. When he opened the big black Bible that usually lay beneath a lace-edged cloth on the chest of drawers, his mother would exclaim:

'Jesus Mawr, why don't you do something else, boy! A maniac you will get, reading that always. There's odd you are! Get to look black and sour as an old preacher you will. Indeed, sluts are the girls today, but glad to see you find one I shall be, for make you forget the Bible she would.'

'I'd rather stay in,' he always repeated sullenly.

She treated him with some interest now that he contributed to the upkeep of the house; since he had gone to the pit she had an extra drink every time she went to the Royal. But she did not like the way he looked at her, the dark gleam of censure in his eyes. She always felt there was some strange and strong being behind those brooding eyes of his, a power that watched her and tried to enter, too, her own dim being. She writhed away in dislike from her son and wanted only her own world of work and drink, without thought, but she could not escape and was secretly fearful that he would conquer her some day.

She had become big, florid and rather terrible as she aged, and her chin was as dominant as ever, the glance of her sharp eyes as hostile, her voice still strident in contempt of all things. Her son looked at her as she went out for her evening's pleasure, carrying her rush-bag, an old fur round her strong neck, a warrior's pride in the set of her shoulders, and vaguely he thought of the strong hills that surrounded them, the glint of the rocks, and the hard nights of winter that came down in the Valley with the winds. She was of the old pure Welsh blood, and he of her descent would in other days have sung poems and carried his harp from village to village, a bard bred of the rough hills and wild people.

So, after the little tirade at his austere mode of spending the evening, now she went off to her pub, and he turned to the Bible. Lately he had begun to read the Book right through, carefully. The reading of the Scriptures gave him such joy that he often sprang to his feet and in an exalted chant cried aloud those verses of flame and marble. In these moments his voice became an imploring music and he would throw out his arms as though he would gather to his breast all the delight and ecstasy of the world.

When he was fifteen Martha was certain that she had brought into the world a son who would become daft and a source of misery and disgrace to her. She had suddenly come upon him one night as he was declaiming from *Lamentations*, and her being was moved to a strange fear within her.

CHAPTER IV

One evening as he sat, as usual, with the Bible between his knees he heard the sounds of a commotion outside. Brawls were common in the street, and following the custom of the dwellers there he went out to join the crowd.

The people were gathered outside number 17, and from their midst came a man's curses and a woman's shrieks of abuse. He pressed forward through the people, who were observing the little drama before them with an air of solid interest.

Crouched near the gutter of the roadside was a girl of twenty, snivelling, and with a blood-smeared wound over an eye-brow. She had just been ejected from number 17, her home, and on the pavement, waving his arms and engaged in verbal warfare with Mrs Williams, Martha's companion in liquor, stood the girl's father. Reuben put his hands in his trousers pockets and listened.

'A respectable family mine has always been,' the father shouted, 'and a clean house I will keep it. Let the bitch rid herself of her dirt and find her own reward again. Impudent was her tongue always before she went away, and now she is fallen, creep back like a poisonous snake she does. Ach y fi, think you I will let her touch my other sons and daughters!'

Mrs Williams, hefty and muscular as a navvy, shook her fist in his face. Her pale, doughy face was lit up by the angry glare of her protruding eyes. She tittered, in a voice of lashing fury:

'Ha, you are the one to cast out a poor girl! A man of the chapel you are, to be sure. But don't you forget, Rowland Roberts, how it was with you when the little servant of the manager miscarried because chased she was by old Butcher Jenkins' bull! Then a man of God you became, for did not God save you from disgrace when the little servant died? Ha, forgotten these things are you think, but a good memory for the badness of the men I have. Take you your daughter back as repentance for the little servant.'

Reuben recognised the girl as Ann Roberts, who had left home some months before to become a servant in Cardiff. He stared at her as she cowered weeping on the ground, wiping away her tears, her hair loosened and her blouse torn. The blood on her forehead hurt him.

But the father continued, his thin emaciated face as sharp as a hatchet:

'A female's lying tongue and imagination you have, Sarah Williams. Bowen the lampman it was who went out with the woman at that time.' His voice rose dangerously, 'And don't you interfere in my affairs. *My* daughter that slut was and *my* name has she brought low. Know well enough you do, for help spread the knowledge you have, how she walks the streets of Cardiff. Think you a deacon shall take into his home a woman of evil! The truth it is that from my loins she came, but answer for the slut must I now she has become as the beasts? Out of my dwelling I cast her, for her body has become the possession of other men.'

Loud cries of protests greeted these remarks. Mrs Williams cursed him in further violent terms; it was as though she wanted to break upon him great crushing stones of wrath. But he stood tall and bleak and unmovable in his religious righteousness, his lipless mouth clenched shut. Behind him, in the doorway, cowered his wife, small and afraid, with her starved and shivering face glancing out in fear, her nose twitching. She was ignored by everybody, for she was half-daft and only an echo of a woman. But Mrs Williams suddenly burst out, pointing to her:

'Look you at her, your wife! There's a fine tale of what your nature is! A pretty little thing she was before she lost sense and married you. Ach, my man, a whip across your back you ought to have. A scab on the street you are.'

Someone called from the crowd:

'Now, now, Mrs Williams, does he not supply the bread and the wine for communion in the chapel?'

Rowland Roberts cried angrily:

'A vulgar street this is. Drunkards and atheists inhabit it, and the stink of the damned is about its doorways.'

Then suddenly his daughter leaped up and bawled:

'What do I care if he won't take me back! Lying were

those tongues that said I had become a whore. People, bad company I got into but now I came back to lead a new life. No money have I got, for a fool I was in Cardiff. But driving me back to badness he is. A cruel father he's been and burn in hell for ever he ought to.'

She burst into a howl as she finished and her head dropped sobbingly on her breast. In the fading light of evening her face had a yellowish pallor, and her hands plucked agitatedly at her throat. Then she raised her head and gazed round the crowd with wild, frightened eyes. She suddenly turned and, screaming, beat her way through the people and fled down the street.

Mrs Williams continued her abuse of the father. And the crowd pressed closer round him, threateningly. His strict method of enforcing obedience from his family was well known.

Reuben crept out of the crowd and went in the direction Ann Roberts had gone. He hurried. At the end of the street there was a wide stony path that led down over the hill to the main Valley. He hurried down the path but could not see her, for it was getting dark. On the little bridge he stopped and gazed about. He would have seen her if she had continued on the path to the Valley. He called:

'Ann Roberts, Ann Roberts!'

Banks of tall bulrushes fringed the river. He saw a head raise itself among them, some distance from the bridge.

'What d'you want?' screeched Ann Roberts. 'Go away and let me alone.'

But he jumped on the bank and went towards her, half-fearfully, for he did not like the sound of her voice. She was sitting on a large flat stone among the rushes and her face as he approached looked up at him with curiosity and anger.

'Reuben Daniels!' she exclaimed.

Even in the dim light he could see her eyes were red and swollen with weeping, though her mouth was drawn back in a rather vicious curve. He remembered his mother once saying what a little ruffian she was. But he looked into her eyes, that were so wild and swollen.

'What d'you want?' she demanded again, angrily.

'Sorry for you I am.' He gazed at her helplessly. 'I only wanted to help you, if I can,' he continued. 'I thought... I thought that kill yourself you were going to, when you screamed at them just now – '

She laughed stridently.

'Hate them too much I do,' she answered. 'Glad he'd be to see me dead.'

'What will you do now, then?' he asked.

She began to weep once more. 'Drove me to bad things he did before, and now he won't let me come back.' Then she rubbed her eyes and nose on her sleeve, tossed back her hair, and her face became vicious again. 'Ha, I'll bring disgrace on him, I'll make him hang his old fox's face lower still in the chapel, the old b—.'

He did not quite understand. But he hated to see her face, that could be soft and pretty, contracted so vengefully.

He sat down beside her on the flat stone.

'Don't you be like that,' he pleaded gently. 'Forgive him you must.'

But again she laughed. And she suddenly turned to him

and looked at him directly. 'There's odd you are, to follow me down here,' she said. 'But a funny boy you were always. Say what you want with me.'

'Wanted to help you I did,' he answered, avoiding her keen gaze.

'And a ignorant little boy you are too,' she said, grinning.

It seemed to him now that she could very well do without his pity. But he remembered her yellowish face and her piercing voice as she screamed at her father. He did not know what evil she had been up to while she was away, he did not understand, but he felt that whatever it was he would still like her and stand by her; she seemed so alone.

She looked at him furtively. 'Well, if help me you want to, any money have you got?' she asked suddenly.

He searched his pockets. 'Only two shillings I have on me, but more I have got in the house. Say how much you want.'

'Go back to Cardiff and have enough for a day or two I must. Then work I'll be able to find.'

'About sixteen shillings I've got,' he said. 'You stay here and I'll fetch them.'

He stumbled away among the stones. Night had come on and she sat alone in the darkness with her own thoughts. When he came back and put the money in her hands, she said:

'Come you and sit down beside me, Reuben Daniels. A friend you have been to me.'

He sat down at her side. She put her face against his.

'A good boy you always were,' she whispered. 'Not like those other scamps in the street, who used to chase me.'

He sat still.

'Like you I do,' she continued softly. 'Say you like me.'

'Yes,' he said.

Her mouth slid round to his. He did not move and he felt her lips cold and damp against his. Then she leaned back, flat on the stone, drawing him down with her. He felt her breasts pressing upon him.

'Like you I do,' she kept on repeating.

Something sprang into being within him, crept like a flame to his chest, along his arms, to his mouth and eyes. But he kept rigid in her embrace.

'Cold you are,' she complained in a whisper.

He wanted to do something to the girl by his side, but though he ached to press to her the flame that was burning within him, his body felt like stone and his arms like iron. He kept silent and rigid.

After a few minutes she sat up and laughed.

'All right,' she said. 'A proper little gentleman you are to give me this money.'

He drew himself up slowly and avoided looking at her.

'Can I go now?' she asked.

He nodded, and without another word or gesture she went.

For some time he sat there meditating. Now she was gone he wished her back again, there by his side, her arms moving over his body, her breasts pressing upon him. He trembled at the thought of it. When he went back to the street there were groups of people still discussing the little affair at number 17. Reuben saw a certain young man squatting on his heels alone outside his home. He went to him and said:

'Saw you Ann Roberts tonight, Dai Davies?'

The young man spat, and then winked at Reuben.

'Ay, a little beauty she is,' he said. 'But there's a fool, to come back home.'

'What was she at in Cardiff?' asked Reuben. 'Working she was there?'

'Ay, working – in a way,' Dai Davies said, smiling evilly.

'Tell me how.'

Dai Davies, as is the way of young men, was quite willing to display his knowledge of those bypaths of life that were unknown to Reuben.

And Reuben lay in bed that night with his mind sickened. Besides his new knowledge of the traffic of human bodies, he could not sleep, thinking of the eighteen shillings he had given to Ann Roberts, to help her get back to her trade. Finally, he lit a candle and took up his little bedside Testament. And reading page after page, he again found comfort in the life of Jesus Christ. He fell asleep with a troubled smile on his face.

CHAPTER V

On Sundays Reuben went to chapel for the three sessions. But he did not like Mr Hughes-Williams' sermons in the morning services; the preacher droned through it, pausing to wipe his spectacles often, and there was not a spark of the fire that burned in his evening sermons, when the chapel was always crowded.

The squat chapel with its heavy wood gallery and gas lamps, that blackened the walls, smelt of damp and distemper. In the summer the air was stale and warm with human breathings used and reused, and in the winter evenings the only warmth was that which came from the gas lamps and the ardour of Mr Hughes-Williams' sermons. But the chapel was successful; every pew was let. For Mr Hughes-Williams belonged to the old hierarchy of Welsh preachers; the damned were damned everlastingly, with words of terrible strength, but the holy, attending chapel faithfully, should always sit, in their garments of white linen, on little stools about the everlasting Throne. There was always comfort for the minds, if not the bodies, of the members.

Reuben respected Mr Hughes-Williams, but he did not like him, especially the feel of his damp fleshy hand when the minister patted him. But the boy was favoured, the minister often asking him to give the opening prayer of the Tuesday Penny Readings. They liked Reuben's prayers, and already the deacons looked at him with interest. Mr Hughes-Williams said to the father: 'A minister you ought to have made him, Mr Daniels.'

Hugh looked at the preacher with shame.

'You know how it is with me,' he said. 'A trial and expense is Mrs Daniels.'

'Yes, indeed, sore must be your life. Know now you do how the Evil One plays tricks with a drunkard. Blind in your drink he made you, Hugh Daniels, when you took her for wife.'

Hugh's chin dropped disconsolately.

'Send you the boy down to me on Thursday and I will talk with him,' continued the minister. 'See if there's anything in his head I will.'

So Reuben went down to the house of the preacher. The door was opened by Mrs Hughes-Williams, who sent him to a little shed built out in the back garden. The minister was there, wearing a bibbed white apron and hammering nails into a boot fitted upon a cobbler's last. He looked over his spectacles at the Sunday-clad Reuben and exclaimed:

'Dear me, forgot I did that you were coming, Reuben

Daniels. Well, sit you down and wait until I've finished these old boots. Want to go out in them tonight does Mrs Hughes-Williams.'

Reuben looked about him. This was the minister's work shed. A few umbrellas lay about. Mr Hughes-Williams was a handy man and his work as a repairer of umbrellas was well-known. When speaking to chapel members he would often remark upon a defect of the accompanying umbrella and offer to repair it, even to a new cover. It was delicately understood that no payment in cash was to be made, but the minister accepted such gifts as the customer could make – a fowl, or a sack of garden-grown potatoes or turnips, a piece of home-cured bacon, or a couple of jars of pickled onions. Mr Hughes-Williams' pantry was always well-stocked.

He drove the last tacks into the boot, blackened the leather of the pair, and, after a satisfied sigh, spat on the floor. Then, taking off the apron he told Reuben to follow him.

They sat in the front room of the house and Mr Hughes-Williams, laying his hands over his stomach and twiddling his thumbs, asked:

'Read the Bible you do every day?'

'Yes, Mr Hughes-Williams,' replied Reuben, gazing nervously at the minister's pondering purple lips.

'Recite some of it from memory you can?'

Reuben said he could and the minister asked him to begin. The boy, gazing out of the window, recited from the Book, and as he went on, Mr Hughes-Williams closed his eyes and his thumbs became quiet. In his clear voice, that seemed to have the warmth of sunlight, Reuben continued, going from Exodus to Ecclesiastics and Revelations, and expecting any moment to be told to stop. But the minister was silent, except for the slight snore of his heavy breathing. After half-an-hour Reuben had exhausted his repertoire and waited expectantly. But the minister did not open his eyes, and his mouth had dropped open.

Reuben gazed at him angrily as he realized he was asleep. He went over to the man and shook his arm. Mr Hughes-Williams awoke slowly and heavily, opening one eye first.

'Dear me,' he exclaimed, 'dropped off to sleep I did?'

Reuben looked at him with indignant eyes.

'Very tired I was,' the minister droned. 'Been working very hard in the shed all the afternoon I have. A busy man I am. Begin you again, boy bach, and I will listen closely.'

Reuben did not forget the respect which is due to a minister and he began again, though in a voice that had lost its tender warmth. When he had finished, Mr Hughes-Williams nodded his head several times.

'A good memory you have got,' he commented, thrusting out his fat under-lip judiciously. 'Know you do the genealogy of the patriarchs as it is written in the fifth chapter of Genesis?'

Reuben did not and the Minister looked at him triumphantly.

'Ach, knew it I did when I was twelve. There's a tricky piece for you to remember! Put me on a chair and make me recite it my old father used to.'

Reuben was silent. Then the minister asked suddenly:

'A good boy you are? Not mischievous with the girls?'

'No,' Reuben said quickly.

The minister's little eyes rolled in their sockets as he said:

'Careful of them you must be, for disposed to evil some of them are. After me they used to run when I was your age, and there's persistent they were when they knew that going in for the ministry I was!'

Mr Hughes-Williams continued in reminiscences of his boyhood and Reuben listened to the droning voice and wondered when he would be allowed to go. Finally the minister went away and brought back a teapot and a couple of cups on a tray.

The two drank weak tea together, the minister sucking up his with thirsty gusto and during the interval complaining of the noise made by the boys who sat in the back seat of the chapel gallery.

Reuben departed afterwards with a volume of Welsh sermons.

He thought he would take a walk up the mountain before going home, and he began to climb the lower slopes quickly, for night was already darkening the far reaches of the Vale. After the stay with Mr Hughes-Williams his being longed for the exaltation that always came to him when he stood or ran across the top of one of the hills.

He often sat on the crest of those hills and, gazing broodingly over the Valley outspread beneath, a sense of strange power and desire would throb within him.

The air was always clear there and in the calm of evening the life of the Valley seemed far away and dim. The last song

46

of a bird sometimes rose and fell thinly. Reuben would fall back and gaze dreamily into the mysterious heavens, and then the thoughts that came to him were like arrows of flame in his exalted consciousness. He longed to be gathered into union with some unspeakable bliss, a splendour that was all gold spaces, stars, and singing, and the beating of vast wings through scarlet clouds and opened heavens. In these ecstasies a sound like a moan of despair escaped his lips and his muscles tightened.

One evening he seemed to hear his name whispered in the depths of this ecstasy.

'Reuben... here... Reuben.'

What was that call? It was a murmur faint as the shudder of leaves and with anguish he strained to follow the sound. In vain. He opened his eyes and saw that he was still on the hill-top and that it was almost dark. Had he been sleeping! A desolate sadness came over him. Ah, if he had been able to follow that voice! Listening to it, his being had seemed like the full bud of some hot flower trembling for release.

This evening, in a state of acute depression, he wandered moodily over the curving brows of the deserted hill. But the vast sky and the loneliness filled him with dread and foreboding.

What was he seeking? There was something he must do, there was a world that he did not know. He gazed into the Valley, at the grey clustering houses, where the people lived out their lives. And everything appeared sad and mournful to him and the life sunk there seemed to be terrible and without meaning.

47

He walked on in his sudden misery, thinking of his own life – day after day in the pit, chapel on Sunday, and in the evenings his lonely readings. Yet the golden warmth that flooded him in his dreaming, that seemed to form songs and flaming words in his mind, so that his tongue longed to cry them aloud!

But tonight he felt no exaltation on the hill-top. He thought of his visit to Mr Hughes-Williams and his disappointment became anger.

He had expected some intimate revelation of religion from the minister, a talk, as between disciple and teacher, on some subject of Holy Writ.

Clasping the book of Welsh sermons that had been given him, he wandered on in the dying light, his face sombre with mistrust and anger.

Presently he saw the figure of a man squatting near the path and surveying the Valley beneath in an attitude of brooding calm. But a voice issued from the figure and Reuben paused to listen. With strange and shrill declamation the voice was repeating:

'Tomorrow, and tomorrow, and tomorrow,
Creeps in this petty pace from day to day,
To the last syllable of recorded time;
And all our yesterdays have lighted fools
The way to dusty death. Out, out, brief candle!
Life's but a walking shadow, a poor player
That struts and frets his hour upon the stage,
And then is heard no more; it is a tale
Told by an idiot, full of sound and fury,
Signifying nothing.'

Reuben listened wonderingly and fearfully. There was such strangeness and hopelessness in the voice. He approached quietly: the man turned round with a start.

'I heard you,' Reuben said simply.

The man gazed at Reuben intently. He was young and pale, with a rather terrible smoky pallor, and his eyes had a dull burning that was like a fever. His thin body was clad in garments of rough tweed and the hands were emaciated and nervous. The intensity of his gaze troubled Reuben.

'Sorry I am if I've disturbed you,' the boy said, 'but there's wonderful it was to listen to you!'

The young man smiled suddenly. 'Do you know the passage?' he asked.

Reuben shook his head.

'Who are you?' the young man continued. 'Sit down and let me see your book.' He peered at the volume. 'Sermons!' he exclaimed in a voice of contempt. 'You are going in for the ministry?'

'No, I work in the pit.'

'Why do you wander over the mountains with a book of sermons?'

Reuben explained how he often came to the hill-tops, and in a sudden access of liking for this young man, who looked so pale and unhappy, he told him of those secret dreams that haunted him and which he could not understand.

'Why don't you clear out and go away,' the young man said. 'You're wasting your time here if you feel you're so different than the rest of them.'

'What could I do then?'

'What can you do here?'

'Like to lead the people I would and make them happy,' Reuben said with grave intensity.

The young man smiled a little. But his smouldering eyes glanced at the boy searchingly. Then he gazed down the Valley and after a silence muttered to himself:

'There are no stones that can bruise the feet of flame, and the hands that shall grasp the stars are born of the earth: if a man speak as a god and continue in his saying there will be such astonishment among the angels!'

Reuben looked at him, perplexed. The young man turned to him again and said in his strange throaty voice:

'I envy you your ideals. I hope to Christ you'll be able to keep them. I had such ideals once, I think; longed to dedicate myself to the people and sweat myself for their advantage. But now...' He uttered a little cry of laughter that seemed to tear his voice, '...well, I'm told that I'll be dead in a few months, or a couple of years, perhaps, if I'm careful, then the people seem only worms, like myself.' His eyelids seemed to stretch themselves, shudderingly as he gazed at the staring Reuben.

Reuben said, out of his experience in reading the Bible:

'But something more than the flesh there is. There is a glory...'

But the young man laughed again:

'We are clothed with flesh for our joy: why should mine rot before its time?'

Reuben felt that the young man's state of mind was beyond him, but his heart throbbed with pity and sympathy for his suffering. Those eyes, smouldering with their flameless light, and the pallor of his thin face and fleshless fingers roused suffering in him, too. He said simply:

'Let me be your friend.'

It was almost quite dark now, and the young man peered curiously at Reuben.

'Yes,' he replied after a little scrutiny, 'perhaps we might be able to find some meaning together. But you are young.'

'I am nearly eighteen.'

'And I am twenty-three. Five years, and so much difference! I already in the grave and you so vivid with your health and intensity! How wonderful is the earth! I was born with this body, that has grown cell by cell in spite of the implacable germ that is now ruining all the good work. A certain perception of beauty was given me and as I was preparing to enjoy its delights, the worm of doom crept out and showed all its delicate labour. And there you sit, bright and eager, and offer me your friendship! The earth is kind. Ah, far better if I stay alone in my brooding and scorn the earth. I can only corrupt that which is offered me in pity.'

He lapsed into sudden silence again, gazing away into the Valley, that had begun to tremble with little points of light. Opposite and beyond, the barren hills had become faint and shapeless in the grey dusk, a sullen calm about them. Reuben said quietly:

'I want to live. But no one to help me have I found.'

The young man muttered:

'I have lived. But in the shadow of death. All that I see and think is in the reflection of that shadow.'

'Ill you are then?' Reuben asked.

'My lungs are rotting,' the other answered brutally, and

51

as though he took pleasure in revealing the fact. He stood up. 'I ought not to be out here now. The night air. But I had to come out. I stayed in all day and then, as I was trying to forget, reading a book, the house became like a nightmare to me and the people there became creatures of stone and iron. I seem to get a little courage, looking over these hills.'

'There's peace I have among them too!'

The young man looked at him with some disgust.

'A healthy little beast like you,' he said, 'ought to be enjoying yourself down in the Valley among the girls at the street corners, or in the pubs. Wandering about the hills alone, at your age, carrying a book of sermons! What sort of a man will you be!'

Reuben looked at him in pained surprise. But he said, with sudden intuition:

'My soul is as sick as yours, perhaps.'

'What use can I be to you then?'

The young man's face, with its smoky pallor and emaciated contours, looked down at Reuben with some amusement. And the boy looked back at him, his face eager with flowering youth.

But in the deep burning of Reuben's eyes too was the lost and troubled brooding of a restless, unhappy soul.

'I am not a good angel of light,' the young man muttered. 'There's not even the dullest glimmer to my lamp. It is corroded and tarnished with decay.'

The vast night swept over them softly, and with chaste, slow rising, the moon appeared over the brow of a far hill, cold and white in her full nakedness.

They looked towards her as she rose over the hill in her

pale light, leaving a dim trail of gold behind her and over
the quiet hills.

'Beauty!' said the young man. He turned to Reuben. 'Tell
me, is that beautiful, that rising of the moon?' There
seemed to be horror and dread in his voice.

'Beautiful it is, indeed,' Reuben answered. 'So white and
pure she looks, the moon.'

'My being leaped towards her as she first appeared,' the
other said, half-whispering in that voice of dread, 'and then
I thought, She is like a ribald woman showing her
protuberant belly to the world. She appeared to me com-
posed of fat and gross flesh.'

Reuben looked at him in perplexed silence. A fit of
coughing shook the young man with frightful violence. He
writhed and spat, his body bent forward and his face
stretched out convulsively.

Reuben could not bear to look at him. He turned away.
And to him too, listening to that terrible diseased
coughing beside him, the night became horrible, the sky
a mockery.

When the convulsions had abated somewhat, Reuben
went to him and took his arm.

'Lean on me and let me take you home,' he said, unconscious pity in his voice.

The young man suddenly laughed.

'Quite a little Jesus! Lean on me, ye heavy-laden and
retching consumptives, and I will give you rest. It's all
right, you tender young fool, I shall be quite capable in a
minute or two. But you can come back with me if you like.
Your presence might save me from the wrath of my aunt.'

He lived on the other slope of the hill, in a house that, before the opening of the pits, had been a farm. It stood apart and lonely, some distance up the slope, away from the other dwellings of the Vale, and because there was still a cow in one of the sheds and a couple of pigs in the sties, the occupiers of the house were looked upon as farm people, though the men of the house worked in the pit.

'Oh, live in Bryn Farm you do!' Reuben observed, when the young man pointed out the house to him.

'Only lately I've come to live here. I used to be a clerk in London until this beastly disease manifested itself and I was told to go away. Do you know my aunt and her family?'

'No. Seldom I go to this part of the Valley.'

'You can come and borrow a couple of my books if you like. You seem keen on learning things and there's little enough opportunity for you in a place like this. What a rat's hole it is! It's supposed to be doing me good, this air, or I'd go mad here.'

They descended a slope and opened a gate in a low white-washed stone wall. There was a patch of wasteland before the house, stony and barren of flower or plant now. By the side of the front-door was a barrel which, through a pipe, received the rain-water from the roof. The young man lifted the latch of the door and they entered, directly in the living-room of the house. A short and stout, middle-aged woman rose from a chair and cried in a voice of alarm:

'Where have you been, Philip? There's madness...'

'I have been bathing my soul in the moonlight,' he said, ducking away from her hands. 'It did me good and I met this fellow, who, like me, finds a bleak solace in the hills.'

'Coughing you've been,' she said, looking at his eyes.

'He wants some books,' continued Philip. 'Do you know him? You see, he has a volume of sermons already, which I think very odd. Still, I'm in Wales.'

Mrs Vaughan looked at Reuben. Her face was warm and mellow, the skin like soft, wrinkled leather. Her eyes were bright with a nervous solicitude.

'The ministry you are going in for?' she asked too, with respect, being Welsh.

'No. Lent to me by Mr Hughes-Williams of Pisgah was the book,' answered Reuben, a little irritably, and feeling the volume was out of place with him. 'Work down under I do.'

'Methodist I am,' she said with pride, for Pisgah Chapel was Baptist.

'A fine chapel is Caersalem,' Reuben agreed. 'And intellectual your preacher is, I am told.'

She squeezed her nose with her fingers, glancing at her nephew. 'Too cold he is for me,' she answered. 'Not often does he get the *hwyl*.'

Philip sniffed. 'Chapel!' he remarked.

'Go on,' cried his aunt, with gentle asperity, as he was a sick man, 'happier we are than you old atheists, anyhow.'

They went to the fireplace. The room was large and cosy, with big furniture and rugs over the stone floor. A heavy oil-lamp, brightly gleaming with brass, hung on many chains from the ceiling, and on the chest of drawers was a case of stuffed squirrels.

'Where's Uncle and Gwylim?' asked Philip.

His aunt moved creakingly in her chair.

'In their usual places, I suppose,' she remarked with

55

some anger, meaning the pubs. 'And Eirwen has gone to that magic-lantern place that has just begun.'

'Cinema,' Philip corrected.

'Well,' she said with disgust, 'sit in the dark they do and watch pictures on a sheet. There's a childish sort of entertainment it seems to me.' She turned to Reuben. 'Enjoyable the week-night little concerts in chapel are, aren't they, boy bach?'

Reuben agreed. Philip looked at him and winked.

'Ah, there's nothing like an eisteddfod for making the soul swell,' he said. 'The reciting, the choirs, the pennillion singing – what glory, what enjoyment, what bellowing, blasting noise! Still, as I said, it makes the soul big and strong.'

His aunt said, with pity for his sick body and mind:

'Jeer at everything he does. But a good soul he's got.' She looked at Reuben meditatively. 'Pleased I am that you have come home with him. Brood he does, being too much alone. Come you up often.' She gazed back at her nephew anxiously. 'Go to bed now, Philip bach, and I will bring you the hot milk up. Silly you were to stay out so long.'

But he seemed to writhe under the naked anxiety of her love, and there was weary suffering in his eyes as he looked back at her. Death, Death, the grey waste of his face cried when she spoke to him in her voice of apprehensive love. For all his contempt of life, he suffered and writhed at any tone of voice or the least glance that reminded him of his doom. Reuben watched him and suffered too.

He thought: 'If I could bring the love of Christ into his life!'

56

Mrs Vaughan thought: 'If we had the money to send him away to those foreign parts.'

'I will stay down a little longer,' Philip said sullenly. 'Now, about those books – come and look at them.' He took Reuben to some shelves of books in a corner.

Reuben had no great knowledge of books and Philip was at a loss to know which volumes to lend the boy. Finally they decided on Palgrave's *Golden Treasury*, Shakespeare, and Emerson.

Mrs Vaughan looked at the volumes coldly. 'Books!' she exclaimed classically. 'It's this book-reading that turns people's minds quaint and nasty.'

Just then the latch of the door was lifted and a young girl entered.

'Eirwen,' Mrs Vaughan said, 'for what you went out without your scarf! A bare neck like that at night! Chill it is, you foolish girl.'

She was nineteen, tall, and beautiful. Seeing a stranger in the room, she lowered her lids and gazed at her mother a little angrily. But Reuben saw the dark flash of her eyes, and as she stepped into the room the light of the lamp made her skin gleam like gold. She took off her hat and tossed back her black hair.

'I never feel cold,' she said, rather sullenly.

Mrs Vaughan indicated Reuben.

'A friend of Philip he is. Reuben Daniels. Remember him in school perhaps you do.'

The girl looked at Reuben.

Her glance seemed to go hotly into him. The blood rose to his face and beat in his temples. He had never seen such dark and beautiful eyes. Looking back at them he seemed to enter their depths as into a brilliant and disturbing vision.

'No,' she said.

He did not say a word. Her naked neck and face issued from her garment like a white-flaming flower from a strong lithe stem. He was conscious only of her beauty, and he stared at her with such intensity that she began to laugh softly.

'Did you find the magic-lantern show elevating?' Philip asked, gazing at the two with amusement.

'Where did *you* wander off to this afternoon?' she said to him. Her voice had become gentle and reedy, almost a croon, as she spoke to him.

'Like John I withdrew into the desert for bitter meditation,' he said. There was an ironic twist to his grey lips. 'In the hairshirt of my gloom and sitting in the dust, I came to the conclusion that even a lovely complexion has within its shallow life the capabilities of boils and bright bawdy rashes.'

'There's a fool you are,' she laughed stridently, her body shaking, lithe as a sleek animal.

Reuben gathered the books under his arm.

'Come up to tea now on Sunday,' Mrs Vaughan invited him.

He said he would, and Eirwen favoured him with a smile as he said good-night. She had been scrutinising him secretly from behind her thick, drooped lids.

He hurried up the path on the hill, raced across the top and paused for a moment before descending the other slope.

In the moonlight the Valley beneath him seemed like a strange country of melancholy and ancient peace. The night hid all the raw cuts and the harsh eruptions of the mines. Only the silver-grey roofs and the quiet gleam of lamps and windows could be seen clearly. There was no noise from the colliery, no clank of coal-wagons, and the hills that shut in the still village curved up like the gigantic petals of a sombre and sleeping flower.

Reuben looked down into the Valley.

And suddenly he was filled with a hot and anguished love for this, his country.

BOOK TWO

CHAPTER I

'Reuben,' called Martha from downstairs, 'bronchitis you will have, staying up in that cold bedroom all this time.'

He had gone up to his room after the bath in the kitchen and, leaning his head against the window, gazed out upon the dull wintry landscape with a numb desolation in his heart. He felt so alone: all day in the pit he had been thinking: 'I labour day after day like this and there is no joy or hope in my life.' And he had fallen on his knees at the window and lifted his face to the evening sky.

'Reuben,' Martha cried again, 'what for you stay in that cold room straight after a hot bath?'

He went downstairs and sat at the fire. His face, with its pale strong skin and nervous eyes, was sullen in his abstraction.

'There's peevish you've been looking,' Martha said. 'Bad you feel? Say what's the matter with you.'

He shook his head.

But she enquired as to the state of his bowels, and was so solicitous that he sprang up and cried:

'Leave me alone, will you. All right I am and I'll be able to work regularly. Don't be afraid of that.'

She looked at him in fear. Lately he had become so irritable.

'Not thinking of your work was I,' she almost whined.

She had been drinking that afternoon, he knew. Her face was repellent to him: and she seemed to have become pitiable and draggled in her evil indulgence; her old hard strength was dwindling.

'You were,' he cried brutally, burning to anger her. 'What do you care as long as money you've got for satisfying your sottish thirst? Listen to me. Losing the respect of everybody you are and they jeer about you when you go down the street. The smell of drink is always stale on you and before many years you won't be able to rise from bed. And I hate you. You fill me with disgust. Look at your face now. Old and ugly it is getting. Ach, there's horrible you will become.'

He had caught hold of her arm in his fury, but she snatched it away and shrank back in fear from his thrust-out face.

'Mad you are,' she screeched.

He gazed at her intently. Her red lids were lifted from her eyes in fear. And those eyes looked out at him with such horror that he cried in pain:

'Hurt me you do. See, if you'd only become clean and forget the drink, there's happy we'd be here. Older you are getting and afraid for you I am.'

He went to her and held her arms, gazed deep into her heavy, staring eyes.

'My own trouble it is,' she muttered sullenly. 'Leave me alone to my own business.'

He remembered her rare caresses, the veiled love that had always wavered in her harsh voice when she spoke to him. He remembered her quiet hand over his brow once when he was ill; a flow of cool sweetness had seemed to come from it. And he felt so alone. If only she were different!

'I want you,' he whispered, 'I want to be so proud of you – '

But she struggled from him again, crying, 'Go you out and mix with people. It's mad you will get, always brooding and staring like an owl in a cage.'

He went out: he was suddenly sickened of her and the house. He went down to the river and gazed at the water washing over the pale stones and creeping through the rushes. The water was flowing to the absorbing sea, the night would be gathered into another short day, and he was growing older and older. There was something he must do. There was something gathered in him like a terrible power, a power that he must loosen on the world, before returning, dry and hollow with giving, into the earth.

He turned away towards the main Valley. And he thought of the pale faces of the miners who tramped to the pit with him in the cold early morning. He thought: 'Those faces have upon them something that hurts me. And on the faces of the women in chapel, too, there is the shadow of invisible tears.'

He ran up the little hill and entered the main street. There were few people about; it was a cold, desolate night. The public-house on the corner was lit up with its flaring gas-lamps, and from it came a noise of singing and shouting voices. A drunkard tottered out of the front doorway and sat down, muttering on the step. He began to sing as Reuben approached:

'There's a land that knows no trouble,
We shall meet again on that shore...'

And he spat unctuously as Reuben went past.

The bare streets as he crept on, rows and rows of dirty-grey dwellings, were like galleries sunk in some murky, deserted inferno: when a figure appeared it seemed to writhe past with a numb and secret pain. And Reuben whispered to himself, 'There is a wound in the bodies of men, and the blood flows out, drop by drop, staining the world.'

His mood led him inevitably to Bryn Farm. But as he climbed the hill he knew that his friend would but deepen the ache in his soul.

Eirwen opened the door: she greeted him with her faint smile, that made her sensuous lips seem full of hidden richness.

'Philip is in bed,' she said. 'But he'll be glad to see you.'

He did not look at her when they went in: but he was aware of the scrutiny of those dark eyes of hers, that pierced him with such disturbing intensity. Philip was sitting up in bed; a lamp stood on the table beside him and by its light he was reading a stained and pencilled volume

64

of Webster's plays. He looked up as Reuben entered and regarded his friend with a sinister grimace on his shrunken face.

'You bring the odour of life with you,' he said.

Reuben sat down in a chair by the wall and gazed at him without a word. The other continued, as though musing to himself:

'Look at my hand! It is the hand of a corpse. I look upon it as already dead: I think it miraculous when the fingers twitch or grasp something. Strange how it came into being, strange how its white skin, those bones, that ligament, will become nothing. Why was it created and for a period made to know the feel of other flesh, the smoothness of silk, the cool of the sea, the eternal vases resurrected from the earth? I do not know, you say, and the stony universe echoes your cry.' And he cackled with laughter.

Reuben said, in his young voice of pity:

'No, I believe that a greater life than this there is. Suffering and sorrow but make it more certain. There is a being within us that has an eternal life. I believe it.'

'Ah, beliefs...' Philip said ironically.

'If you believed it, you would be happy.'

'Drug one's pain with God you mean? Yes, to keep one joyful and satisfied there is nothing like believing in God. That is why religion should be kept alive amongst the poor; it is the only bed of luxury into which they can sink their weary bones.'

Reuben remarked:

'Man was made to worship. His nature is such that he cannot stand alone.'

'Yes, you are right. All my life I have wanted to worship. Not a God, but the animal and human creatures that suffer.'

'A God you'd worship then. By the wounds and sufferings of the flesh one shall see a clearer light.'

Philip smiled. He gazed into the air as though he looked upon a happy and tender thing. Then, in a slow voice that was monotonous with weary remembrance, he began:

'When I was a boy I lived in a suburb of London that seemed to have millions of foggy houses, each the same as the other, and stuck together in rows as though for eternity. Creatures with two legs walked in and out of these houses, clad in some grey stuff and with their heads screwed on as though forever they would be in the same stiff position, looking before them with eyes that were like the eyes of dead fish. And I used to think of the naked flesh of a naiad in the waters of her fountain. I lived with my mother and father, and in the evenings when I was lonely I sometimes watered the geraniums on the window-sill of our flat and then gazed down into the dirty street wondering how many more women Jack the Ripper would kill. My mother had the obsessed soul of a wife whose husband has the reputation of consorting with other and younger women. My father would come in about twelve at night and he seemed always pleasant, singing those music-hall songs that are for dolls and people with saw-dust heads that have the eyes of dead fish. Then I listened to my mother's voice cracking in its fury as she abused my father; I crouched in my bed and when finally my mother broke down into sobs I would bury my teeth in my arm until I screamed with pain. She would come to me then and as I pointed to the

66

blood on my arm she looked at me like a madwoman. On her forty-eighth birthday I came home from my first job in the city and found her with her head in the gas-oven. When my father arrived I looked at him and did not utter a word. I saw that he too had dead eyes; they gazed at me for a moment, then he went out and I never saw him again. I lived here, there and everywhere afterwards, in London – once with a little Jewess who did not mind how much I hurt her, biting her, as long as I bought her plenty of turkish-delight. After coming home from the office, invariably I read Nietzsche, or Keats' Letters, Baudelaire – any book that would drive hunger and suffering deeper into my soul. And my youth passed. I seemed to have lived in a frozen world – under ice, my feet buried in clay. Perhaps I have never broken through that ice, never seen the sun. Am I to be blamed for that?'

Reuben whispered:

'I have thought that suffering passes, that nothing can dim the flame that I have, the flame that burns brighter when I worship God. There is something within me that bends my knees to the earth and lifts my head to the sky. Have you never felt like that?'

'Sometimes, when I have seen a particularly beautiful evening sky, perhaps, I've wanted to offer up thanks in my exaltation. But to what? I think: that sky is a natural performance of the elements of light and shade and all its beauty will not lessen the pangs of a slum child crying for bread.'

Reuben muttered slowly:

'The life of man seems tangled and hopeless. But who

knows what divine purpose there is in the world's suffering and cruelty? We must keep our faith shining and glowing.'

Philip looked at him and said with a touch of irony in his voice:

'Futility. You should have been a preacher. You would be a great success in a fashionable church; your style would move the hearts of hordes of well-fed women.'

'I want to do more than that,' Reuben said quickly, with some anger in his face. 'I want to make the hearts of the poor tremble with a new joy.'

Philip turned his head away in weariness and looked staringly and coldly into the air again. He continued:

'Success to your barren task! As for me, I am occupied in watching my bones appear more and more distinctly beneath this fading flesh of mine. And, if you knew how my heart burns in anger against that process of decay! I am decaying before my time! The world has lovely places I have not seen; there are pleasures I shall never know; there are women whose lips torment me as I remember them. Limbs of strong and supple flesh, thighs that throb for a moment against my own, a mouth red and moist as a bitten pomegranate, Florence in the Spring, the cold piercing beauty of the Alps, mornings at sea...'

'Haven't you *ever* been happy?' Reuben asked gently.

Philip was silent for a minute or two. His eyes closed, a vague smile came upon his face. He said softly:

'How intuitive you are! But listen. When I lived in London I used to go occasionally to the symphony concerts. One evening I sat next to a woman who kept glancing at me as though there was something about me that distressed her.

68

I looked at her. She was about thirty, and her face had the evidences of an interesting temperament. She was not good-looking, but there was about her a vivid and sapient awareness of things that was irresistible. When the concert was over I spoke to her. I said, 'Madame, the music of Beethoven has just been played. Were you listening?' She replied, laughing: 'No, I've been admiring the austerity of your face in profile. There was a melancholy calm about it that I envied. Will you come and drink coffee with me?' I went with her, and thus began an affair that gave me all the joys of the blessed and the torments of the damned. She had a little flat in a crescent of houses in Bayswater and a man, a dress-designer who was half his time in Paris, kept her. But the dress-designer was not the Alpha and Omega of her life. After coffee that night she invited me to accompany her home. I went. I remember the gleam of her eyes in the cab. She said: 'I used to know someone like you when I lived in the Midlands, years ago. He died of something or other, he was never strong. But he had just such an expression as you have.' And she looked at me with such penetrating eagerness that I began to laugh. 'Don't laugh,' she said rather angrily, 'I loved him and we were to be married.' After my bare cheap room her flat had a luxuriousness that to me was a dream of senuous ease. I stayed with her all night and at intervals she would pass her fingers over my forehead and eyes and murmur, 'It is there that you are like him.' Once I protested. 'You are in love with a ghost,' I said. But I was too happy to be angry with her. Her body made tangible all I had dreamed of in my lonely nights. In the morning I said, 'You never want to see me again, of course,' but she answered, 'Come to see me this evening and we will talk about Beethoven and Bach.' I went, and we talked of the processes of love. She was an odd creature, a kind of decadent Aspasia. She had no morals. If, looking at a man, the curve of his back or the poise of his head made a certain chord in her vibrate, she did all she could to obtain him for her gratification. After a period her physical desire for me waned. But my love for her increased. I was sickened when I thought of the other men. She tried to comfort me, saying that she desired me above all for her mental satisfaction. We went to concerts together – she had a sentimental affection for music – and we used to read Swinburne and brood over volumes of Beardsley's drawings together. At times she awoke in me a feeling of nausea, but she had only to look at me with those eyes of hers, those eyes that in spite of her art had the shadows of despair about them, and I was instantly her slave. I asked her why she lived such a life, and she answered, 'Because it is sin and I have a grudge against God.' I said contemptuously, 'A cheap excuse. You mean because you are a born harlot.' When I lay in my own bed and thought of the man she was probably embracing, because he had some likeness to a dead lover, I wanted to run to her flat, set fire to those rooms stained and accursed by her orgies, and force her to live with me in some low quarter where there was misery and poverty like a sharp and blasting wind about us. But at times she let me caress her body and all was well again. Then one evening when I went to see her I found her strange and silent, and her face had a pallor that was like death. I asked her what was the matter, but she would not answer and said, 'Let's go to a concert.' On the way she became more animated and, except that she would stare fixedly before her now and again, she seemed her own self. During the concert she sat back with her eyes closed and seemed to listen attentively to the music. But I did not like the look of her face. The last piece the orchestra played was Mozart's *Eine Kleine Nachtmusik*. 'Ah,' she said, as we walked out into the night that seemed full of menace to me, 'such happiness is not for me. You listened to that last music? It was awful to hear such loveliness.' And I could have laughed at her then, because at last she seemed to be suffering. She had a way of gazing at me that made me laugh like a fool, as though I wanted to protect myself. I looked at her closely. And I saw that her face had become ugly, a sort of reflected mental ugliness, a sort of ravaged horror in its exhausted contours. We walked to the Crescent. And she began to talk of her lovers, but in a new, bitter way that pleased me. She remarked that she had passed from male mouth to male mouth like a bawdy story. And she would stop now and again, lift her head to the stars and hum from that sentimental Mozart piece. I remember her stretched throat in the lamplight of those streets. She would not let me enter her flat that night. I asked her what was the matter, but she only stared at me with darkened eyes that afterwards I knew were bidding me an eternal farewell. She left the flat, disappeared. But I saw her about six months later one night in a quarter of London that is haunted by the cheaper kind of prostitute. Her face had become evil and all its paint and powder did not hide the bluish tinge of death that was upon it and the nasty sickliness that showed upon her. I spoke to

71

her, asked her why she disappeared so suddenly, and she laughed like some shameless hag as she said, 'I went into hospital,' and then began to abuse us bloody men. I wanted to help her, but she laughed me off, saying I was too much of a Jesus to help her then. As I left her she called, "Don't worry about me. I'm still enjoying life and I have a gramophone and a few books still." I went home, to bed.'

Reuben cried:

'Stop. You should not think back of those things.'

The other began to laugh softly.

'You do not think there are such things? I tell you that even when still alive the body can become so horrible that even a dog would sicken from it. But of course there is always the soul within, that came from God.'

'You can mock,' cried Reuben, his young eyes burning, 'but that soul shall be purer because of those stains, it shall be like the lily and the snow. When the body will be of earth again that soul will be like a white bird in the Kingdom of God. It will sing the loveliest music and earth and pain will be utterly forgotten.'

Philip gazed at him calmly.

'Ah,' he said, 'what a style! It would make a fortune for you, especially here, in Wales.'

Reuben looked back at him in misery. If he could but bring the comfort of God to that suffering soul! But it seemed a hopeless task.

The consumptive muttered suddenly:

'How much longer, how much longer?'

There was a stricken darkness in his eyes, and the attenuated cheeks burned feverishly. Reuben was suddenly afraid. There was such cold deathly hopelessness in that muttering. He stood up and went downstairs softly.

Eirwen was sitting by the fire, reading and alone. She looked up quickly as he entered the room.

'Ill he seems,' Reuben whispered.

'He's got one of his bad bouts on,' she answered, rather carelessly, without moving.

'Perhaps he wants something,' he urged tentatively.

She got up, and with her easy graceful walk went to the stairs and called out:

'Philip, do you want anything, cariad?'

The Welsh endearment fell with strange tenderness from her mouth. And while she called she looked at Reuben with her eyelids lifted.

'Only peace,' Philip cried back.

She smiled at Reuben, showing her fine strong teeth.

'Odd he is,' she laughed. 'Think I do sometimes that take pleasure in his state he does.' She went back to her chair.

'Come and sit by the fire,' she invited. 'About what were you two talking all this time?'

'He was telling me of his life in London,' Reuben answered cautiously, sitting down, rather unwilling, on a stool by the fender.

She looked at him meditatively.

'More than he's told me that is,' she said. 'Close about his life he is with me.'

He gazed at her furtively. In the soft light of the oil-lamp the beauty of her face was chaste and tender, the sensuous lips delicately curved. As she breathed he noticed the quivering of her nostrils.

73

She looked into the fire.

'There's quiet you are,' she murmured softly.

'Quiet the house makes one,' he answered quickly. 'Away up here... lonely it is – '

'Yes, lonely,' she repeated. 'Until half-past ten only Philip is here tonight. But I am accustomed to being lonely.'

There was a hostile quiver in her voice. Her body seemed taut with rich life, as she leaned forward and gazed into the fire, her full stretched neck bearing up proudly her gold-gleaming face.

'Like to go away you would?' he asked.

'I wanted to go and learn singing, but too poor we are, so I have to stay here and sing in the little eisteddfod of this and that chapel.' She spoke angrily and bitterly. 'I want to go to London, Paris, Italy – sing in opera and big concert-halls.'

'A grand life that would be,' he said, and gazed furtively at her. He was rather afraid of her, in the atmosphere of her vindictive female ardour, her passionate flaming vitality.

She turned and looked at him with sudden curiosity:

'Religious you are, aren't you?'

He disliked people thinking he was entirely religious. In the Valley religious boys were objects of derision to other boys and girls. But he hated telling people the ideals of his being, he hated to speak of the ecstatic life of his soul, that was so secret and indescribable. 'I don't know,' he said sullenly. 'Difficult it is to be religious.'

She continued to look at him with her dilated naked eyes. He was clasping his knees, gazing intently into the hearth, his pale face, its strange muscular tenderness shadowed, as

74

though abstracted in a dim dream remote from her.

'I've been reading those Shakespeare plays Philip lent me,' he murmured.

She moved in her chair as though she trembled.

'Shakespeare...' she repeated, in a barren voice. 'Oh, I know... poetry.'

'Lovely they seem,' he said. 'Such words – '

His voice was soft and strange, his face turned from her, its male power so tender and abstracted in shadow, a profile of pale beautiful stone.

'What are they about?' she asked, her voice dark and quivering, and, hesitating, added, 'Love, I suppose!'

He looked up slowly and saw her burning eyes.

'Some are,' he answered, his throat beating.

He seemed to crouch on the stool before her, as though afraid and fascinated, gazing at her, a faint, nervous smile on his lips.

She lifted her head and her face seemed to lift and contract with pain.

'I like you.' Her lips moved in a hardly audible whisper, as she repeated, as though in a croon, 'I like you. Different you are. I like you.'

She got up, with her proud, graceful movements, like a languid imperial cat, and knelt down on the rug beside his stool. He stared at her, and he did not move even when she laid her hands on his knees and lifted her face up like some distorted flower to him.

Then he muttered swiftly, 'Don't look like that! Don't look at me like that!'

She cried, in a voice that burned into his brain:

75

'Kiss me, kiss me. On my mouth. Kiss me.'

Slowly he bent forward, slowly and vaguely, as though he were being sucked down into darkness and sleep, obeying that drugged voice.

Her lips were moist and devouring. She clasped her arms round his shoulders and drew him down to her with a vehemence that seemed to snap his nerves.

'Let me go,' he cried suddenly.

He did not want her then, the pressure of her breasts against him, her keen skin, her vehement hands – he did not want them then. Not then. But the blood raced madly through his veins, his eyes were hot against their lids and his limbs were taut and strung with a fierce strength.

He had kissed her mouth with a desire that was like a burning seal.

But he did not want the terrible passion of her arms, her body.

'No, not now,' he cried, escaping from those arms.

She looked at him, wrath and shame mingled on her face. But her eyes were dilated with a dark, numb appeal.

'Do you hate me now?' she whispered.

He leaned against the table.

'No,' he said, then began to laugh nervously.

She got up slowly. Then she smiled too.

'Coy you are,' she said.

'Careful you mean,' he laughed.

She shook herself like some lithe silky beast.

Later they sat again before the fire. Reuben had taken a book of poems from the shelves in the corner and was reading Wordsworth to the young woman, absorbed in his task and oblivious to her constant yawns.

She gazed into the fire, dreaming. When he had finished reading he looked up and saw her thus.

Her face was still and calm, her body in repose. And she appeared to him like one of the chaste women of the Bible – Ruth or Esther, whom he admired and loved.

And she was beautiful – he could see it.

Before he departed he whispered to her:

'I love you too, Eirwen fach. But with a holy love.'

And as he walked home he chanted a psalm to the sky and the stars, in a voice that was like crystal, his eyes full of a mystic peace and serenity.

CHAPTER II

The image of Eirwen became tangled in the thoughts of his waking and sleeping mind. When he woke in the dawn to go to the pit he could dimly remember that her vague secret smile had been with him in his dreams. And he thought of her, too, in the pit, as he heaved the coal into the trucks and as he silently devoured his bread and cheese.

He saw her clearly against a starry deep blue sky, her face pale as an angel's, her eyes as though lost in the contemplation of sweet holy things, and her fine breasts, firm but with the soft contours of youth, seemed to move as though her soul stirred in a chaste ecstasy.

It was thus he saw her.

But her image did not interfere with his studious evenings. He took down the Holy Book as usual and sat by the lamp, his forehead resting on his hand, or perhaps he went for a religious talk with Old Morgans, who had a bakehouse and was engaged, while the bread baked, in copying out the Bible in his own handwriting and in red ink. Reuben had known him since he had been able to carry his mother's tins of dough down to the bakehouse.

Now he would knock at the bakehouse door, when the time for receiving the dough for the evening's baking was past, and all was quiet, save for the scratch of Old Morgans' pen. The saintly old man, rudely called Moses One Leg by young boys, would stump across the stone flags of his bakehouse and open the door, his fierce eyes glaring through the spectacles set half-way down his aquiline nose. But, because Reuben was familiar with the Scriptures, he was one of the few allowed to disturb the old man's sacred labour.

'Come you in, boy bach,' he was always welcomed.

Reuben liked the warm cosy atmosphere of the bakehouse, the whitewashed walls and the crisp smell of baking bread, and Old Morgans himself, who had a long white beard of stiff hair that reached to his corduroy trousers and which was sometimes singed when he poked the fire.

'How far have you got now?' Reuben asked, looking at the copybooks on one of the tables.

No one knew, exactly, why Old Morgans was copying the Bible into those cheap note-books; if anyone asked, that person was told, angrily, to mind his own business. In his youth the baker had wanted to be a minister, and his wife was a grim and icy woman with a contemptuous horror of men. She encouraged his holy task in the bakehouse, where he could rest his wooden leg unseen of her.

'A good sermon you had from Mr Hughes-Williams on Sunday?' he asked Reuben.

'Well,' Reuben said meditatively, 'sweat very much he did. But empty sound seem his sermons to me lately.'

'Yes,' Morgans agreed, his nose twitching with disgust, 'a patchy old windbag he is. Odd it is that his chapel is so full. But a fashionable style there is to his sermons. Popular is his trashy manner always. But examine you his sermons closely and dafter than a lunatic's babble you will find his thinking.'

Reuben sat on a stool and folded his arms.

'Better sermons I could give, I think.'

The old man looked at him sadly:

'Like me you are. A natural minister of God, but too poor to be made lawful and be honoured in a pulpit of oak and cushioned seats.' He raised his head and his beard of stiff hair stuck out proudly. 'But a ministry there is which is honoured better in the eyesight of God – the ministry of poor men who help each other without noise and live a life that is pure as a baby's sleep.' He looked into the air in the manner of a preacher, stroked his beard, and continued, 'Who shall deny that I do more good than Mr Hughes-Williams? Fiery are his words and listen to them closely does his flock, their eyes wide with fear and their mouths open with surprise. But there's a fine lot they are out of chapel – there's private lives they lead except on Sundays! So where is the influence of his words? Weak, weak he is. A better man even am I. More good I do by looking carefully that the bread in this oven shall not be burned, that the loaves of the hungry people shall come forth brown, but not black, their crusts risen beautiful and crisp because of the right heat of my oven. Even more good I do when I allow the rude children who call me names to come in and drink of the water of my tap when they thirst at their play. Even stronger was I when my leg was poisoned and I said, "Let it be removed, for God in his mercy has thus chastised me for a sin of my youth." '

'Yes indeed,' Reuben answered, in the grave melancholy tone that Welsh people adopt when they discuss ministers, 'easy-going preachers become when they are certain of their wages. There's different they are to the old saints! Bare should be the fact of a minister of God, hungry his stomach, subdued his flesh...'

Old Morgans spat into the cinders beneath the oven. 'Empty words!' he said surprisingly, for Reuben was but pandering to the baker's love of mournfully deploring the habits of ordained preachers. 'A hungry man is a sore sight to God. Fields of wheat and lovely animals were created by him, and the art to make them into delicious food he craftily placed in man's mind. And the flesh...!' He looked at Reuben with large shining eyes. 'Meant you the love of women, boy bach?'

Reuben nodded his head gravely. The old man's voice took on the resonance of strong bells:

'God is in that love, and the marriage-bed that has respectful love as a mattress and moderation as a quilt is the bed of the true religion and a welcome picture in the eyes of God. Do not scorn the flesh, or misery will come upon you like a whip. *Rejoice, O young man, in thy youth.* In the joys of the flesh a clear light will come to you.'

Reuben said meditatively:

'Light you have had in abundance perhaps, for the voice of a wise man you have.'

81

Morgans cackled with dry mirth.

'Plenty of light I had,' he said reminiscently, 'but a long time it has had to last me too.' Then suddenly he lifted his wooden leg and pointed to it. 'Respect for the flesh that has given me,' he continued. 'Aged I was before my time because of it. There's often I have said to myself, *"the golden bowl is broken, and the pitcher is broken at the fountain, and the wheels broken at the cistern."* Proud and a strong young man I was, and lusty my joys. Because of them better understanding of religion and ministers I have.'

He raised his hand like a prophet and his brows contracted with dark wrath.

'Yea,' he continued, 'the ministers have no knowledge of life. They have given themselves over to a comfortable holiness as to a corrupt harlot who pretends chastity. They borrow their words from the books of their cosy libraries and there is not in them the flame that shall burn up the evil of the world. They do not go forth into the wilderness of suffering and gather from men the cry of their ailments and from women the tears of their griefs. But in the mornings they take their tea in bed and in the afternoons they sleep on their soft sofas before their drawing-room fires! If industrious some of them are, it is for the benefit of their deep pockets, wherein often, as aforetime, lie thirty pieces of silver. Ah, but there's a power in the land they could be! I would cry to them, Gird up your loins, leave your carpets, beds, books and comfortable wives, and go forth into the dark world, a torch of fiery light in your hands, the naked power of God as a great music in your voices!'

82

And he hit his hands together and stamped his wooden leg with righteous fury. He was fond of denouncing ordained ministers to people who visited him in his bakehouse. Reuben looked into the eyes that glared at him from beneath twitching brows, and he was filled with respect for this old man, who was so laboriously copying the Bible and whose disputes with his wife were well known.

'Think you the Corinthians have the true light more than the old chapels?' he asked, knowing the baker's liking for that sect.

'Ah,' Morgans answered, 'they are the real children of God. No stink of money is there about *their* simple halls, no communion sets of silver have they, no pews of costly wood, no coloured glasses in the windows. But in their worship there is a purity as of a morning wind.'

'Do you give the sermons there sometimes?' Reuben asked. He knew that any member of the sect, male or female, was allowed to occupy the rude pulpit when the Leader, their unordained minister, chose to be sacrificial.

'Yes, honoured I am often by a request to take service,' the old man declared proudly, 'and complimentary everybody is afterwards. And there's fervour I rouse in the congregation! Their faces shine like the faces of angels and afterwards they do sing as though they were in Heaven.'

'Yes, a very lively lot they appear to be,' Reuben said reflectively. 'Even sing hymns and pray in the pit they do. You know Isaac Evans? Near me he works, down-under. Heard him pray often I have, thanking God for giving him a good seam to work on. And, indeed, lucky he is, for one of the best workings in the pit he has got.'

'Attends evening service very faithfully does Isaac Evans,' Morgans said. 'And there's a holy and simple life he leads; and a bachelor he is. A lot he must put away every week! But no style is there to his praying when he gets up in chapel, no warmth. Too holy he's always been I think. Nothing to repent of has he done.'

'Think you then one is a better preacher after having done a little sin?'

'Yea. A pleasure there is in most sin and a better pleasure in repentance. And God did not say, *Let the earth be a good place*. His place above the sky is good, and different the earth had to be. How should men delight in Heaven if they have been familiar with it on earth?'

Reuben meditated.

He had heard men discuss things in the pit and his being had shuddered at the filth of the world. But he did not think of his own body as a vessel of sin. There was one sin the men spoke of constantly and it had troubled him most – the sin with women, while one was still in a single state. The men spoke of women with lewd words, laughing enjoyably, and he had been troubled by emotions that made the blood run hotly through his body.

For he had thought of his body as a thing dedicated to chastity, a song of purity, a star of white flame, a flower of Christ.

Old Morgans sniffed noisily.

'The bread is nearly done,' he said and reached to the top of the oven for a long shovel which he used to draw forth the tins of bread. 'Come you up to the Corinthians one Sunday evening, Daniels bach. Wasting your time you

84

are in Mr Hughes-Williams' chapel. A stomach for more satisfying religion than is taught there you have.'

He washed his hands, combed his flowing hair, and put on a white apron.

'There's a lovely smell the bread has!' Reuben remembered, getting up to go.

'The blessing of God is upon this bakehouse,' the old man said fervently. 'Ancient is the oven but never does it go wrong. Refuse custom I have to. There's jealous Thomas Watkins is! A new oven he has, but next to nothing is his trade. But a churchman he is, so not surprised am I.'

Reuben promised to go to the Corinthians' service one Sunday evening and the baker told him he should sit in the front seat, next to him.

And as he walked home he thought again of sin.

What were those sinister thoughts that escaped his mind when he woke in the morning? It was as though in his sleep he had been thinking of things that flew like figures of shame from his waking mind. Once in the night he thought he opened his eyes and saw in the air before him the face and throat of a girl. Her hair was loose and fell in threads over her drowsy eyes, her lips were heavy and dark, her thick white throat pulsated with a movement that fascinated him. And about the image there had seemed a subtle delight that was terrible and evil. A cry had escaped his lips and, waking fully, he had listened fearfully to the loud throbbing of his heart.

He began to hurry and once or twice turned his head, as though he expected to see again in the darkness that beautiful face of sin, the passionate throat.

His father was in when he arrived home. Hugh sat at a table making spills of paper, the jam-pot that held them before him. They were used for lighting the lamp and his pipe.

'Well, Reuben, and where have you been tonight?'

'Talking with Old Morgans the bakehouse.'

Hugh gazed at his son.

'For what you like to talk with elderly men like him so often? And a contradictory old turncoat he is. Tried all the chapels in turn he has, and when the deacons won't let him be bossy, critical and jeering he becomes. What chapel now is he favouring?'

'Corinthians.'

'Aye, more freedom he would be allowed there. But cranky lot they are. Believe they do that God is more pleased if they go out of their minds and make a noise like screeching lunatics.'

'Think I will attend their services for a while.' Reuben said. 'Stale and profitless I find Mr Hughes-Williams' sermons lately.'

'Now, now,' Hugh protested, 'an educated man is our minister.'

'A fine repairer of umbrellas he is,' Reuben answered, 'but no art is there in his sermons.'

And he took down the Bible, opened it, but thought of Eirwen, until his mother came in and chattered tipsily of her neighbours.

CHAPTER III

Reuben went often now to Sunday tea at the Farm. He was considered a pleasing young man by Mrs Vaughan, who was worried because of her daughter's indifference to sacred matters. True, he was only a pit-boy, and her daughter had ambitions for her voice, but he was so unlike those hooligans who smoked and spat about the street-corners, and he had a definite place in a chapel too.

Reuben walked there today in a mood of dim expectation. He would ask Eirwen to walk out with him after chapel. That was the correct thing to do if one intended to court a girl.

But when he asked her, as they sat alone in the parlour before tea, she answered with an indignation that was both mocking and arch:

'What do you mean, Reuben Daniels? Not courting, we are! But people will say so.'

'I thought you wanted me for a boy.'

'Go on. Why?' she asked, lifting out a languid hand and stroking the leaves of a luxuriant aspidistra near.

'The other night – ' he began in a subdued and pained voice.

She tossed her head. But her cheeks burned.

'Thinking of you I've been,' he whispered. 'You said that you liked me and you let me kiss you. I kissed you. You remember.'

She bent her face, her eyes closed: her cheeks were flushed as though in a sweet shame.

'You let me kiss you and hold you,' he repeated, watching her, his great eyes hungry beneath their nervous brows.

'And behaved like a little minister you did,' she said, tossing up her head again. 'Like a little minister who has just begun in his first chapel.'

'Now, Eirwen Vaughan,' he protested, 'don't you have loose thoughts.'

'Not ashamed of my thoughts am I,' she answered proudly, curling her arrogant nose. 'But a bit too soon it is for *you* to understand them.'

She crossed her legs before the fire and scratched her head, moving her arm with decided but always harmonious gestures. And as she lay back indolently in her chair, in her purplish Sunday dress, she seemed like some vivid flower lifting out disdainful petals in a place of respectable pale ferns.

'Not much knowledge of the female mind have I yet,' he admitted humbly.

'A costly knowledge that is.'

'Let me learn though.'

She looked at him subtly, down her long lashes. She liked the eager, vital earthliness of his body, the visionary face that had the shadow of melancholy upon it.

'But you will come out with me after chapel?' he asked quickly, hearing Philip's voice.

'All right. Meet me by Lewis the Milk's shop.'

For they attended different chapels.

Philip came in, coughing and ironic. He looked with a jeering and amused grimace at the couple.

'A Welsh Venus and Adonis among the aspidistras!'

'Who were they?' Eirwen enquired languidly, getting up. 'Bad people, I expect, judging by your face. There's a grin!' And she went to help her mother to prepare the tea.

'She's a slut, she is,' he said coarsely to Reuben.

Reuben turned, displeasure on his countenance, to the fire.

'Lovelier she is than any woman I have seen,' he said sadly.

Philip looked almost gay today. His face shone with a pallid and watery laughter. He sat down and began to sing, in a cracked, uncouth voice, an operatic air.

When tea was ready they were called into the living-room by a hoarse scream from Mr Vaughan who, when he was in the house, seldom moved from his specially-made armchair, which held his massive proportions as no other chair could:

'Clap your noise, Philip, and bring Hugh Daniels' boy bach in to tea.'

They found him already seated in his armchair at the table and removing scones at a great rate. Mrs Vaughan had been known to say, 'If it wasn't for his appetite a row of houses we'd be owning now.'

The table was rich with the Sunday china and the delicacies dedicated to that day. The Sabbath tea is an ornate function in the Valley; there are jellies, special pastry and meat patties, in addition to the lesser luxuries – scones, toast, plain Welsh cakes, and muffins. And the woman of the house is disturbed if a visitor fails to taste all of these good, wholesome delicacies. Let there be plain teas on other days: the meal before Sunday evening chapel must be a good one and must be eaten.

Mrs Vaughan poured out the tea, calling to her husband, 'Bread and butter, William Vaughan, bread and butter. Leave one little scone for each of us now.'

His shining protruding eyes roved over the table restlessly. He loved Sunday tea.

They sat down at the round table beneath the glittering oil-lamp. Eirwen looked sardonic and proud, as she always did when there was a visitor to see her father eat, and her brother Ben, a little older and with some of her beauty, brutalised, set about his meal with silent avidity too.

'Can you tell me, Reuben,' asked Philip, slowly cutting his muffin, 'if there is any connection between the stomach and religious inclination?'

'There's a question!' Mrs Vaughan protested. 'Don't you take any notice of him, Reuben. Teasing he is.'

'Because,' Philip continued, 'I have noticed, especially in Wales, that religious people eat substantially before a service and also as substantially when they come back to supper. I am not sarcastic; it is pure intellectual curiosity. Does listening to the service, the hymns, the sermon, and the praying, create a stomachic void that the worshipper tries to guard against before the service – though ineffectually it seems, judging by the supper afterwards – or is that void created by loss of psychic force through actual worship, the strain of trying to establish connection with spiritual things?'

Mr Vaughan for a moment stopped blowing into the hot tea in his saucer.

'Worship better one does if the stomach is well-filled,' he said, his glance pouncing on the dish of patties, 'and natural it is that one is hungry after, when the old services last for over two hours!'

Eirwen said, curving her derisive lips:

'And most of the people eat sweets in our chapel. See them put their handkerchiefs to their noses and slip a peardrop or a black-and-white into their mouths!'

'Now, now,' Mrs Vaughan cried, her soft eyes glancing ashamedly at Reuben, 'there's a jeering talk this is. Leave your chapel alone.'

Reuben laughed:

'Don't worry, Mrs Vaughan. Too solemn as a rule are people when they talk of chapel. A place of laughter as well as worship should chapel be.'

'Strange words from a religious boy!' Eirwen said in a biting voice.

He looked at her, pain in his face. She was staring at him, her elbow on the table, her chin resting on her hand.

91

There was a cruel glitter in her contemplative eyes, her lips were curled down mockingly. And she watched him all the time, with her gaze that was restless to destroy his peace.

When tea was over they went to the parlour, Eirwen and her mother coming in after the tea things had been put away. Eirwen sat at the piano. Her father lay sprawlingly on the sofa.

'Hymns now, Eirwen,' Mrs Vaughan said, 'or something out of the *Messiah*.'

'I'm not in a mood for hymns or the *Messiah*,' Eirwen answered, rather impatiently.

Finally she sang old Welsh folk-songs – melodies full of Celtic longing and hopelessness, love-songs that seemed to swoon within their melancholy music. She had a rich contralto voice, and it lingered over the sentimental songs with a plangent emotion that Reuben listened to in a dream of exalted rapture.

Mr Vaughan called sleepily from the sofa:

'A lighter touch there ought to be in your voice, Eirwen. Too much honey you put in your singing.'

Eirwen left the piano – she was very sensitive about her voice – and sat by the fire.

Reuben looked at her, his eyes dark in ecstasy. Her voice had gone into his soul like some trembling utterance of passionate love. He suddenly thought of a line of poetry he had read in one of Philip's books:

'*Lean back thy throat of carven pearl...*'

And he quivered exultingly.

Then he wanted to be alone with her so that he might

hold her, and press his mouth to hers until they would cry out with the pain of it.

Philip, who had been sitting back with closed eyes said suddenly, into the darkening silence:

'They say that when a corpse is cremated it behaves, before it is quite burned, like a live body, jumping and lifting its arms in quite a lively fashion.'

Mrs Vaughan uttered a loud, shocked cry.

'Philip! There's awful thoughts you have! Dear me, well... there's taste – ' She subsided into a horrified, agitated silence.

Mr Vaughan sniggered fatly on the sofa.

'Information of that kind interests me,' Philip exclaimed. 'I get a sort of bleak comfort from it.'

Reuben looked at him with pity and fear. Philip's shrunken face, with the skin tight upon the bones, had upon it a brownish tinge as of shrivelled fallen leaves, and the eyes seemed to burn up in the dim room like a conflagration. Reuben saw the skull beneath that thin brittle flesh and shuddered. And he saw too, Death as a terrible devastation, a splitting of the dry earth into unfathomable abysses, a grey desolation wherein all life perished and there was no sun.

His heart throbbed. Then he prayed in his soul:

'Jesus, where art thou? Be near me now, be with me, as thou wert with thy disciples at Emmaus, for I am sick at heart.'

He often prayed thus when horror came upon him. And as a rule he was comforted.

Later he accompanied Eirwen and her mother on their

long walk to chapel; Mrs Vaughan, walking between them, talking with mournful grief of Philip's hopeless state. Nothing could be done for him now; it was too late. He might die in a few months or he might last a year. And he was dying without the comforts of religion.

'The way he was brought up it is,' she almost wept. 'A fool my sister was to marry that ruffian in London. Not a fit man to make a home and be a father was he. There's an evil day it was for Janet when he made her run off with him.' Her kind voice trembled with unaccustomed rage. 'The whip he ought to have; he ought to be stripped and tied to a tree and whipped, like they did to Shenkin the Goat in Cardigan.'

They parted in the Square, Mrs Vaughan and her daughter joining the little crowd of people who were making their solemn way down the street that led to Caersalem.

Reuben walked to Pisgah with tender joy in his heart. Ah, Eirwen was a girl to be proud of. Who in the Valley had such beauty! She had the beauty of the little ewe-lambs, of the rose-bush heavy with white blossom, of the young moon slender and shy in the night. They would go hand in hand through life and God would shower upon them a plenitude of blessings. He scarcely listened to Mr Hughes-Williams' sermon. And after the service he hurried to be the first in the doorway of Lewis's milk-shop.

Half-an-hour later she appeared, sauntering along, swinging her umbrella.

'A long service you had!' he remarked.

'No. Delayed I was in the vestry afterwards. They want

94

me to sing for them in a concert.' She was pleased; any opportunity to display her gifts on a platform gave her a voluptuously taut pleasure.

'Where shall we go now?' he said. After chapel most of the boys and girls walked up and down the main street, up and down everlastingly like little beasts condemned in a cage.

'I don't know,' she said, meditating.

There were the mountains, but their bare walks were not inviting in February; and there was the Lane – but the Lane was doubtful because of its character. Had not a minister denounced from the pulpit its dark looks and obscure meanderings wherein, he had been told, Satan loitered as though he were in his own dark kingdom!

'What about the Lane?' Eirwen murmured, sliding the ferrule of her umbrella along a division in the pavement.

'The Lane!' he said slowly.

'Yes,' she said with sudden gaiety, as though it were a prank. 'Fun it will be. They say crowds go there after chapel now, since the minister of Noddfa spoke about it.'

He went along with her unwillingly.

Once in the Lane, which bordered a brook and contained almost the only trees in the Valley, the adventure did not seem so wicked. A kind darkness hid everyone. People wandered about in couples, but some, alas, were alone, and one could hear subdued whistles, sighs, and suppressed, throaty laughter. Eirwen herself laughed softly, as they wandered deeper into the gloom.

'There's a place!' she whispered.

He put his arm about her waist.

'That's right,' she said, and sighed.

'There's love you I do,' he whispered, drawing her yielding body, that was supple as a healthy sapling, closer to his side.

'Shall we stop here?' she said, stumbling against a tree in a little space that appeared deserted. She stooped and felt the stony earth. 'Damp the ground is,' she then said.

But he did not offer to take off his overcoat and lay it over the dampness.

In each other's arms they leaned against the tree.

He began to talk, in a voice that was quiet and slow with dreams and visions of their life together:

'Like a little heaven on earth it will be. A home of our own, where we'll have books and a piano and a cat and peaceful meals in the evening.'

She allowed him to go on and when she had an opportunity lifted her warm face to his.

He kissed her with a gentle, chaste desire, a virginal kiss.

But suddenly she clasped his mouth with a mature dexterity that held it fast. Her arms tightened like snakes about his body; he was held in the tentacles of her physical vigour as a drowning man in the supple arms of an octopus. He began to squirm for breath.

She loosened his mouth, a moaning sound escaping her lips. Her head fell back and in the darkness her dim white throat pulsated before his staring eyes like a dove throbbing in death.

'Eirwen,' he whispered, 'don't, don't...'

There was a wild sweet perfume about her breasts; he

buried his face in it, and he felt lost in a darkness that gleamed here and there with a glitter as of silver flesh, pale fire and marble columns that rose, thick and strong, to a sky of black night...

She raised her hand; she breathed into his ear:

'Now...?'

He quivered, slowly lifted his face, and stared at her.

'Say that you want me at last!' she whispered in a hot voice.

She could not see the lost despair in his eyes. He did not know what word to utter. The perfume of her breasts crept into his veins, but there was within him, also, a stony horror that was as an arrow from God.

She became physically urgent: he muttered:

'No, no... Eirwen... I mustn't.'

But again she clasped his mouth and tightened her arms about his body. It was as though he was being borne away into the depths of a perfumed sea where he must at last swoon into the awful bliss that was closing about him.

Lifting away her head for a moment, so that she might draw a deeper breath, she cried softly:

'Little preacher, I'll show you...'

The horror that was almost submerged within him suddenly split into violence. His eyes flared; and as her mouth in its sucking grimace came near his again, he thrust her away shudderingly.

'No, no,' he stuttered madly. 'Evil, evil... Leave me alone!'

She stood still in rigid silence, thrust back against the tree. Then he cried in despair:

97

'Why must you be like that! I love you. I love you as I love the little lambs on the hills in Spring, and the flowers and the moon. But always you must show evil. Go away from me; I will not go down to your filth.'

She seemed to gather and crouch in anger, as a beast crouches to spring. Her voice shot out, like a serpent's hiss:

'You little fool.'

He stared in surprise and pain. She added viciously:

'Yes, that's what you are. Lambs and flowers indeed! A little lamb *you* ought to have been, bleating for its mother. Thought you were a man I did. There's a mistake I've made.'

He cried furiously:

'Someone as bad as yourself you thought I was.'

She turned and began to walk away. He followed her.

'Let me go alone,' she said, drawing herself away.

'Not in the Lane,' he answered.

But she darted among the trees and was soon lost to him in the darkness.

Reuben walked home slowly. Angrily he thought of her. Then he could have wept. And he gazed up into the far cold sky and shuddered at the dark emptiness. The world seemed full of darkness and evil and now there was no message of stars in the sky. Then he brooded: why is there misery within me because I would not submit to her temptations? Her beauty is pure and with her I could live my life and be happy.

He flung back his head and hurried home: he would have patience with her and in the end the spirit of God would be over their union.

Martha was about to lay supper when he arrived and she

looked him over with an examining scrutiny, particularly his boots. Hugh, sitting in his armchair, glanced over the top of the Family Bible.

'Where have you been?' Martha demanded.

Tonight she was tidy and respectable, in a spotless apron, her blouse fastened with her Sunday evening Cameo brooch and her hair done properly.

'For a walk,' he said shortly.

'Where to?'

He looked at her.

'For what you want to know? Content enough to be ignorant of where I go you are usually.'

She said accusingly:

'In the Lane you've been.'

'Who told you?'

He flared suddenly.

'Never mind,' she said.

Stern and righteous wrath sat austerely on her face tonight. 'But seen you were entering that place with a young woman. Ach, there's a surprise it was for me!'

'Why?' he demanded angrily.

'Why! In the Lane! On Sunday night! Where all the lowest go, where all the mischief in the Valley is done!'

Hugh cleared his throat nervously and put in:

'Now, now, Mrs Daniels, innocent people take walks in the Lane too.'

'When?' she cried, raising her voice in denunciation. 'Not by night! Who is there respectable that walks within it? Ah, don't argue with me. Well enough you know what a shameful reputation it has got. And there he's that has got such a holy name, walks with that slut from Bryn Farm! Ach y fi, not a hypocrite I thought you were, Reuben Daniels. You, with your nose in the Bible always, walking in the Lane with a flighty piece of goods such as Eirwen Vaughan! Shocked I was when I was told.'

He cried in indignant wrath:

'Often enough you've told me that you wished I'd find a girl to go out with in the evenings. When I stay in to read the Bible nag at me like that you do. And there's filthy gossip it is about the Lane! Nothing shocking I saw there.'

'Can't you walk in the streets with a girl? That's what respectable couples do. When I was a young woman no courting couples would go further than the main street.'

Hugh shut the Bible, unlatched the back-door and went out. Martha continued in a quieter voice:

'And what's this business with Eirwen Vaughan? Thought I did that you went to Bryn Farm to see that young man who is bad. Is it serious you are with the girl?'

He gazed at her suddenly. Her face for once had lost its bleary looseness, and her pale blue eyes shone with purified brightness. It had been one of her rare sober days.

'Don't you like her then?' he asked, his voice beginning to tremble.

'Not the sort for you she seems, and a name for being too easy she has.'

He leaned to her.

'Don't you want me to go out with a girl?' he asked, a sudden smile flooding his intent face.

She turned her head and went to the cupboard at the side of the fireplace for the supper dishes.

'Don't you?' he repeated in a thick quivering voice. He knew she had turned from him to escape his eyes.

'It's the way of young men,' she said with something of her old jaunty indifference.

He went to her and laid his hands on her shoulders as she stooped down before the cupboard.

'More to me you are than anyone else,' he whispered. But the pain in his voice was too naked.

'Oh, go away with you,' she cried impatiently, shaking herself free. 'Do as you like, but respectable keep your name.'

He did not utter the ironic retort that came to his lips. The touch of her shoulders burned in his fingers and he went upstairs in a passion of joy and pain.

Hugh came in just then. He looked at Martha over his spectacles, shame in his mild eyes. Martha glanced at him, a sudden flush on her cheeks.

'Well,' she asked, with a slight toss of her head, 'for why you look at me like that?'

He opened his mouth tentatively, and then decided not to speak.

'I suppose,' she said, with dour arrogance, 'thinking you are that no right have I to speak to Reuben about the Lane.'

He went to his chair and dropped his head in shame.

'There's a dark night it must have been when I met you there,' she said, and laughed stridently.

CHAPTER IV

The Corinthians' chapel was a crude, roughly-built structure of wood and corrugated zinc. It stood on the mountain-side, where the land was free, and in its isolation it was a symbol of the simple and proud faith of its worshippers.

In winter the winds from the hill-tops howled and tore about its meagre walls and foundations, but never did it suffer any damage. God, they said, protected this ugly little shed that had been built with such holy love and care. For members of the sect built it themselves, after their usual work had been done, and though mocked and derided by many, it was a lesson to see them toiling up the hillside from the main street, carrying the various materials and singing hymns and uttering prayers as they progressed. So the simple chapel was built without payment or monetary profit, and furnished by labour that received no earthly wage.

But God rewarded these zealous people with visions and

ecstasies, sermons of fire, and souls that burned with a fierce joy. And from their exaltations they could see clearly the defects of the lawful chapels in the neighbourhood, which they denounced with righteous contempt and courage.

Reuben climbed the hill with Morgans the Bakehouse one Sunday evening, curious to know the manner of the Corinthians' worship.

They entered the chapel, which was already full, though they were early.

'See you,' said Morgans proudly, 'how Corinthians come to their chapel without ringing of bell or watching of clock! And sometimes we are here until almost midnight. There's a triumph for you, to keep people from their suppers!'

Those already gathered in the chapel were singing hymns, quietly, swaying their shoulders with a slow rhythmic motion.

'Softly they sing,' Reuben observed. 'Told I was that the Corinthians were very loud in their hymns.'

'Reserving their strength and power they are until later,' Morgans answered. 'Wait you, and you shall hear how Corinthians can sing.'

Several people turned to them as they walked down the aisle, who called out:

'God is with us, brothers.'

'Glory to God, Morgans the Bakehouse.'

'Jesus be with us, dear ones.'

'Let there be light tonight,' cried one woman, in long fervent wail, above the quiet singing.

'Yes, indeed, let there be plenty of light,' another answered.

Morgans occupied the first bench, near the pulpit. Before sitting down he knelt on the floor, and Reuben did likewise. They prayed silently.

Oil-lamps shed a soft light; the rough, homely pulpit was a raised platform with a little ladder at the side; and nailed on the wall above the pulpit was a banner that had painted upon it a large blue eye set in a triangle from which conical yellow flames sprang, and underneath the words:

THE EYE OF GOD SEES ALL.

Morgans and Reuben joined in the singing – old Welsh tunes that never fail to fill their singers with mystic joy. Soon the chapel was crowded, each bench filled tightly, so that the place began to get warm with human breathings. Presently the Leader walked down the aisle and mounted the little ladder. Arriving on the platform, he raised his arms and called out:

'The voice of Jesus be with me tonight.'

The people answered:

'The voice of Jesus be with you tonight.'

They began the service with a hymn. And now they sang religiously and properly, so that the noise of the little organ at the side of the pulpit was quite lost: they sang with their chests, their stomachs and their legs in the singing; their voices mounted up in a terrific roll of earthly thunder. God was certain to hear such singing.

The Leader gazed over his flock with shining eyes. He was a lean young man of thirty with a big head balanced like a ball on the thin cane of his long neck: his gleaming eyes protruded and rolled in their sockets, beneath them a sharp and nervous nose that twitched continually, except when he was preaching.

Reuben looked up at him inquisitively. That was the famous young man, who formerly was a quarry-man but had so impressed the Corinthians with his sermons that they had chosen him for their Leader, giving him a little cottage and two pounds a week, promising ten shillings more if he got married.

Reuben thought the young man looked ill and nervous.

But there was no sickness about the Leader's prayer and the sermon that followed.

A being that writhed and sprang about the pulpit like a wrathful angel seemed to possess him. The words that poured in torrents from his mouth dropped like stinging hail in the chapel. A tremendous force shot the words out. And wildly his head spun about on his thin neck like a globe of fire, his hands invoking the heavens with frenzied clawing.

Reuben listened attentively. But he could gather no revelation of divine wisdom or love from the sermon, he could not gather even sense or a coherent statement. But there were sentences of Holy Writ delivered with a power that sent them flaming through the chapel, and then utterances that sang themselves from the young man's mouth in a voice that was exalted to unearthly music.

The people punctuated the sermon with various exclamations of encouragement, fervour, or gratification. Now and again a woman moaned as though in acute distress.

105

'Jesus, Jesus, Jesus,' another repeated continually, as opportunity offered in the short pauses of the sermon.

'Glory, glory...'

'Heaven is with us...'

'Yes, indeed, dear God,' a man wept.

The chapel became very warm; sweat oozed over the faces of the people. The flames of the oil-lamps seemed to tremble in the charged atmosphere.

'God is here,' groaned one stout man.

'Ah, yes,' cried a woman ecstatically, 'He is here with me too, brother.'

And still the Leader writhed and foamed amid his torrential phrases, now and again remaining static for a few moments while he gazed upwards with glaring eyes, as though he beheld a terrible vision in the roofing.

He concluded like some great actor in a last death scene. Sobbing, he bent his body in convulsed contortions and hung over the pulpit limply, his voice breathing out like a sad sigh, weary and heavy with tears.

At last, sinking back in the chair, he murmured in an exhausted whisper:

'Amen, Amen, Amen.'

Then the people broke forth. They lifted their voices in a hymn that swept up to heaven in proud and passionate worship. Again and again they repeated the last verses, until the Leader, refreshed by a rest and a tumbler of water, got up and lifted his arms.

'Pray,' he uttered intensely, 'pray, dear people. Kneel down with me, dear brothers and sisters, and we will confess and pray for forgiveness.'

Each person uttered an individual prayer. Some sobbed, others whispered, but many let their voices peal forth in loud lamentations of divers sins or in passionate demand for intimate contact with God.

Oh, the bliss of being in that state! They were in Heaven already, here on their knees in the chapel, moaning and crying as their bodies writhed in an ecstasy of repentance and certainty of God's wonderful love and interest in their case.

'He is with me day and night,' cried a young woman, happy tears falling down her cheeks. 'Oh, how lovely it is to have him in my heart like this! Oh, God, God, God, how I love you.'

A man, thin and austere of countenance, lifted his voice:

'Keep me still from drink and sin, Dear One. Five months now have I been free of them and wonderful has been my health.'

And the exudation of this ecstasy of the body and spirit mounted up so that the unventilated air quivered and smelled of exerted humans.

Reuben's lips, too, moved in prayer. He had listened in wonder to the anthem of piety about him and he was moved to his bowels by the strength and intensity in the people's words and voices. Here were people who displayed their religion with proud and fervent emotion, and in their prayers there was the utter abasement of the poor human being before the mystery of the Divine.

He bowed his head and, his body warmed in the glow of that abasement, prayed with words that rose like a poem to his lips. Old Morgans at his side was uttering a noble prayer too, and a woman kneeling the other side howled in detail the physical success of her conversion to God's True Religion – she had been rid of an ulcer and the shingles since God took her for his own, the rash disappearing, though all medical treatment had been in vain.

Thus the anthem of the Corinthians rolled up to heaven.

Old Morgans turned to Reuben proudly:

'There's burning zeal for you, boy bach. Hark at them as they lift their holy voices to our Father! There is the ancient worship of the world in their prayers. No petty and fashionable ornaments are in these services.'

And his eyes, too, shone with glowing pride.

'Strong and fiery is their worship,' Reuben added in a voice of awe. 'Ashamed of my weak doubts they make me feel.'

The Leader shrieked above the din:

'Stop now, dear people, and we will sing the fifty-fourth hymn.'

The organ struck up and the congregation concluded the first service with voices strained to cracking point, their gusto undiminished, their faces lifted up, flushed or pale with rapture.

'Stay you to the second service?' Morgans asked Reuben.

The second service was for likely converts who, admitting their desire to be 'saved' would be received publicly into the fold of the sect. But Reuben thought he did not wish to witness this initiation immediately. During the praying he had felt his mind sinking into the fervour about him, and if it had continued he knew that he too would have been lost in its intensity and wild worship. And he felt that he was not prepared for such conversion yet. There was a terrible force in this worship which frightened him, a force dark with violent ecstasy and exaltation, that sent the mind quivering amid broken spheres of split radiance and flaming skies, that opened before the inner vision a kingdom of unearthly emotion, where landscapes were voices of strange chants, where music was carved into symbols of crystal colour, and stars opened into faces of inspired beauty, and the mind dropped at last into a deeper darkness that was like sleep. Had he not known those exaltations and visions in his lonely vigils on the mountains and in the depths of the night when he had wakened from troubled dreaming? And he did not want to identify his visions with the Corinthians just yet.

'Not tonight,' he answered.

'But lovelier is the second service,' Morgans insisted.

'Let me come again another Sunday,' Reuben said. He knew that Morgans was anxious to father his conversion to the sect.

'You have not heard the call yet?'

Reuben shook his head and left the disappointed old man. Few people had left and on the faces of the remaining congregation there was impatience for the second service to begin; most of them were humming and tapping their feet in the measure of a familiar hymn.

The cold night air cooled his head; he started on the walk to Bryn Farm with slow steps, for he did not want to arrive early and disturb supper there.

The hills crouched like long supple beasts asleep and

over them the wide sky stretched in a vast and flawless arch of darkness; tranquil peace lay over the Valley and as he climbed higher his soul became calm.

He thought: Here the Voice of God is heard best.

And then he thought of the people below in that chapel he had just left, crying out their repentance and desire for spiritual grace. 'Even their prayers,' he muttered, 'are the prayers of the human race longing for peace.'

But now there seemed to him error and delusion in their noisy outbursts. Not thus was inner harmony and grace achieved. Those gifts of the spirit were not hidden in such turbulent displays. 'A man should arise from among them,' he whispered, 'and teach them that peace and holiness shall come to them best in the silent prayers of their thoughts and in the quiet meditation of their souls.'

He stopped and gazed about the lonely hill. Then suddenly he cried aloud:

'There is a vineyard in the soul that bears such lovely fruit! Silence and shadow is under the trees and there one can rest and taste of Paradise. Labour to cultivate that vineyard, O men and women, and you will gather the precious fruit and, lying in the cool shadow, eat of a heavenly food...'

As though ashamed of this sudden outburst, he hurried on. The desire to speak aloud thus often came to him in his wanderings, and when he gave way to that desire he was surprised at the ease with which the words flowed from his mouth.

He arrived at the Farm with mystic peace in his being, his face pale and visionary, his eyes gleaming with dreams.

Philip, who sat in a chair by the fire with the inevitable book on his knees, looked at him with amused dislike on his face.

'I can see you've been at religion again,' he said, gratingly. 'There's artificial sunlight all over you.'

Mrs Vaughan uttered a 'Tut, tut' of distress.

'There is nothing artificial about my religion,' Reuben answered, smiling and firm in his peace. 'It gives me contentment and faith and strength to live.'

'Clever chap,' Philip commented, 'to be able to get all those together. You can ask no more of life, surely.'

Reuben looked at him, his eyes gentle with pity.

'Ah,' he said softly, 'if only you would believe in my faith! Why don't you believe even in the faint hope that it is true?'

'That's what I was saying,' Mrs Vaughan broke in. 'Easy it is to say there's no God and become a dry old atheist. But even if there is no God, safer it is for our peace of mind to believe otherwise, and more comfortable life becomes. Dear me, there's miserable I'd be if I believed there was no God! Think I would that same as the animals we are, and married life is like they behave and without any meaning. Indeed now, a father Philip should be and he'd change his views then, for there's faith a child gives one!'

'I should have thought,' Philip said, 'that in the case of a woman, having a child gave her a deeper consciousness of earthly realities.'

Mrs Vaughan looked at him over her glasses.

'Philip bach,' she said, ignoring his observation, 'you haven't taken your cod-liver oil since breakfast.' And she went to get the medicine.

'Where is Eirwen?' Reuben asked.

'Probably where you ought to be – in the dark corners of the village, stirring up young blood.'

Reuben laughed at the contemptuous grimace on Philip's lips.

'I suppose you've been to chapel,' Philip said.

'Yes, to the Corinthians.'

'Ha,' the other exclaimed in a biting voice, 'what an entertainment!'

'Have you been to their services then?'

'Yes, I have. Talk about a reversion to our barbaric forefathers! There one sees in all its simplicity the grovelling of the savage before the mystery of life. And aren't they happy in their howling and grovelling! With what joyful abandon they cast away their civilised conventions and enter into their natural state! But there's a certain old and sinister beauty about the abandon which they put into it. I was both edified and entertained at their exhibition.'

Again Reuben felt that this young man's ideas were beyond him, and his case hopeless indeed. But he protested simply:

'I don't understand all that you say to me. But always you cast slurs and doubts on religious worship. Man is man whether he is a savage or civilised and their worship is the same though they might have a different manner of expressing it. And whatever you say doesn't affect my reverence for God: I burn with the thought of him and a firm faith in his power I have.'

Philip glanced at him along his thin nose.

'All argument on religion is futile,' he declared with

bored resignation. 'I suppose each man must work out his own philosophy of it, according to his lights. It's all very tiresome to me now. One of the finest poems I've read says:

'I think I could turn and live with animals, they are so
placid and self-contained,
I stand and look at them long.

They do not sweat and whine about their condition,
They do not lie awake in the dark and weep for their sins,
They do not make me sick discussing their duty to God,
Not one is dissatisfied, not one is demented with the
mania of owning things,
Not one kneels to another, nor to his kind that lived
thousands of years ago – '

So the two young men concluded. Later Eirwen came in, her cheeks glowing from the climb up the hill in the cold air. She nodded to Reuben and went upstairs to put her Sunday coat away, as her mother insisted. When she came down again her face was pallidly beautiful.

'Powder on Sunday night!' Mrs Vaughan exclaimed. 'What next, you silly girl! Ach y fi, there's foolishness.'

Reuben saw Eirwen's brows draw together in anger. She did not answer, but came and sat by the fire between the young men and lifted her lips ironically to Reuben.

'Well, Reuben Daniels, where have you been tonight – chapel as usual? A girl I know said to me there's a rumour about that you can recite the Bible by heart.'

Her cruel lifted eyes flickered with little golden lights.

113

He looked back at her, unperturbed at her jeer. Her shapely face seemed to burn with an inner white fire.

'I wish I could recite it,' he said simply.

And as suddenly she altered her tactics, as she gazed at him. Her voice was warm and vulnerable when she continued:

'Come and hear me sing, Reuben, at Caersalem's concert.'

And when he looked into her eyes again they were like dark flowers opened to him in sudden desire.

His heart ached. Why was she so strange, mocking him one moment and looking at him with such naked love the next! She sat there, crouched in her burning loveliness, lifting her heavy lips to him, and he looked back at her with pain dark and quivering in his eyes. And he loved her with a quick, passionate love that lay like dread in his heart.

For he knew that she would drag his soul down into the pleasure of that garden of the flesh which he had looked upon in dreams. And there was some other call in his soul, that rang, swift and clear as a trumpet-call, crying of proud hills, glinting rocks, woes of men, and, at the last, rapt, triumphant faces.

Slowly he lowered his face and looked into the fire. Philip was saying:

'I should go to hear her if I were you, Reuben. She is very imposing on a platform. One day, if she's cute enough, she'll sing opera before crowned heads. You can see she's already developing all the aspects of the successful prima-donna.'

Eirwen laughed softly, her face wreathed at that prospect.

114

Reuben got up.

'Don't forget,' she whispered to him at the door. 'And are you angry with me still?'

He shook his head.

'Reuben bach,' she added, laughing, 'there's quaint you are.'

CHAPTER V

Yet still he was unhappy, silent, in a world of dream that was shadowy with a piteous melancholy.

He saw the days march down upon him with monotonous certainty, an endless succession of tramps in the dawn to the pit, the descent in the cage with the thought of annihilation always insistent in his mind, the grovelling and the picking by the pale gleam of his lamp, the weary tramp back and up into the grey world, to evenings that would become desolate and barren too; and forever, forever a silent torture in his vanquished soul.

His days in the pit became hours of brooding and torment, his mind shadowed with a hollow and erosive pain. Yet he achieved distinction in the labour of the collier. The seam of coal that he and Hopkin Watts worked yielded plentifully to their energetic application, Reuben's wages increased, and Watts would bring large slices of good fruit-cake and roast pork for their mutual ten-minute meal.

But the old miner, proud of the unwearying muscular strength of his young 'butty,' knew nothing of the monotonous meditations that wore away Reuben's soul so that this chamber of hot darkness inside the earth became a tomb of stifling and cramping horrors. Perhaps death would come to him early, he brooded. But not bloodily, terribly, as it came to some men in the pit, as it came to Elias Evans, from whose body he had helped remove the fallen rock that had crushed it to a red mess. But death like slow, faint music, that would beckon his tired soul over the hills to a lovelier land.

'A broody nature you have,' Hopkin Watts remarked, loosening his belt as they paused for a minute after their meal. 'And thin your face is getting. What for is it so white too?'

Reuben shook his head.

'Haven't you found a little woman yet?' the collier enquired, looking down at Reuben with his watery eyes.

'No.'

Watts pulled off his vest again, which had covered his sweating body for the meal.

'Evil are women's natures,' he pronounced in his dour fashion, 'and damned is a man that takes to them with extravagance, allowing the sluts to be God, food, and drink to them. But a comfort and a medicine they are sometimes. And thinking I am that one that is not too quiet and not too greedy you need. Looking for one you are?'

Reuben smiled faintly at his considerate boss. He had seen the four healthy daughters of Hopkin Watts – four

117

single young women with a bouncing gait and great capable thighs.

Watts reached for his pick.

'Saying my daughter Maggie was the other day that a lonely young man you look, and then Sarah said, there's a sad face you've got and marry young you ought to. Interested in you they seem. Come you up to tea some Sunday and we will make a little musical party afterwards.'

'Perhaps I will, some Sunday,' Reuben promised, in an unwilling voice, taking up his shovel.

And he wondered if it was the lack of women in his life that made him sullen and miserable. Eirwen had given him no happiness that was not shadowed with a vague pain. And as he thought again of her gleaming face, with its eyes in which night lay like a rich slumber, his vitals moved in sick anguish. No, he would not give himself over to the dream of possessing her. That was the holy joy that made the wedding-night a song of earthly beauty. But he would not possess her body in the furtive darkness of sin. He thrust thought of her from him.

It was the silence and the terror of the world that made his being ache in darkening reveries. The tramp to the pit in the dawn. Then the grey light lay like steel swords behind the clouds and the hills seemed to crouch as before a menace suspended over their brows. There was no loveliness in the dawn as it was loosed upon the arid hills; and the pale shrunken faces of the miners tramping in procession about him were always shut and mute in that hour of the ashen-coloured world.

Ah, the world was grey with misery and desolation. The

toil of the colliery was not beautiful to men; it bruised them, maimed them, rotted their lungs, and their reward was the poverty of slaves.

'And where was the voice of Christ?' Reuben asked himself.

Then one early evening he wandered up to the Farm, to Philip, who was as a thorn in his flesh too.

Philip was in bed again. The flesh had dwindled from his face, and Reuben suppressed a cry as he gazed on the protruding bones from which substance had fled as though in horror.

'You see, I'm not to be denied the whole symphony of pre-decay,' the sick man cried, with his mordant grimace, as he observed Reuben. 'I insisted on having the mirror brought me this morning. And for an hour or so I meditated upon the curious composition of man.'

Mrs Vaughan hovered anxiously about the bed, settling the pillows and murmuring sadly:

'Now, Philip bach, don't think and talk so much. Let Reuben read you some book or something. Make your mind quiet you want to.'

Philip cackled with amusement his hearers did not share.

'Why should I go out in a drugged state?' he demanded. 'I will not have the entertainment of my last woes filched from me.'

Reuben cried, out of the depths of his soul:

'Jesus Christ bring you peace.'

Tears ran over Mrs Vaughan's cheeks. She sank on a chair and her body swayed in anguish.

119

'Oh, hell, leave us,' Philip muttered irritably.

She looked at him wildly but went out.

'How women put their very bowels into the rites attendant on death,' he exclaimed, as the door shut. 'I hate to deny her an operatic spectacle, but I insist on dying in my own way, reasoning out the process.'

Reuben whispered fearfully:

'Why?... Are you – '

'I am going at last,' Philip finished, with morbid amusement at Reuben's gravity. 'The last vestiges of flesh are leaving me, as you can see, and I can scarcely lift my hand.' He slowly turned his head away. 'That minister from my aunt's chapel came up to see me yesterday. There was a bright cheerlessness about this discourse, remembered, I should think, from a shilling sermon. He spoke for twenty minutes and all the time I was fascinated by a large boil that was ripening on the side of his neck. So when he stopped I told him of a good way to shift boils from one's skin. He listened politely, and even promised to try the method. And when he had gone I was thoroughly ashamed of my vulgarity. After all, he was doing his best for me.'

Reuben smiled, bleakly.

'So don't try and comfort me,' Philip added.

'Shall I read to you then?'

'Yes. Go and get the volume of Swinburne on the shelves downstairs.'

When Reuben returned with the book he asked:

'Which shall I read?'

'Find the one called *The Leper*. It's suitable to my memories.'

120

Reuben began:

'Nothing is better, I well think,
　　Than love; the hidden well-water
Is not so delicate to drink:
　　This was well seen of me and her – '

He finished and was silent, thinking of this strange poem,
that seemed to him to be heavy with a kind of evil grief.

Philip was muttering, as though to himself:

'I wonder what became of her. Ah, we should have been
such lovers! I would have tended her, too, even when "the
body of love wherein she abode" had become leprous also.
Ah, with her, her bright disillusioned mind joined to my
mind, I would have reached down into the roots of
humanity – we would have become eternal with knowledge,
she with her perception and experience of evil, I with my
thwarted idealism – '

A tortured bitterness was in his eyes, and he was silent
for some time. Then, turning to Reuben, he asked gently:

'Do you love Eirwen?'

'I don't know,' Reuben said, hesitating. '...She is lovely,
isn't she?'

Philip's laugh was like a croak as he answered: 'She is
lovely in a primordial way. Her type of beauty is of the sort
that is formed with the rocks and the trees and the mineral
substances. Love with her would be entirely of the earth,
like the nuptials of the animals and the birds.'

'You mean she has no intelligence?' Reuben asked
gravely.

'Oh, well, she can sing quite well and cook very decently. Married life with her wouldn't be so bad. Eatable meals and music in the evening! I will be just.'

'I like her,' Reuben said intensely, – 'only,' he paused, embarrassed, – 'she is too fleshly...'

'She worries you with that?' Philip asked, his eyes beginning to sparkle with enjoyment.

Reuben's brow was dark.

'Oh, I understand,' Philip said with strange gentleness. 'But, Reuben, *you* are much too spiritual. Strange how two extremes are attracted like this!' He gazed scrutinisingly at Reuben. 'I think you'd forget all this snivelling over your little world if you surrendered yourself a little to her charms.'

But Reuben said morosely: 'It seems evil to me – '

'Ah, I forgot. The chapel. Evil, that's it, evil. Something repulsive swathed in dirty rags. Not such joy as floods the world with delicate colours, unwritten music, rest.'

Reuben said nothing, and presently Philip asked:

'What are you going to do with yourself? Have you decided yet?'

'I don't know,' Reuben murmured disconsolately. 'But there is something in me that cries for expression and I want to work at something that would make people happy and bring them eternal joy.'

'The old desire!' Philip answered ironically. 'Contact with people, desire to enter and serve their consciousness. Each of us wants to be a Christ.'

Reuben cried swiftly, 'Yes, that is what I want to be. I want to go among the suffering and the poor and help them not to mourn, I want to speak to them as Christ spoke to them – '

'But you do not know enough of people yet,' Philip answered gently. 'You ought to go away and bury yourself in the miseries of great cities, starve and battle in the economic struggle of existence. *You* might find a splendid light then. I didn't, though that, I think, was the fault of my own nature. Also this disease, which disgusted me.'

'I think,' Reuben said slowly, 'it is as well that I stay here and try to find my work in religion. There seems a loveliness in religion – '

Philip shook his head. Then he said:

'You Welsh! A race of mystical poets who have gone awry in some way. Alien and aloof in your consciousness of ancient austerity and closing your eyes to the new sensual world. To me there seems to be a darkness over your land and futility in your struggles to assert your ancient nationality. Your brilliant children leave you because of the hopeless stagnation of your miserable Nonconformist towns: the religion of your chapels is a blight on the flowering souls of your young. When I think of Wales I see an old woman become lean and sour through worrying over trivialities, though there are the remnants of a tragic beauty about her nevertheless. And you, Reuben, with your helpless pity that is instinct within you, pity for the submerged classes I suppose, why don't you work that pity into a burning rage and strive to destroy that which angers you? Instead of worrying over a dead religion.'

But Reuben cried with sudden wrath:

'That religion is not dead. It is the glory of Wales.

Dwindling its fire might be, but I want to be as a fan before it. It is that worship which shall make the Welsh people take on joy like a heavenly robe...'

'Oh, dear,' Philip interrupted in a weak, wavering voice. Then, dismally, 'Ah, the Bible! Yes, awry was the word.'

Reuben lapsed into silence, and his brows were knit sombrely. Philip stretched his head round and gazed at him. Then he spoke, and now his voice was gentle and sad:

'Reuben, I am dying. But I think I have lived and that is more than mobs of people much older can say. Always I've sought for consciousness of life, deeper and deeper consciousness, especially of suffering. When I lived in London I used to seek contact with people who were maimed and diseased, people of criminal instincts, people who sold their bodies for the gratification of others, the stunted, malformed, people who were consumed with hate and vengeance and lust. I've lived with such people and also with nice quiet people of respectable habits. But from neither one lot nor the other have I gathered any admiration for life. Injustice, ignorance, folly, and cruelty – these I have seen and experienced too well and into me also they have passed like sin. But worst of all those evils the one that is the most common – indifference. People will not stir to force a vision into realization. Day after day comes wretchedly for them and the golden kingdom is still in the skies. Ragged children still press their noses to the windows of opulent shops and a woman starves in a slum though there are loose bricks in the walls of the tenement. That woman might cry a little before going to sleep but in the morning she will get up and scratch her head and hope

124

for the best. And the nice quiet people of respectable habits grow monstrous vegetables in their souls; they are choked with smooth pulpy horrors. But they live with unctuous ritual in their monotonous suburbs and every Sunday they appear in their bits of parks with faces suitably cleaned of all moral sin. If you would go to the starving woman and say, "Come, we will go and get bread even though we have no money," and to the bank clerk, "Let us go and demand an interview with the Bishop of London," they would certainly laugh and turn their backs on you. And who can be blamed for their respective lives? Why, why this evil status of humanity?'

He laughed with hollow amusement and added gratingly:

'What naive questions! Christ, what an idiot I am to worry over those past nuisances, here on this bloody deathbed. And there you sit, you little fool, and stare and stare at me with those mad eyes of yours and listen without protest to all I say. Why don't you exclaim, "Of *course*, you are warped in mind and body and your vision does not embrace the grandeur of life. There is grandeur and nobility for those eyes that can see. And God is always above with a loving smile!" Something like that. But don't stare at me so. Your eyes disturb me. I spoke to you like that because I wanted you to know how useless and barren *I* found contact with people. Ah, if one could make a little tent of serenity for one's own life and live in its shadow with a playful young girl and be unaware of the stinking world – that is the ideal worth thinking about.'

'We must have strength,' Reuben whispered, 'strength to

examine the errors and deceits of men and profit by them. Mock at God as you will, but I have faith in me that tells me he lives and suffers for the world.'

But the other turned again to him his eyes that were cold with death, and continued:

'You will go on delving into religion, as some delve into pernicious sexuality, and as I delved into the folly of trying to find a meaning to things. But one day you will sicken of all this feverish mystical ecstasy, you will sicken to the last emotion of your being, and then the trials of the soul will come upon you and you will stand or fall according to the texture of your strength. And the gods be with you then, for it seems to me that you are more a slave of instinct than intellect. Yours is not the nature that will escape into contempt.'

Reuben looked at him in fear; Philip seemed to be peering into the secret tabernacle of his soul. And he cried in anguish:

'I am afraid, Philip – sometimes I am afraid of life and pain. The other day in the pit I helped to roll a stone away from a man that had been killed by it. And my soul seemed turned to iron. Afterwards I went into a dark space and tried to pray, but I couldn't, and when I came up from the pit I was frightened of the world.'

Philip had closed his eyes.

'Ah,' he cried, in a mocking, chanting voice, 'the sword of flame is within the sky and the hills shall shake with thunder.'

'What do these words mean?' Reuben asked, trembling.

An exhausted smile moved Philip's lips.

126

'Nothing,' he answered, breathing with difficulty. 'I'm speaking nonsense. You and I ... In the hospital of sick souls. Beds of barren earth. Bodies of straw. Carve from the grey stone of faith an image of the Lord. Eyes on the belly. A serpent in the loins. There is a rusty-coloured goat in the fields of asphodel. Laughter in the divine courts. By the wharves of hell huge ships sway beneath the heavy eyes of oily stars. Odour of rotting flesh and violets. But ribs of music close round my bowels...' He laughed in a kind of horror.

Reuben rose slowly from his chair. He wanted to pray, pray for this weary soul that was fading from the world without any faith. He hardly listened to Phillip's hushed rhapsodical voice chanting mad things that had no meaning. He went on his knees and prayed quietly:

'Lord, be with this soul in its affliction and fill it with peace as with the Balm of Gilead. Heal with the ointment of thy love the wounds of the world that have torn this soul. Jesus, thou who suffered in flesh and spirit for the woes of men, be near him as he lies in torture and anguish: lay thy hands that are cool with love on the heat of his brow, quench the agony of his full heart...'

And Philip was continuing rhapsodically, his eyes shut:

'...and my limbs stretch in wet clay that is warm as a woman's breast. Death veiled between bushes of rosy clouds. Elbows on the peaks of crystal hills. Head in a sky of mud...'

'Then shall he be in Paradise. Amen,' concluded Reuben and got up.

But Philip continued to gabble and Reuben went to the

window, his soul lifted in his prayer as though on wings of trembling strength. Evening had darkened the sky and the hills were remote in its tranquillity. Hushed were the landscapes of the world; and it seemed to him that death was beautiful in this peace and calm, that suffering might be forgotten and the bruises of the flesh healed.

Mrs Vaughan came into the room with a lamp.

'Behold,' cried Philip, opening his eyes, 'a lamp in a woman's hand!'

And Reuben looked at the shrunken yellow face of the dying man and went downstairs without a word.

Mr Vaughan, obese and snoring in his big armchair, lifted an eyelid as Reuben went through the living-room.

'God will give him peace,' Reuben said fervently.

'Aye, and he needs it.'

'He will rest in the bosom of Paradise, cleansed of the evils of this world,' continued Reuben exultingly.

Mr Vaughan dropped his eyelid and was silent. And Reubèn went out. But leaning on the gate at the end of the piece of waste land was Eirwen, her head bare, an empty pail on the ground beside her. She turned at Reuben's approach. Her eyes glowed beneath the repose of her smooth brow, her pale hand played carelessly with a string of amber-coloured beads on her breast. She breathed softly:

'Where are you going?'

And it seemed to him at that moment that this girl had about her the beauty of hell. He answered, denunciation in his voice:

'What is it to you?'

'Chapel, I suppose,' she laughed.

He drew nearer to her. 'Eirwen Vaughan,' he cried, 'do not mock at those who fear God. There will come a time when you too will bow your knee and cry to him for peace; for a soul such as yours gathers woe to it as surely as age shall wrinkle your living flesh.'

His pale face had the austerity of marble upon it, his voice issued from his throat like a thread of flame. She bent her dark heavy eyes to him, her lips opened, and her breath passed over his face like a warm, caressing breeze. She said, and in her voice too there was an answering exultance, though her lips mocked:

'I was reading in one of Philip's books that in a town in Greece they worshipped the statue of a beautiful woman. And when the young girls of the town reached a certain age they went to the gardens of the temple and offered their bodies to men. That was the way they worshipped the statue – by sacrificing their virginity to strangers. What do you think of that, Reuben Daniels?'

He stepped back and lifted his hand.

'Go from me,' he cried madly, his eyes flaming. 'There are people who are as the beasts of the field.'

She opened the gate for him and, with laughter, watched him retreat from her.

'I love you when you are in your holy rage,' she said amid her laughter, 'for like a beautiful angel you are then.'

He turned without further words and strode away.

He fled over the hill with hurried steps, breathing heavily, his being afire. And now he wanted to cry aloud words of wrath and devastation, for suddenly the world seemed to be reeling in an embrace of sin. He saw before him the face of

Eirwen, an evil smile twisting the dark red mouth. And his hands clenched and violent words rose to his lips.

He began to descend the other side of the hill. Then he saw, in the distance, lights in the windows of the Corinthians' chapel. Ah, there he would go and pray, pray and again find peace in the Lord.

When he arrived, the Corinthians were occupied in that holy labour. They were on their knees, praying as the spirit moved them. Some moaned, some chanted, some were loud in ecstasy, some wept noisily. Reuben crept to a seat and knelt. A man beside him opened his eyes and, looking at Reuben with widened eyes, exclaimed:

'Brother, beautiful are the dwellings of heaven. Been in them tonight I have.'

'Amen,' replied Reuben.

God was in this chapel. Reuben felt it. There was nobility and sacredness in the prostration of the Corinthians before the presence of God. A woman lifted her voice in a song that wailed round the chapel and entered into his very entrails. The young Leader knelt in the pulpit and cried loudly:

'Jesus, in thy robe of gold and crown of stars come down to this little chapel and fill us with the light of thy presence. Thou wilt lift us up and our strength shall he renewed in thy wonderful love...'

A young woman leapt up and stamped up and down before her seat, screaming:

'I have seen him, I have seen him. He opened his arms to me and like the sun was his face. Oh, people, my soul is blinded by his love.'

Then she fell back on the seat and groaned, her body stretched out, foam gathered about her spluttering mouth. Presently she regained her normal faculties and went down on her knees again.

Reuben bowed his head to the floor. His being was wrung in the anguish of this straining for establishment of union with the Divine. The wails, groans and cries of the people moved his belly, and through his mind swept flashes of blue light, fiery wheels and phrases printed in lightning. Then his body was pressed between burning stones, wet hair seemed to sway into his mind, and he was entangled in long golden whorls of curling radiance. The heavens burst, and ensconced above tablets and pillars of fire, God sat on a throne of burning ice, robed in mist, his face translucent and white with love... Reuben's head reached the floor and earthly consciousness rushed back through him. He opened watery eyes.

'Glory, glory, glory,' the man beside him was crying. 'Ah, a royal happiness is mine.'

Reuben rose to his feet. A great power swelled in him. He began, with words that had the swift flame of the Scriptures upon them:

'Behold, I have looked upon the face of God and I have seen eternal love upon it. People, I cry unto you, Rise up and let your hearts be flooded with joy. Let the earth be a new earth to you: thirst no more, dry all your tears. The dove of the Lord shall flutter to you and rest in your hands. We shall have love like the power of kings, love like the faith of the little children, love like the precious stones, like jasper stones, like rubies of eternal worth! And the dove shall be as a sword in our hands too, a sword that shall slay evil and the corruption of men. Listen, people...'

The noise faded, ceased. They all turned to him, their faces uplifted, mouths open and eyes staring. And the words flew from him like a flight of the doves of which he spoke. He continued in the strange silence, his eyes shining as though they had looked upon the incomparable glories. And the old men and the women even forgot to punctuate the discourse with their usual exclamations of encouragement and gratification.

He finished in a blaze of Biblical imagery. Then *Amen* said the old men and the young, and *Amen* sighed the women in rapt, hushed voices. The young Leader said to him from the pulpit:

'Brother, the voice of God has spoken through you. The Corinthians open to you the doors of their chapels. Come to us and we will welcome you to our pulpits.'

But Reuben, with bowed head and tired eyes, slowly went out from among them. Outside, he shuddered in the cold air of the early spring. He raised eyes, that were heavy with agony, to the calm heavens.

'Oh, God, take not your spirit away from me,' he breathed.

For the exaltation that was within him was flowing from him as though the blood was flowing away from his veins.

He entered his home like a pale ghost. His father was nearly asleep, alone before the fire in the kitchen. He looked at Reuben vaguely as he wakened.

'Where is my mother?' Reuben demanded in a cold voice.

132

'Ach, Reuben, don't you ask unnecessary questions,' replied the father, sniffing with disgust and looking for his spectacles.

'I forgot...' Reuben muttered, clinging to the table.

'There's white you are!' Daniels exclaimed, getting up in haste.

The father caught him as he fell, muttering in a drugged, incoherent voice:

'The stones of jasper... the dove... the sword of the Lord.'

CHAPTER VI

From then a new life began for him.

His soul was laved in a constant torrent of fierce exaltation. He attended the various services of the Corinthians,
cast himself into their fervour with an abandon that astonished even them. And he was happy. The fabric of the world
took on the trembling harmony of a vision, the universe
chanted a mystic song. His austere face, that had been thin
and grey as any collier's, had now a wild beauty upon its
pale lineaments.

Martha watched with veiled alarm this vivid change in
him. And she hated the proud accusing look of his violent
eyes.

'Glaring at me like a nasty-tempered bull,' she protested
one evening just before her preparations for her evening
jaunt.

Hers was the sin that troubled him most now. People

jeered at her, knowledge of her drunken habits was common property. And he could not ignore her. How could he enter into spiritual bliss when his mother dwelt in the darkness of one of earth's worst evils? Here in his own home was a task for him.

'You know why I look at you,' he said, darkly.

'You be respectful,' she answered, asperity hardening her eyes. 'There's interfering religion makes people!'

'Interfering!' he said. His voice was hot. 'You must listen to me.' He caught her hands in his strong grasp. 'I want you to forget the drink. For me. Think how everybody knows about you, and they laugh at me because I'm religious and you are like this.' In his fervour he talked in the old way, the Welsh way that conversation with Philip had changed in him. 'Mam fach, say that you will do this for me now. There's worry I do about you. Think, now, that you are getting awful! Ill and ugly you will become and no peace will there be for you when old you are. But I will work very hard for you and take care of you.'

She looked at him. Her earthen face was inscrutable. She loosened her hands impatiently from his grasp. And she answered:

'There's a silly goat you are! Think you the habits of a lifetime are changed by a little preaching? And who says that awful I am getting? Some would say that awful *you* are getting, with your old religion. Ach, leave me in peace.'

She turned away. But he caught hold of her arms.

'Come with me to one of the Corinthians' meetings,' he begged. 'Such lovely preaching and singing you will hear! Forget the world you will and there's peace one feels then.'

135

'Ha,' she cried, 'heard I have about those meetings. Nice behaviour goes on in them! Know you do that out of their minds one or two Corinthians have gone? Remember I do how Mrs Hopkins, the haulier's wife, come from one of their meetings and stripped her children to beat old Satan out of them.'

'Fools and weak-minded people there are everywhere. If you knew what quiet there is in your soul after you have been to a service!'

But her face was full of dour scorn.

'Each one to his own taste,' she muttered, settling her old weather-beaten hat impatiently, 'and no interference. Meddling in other people's little pleasures! Fussy, croaking big toads!'

'Who?' he demanded angrily.

But looking into her pale eyes, that seemed shrivelled and pitiful in the sagging drink-sodden flesh of her face, he wanted to cry aloud of the hurt in his love for her.

She went out with a proud, granite-like composure, in her shabby carelessly arranged clothes. Reuben's heart was full of anger and pain as he watched her. And it seemed that there was not one soul in the world to companion his. Not one that would share, with perfect intermingling, his joys and sorrows.

Even in the raptures of the mystical exaltations that his soul enjoyed there was a loneliness that was, he thought now, terrible. His soul came alone, a wanderer from earth, and, returned, there was stony scorn on the faces of those to whom his heart quickened most.

Alone! He would be forever alone.

But there was his task. Contempt and scorn and indifference that he must conquer. To strike into the souls of the scornful and the slothful sparks of divine light – that was his task.

He went out.

In the early spring dusk the Valley stretched vague as a slatternly woman abandoned to wretchedness; the March clouds lay sullenly about the sky, and, their pit-broken flanks grey in the falling light, the ancient hills seemed to complain dimly of the evil that made ugly and filthy their once-fair flesh.

He descended to the main part of the Valley, where the better houses gathered together thickly, crouched close to each other as though for company beneath the morose hills. In the windows of the few shops greasy lights began to flicker; and at the corners groups of colliers squatted on their heels as they spoke together, joyless and brave.

Quickly he went through the streets, his brows drawn taut above the restless gleam of his observing eyes.

Ah, that the voice of God would thunder from the heavens and quake through the beings of the people! He passed public-houses, the shed where silly pictures were displayed upon a sheet, fried-fish shops, big squat chapels of firm stone, and houses, houses, that were as tombs of the dead. And his voice trembled for utterance, he wanted to cry of the glory that was not in the lives of the people about him.

He ascended one of the hills with quick breathless energy, his limbs bathed in a glow that gave him an acute sensation of eternal power. Arrived at the top, he sat down and stared below into the Valley.

Jesus Christ! The world was grey and lost, sunk in apathy. He pressed his teeth into his knuckles and shook, his limbs trembled and stretched themselves. And he cried aloud:

'The people thirst, and there is no water in the wilderness – where is the rock of Horeb that shall bring forth water for the parched, and the man of God that will lead the people to the promised land?'

For a time he stayed there on the lonely hilltop in austere meditation, his body quickened, flooded with supple power. Then slowly he descended, his feet noiseless on the soft Spring grass. The bed of the Valley was fading into the dark blue shadows of night, but thin light still lingered on the hills, the curved outline of their brows defined sharply and sinuously against the sky.

Huge rocks were scattered here and there on the lower slope of the hill. Reuben, occupied in his holy meditation, wandered down among them silently.

Suddenly, coming round a rock, his brooding eyes beheld a young man and girl lying in the shadow of the stone. Embraced in the proud simplicity of flowering passion, beautiful and abandoned so that even the wrinkled rock seemed to gleam and lean to them its shadow as a protective benediction, they had neither eye nor ear for the world.

Reuben stopped still, and stared at them. Then, turning quickly, he hurried away.

His heart throbbed like a wounded bird. He muttered:

'Christ, keep thy face ever before me.'

And he hurried down into the Valley.

He went to Morgans' bakehouse and knocked. The baker opened the door a little way and cautiously peered out. But he welcomed Reuben.

'Step you in, Reuben. Refreshing it is to see a Christian face. But, boy bach, overcast as an atheist's face is yours tonight: say what's the matter.'

As usual, Morgans had been employed in his task of copying the Bible into exercise books. But he shut the books now and put them away in a biscuit-tin that stood on a high shelf. Then with his bony fingers he briskly combed up his beard and sat down opposite Reuben.

'There's a lovely little testimony you gave last Sunday,' he said admiringly. 'Like a bard you were.'

Reuben's face brightened.

'You think I can speak well in the chapel!'

'Yes,' indeed. And poetical is your style. Talking about you we are in the chapel. Our Leader said, "As good as the Psalms is his speech." '

The old man scrutinised Reuben and added softly: 'Say now, if our Leader left us to go to another chapel, how would you like to occupy our pulpit?'

Reuben smiled. 'Ah, too ignorant I am, and people will not listen to me closely because I am so young.' But his voice was eager and excited.

Morgans cried, with uplifted hand, in a preacher's manner:

'An inspired power comes from the mouths of the young. The old men and the old women are grey and bowed with experience and crooked as a rule is their vision of divine things. The world has cracked the rock of their strength, and they quake and crumble under the blows of life. But the young go about in the shining armour of their trust, and under their eyelids there are stars and in their breasts the sun of summer. Not grey wisdom flows from them, but beautiful faith like golden sunlight, which the cold bodies of the older people yearn and pant for.'

Reuben smiled gently. 'A good preacher *you* are,' he said sincerely. 'How is it that you have not taken the pulpit?'

'People will not listen to me,' the old baker answered rather angrily. 'I have been in the pulpit once or twice in our chapel, but though my words have shone with glory, I could see the laughter hidden behind the people's faces.'

'Laughter!' repeated Reuben. 'Why laughter?'

Morgans' crisp beard stuck out, his nostrils quivered.

'No confidence in me the people have, it seems. Believed in many creeds I have in my time and attended many chapels. A turncoat they call me, because I am looking for the True Light and have found that Light poor and dim in most chapels.'

'Yes, true that is,' Reuben agreed. 'Religion is mocked in the chapels. Make Jesus Christ into a man with a frock-coat and a liking for scandal some of them do.'

'Ah, good that is,' Morgans declared with enjoyment. 'Yes, indeed, imagine they do that the Man of Sorrows is like their own preachers.' He leaned forward. 'And a little too scandalous some of the prayers of repentance are in our chapel too, I think. Too much into detail some of the women go when they are carried away by their fervour. Seem they do to take pleasure in telling everybody how Satan worked in them. Ach y fi, ashamed I've been to listen sometimes.'

Reuben looked at his hands meditatively.

'A religion simple as the Sermon on the Mount I should like to preach,' he murmured.

'And do it you can,' Morgans cried with warmth. 'A place there is for you in the religion of Wales. Youth, strength and inspiration you have in abundance. Religion waits for such as you and Wales is ready for a revival.'

Reuben's voice quickened.

'You believe I have the power – ' he cried.

'Give yourself over body and soul to God,' the baker answered vehemently, 'and let yourself be carried away with the Glory that you see. And the people will harken to you as you speak as out of a cloud of fire. But keep you steadfast in faith. Never question the power that will flow out of you. Keep your mind open to inspiration as the flower is open to the sun. For it seems to me that you are a chosen vessel.'

Reuben lifted his head. 'Oh,' he murmured, 'if I could lessen the sorrows of the world!'

Morgans got up. 'Always attendant on the flesh is woe,' he uttered with a sigh, 'but set fire to the darkened torches of the spirit you can.' He looked at his watch. 'Now, Reuben bach, see to my bread I must. This earthly work the Lord has given me and I must do it well. Truthfully can I say, no bread is baked like mine, no crust rises so lovely. For I watch my baking as the eye of Moses watched his people in Sinai.'

'And there's peace I find in this bakehouse!' Reuben said.

Morgans put on his apron.

'Think you over what I have said about the pulpit in our chapel, Reuben. For talk there is that our Leader is going to another district.'

Reuben went home excitedly. He entered the living-room eager to tell his father.

Eirwen sat in the arm-chair by the fire, talking to Hugh. She wore a black hat and a black scarf, and as she entered the room she turned to him a face that was quiet and grave.

'I came to tell you that Philip died last night,' she said softly.

He sat down and looked at her sombrely.

'Poor Philip,' he muttered.

And as she told him in her cold, quiet manner it was as though an icy blast entered his soul. He saw again the shrunken and yellow face of Philip, with its devastated eyes and mocking mouth: and his heart ached with grievous love.

'He is no longer suffering,' he cried suddenly. But his voice seemed to echo with despair. 'He shall have quiet and peace evermore.'

'He raved so much before he died,' Eirwen continued in her hushed voice, – 'cursing everything. Then he got so weak, he couldn't use his voice, and his eyes were awful – ' Her voice faltered in her throat. 'How shall I forget the way he looked at us then! Afraid it has made me.'

She looked at Reuben's pale wild face and she shuddered in herself.

'A terrible grief was in him,' Reuben muttered.

And though he knew Philip was dying, this announcement of his death hurt him to the depths of his being. There was only silence and desolation in that diseased body now: its passionately crying soul had fled. Whence, whither? With all his imagination Reuben could not see Philip treading the gleaming floors of Heaven.

'He shall live on a star where there is rest like music,' he cried with sudden rhapsodic certainty, startling Eirwen.

She looked at him with some distaste.

'He didn't believe in such things,' she said coldly. 'I heard him say once that he wouldn't make the worms very oily or the earth very rich. Because he was so thin. There's ideas he had!'

But his eyes were heavy with tears. He gazed at Eirwen as through a mist and saw her grave face, that seemed chastened by her fear.

'If I could have made him believe!' he cried.

Eirwen was affected by this regard for her cousin; she began to search for her handkerchief. And Hugh looked over his spectacles, sniffed in embarrassment, got up, and went upstairs silently.

'We all loved him,' she trembled, 'although he was so rude, sometimes.'

And for a while they were silent in their tears and lamentation. Each thought of the dead man. He seemed to be here in the room, they saw the faint smile on his pale lips, the stretched ironic eyelids. His shadow was upon them.

Eirwen gazed at Reuben mistily. His face was bent, his hand was in the black disorder of his hair, as he sat at the table. She went to him and took his hand.

'Never mind,' she said, 'he won't be ill any more. Perhaps it is best that he is gone. And God is sure to forgive him his blasphemy, because he suffered so much.'

He looked up. Her face was pale as an angel's, her large eyes soft as the eyes of a trustful heifer. With gentle strength she drew him up from the chair.

Inscrutably he gazed at her. Her lashes were still wet with tears, her lips poised in the sweet grimace of lamentation.

'So upset I've been because of it all,' she cried.

She leaned to him as though she was utterly wearied. 'And I've thought of you a lot when I've sat by him in the night.'

She leaned her body to him. There was the same old perfume about her, the same urgency in her softly pressing breasts. His arms crept about her: she lifted her mouth to his. And now a chaste grace was in her tearful abandon.

Dimly he was aware that she was kissing him. But, ah, so delicately – such kisses as angels might give. And again he was aware of a hot strength crouching within him, crouching like a savage beast that yet will not spring to its prey.

Then she passed her hands down the sides of his body, sighing with faint languor from her thick throat:

'Lovely you are... Reuben... I've thought of you so much...'

With violent hunger he pressed her body to his – his mouth upon hers so that she felt the wandering desires of her body sucked up into one long inarticulate cry of lust.

But as violently he thrust her away. And anger came upon his face and darkened into hatred.

'Leave me alone,' he cried. 'Why will you always tempt me with your evil snares!'

144

Her face became dark with disgusted amazement.

'A funnier boy never trod this earth,' she declared.

But he looked at her with contempt and exclaimed in a voice that pealed forth proudly:

'My life will be given to joys that are not of the flesh. And you are given over altogether to the flesh, Eirwen Vaughan. Leave me alone.'

She kept gazing at him from under her drooped golden eyelids. And his voice trembled as he continued to denounce her. When his fervour ceased, she muttered calmly:

'A fool, a blind fool, that's what you are now, Reuben Daniels. But wake up you will one of these days.' Her red lips smiled spitefully. 'Then you'll remember me and be much angrier than you are now. Oh, Reuben bach, my little preacher, you were not made to stand in a pulpit. Too much looks you have. Unsettle the women in the wrong way you would...'

He shook with rage.

'Go away!' he cried.

And he went up to bed that night in a passion of angry grief. He prayed by his bedside with increased energy – for the peace of Philip's soul, for chastity to occupy Eirwen's mind, for inspiration to impart Light to the world. Hugh passed the door of his son's bedroom and shook his head gloomily as he heard the voice within; Martha passed and snorted some tipsy exclamation. Finally Reuben, shivering in his flannelette night-suit, crept into bed and, his face white and mysterious like the moonlight, fell into broken slumber. And he dreamed.

145

He seemed to be sitting in a lucid sea of icy water, watching naked bodies flow up and down before him. Bodies that were pale and emaciated as they floated in the clear green depths, their faces white, silent, and dead. And the sound of the moving water was as the passing of dead ages and he listened with dread and fear alone in his soul. Dread and fear, for in that icy eternal sea he alone lived, in a body that was hard as iron, with eyes that were frozen. 'They are dead, they are dead,' his mind cried despairingly, as he watched the mysterious naked bodies float past. 'I shall live companionless, alone in this cold sphere.' And as the cry fell like broken syllables of doom through the frozen chasm of his mind, he woke.

He shivered on the bed; all the sheets had been kicked to the floor. But his head was bathed in sweat.

He lifted the blankets and rolled in them. Soon he was warm and slept again. But again he dreamed.

He lay with a creature whose body was fibrous and damp as the thick stem of a monstrous resinous plant. A perfume that was as the heavy odour of desire was exhaled from her, and the lithe strength of her slender body lay in his arms like all the sin of the world. His voice shouted within him, 'The flesh dies, the blood is poured out, the soul is the shadow of a cloud,' and his body clung with desperate abandon to the warm creature within his arms. He lifted his face to her and it was as though his head moved amid huge sticky leaves gleaming with an evil strength; his mouth moved hungrily for her mouth, and he lifted his hot eyelids... He saw abhorrent curved-back lips that were pale as with death, eyes that under snake-like

146

brows held evil as hellish laughter, dark flesh that shone –
and his mouth swayed to hers in awful delight...

He woke again, with horror, his belly stretched in sickness.

Starting up, he cast away the blankets, and leapt out of
that bed of abominations. Then he threw off his night-suit
and stood naked, his body covered with sweat. And the
thought of going down to the river and immersing his
unclean flesh entered his mind.

But he fell on his knees, praying madly and weepingly,
he fell prostrate on the cold linoleum and lay in the throes
of repentant grief. For his dream had been real to him and
he had given himself over in sinful delight to that wanton
woman.

His voice rose, he writhed and twisted on the floor.
Hugh, opening the door and carrying a candle aloft, gazed
at him in fright. But before Martha appeared he had cast a
blanket over his prostrate son, exclaiming as she came
blowsily into the room:

'Dear me, a fit he must have had.'

She gazed at both with dark wrath.

'Yes, a religious fit such as ends people in asylums,' she
pronounced acrimoniously. 'What have I said in the past,
Hugh Daniels? When you have given him the Bible and
encouraged his weak mind to dwell on those old daft tales!'

She stood dourly in her flowing striped nightdress, her
mottled face angry at this disturbance of her tipsy rest.
Reuben, lifted to his feet by his father, gazed at her with
glittering eyes.

She drew back a little from his mad gaze, lowering her
eyelids. Then suddenly he went to her, his head stretched

forward, a strange light in his eyes. He took hold of her, and his hands were like iron on her shoulders. But his face had upon it a child-like simplicity.

'You will cast away your sin,' he muttered in a strained, muffled voice, 'you will come to me fairer than the morning and rest with me in the evening.'

She gazed at him in fascinated dread. And, his voice rising in rhapsody, he fell at her feet and swayed in his chant:

'I have waited long for you. But you will forget your sin and we will go together over the hills of suffering, through the waters of Jordan, and there will be peace for you at last – '

But she fled, uttering a low moan of fright and horror, and Hugh, as though in a trance himself, was left to deal alone with the transported Reuben.

He put his son into bed, opened the Bible that always lay on the little table, and read in his gentle voice the calm verses of Ecclesiastes until Reuben dropped into a heavy slumber.

And he was troubled no more with evil dreams that night.

BOOK THREE

CHAPTER I

Yes, Wales was thirsty for a Revival.

Ten years had passed since the last, and the time for another was at hand. The ministers said so, denouncing the building of cinemas and the fondness of young people for dancing in couples; the deacon sitting in the Big Seats of the chapels agreed and in their prayers in the second meetings prayed avariciously for its coming.

Religion was getting monotonous as it was. Who would come out of the youth of the land and pour a new vitality into souls that were stale, with the whip of his tongue drive again to the chapels the backsliders carelessly sliding away to the damnation of modern pleasure?

The ministers and the deacons lifted their voices in continual prayer, remembering the excitements and fervours of the last revival.

And now it seemed that God had harkened and decided

also that Wales needed a quickening, an enlivening of its ancient religious life.

Wherever the ministers gathered together in the Valley they spoke of the young man, Reuben Daniels, who with his beautiful prayers and powerful sermons was filling to overflowing the hillside chapel of the Corinthians. Already there had been scenes of remarkable zeal at the chapel – converts throwing off the shackles of their sins with clamorous ardour, and paricularly there had been heartening success with young men and women, owing perhaps to the youth of the evangelist. Queues, it was said, waited outside the chapel long before the door was open. And the public-house keepers were quaking in their boots, the owners of this new pleasure, the cinema-halls, went about with uneasy faces.

The ministers waited for developments. Religion would be again the glory of Wales and the ministers a greater power in the land. They waited for the flame to spread: some invested in new frock-coats on the surety of what already had happened.

And in the little chapel on the hillside God worked his wonders. Surely one evening those frail walls would split and burst with the swelling power that was manifested within! It was lovely; the soul within one rose up strong and flaring with the holy fire, and the tongue in one's mouth was loosened and, after repentance, pride in God sat like a kingly strength in the bosom.

They poured into the chapel in enthusiastic profusion at evening service – those who came in groups singing loudly as they made their way up, waving their Bible-grasping

150

hands to the sky. Ah, they would show God that he was not forgotten on this sin-filled earth, they would show him how passionately and rapturously they loved him!

The long weary hills that shut in the black Valley looked down inscrutably at these little singing mobs that climbed to the chapel like ants in their hasty profusion. How much longer, how much longer, seemed to be written on their lonely, contemptuous brows. The hills, shut in the Valley, lay in sombre wardership about these creatures clambering so fussily upon their slopes: and there seemed to be hate beneath their impenetrable gaze.

But the ants were unaware of it.

'Oh, God is surely here with us, brothers and sisters!' cried one man in a group of about a dozen clambering to the chapel. 'Think you, how lovely is the world: Look at these mountains and the grass thereon, and the clouds, and the water coming out of that spring. God gave them to us. Ah, the great God gave them to us, glory be his name, Alleluia, Jesus Christ be blest. Sing, loved ones in Jesus, sing!' And he struck up:

'*The dwellings of Jesus are here below*
If we would look, if we would know – '

So, singing lustily, they joined the queue gathered at the door. An hour before the actual performance was supposed to begin, the door of the chapel was opened and the crowd swayed into the front seats. These fortunate ones entertained themselves for that hour in tireless singing, to the beat of their stamped feet and clapped hands.

151

Soon the chapel was packed to the doors. About the pulpit, crammed in every corner, the crowd frothed, never ceasing to sing. When Reuben Daniels appeared on the little platform cries rose above the hymn:

'Greetings in Jesus, brother.'

'Oh, fill us with lovely fire tonight.'

'God stands behind you, brother Daniels.'

Encouraging were their cries. They had come for fire to warm their stale souls and they must not be denied it. They must not go back to their dark stuffy hovels without the certainty of God's hot affection lit in their barren souls.

Reuben went on his knees and the singing ceased. He began the prayer quietly, his voice trembling in its vague chant, but as he went on, the words came forth triumphantly shining with Gospel pride.

'I climbed to thee, O Lord, and there were thy people arrayed in the strength of worship, loveliness upon their faces, the songs of angels upon their lips. Ah, the splendour in their singing! Thou, God, listened, and the heavens shone for us...' (The April sunset had sent the suitable message through the windows.) 'A ray that was rosy like the light of Paradise lay as a benediction upon our heads. Let us keep that light about us, let it make clear our darkest hours, let it be the sun that shall pour healing upon us. We bleed, our knees tremble, our mouths are full of the dust of toil, but thou pourest thy marvellous healing upon us and our bruises are like white flowers, our weary bodies stand like happy emperors; and we are full of joy.'

The voices of the people took on rapture as this sacred flattery was issued to them. Yes, they were God's children,

152

they would not be orphans any longer, every cell in their bodies loved the Father who sat enthroned above all earthly splendour and promised them rewards more eternal than earth could give. Money, a mansion, holidays, clothes, foreign lands – bah, what were they compared to the bliss in Paradise that they were earning by praying thus on their poverty-clad knees?

They sang with riotous abandon:

> *'Happy land, happy land,*
> *Where God's faithful noble band*
> *Love and sing*
> *Round the King...'*

And, set to familiar tunes, other hymns by their own poets.

The crowd overflowed beyond the front-door and the hymns were continued outside.

And Reuben stood, a young god, on the platform and gazed in a brooding ecstasy over the people gathered beneath him. He was removed to a sphere beyond earth, he was exalted to a station where inspiration was about him like a golden cloak quivering with ardent stars: he heard his voice speak out of him as though it issued from a still more exalted sphere – he was but the trumpet that received and issued the Word. Pale and gleaming with mystic ecstasy, he stood in that little rough pulpit, a seraph clad in comely flesh, receiving the divine message.

'Ahr-r-r-r – ' cried a certain young woman, carried beyond herself by devotion, as the last hymn died away, 'I have come to thee at last, Jesus, and thou hast not turned me away...'

'Glory to God,' several others cried.

'But thou hast taken me to thy breast and led me to salvation,' she continued in a strange wail.

Everyone gazed with glazed eyes at her.

'Praise be to Jesus for saving Catherine Pritchards,' an elder sister screamed. But there was a jeer in her voice.

Converts were supposed to wait until the after-meeting to declare their successful entrance into bliss. But some could not control themselves until then and the course of the first meeting was often interrupted until their declarations subsided into, perhaps, a soft moan of converted joy, or complete, tranced silence.

'Praise be to Jesus for another soul,' echoed the others.

Reuben gazed with the love of Heaven at the entranced Catherine Pritchards, who stood with eyes raised to him rapturously, her white face winged in frizzed golden hair.

'Sit down now, sister, and be at peace,' he called to her gently.

She sat down submissively. But her eyes were full of adoration, her arms crossed claspingly over her breasts. Then the performance continued with accelerated zeal.

Long, long hymns repeated and sung with proud vigour, ceaselessly interrupted with the holy cries of those who beheld visions. The flesh of the people became the tissue of God's Word; though of earth they were denizens of Heaven, as they galloped round the universe in the elevation of their singing. The organist, an elongated young man in a high stiff collar, sweated and steamed in endeavours to keep pace with the voices. Ah, Heaven itself was let loose in the rocking chapel.

Reuben rose to deliver his address. He chose a text from Proverbs: *'How long wilt thou sleep, O sluggard? When wilt thou arise out of thy sleep?'*

In jewelled rhetoric he called to the world to awaken from the sloth that was slaying the precious soul within. He began in a voice that was like a cool brook running among polished stones; but speaking of the world, he blazed forth as charging clouds burnt through with lightning. And chanting of the woes of Christ, his face was transfigured with love. The words rushed to his tongue in unhesitating ease and he was aware of a power that flooded his veins with intoxicated flame.

The people moaned in the gratification of religious pleasure; some were audible in abandonment to weeping, others, occupied in private trances of their own, uttered little noises of devotion. The sermon lasted beyond an hour, but time was nothing and fled unheeded.

More hymns and the rattle of the collection-plates as the pennies were showered into them. A prayer, and the first service was over.

But no one went out. In fact, those outside made extra, though futile, attempts to press themselves into the sweating chapel. The people knew each other, and conversion, with its attendant confession, is sometimes interesting.

There were twenty-two converts that night. Reuben began the prayers and other members of the chapel were loud also in fervent demands that God might move in his mysterious ways tonight. Soon the conversions began.

Catherine Pritchards was not to be denied the full glory of repentance. Her declaration in the last service had been

155

much too short. She stood now in the unappeased splendour of her rejoicing face and gilt hair, and continued, above the sighs and muttering prayers of others:

'I saw him as I lay in bed one night, dear people, crying because I had used wicked words quarrelling with my father. Oh, yes, I saw Jesus. Lovely he looked at me. He said: "Hard your words have been and though your father is in evil ways a daughter must not provoke him to further badness by angering him with her tongue. Think on me and lead your father to me gently too." Like that he spoke, brothers and sisters, and faded away between the chest-of-drawers and the window. And I jumped out of bed and went downstairs to my father, who was in a drunken way. " 'Dad bach,' I said, 'sorry for what I said I am.' " And I took his hand and said further, " 'Let us pray together to Jesus.' " He thrust me away, but I prayed alone, there in our little kitchen. And I will lead my father to the Blessed Courts, he shall come to Jesus, he shall sit with me here. Has he not got an awful bout of rheumatics already, because of that bad beer! Jesus will help me to bring him here, he will strengthen me. Oh, Jesus, lovely you are, strong and powerful you are...'

Everyone knew Catherine Pritchards, who lived alone with her father, a fireman in the pit. She was near thirty, and six years had passed since she had given birth to a stillborn child. It was not known with certainty who the father of the child was, but scandal blamed a young preacher who had left the Valley shortly after the birth. Catherine had maintained a sullen silence; but now and again she would attend assiduously the established chapels, in the vain hope of obliterating her sin in the minds of the people. So she had come at last to the Corinthians, who are famous for their mixed congregations. But no word of her well-known sin stained her confession now, and she stopped speaking in a gaping silence.

Reuben looked at her. He saw her white face that had the melancholy of suffering upon it, her saddened mouth. He cried to her:

'Be with us in Jesus, sister, and we will work together for the glory of the Word.'

So she was received into the Courts of the Saved.

Conversions continued. Old Sam Williams the Sack, who was accustomed to attendance in a very earthly Court, for frequent pilfering of coal from the wagons at the side of the pit, was now received into the Greater Court. He fell down to the floor in his piety and beat his head against the uncarpeted wood. A grey, shrivelled old woman lifted a poor little voice that became shrill as she described the subsequent significance of her dry life when Jesus came to her 'big, and took her to his breast.' Several young women strove to outdo each other in the passion of giving themselves to God; they foamed at the mouth in the fury of their ardour, hats came off and hair was loosened, their bodies shaken in the convulsions that often attend this process of being saved.

And so, drunk with the divine frenzy, this sacred madness, the people sang with unabated intensity a last long hymn.

Reuben stood still in the pulpit. His face was pale and exhausted now, though his eyes shone with the light that is not of this earth. He had writhed like a god in vehement transport of ecstatic prayer and like an inspired young man of earth he had chanted of the bruises and the desolation of his fellow-creatures. And the people had taken fire from him, they had sucked with hungry avidity his divine inspiration. Now, exhausted and calmed, he knelt and asked each to repeat the Lord's Prayer.

Thus, with that simple chant, they finished.

Catherine Pritchards came to Reuben as he stood alone for a moment after descending slowly and tiredly from the pulpit. She said to him happily:

'Brother, I have truly heard a Man of God tonight! Right down into my soul your wonderful words went. Dear Reuben Daniels, great you are, and a faithful sister I am going to be here.'

He thanked her for her praise. She continued with increased fervour, her obsessed pale blue eyes fixed on him:

'Let me do service for the chapel. Let me work with you, brother, however humble a task you give me. Oh, Jesus, I will do it well.'

'Come up to the Thursday meeting, when the members meet,' he said a little wearily, and bidding her goodnight he went into the little vestry.

And the people went home joyfully to their dark miserable dwellings, to their stuffy uglily furnished houses, to their children gathered about the sordidly bleak streets, to the malformations of their hovel existence. But what of that? God loved them, he was above, benign in his Heaven that they would reach some day, to dwell there evermore in the comfort of the freed spirit.

Reuben, when he was at last released from the congratulations of the members went home in weary calm. He was content with what he had done, proud of his success, full of gratitude for this power of leading people to God. Twenty-two converts in one evening – five of them notorious backsliders into various worldly sins!

It was half-past ten; Martha and Hugh had eaten their supper, and now Martha dozed by the side of the fire while Hugh meditated, an anxious frown on his brow, opposite her.

Reuben came in and looked at them without a word.

'Just come from the chapel you have?' Hugh asked.

'Yes. We had a good service.'

Hugh looked at his son unhappily.

'You know that religious I am, but too much of it you are having lately. Unnatural it is.'

Reuben sat down, his brow darkened. His father knew nothing of the Vision that burned within him, of the voice that urged him to conflict for the salvation of the people. He muttered:

'I have a task to do.'

Their voices awoke Martha. She cried out with some violence:

'Where have you been all this time?'

He lifted his still, weary face to her.

'You know where I have been.'

'That chapel!' she went on, with temper.

He sat at the table; his stomach craved food.

'Do I hear right,' she continued, 'when told I am that you are going to leave the pit for those yelling dolts?'

He sprang up. Nobody could rouse his temper so swiftly as Martha.

'Be quiet,' he cried, yellow under the eyes.

She laughed harshly. Hugh's chin sank despairingly into his neck. He murmured, 'Now, people, use gentler words on a Sunday night!'

Martha turned to him. 'Are you going to sit there quiet, like a cold flat-fish, and let your son give up a manly living for those old idiots?'

'A talent for preaching he has, they say,' he answered mildly, 'and come out somehow it must.'

'Yes, come out like a bad old family rash,' she said spitefully. 'Well I remember how some of your people were taken foolish when the last revival was on. Your sister Siân, it was, wasn't it, that cut off her hair because tended it in vanity she said she had, and went about without a hat to show her lunatic's sacrifice?'

'Hush, woman,' he commanded her sternly.

She tossed her aroused head.

'And very religious she is still!' she jeered. 'More faith in the bottle she has had for a long time now.'

'Rest your serpent's tongue!' he cried, with anger that was strange to him.

She turned on Reuben.

'Don't you do this thing,' she almost screamed. 'No one from me must wear the black of a preacher. Do you stick to the black of the pit, which will bring you more comfort than the other.'

He looked at her with flaming eyes.

'I intend to do it,' he said.

160

She stared at him.

'Who are you to tell me what I am to do?' he asked cruelly. 'Not often have you troubled yourself like this.'

Then he said further – but now his love for her was naked in his voice – 'What have I been to you? Have I not been always alone?'

She drew away from him, from the bright, haunting regard of his eyes.

His face was ashen. 'Ah,' he cried softly, 'you will come with me yet.'

But in a sudden wail she exclaimed, 'Awful this is. Why is it he is not built like other boys! Drat me, gaudy and flighty is Eirwen Vaughan, but rather I would that he married her tomorrow. There's slack she's been!'

At this mention of Eirwen he again trembled with rage. But he sat once more at the table and began to eat with added hunger. There were cold meat pies, sausages, jelly, and jam tarts. He ate well, though sullenly, and afterwards offered up his usual prayer.

Martha had returned to her chair and was gazing broodingly into the fire.

He bade them good-night and went up to his bedroom. After he had stripped he lay prostrate and prayed with gathering emotion. It was now easy for him to enter into ecstatic trances wherein he might hear God's voice. He entered into one tonight and soon was scaling the pinnacles of a lovelier world than this.

Thus Reuben Daniels began his work for Christ.

CHAPTER II

He left the colliery.

The Corinthians paid him two pounds per week, presented him with a ponderous Bible that had brass clasps and was ornamented with useful oily-looking pictures, and congratulated themselves on possessing such a golden-tongued preacher at such a reasonable salary.

They looked upon him as one of the natural prophets of God, one of those who come out of the people, simple and lowly, who speak as the dawn flows over the earth, as the stars appear, and the flowers grow, natural and primeval.

'He is one of those Christ would have for disciples, if the Man of God walked in the Valley,' said Morgans the Bakehouse.

They were busy, arranging a series of special meetings, to present him to the Valley at large and to attempt to fan into a conflagration the religious fire already begun.

Reuben was remote from this fuss, he was not expected to occupy himself in these careful arrangements for his appearance before the larger public. He was supposed to spend his time in deep meditation and preparation for display of his powers. This he did.

Mostly by wandering over the hills for hours. For in the house his holy serenity was broken by Martha's presence. He could not bear the dark hostility of her face. But on the hills his soul ran quick with sacred passion and he was in frequent contact with invisible beings and heard voices that had no earthly sound. His pale wild face lifted to the sky, he would pause and strain his widened eyes to some choric vision among the clouds. For him, too, the mountains and the islands were moved out of their places and the people of the earth hid themselves in the dens and among the rocks, fleeing before the face of the Lamb.

The people must cleanse their souls, so that the face of the Lamb would shine forth in well-pleased satisfaction.

And the chanting song of Reuben's voice was often lifted amid those patient hills whereon he wandered like John in the desert, beholding God everywhere.

Often his wanderings brought him to the hill upon whose lower slope Bryn Farm stood. One early afternoon he saw Eirwen lying in the shade of a flowering cherry-tree that grew in the back-garden. She was reading a book, lying flat on her stomach, occasionally kicking a leg into the air. For some time he watched her from the upper slope, his face cast in vague sorrow. Presently he made his way slowly to the farm, to the front entrance.

He hadn't been to the Farm since the day before Philip's

funeral. Then he had gone to look upon his friend's face before the coffin-lid was screwed down, and immediately after he had fled, his soul cold at the sight of that face that had upon it evil contempt like a grimacing mask. Now he knocked at the front door,the peace of God upon his brow.

Mrs Vaughan opened the door and cried, 'Reuben Daniels! Indeed, now, an honour this is.'

She swept her apron over a chair for him, fetched a glass of small-beer, and looked at him in admiration.

'There's different you look! Not so broody. Happy you are since you went over to the Corinthians? Well, well, there's success you are having! Heard we have of your heavenly preaching.'

He drank the small-beer, listening to this woman's admiring praise. If Martha were like her! How complete his joy would be then.

'You must come to our chapel and hear me,' he said.

'Indeed I will. A little weary of Caersalem I am getting lately. Above my head the sermons seem to be. They say that awful success you are having with bad people. Proud you must feel converting them.'

He smiled religiously. 'It is not my power that converts them, but the power that flows from the Throne in a river of Eternal Life. Perhaps for a time I am the vessel of that power, and I pour it out as God directs me...'

She sat and listened, entranced. Reuben Daniels speaking a little sermon alone with her! She sat in expectant silence and leaned her ear to him.

'...and I shall not be dumb while he commands me to speak, while he commands me to trumpet his message – '

164

His eyes began to shine and for a little while Mrs Vaughan was given quite a Sunday treat.

He finished his small-beer and asked, 'Where is Eirwen?'

Her face became melancholy. 'Out in the garden, wasting her time reading one of Philip's books.' She looked at him with a sad appeal. 'Hoping I was that you would settle down with her, Reuben bach, for a steadying influence she wants. And now old Lewis the Cauliflower's son is after her and she seems to incline to him. But disturbed I am at the affair, for a ruffianly name has the boy.'

A little glow of colour appeared on Reuben's spiritual cheeks.

'Serious the affair is?' he asked.

'See each other often they do and given her a gold brooch he has.'

Reuben was silent. He knew the son of Lewis, who owned the Cauliflower, a prosperous public-house. The young man was occupied in the business of the beer-house and had a reputation also; and, as such people are sometimes, he was handsome in a dashing, fleshy way. Reuben was filled with horror at the thought of Eirwen in contact with him.

Presently he went out to the garden and approached Eirwen, who was intent on her book, lying in an abandoned fashion on the patch of grass about the tree. He called softly:

'Eirwen Vaughan!'

She turned round languidly. For a few moments she regarded him with a faintly insolent smile on her lips. Then she said, 'Well, Reuben, have you come to try to whip my sins out of me? You always said I was full of them, and an expert on things like that you are getting, it seems.'

He was beyond the jeers of the ribald now. He looked back at her, a chaste pleasure in his face.

'Eirwen Vaughan, you are one of God's loveliest flowers of earth.' She stared at him curiously. 'And who shall pluck you and cherish you for eternal delight?' he asked softly.

She lay in indolent grace beneath the flowering cherry-tree. A blossom dropped through the sun-warm air. He picked it up and put it in her hand. He sat down beside her and looked into her face, that gleamed with young vitality, at her flaunted throat and her supple shoulders. She watched him from beneath her eyelids. He said:

'How lovely you are!'

A faint derisive smile flickered over his face. But she was silent, looking at him cruelly and with vanity.

His head dropped to hers, rested on her shoulder, his lips grazed her ear. 'Your heart is not wakened yet. The desire of the flesh is deceitful as worldly wealth. If you will go to men for the love of their bodies, your soul will be filled with dust and ashes.'

She moved away her head and looked at him sardonically.

'Is that the way Corinthians make love?' she asked, strange laughter in her voice. He got up.

'I am not making love to you,' he answered in his exalted voice.

Her body trembled as he moved from her.

'Oh, well,' she said, 'odd and quaint you were always.'

'What is this publican's son to you?' he asked coldly.

She burst into sudden laughter.

166

He watched her supple body shaken by mad laughter. Anger rose in him. 'Be quiet, girl,' he cried austerely, 'you have the noise of a fool.'

She sprang up. 'And you have the manner of an idiot, Reuben Daniels.' She stood quivering before him.

He bowed his head. 'Forgive my harsh words,' he whispered.

She looked at his young, wild hair, the sorrow of the pale face beneath it. 'Pity you are not different,' she said stonily, 'for I have had love for you and wanted you for a lover.'

He cried out in sudden rhapsody:

'But I have given myself to the love of God and I shall labour for him. How can I do that if I let myself be filled with the beauty of your flesh! No, no, a sacrifice of that I must make. In the labour of God my pleasure must be.'

She sat down again and, clasping her knees, looked at him with desire keen on her face. Always she had been attracted to him, always she had wanted to cool her desire in the ecstasy of his spiritual love. He could strike from her desire a deeper pleasure than any of her various lovers gave her; he had the sacred fire in a body that was firm with chaste strength.

'Reuben Daniels,' she exclaimed suddenly, 'you are lost.'

He looked at her in dark anger.

'Lost!'

'Why,' she wailed in real despair, 'will you be so mad?'

He turned away, saying scornfully, 'You know of nothing except the things that lead to damnation. It is you who are lost.'

167

She called to him. Her brows were drawn in a strange expression, and from under them her inscrutable eyes burned as though recoiled into some inner vehemence. Her voice issued in a reedy whisper:

'One day you will want me, Reuben. I know it. You will come for me and I shall be waiting for you. You will love me for the pleasure of my flesh and I shall have you for a lover.'

He shook his head and turned away without a word.

'I know it,' she called after him exultingly.

He resumed his meditations on the hills. By evening he would return to the house and eat of the meal that Martha silently and disdainfully put before him. Then perhaps there was a service in the chapel, and there he would be occupied for the rest of the evening, delivering oratorical value for his two pounds a week.

'A disappointed woman I am,' Martha would sniff to her cronies. 'A good collier he was getting and no bad habits he had.' She would complain until absolute consolation was reached.

And the Corinthians continued their preparations for the scourge. There was much labour to be done, while the repentant iron was hot. For obviously, judging by the increasing numbers who poured out their emotions in the chapel, the people, to the bowels of their souls, were sick of their monotonously sinful lives. They raised the membership fee, bought a larger organ, and spoke of building a huge chapel.

But the special meetings must be prepared first. They arranged, after some difficulty, to rent Hopkins's field, which was in a central position, being near all conveniences and having at one end a pool of flowing water, in which, it was proposed, converts could be dipped in Baptism – an open-air novelty that would be certain to attract large crowds. Old Hopkins the butcher had at first been unwilling to rent his field to a sect that was outlaw and took upon themselves airs that were not Methodist, but an extra shilling was offered over the usual five charged to the lawful chapels when they used the field for sports after the annual Sunday-school tea.

'Ach,' Morgans the Bakehouse exclaimed, as the contract was concluded, 'regretful you will be that you didn't give the field for nothing, when you see the wonders that will be done there.'

Mr Hopkins fingered his big gold watch-chain and answered coldly, 'See you that no damage is done to the field and that people take no advantage of the hedges.' And he insisted on them paying the whole of the rent in advance.

A marquee and also one or two smaller tents for possible overflow meetings must be obtained. The Corinthians borrowed money to pay for the loan of these – the large collection-plates would be certain to bring in more than was spent. A refreshment stall, stocked only with the home-produce of members, would be set up in one corner of the field. A band must be engaged. Flags and banners were to make the field bright and festive. Then announcement bills had to be printed. More money was borrowed, in cheerful certainty of success.

Committee meetings followed one after the other in the

chapel, and, in the usual Welsh style, matters were discussed without settlement, postponed, debated with heat and noise, often interrupted by a prayer or a hymn as a member was so moved, the women particularly being unable to settle the question of the refreshment-stall, so that April passed and May was advanced before things were well in hand.

In the meantime converts were accumulating and soon there would be no room in the chapel for those who were still in sin but desired to better themselves in a Sunday evening service, the favourite time for penitential confession.

Reuben Daniels went on from glory to glory. His orations were splendid in the Biblical manner: people compared them to the Revelation of St. John. The Bible was his unfailing friend and he drew exhaustless inspiration from it; he read nothing else now. And his youth and simplicity assisted him. His face was pure, and no scandal, beyond the drunken habits of his mother, was attached to his name. People were reminded of the youthful Jesus.

The flock already gathered in faithful membership worshipped him. His simplicity among themselves, his regard for the old and feeble, his comradely love for the young. And in the pulpit he was beautiful, beautiful. There it was as though great white wings beat about him, his face was glorious to look upon, his voice a poem of divine love.

He moved them to tears, exclamations, sobs, hysterical noises, swoons, trances of peaceful bliss, as no one else had.

Of the converted nobody was louder in praise than Catherine Pritchards, no other looked at the young Leader with such eyes of adoration. Since her conversion she had attended nearly every service, week-days as well. She soon occupied a position in the chapel, for she had a governing personality and a well-turned tongue. She could sing, too, in a full swelling manner that had some power, and she suggested in a committee meeting that advantage should be taken of her voice during the special meetings. She dearly wanted to be on the platform with Reuben.

She always found an opportunity to speak to Reuben, and she would go to him, her pale blue eyes sparkling, her big-breasted body gathered up taut and quivering, and say:

'Brother, what a pleasure it was to hear you tonight. And, what a lovely life mine has been since you converted me! Serve Jesus I shall with all my strength.'

Her eyes constantly sought his and when, perhaps, he would bend and speak to some old shrunken woman with a back shaped like a lemon, she would lean to them and listen closely to his words. And she dressed better than any other member, though she dared not wear jewellery in the chapel.

'Come you and speak to my father some day,' she asked him. 'Listen to you he would, I'm sure.'

He nodded vaguely and she added an invitation to tea. He promised to go some day.

And Morgans the Bakehouse was proud as a king at Reuben's success. His eyes too had a frenzy that had been absent for long. He was in the habit of saying:

'The faith of the chapels is weak-kneed and the ministers thereof given over to the vanities of easy living. But we have the ancient worship of the children of God and there

171

is no corruption amongst us. The promised land is at hand; our souls shall feed on the milk and honey gathered at a holy source.'

And his pride was such that he refused to bake the dough that came from the houses of the lawful ministers.

By the end of May all the preparations for the scourge against sin were ready. Soon Wales would again be a kingdom of God.

CHAPTER III

The scourge began.

The first meeting took place on Sunday evening and until the following Saturday the field was occupied with an enjoyable battle between the forces of Good and Evil. Good won; indeed, Evil put up a poor fight and fled in shame from the splendid marquee, from the inspired youth within, and the music of the brass band, from the baptismal pool, and the banners of that sacred field. Good prevailed, and a new reign of Godliness seemed to be at hand in the Valley.

On the Saturday before the opening meeting the Corinthians put the finishing touches to the field and its contents. Men and women worked with singing eagerness, the noise of their hymns mingling with the Saturday evening clamour in the near main-street. People made their way to the field and peered curiously through the hedges: they had read the posters scattered over the Valley:

173

SALVATION!

COME TO HOPKINS'S FIELD
AND GIVE YOURSELF TO GOD.
HE IS WAITING!
COME AND HEAR THE YOUNG EVANGELIST
REUBEN DANIELS.
EZRA'S BAND WILL PLAY SACRED MUSIC.
COME AND BE WASHED IN THE BLOOD OF JESUS
REFRESHMENTS.
SILVER COLLECTION ON SUNDAY EVENING.

Everything seemed to favour success. The late May weather was fine and warm, there had been no hitches in the labour of arranging the field; the refreshment-stall, in a little tent of its own, was laden with home-made food and drink, and much publicity had been given to the venture – in pit, public-house, chapel and street-corner.

A crowd on Sunday evening was assured. For not often is the arid Sabbath of the Valley visited by an entertainment beyond the customary chapel services.

The gate in the hedge was opened an hour before the service began, and, assembled in the field, the band played old Welsh airs. It was not long before the marquee was filled; the benches with no back-rests and the chairs creaked with a comfortable mob fresh from Sunday tea. And the band played with grace the sad old tunes – those hymns that never fail to quicken the spring of mournful tears ever bubbling in the hearts of the Welsh people. Soon, too, the voices of the waiting people were raised in swelling singing.

At six o'clock the tent was crowded. Those unable to obtain seats squatted on the grass of the aisles. A section of the marquee had been reserved for Corinthians, and this too was filled; these already Blest Ones led the singing and by their frequent ejaculations of pleasure showed the others how complete was their fortunate state. The brass band took its place beneath the rather flimsy-looking platform: six kitchen chairs and a little table, upon which rested the Book, and a jug and tumbler, completed the furnishing of the platform. No banners adorned the marquee; all that expensive display was outside.

The voices of the people were raised in expectant pleasure.

Grey colliers, with bleak faces forever strained to some vision that would spill something remarkable into their lives, their wives worn with labour – ah, will the sun never again quicken their shrivelled roots? – their curious sons and daughters eager for ecstasy: they waited in singing expectancy for a kingdom where they would rest forever in bliss.

Thus the faces before Reuben Daniels as he sat in his chair on the platform and gazed over them. Entranced in love he sat there like an angel chained in pity to the earth.

Also on the platform were the important men of the Corinthians' chapel – Morgans the Bakehouse, shining and prophetic like a Biblical character; Samson Jones, tall and thin and trembling – since his conversion his fervour was such that his limbs were affected as though with an ague;

175

Zachariah Evans, whose eyes were always cast down in public because of his sister's ill-fame, but who could pray with such abandon that hearers were moved to weeping; Bangor Davies, small and fussy and fused with eager fire – he could lead singing as lightning leads thunder; and then, the soloist, Catherine Pritchards, robed in puce velvet, a yellow hat on her flaming hair, satisfaction like a queenly pride on her glowing face – she had realized her ambition. Morgans the Bakehouse stood on the edge of the platform. His venerable beard thrust out proudly, he began:

'Brothers and sisters, the time for a revival of God's power is at hand. The voice of God has spoken to us in our faith, saying "Behold, the earth is stuck fast in sin, and in places where I look abominations flourish like evil serpents." ' He raised his arms and cried powerfully, prophetic doom in his voice, 'He that hath an ear, let him hear what the Spirit saith unto the churches. Behold, he cometh with clouds; and every eye shall see him, and they also which pierced him: and all kindred of the earth shall wail because of him.' He paused, and a Corinthian repeated moaningly, 'Yea, they shall wail because of him.'

As in answer, a slight groan and shudder went over the crowd.

Morgans the Bakehouse continued proudly, 'But we shall be ready for him. Oh, yes, our souls will be arrayed for him and lit like lamps in the darkness of the earth.' He went on more swiftly, as inspiration came upon him. 'Lamps of heavenly oil in our hands we shall light up the evil of the earth. Into the darkness of corruption we shall go and our bodies shall be bruised in the battle for our heavenly

176

Father...' Thus inspired, he would have gone on at considerable length, but he was interrupted by a young man in the front seat, to whom the cloud had come already, who stood up frothing in frenzied contortions and lifted a leg up and down again, moaning. He was Isaac Watkins, an idiot: he had craftily slipped out from his home to attend the forbidden meeting, for after various former conversions his parents had denied him the joy of religious services.

The Corinthians would have preferred their first convert at the Special Meetings to be someone else. Still, even an idiot is a beginning. Morgans the Bakehouse cried to him:

'Peace be with you, brother, and sit you down.'

One of the others went to the moaning young man guided him into his seat, sat beside him and held his hand. The idiot suddenly shrieked, 'Jesus, Jesus,' and then was silent, a look of abysmal vacancy on his face.

Morgans the Bakehouse finished, 'So let us go on from strength to strength and make a new Jerusalem among us... Now, dear people, Miss Catherine Pritchards will sing a sacred solo, with the band.'

When Miss Pritchards advanced, regally a Blest One, to the front of the platform, the attendant hush seemed rather chillily sardonic. Ha, she was a fine one to save, with *her* past. And so proud and unashamed on that platform!

She sang an old air, *Light of my Life*, with an intensity that drowned any defects. Truly, there was a terrible strength in her voice. A voice that went down into one and disturbed the stomach. The music of the band was suitably subdued.

Then the hymn-singing began. In time, for the people

177

were getting restless and eager to contribute. Are not these services meant for the movings of one's spirit, when one can give way utterly to religious joys?

They sang with all the emotional abandonment of the Welsh. When at last they had finished, the air was charged with excited fervour.

Zachariah Evans began the prayers. He prayed for outpourings of divine forgiveness. The world was shocking with sin. A sensation was caused when he referred to his sister, the harlot, and prayed with sobbing simplicity for her conversion to a virtuous life. His honest grief in this allusion to his private woes moved the people to admiring exclamations.

Sin must not be concealed, it must be brought forth and exhibited in the Redeeming Light.

He called to the people to go on their knees and lift their voices in their own supplications. This was done and soon the tent shook with hundreds of mixed prayers.

Reuben got up.

Tall and beautiful, his face as the face of a seraph lit with pale fire, his black hair like fierce black flames, his lifted hands keen with restless power as they accompanied his inspired oration, he cried:

'And he shewed me a pure river of water of life, clear as crystal, proceeding out of the throne of God and of the Lamb. The river is flowing for us, the water of eternal life is flowing from the Throne for our thirsty hearts. Brothers, brothers, let us drink it. Out of Heaven the winged angels are coming, clad in their robes of blue light, their arms bearing vessels of gold, and they whisper to us, Drink of the heavenly water and thirst no more. And the tears shall be wiped from our eyes, hunger shall go out of us, sorrow shall flee from our souls, and joy burn clearly where there was desolation. Joy, joy, brothers and sisters. Are we not born for joy! Was not the earth aforetime a garden of delicious flowers and tender fruit, where men might labour in simple joy and there was no greed? But now that garden is not where our dwelling of bricks and mortar is built, for the earth is given over to greed. But within us we can cultivate that garden! There shall the fruit and flowers of Paradise be, and the well of the water of life, and the rest from weariness and the forgetting of tears. Joy, Joy for us! Who can take from us that joy? Lift up your hearts in singing, let your soul echo like cymbals, let your voices be proud as the sunlight leaping over the earth, be proud in God, strong as the rocks and hills in faith, and we shall enter victorious into a new earth, victorious over suffering and sin and greed, we shall be the children of God...'

Thus Reuben Daniels continued. Well might the people say it was like hearing a new Bible. They rocked in satisfied pleasure, listening to his passionate voice lifted up thus. And he was raised beyond his normal consciousness, the words flowed from a source that was as a flaming tabernacle in his exaltation. Yet always he was aware of the faces staring up at him, faces rapt and avid and content as they devoured his oration. Once he paused for a few seconds and the faces contracted as though in vague dismay and then as he resumed opened again into rapt sucking expressions, like the faces of babes sucking milk.

He moved them. Their ancient consciousness, their

tribal worship of the prophet, the sacred bard of the tribe dwelling in the hollows of the mountains, the mystery of his primeval voice echoing the declamation of God to the crouching people, stirred them to fearful wonder.

That wonder became a frenzied ecstasy when at last Reuben dropped back to his seat and the singing was resumed. Bangor Davies led them in a fury of leaping ardour.

The silver pieces dropped gratefully into the many plates. Morgans the Bakehouse listened and was comforted of his anxiety over the expenditure.

Again and again the last verses of the hymn were repeated with undiminished ecstasy.

Then individual emotions were loosened at last. An elderly woman leapt up with surprising agility and cried shrilly, 'Blessed is the Lord Jehovah, tonight he has shown himself to me. Left my chapel twenty years ago I did because a lot of cats were the ladies when in jail my husband Amos was put. Sick of the worship of the chapel I was, and I lost sight of Jesus Christ. But now I have come to him again. I have seen him with his Father!' And she screamed, 'Holy One, stay you in me like this for ever.'

Others excelled her in example and confession. The band struck up and a hymn was begun. In the pause after a verse Reuben Daniels cried with vehement earnestness

'Oh, people, put away pride from you and confess Jesus. He is waiting for you. Ye that are weary and heavy laden, come to him. He is waiting.'

He descended to the space beneath the platform and, the band behind him like a chorus, cried out in a chant the invitation to the Lord.

Many converts rushed to the space and dropped to their knees. Young women clasped frenzied hands and declared their contrition, young men denounced themselves for their errors and bigotry. Their elders, too, were not to be denied salvation. In a few moments the space was filled with a writhing crowd of converts.

'Jesus, Jesus, Jesus!'

'Oh, how beautiful it is.'

'Tonight I have been born again!'

'Fire is within me!'

'Like stones in me my sins weighed me down, but now I am light as a feather!'

'Jesus Christ is mine!'

'Saw his face I did when Reuben Daniels was preaching, and there's love for me was on it.'

'He smiled at me and said, "I thirst for you. For you I went into Gethsemane and was nailed to the Cross." Jesus said it to me and like a child I became.'

One of the young women fell flat on her back and then writhed over and over uttering little screams of ecstasy. Reuben paused in his chanting and gazed at her intently for a moment or two. Then he dropped beside her and took her hand.

It shook in his grasp with swift strength. Her eyes were closed, her mouth worked foamingly and still her body writhed as though she were in an orgasm of pleasure – for her face showed plainly that it was not pain or anguish she was enduring. In a low voice Reuben said to her:

'Be at peace, dear sister.'

And he placed an arm about her shoulder and pressed

his hand on her convulsed brow. Her body moved in one last violent spasm and then, sighing, she opened her eyes vaguely and sat up.

'Oh,' she cried, 'the angels were about me. How lovely they were. Why must I leave Heaven and come back to this old world!'

Jacob Williams, the blacksmith, a man of dignified stature and bleak features, stood up and made a testimony in his slow, booming voice:

'People, you know how it has been with me. A troublesome home because of the woman's love for the finery of life, till loose in the head she got and blasphemous her tongue, saying this and that about me, so that because of the shame of her state kept away from chapel I did. And I went out of the ways of God. But now I am come back to him: the words of Reuben Daniels made a weeping in me and then suddenly God spoke in my ear: "Shake yourself, Jacob Williams," he said, "a slowcoach in my service you are and lamented I have since you have been so thoughtless about me." Oh, when I heard his voice!' His own stern voice became stonily cracked as he fell abjectly on his knees. 'Great Man in the sky, coming back to you I am. And give me the power to lead my wife Mattie to you also, for sad is her case.'

This example of Jacob Williams, an aloof and dour man who was usually silent about his private woes, though they were known to all, created a further spurt of boiling frenzy. Oh, the divine workings of God! Now was the time to pour out in passionate grief all that was mean, deceitful, cunning and private in one's life. Now was the time to shake and cry in joy at the mercy of the Lord.

The band struck up and a hymn was screamed through at break-neck speed.

The elderly woman who had spoken of the cat-like ladies in the chapel was again possessed of strange beautiful energy. She sprang up on her seat and waved her arms exultingly, shrieking 'Jesus.' Her eyes bulged in her sere face as though she choked in agony. She grabbed off her bonnet and shook loose her scant locks.

'Oh, lovely Jesus is with me again. Jesus, Jesus! Can't you see him?'

The hymn proceeded:

> *'Land of milk and honey,*
> *Land of bliss beyond compare,*
> *We shall be there, we shall rest there,*
> *With never a tear and never a care.'*

Reuben was on his knees in the enclosure beneath the platform. Both enclosure and platform were with converts. On the platform Morgans the Bakehouse led the praying for his own batch, and beneath Reuben prayed in glorious language for a visitation of comfort and peace to the suffering people of earth.

> *'Oh, the joy, the gladness*
> *In that land of flowers so fair,*
> *Crowned with crowns of gold eternal,*
> *With never a tear, and never a care...'*

His face was a marble mask of ecstasy, its lineamemts

183

hard and tense with the pure flame that devoured him. Song, prayer, and music swept about him like a beautiful and vehement storm riding over the world, and he was within it as a static centre of pure ecstasy. Vials of fire, golden doors flung back, a choir of angels within the everlasting halls, opened scrolls whereon were written in blood-red characters messages of divine love, and trumpets from which issued a call that cracked the sky so that the stars trembled and Reuben opened his eyes and delivered another inspired invocation to the people. Never had he been so exalted.

The star convert of the evening was Esau Evans – ruffian, drunkard, loafer, wastrel son of a minister who, with his respected wife, had been brought down to the grave because of Esau's rascally conduct (it was said). Middle-aged now, a character loafing about street-corners, with his red beard, rheumy eyes and long pointed white teeth, his name was used by mothers to frighten their refractory brats; and, more disgraceful than anything else, he never did a day's work, but lived in sin with a half-daft woman who searched for coal in the tips of the collieries, earning a meagre living by selling it to the tradespeople.

He had drifted into the tent with the crowd and sat meekly enough between those indignant neighbours forced to be near him because of the packed benches. Ach, the man was so disgusting that, having no Sunday suit, he attended a religious service in corduroy trousers and a patched, smelly coat. The pleasure of his neighbours was spoiled because of his nearness.

But as the service went on and the sea of singing and

praying rose in a flood about the rocking souls of the people, Esau Evans got up and in a voice whose strength neither ostracism nor loose-living had diminished, loudly declared thus:

'People, people, a vision I have had. Hundreds of swine I saw coming from a pig-sty round about which was darkness. Upon the door of the sty was written Earth, and the nose of my soul was filled with the odour rising from within. And the swine never stopped coming through the doorway and each one made a noise that was like strange crying in my ears. I looked upon the faces of the swine, dear people, and my heart started weeping inside me. Oh, then I saw the errors of my life. How among swine I have lived and grovelled with them. In my vision I lay there among them and the stink and faces of them turned my belly. Then I heard Reuben Daniels saying in his sermon, "The voice of Jesus Christ is crying to the earth." And the vision was no more before me, and as I listened to Reuben Daniels peace came to my troubled heart. Listen to me, people. Well known is my face to you and well known to me is your opinion. I have lived in sloth and enjoyed the husks of the outcast, but my soul is my own within me and my back is not curved through bending before the riches of the world. And I worship God and his holy son Jesus Christ. Here I say it among you who have reviled me, God is in my heart and I love him.'

Strange, strange power of God! Drunkard, outcast, filthy loafer, Esau Evans acknowledged him! The people looked vaguely about them for a moment. Most of them had listened to Esau, though during his declarations little groups scattered

185

over the tent and deaf to others had not ceased to cry and pray among themselves. And the people did not quite know how to take his conversion. Of course it was plain that he was repentant. How feelingly he spoke of the swine in his vision – meaning, of course, his dirty companions in drink and abominations and that woman who lived with him in sin. But they could not quite reconcile themselves to the thought of God with Esau Evans. It did not seem quite proper.

Reuben had no such doubt. Arms outstretched, face glorious with pitying love, he advanced through the centre aisle and arriving at the bench where Esau sat, called to the convert to come out and kneel with him.

Esau, the ragged hooligan, knelt there in the aisle with the ecstatic youth, and the people began to sing again, thinking then how remarkable indeed was this manifestation of God's infinite love and merciful power.

Tears were falling from Esau's rheumy eyes and all his coarsened face expressed the shining of an inner light. Perhaps at that moment he was thinking of his past pure childhood in the home of his father, the minister, and the readings from the Bible every night before bed, while his mother sat still in religious repose, and there was no shadow of sordid life within the room. Who can tell? Immediately after their prayer together, he got up and, after staring round the tent with a strange glint in his eyes, went out slowly and with dignity.

A certain man got up and proclaimed his wonder at this conversion. 'Let us hope now,' he said elegantly, 'that one who was as a sore on our flesh will be cured of his disgusting manners.'

Already it was half-past nine and there was no sign of the meeting coming to an end. The brass band had begun to stir for departure, but after a hurried consultation between the conductor and Morgans the Bakehouse, they stayed and played on.

Several women had to be carried out to the fresh air – some having fainted, others convulsed in emotion so that their faces became yellow and they gasped in choked spasms of frenzy.

> *'Wash away sin, wash away sin,*
> *Jesus is coming with water of life...'*

Until ten-thirty they washed themselves free of it with great success. Never did a happier congregation swell into a happier last hymn. All was joy and contentment.

Catherine Pritchards sang the first verse of this last hymn and she stood on the edge of the platform, taut with the energy she had had to repress for the last three hours. Her voice swept out like a spume of stormy sea water; at last she would loosen on the people the dark strength of her volcanic soul. They answered her in terrific chorus, the men's voices swelling out in thunderous force, and even forgot, in the purity of their worship, her brazen behaviour in the past.

The officials of the Corinthians were all arrayed on the platform, Reuben in the centre, very pale now. He pronounced the last words:

'Peace be with us for evermore. Keep us in the ways of thy gentle son, O God, so that peace shall be in our hearts like a drop of his own sacred blood – '

187

And even filing out of the tent, they had to begin another hymn, which was continued to the main street.

Reuben was silent as congratulations were showered upon him. He sat pale and silent on a stool and seemed to listen to other voices than those congratulating him, his eyes strained out and inscrutable. At last he got up and said to Morgans the Bakehouse:

'I am going alone now.'

Morgans the Bakehouse laid his hand on Reuben's shoulder. 'Yes, go you to bed soon and gather strength for tomorrow night.'

Samson Jones said, 'Eighty-eight converts I was able to count because they spoke up, but others there were. There's fine. Heavenly all of it has been.'

Reuben went out and trembled as the cool air touched his burning head.

The mountains were like black robes flung against the misty sky, and he lifted his head and breathed in the night, conscious of the great pure spaces above him.

He went beyond the houses to that part of the Valley where rocks are strewn over the base of the hill and there is loneliness and silence, save for the sound of the weary river dropping and wandering over the stones. In the thin misty light of the sky the misshapen boulders were like dark blue shadows. An old savage beauty seemed to lurk here, among the naked rocks, with the stark hills stretching up in primitive austerity, and the earth's water, that issued from the breast of the furthest hill, desolate in its murmur.

He went among the rocks and found a little hollow with

a patch of grass. And he cast himself down and lay in utter loneliness in that silence.

His mind was empty of thought, emotion or strength. He yielded up his soul to the high sky and his body was like an empty shell.

The distant murmur of the river soothed his beating nerves, and at last he lay in the perfect abstraction of mindless peace.

Then after a while his lips moved: 'Dear God, let your spirit not depart out of me. Let me not wander in weariness from thy labour.'

Behind one of the rocks Catherine Pritchards waited. She had cautiously followed him from the tent, her soul still hungry for contact with his spiritual vigour. Who can tell the mysterious ways of women? Presently she stood before him, her hands crossed on her breast, her face as an utterance of chaste love.

'My heart ached because of your tired looks,' she whispered. 'I followed you afar, for am I not one of your disciples? Yes, and more than that, shall I not be your sister, you who have no sister of your blood?'

He stared at her in silence and then smiled faintly.

She took advantage of it and sat beside him on the grass. Her fingers interlaced peacefully in her lap, she went on dreamily:

'You remember how Mary Magdalene loved Jesus Christ? Yes, followed him to the Cross she did and stood there weeping with his mother, while the Beautiful One died for our sins. And did he not appear first to Mary Magdalene when he had arisen from the sepulchre? Often,

often have I read the stories of Mary, and wept for her.'

'Why?' he asked gently.

She shook her head and was silent for a while. Her breast moved as though she sobbed within herself, and her head drooped. Then she continued in a low, monotonous voice:

'Before the service tonight I was reading how Jesus was sitting in the house of the Pharisee and the woman of sin came to him in grief and anointed his feet with ointment. There's wonderful it seemed! Weary like yours were his feet, and her tears fell upon them and he let her wipe them with her hair.'

He gazed at her and smiled again.

'You have brought no ointment, Catherine Pritchards?'

She lifted her head. 'Am I a woman of sin?'

'A daughter of God you say you are since you were converted.'

She cried out suddenly, 'Yea, and truly repentant I was that night in the chapel. You it was who brought me again to Christ. You have heard how it was with me years ago?'

He turned his head away wearily.

'How should I know!'

Her eyes gleamed, and her tearful voice became hard and clear as she went on, 'Yes, Reuben Daniels, a woman of sin I was. A child was born to me, and the father of my baby was a minister.' She paused, and as he made no exclamation, continued dramatically, 'And a minister who had lost his faith he was. A trade he made his ministry, and corrupted was his weak mind. But lovely he could be in the pulpit sometimes and foolish I was about him.'

Reuben listened in silence, his head turned away.

'Who shall blame me for my sin? He promised me marriage and I thought: Then will I bring him back to Christ and a great preacher he will become.'

Again she waited, watching, like a cat, Reuben's turned-away head. At last he said quietly:

'What matters the past? We must work now for Jesus with all our strength. We must go out of our own selves and ease the suffering of those who dwell in despair.'

She answered with quick fervour, 'Amen. All our strength we must use for the Lord.'

He turned to her and gazed at her with a gentle regard, a faint smile still on his lips. She leaned over and took his hand, held his fingers in her own strong grasp and suddenly burst into tears.

'Oh,' she sobbed, 'understanding you are. When you look at me a great religious woman I want to be.' Her voice was strangled in her throat, her eyes protruded fanatically, her breast heaved – she seemed to be internally struggling with several emotions, and, rather alarmed at the evidences of it, Reuben took both her hands and knelt before her.

'Be at peace, Catherine Pritchards,' he murmured soothingly, 'let your spirit be quiet.'

She pressed his hand to her cheek convulsively, then kissed it again and again. He did not resist, thinking it would calm her.

It did not. She burst into a further orgasm of emotion. It was not sobbing and it was not ecstasy, but a strange agitation of her being that made her bosom shake as though she were in active pain. Her voice came thickly from her throat, in a sort of wild chant: 'The women of the Bible followed him and loved him and wept for him. Full of pity and love for them he was. How lovely were his words to the woman who was a sinner! So sweet and pure he must have been.' He said, "Her sins, which are many, are forgiven; for she loved much," and understanding was his wisdom of women.'

'Yes, yes,' Reuben agreed, troubled by her fervour.

She thrust up her face fiercely.

'Press your lips upon my brow,' she cried, a hard anguish in her voice, 'press your lips upon my brow and I shall be made whole again. For are not your lips pure as the lips of Jesus!'

He started back, but her grasp of him was firm.

'Do not say such a thing,' he said sternly.

Then her tears flowed; she loosened him and sank her head to the earth in spasms of grief. And Reuben lifted her and pressed his lips to her brow as she desired, his arm about her shoulders. Her convulsed sobbing ceased, her eyes became as stars, a little sigh escaped her lips.

'Oh,' she breathed softly, 'like the touch of an angel that was.'

Gently he drew away from her and stood up.

'Come, it is late, and I will walk with you to the houses.'

She got up at once and, fastening her hat on her dim gold hair, meekly followed him.

It was midnight when he arrived home. Hugh was waiting up for him.

'Well, well, Reuben, there's late they kept you,' said the father gently.

Reuben sat down and gazed into the dying fire.

'I have been by the river since the service finished.'

'Heard we have how it went,' said Hugh, glancing at his son's exhausted face. 'There's speaking of you the people are!'

'What did mam say?' Reuben asked wearily.

'Oh, well, strange she behaved. Wept she did after Mrs Morris number ten came in and told us about the meeting, and she went to bed straight after and I heard her moaning to herself.'

Reuben looked up, a quick eagerness in his eyes.

'Think you she will repent of her ways?' he asked.

Hugh's grey face was desolate and his voice hopeless.

'Stuck fast all these years in her ways she has and easier now it would be to make the river run backwards. But in her own being the change might come.'

For a while they were silent. Hugh glanced at Reuben furtively. Dimly he was aware of the soul within his son. At last he stirred and said hastily:

'Well, Reuben bach, set about your meat and bread; and cold milk you must have, for no fire is there to boil the kettle. Hungry is your face.'

Reuben slept a deep and dreamless slumber that night, and in the late morning he swam up dimly to consciousness as from the obscured depths of annihilation.

Yet on waking his lips moved immediately with the words:

'And I saw the Holy City, new Jerusalem, coming down from God out of heaven, prepared as a bride adorned for her husband.'

CHAPTER IV

That week his name was heard throughout the Valley.

The people discussed in marvelling voices this youth who had come out of the pit and spoke to multitudes with the eloquence of a great preacher.

The old fearful soul of the Welsh recognised him: ever through the ages there had been men such as he – poets, bards, seers, prophets born to the simple, worshipping people, reared among them and at the suitable period arising to open the scroll of their sacred talent.

Honour must be done to him. So it became the thing of the moment to go down to Hopkins's field and harken to the voice arisen – a beneficial pleasure within the reach of everybody. Did not those already in the beatific state exclaim of the benefits – the worries of life fled, a happiness that made one sin, hymns all day, refreshing slumber... and even improvements in bodily health, too.

The second evening of the Corinthians' onslaught, they assembled first in the chapel on the hill-side and after a rousing little prayer-party on their own, marched down to the public field in singing procession, headed by a large red banner, on which was the message:

THE CYMBALS OF OUR TONGUES SHALL CLAP
HIS PRAISE.

It was a bright, happy procession, for the Corinthians were revolutionary, and did not favour the grieving and funereal demeanour the lawful chapel people assume in their public religious observances. The women were decked as though for a Bank Holiday outing and joy was loose on the faces of the men. Proud in their swollen strength, singing rapturously as they marched firmly through the streets, good it did one to see them, for what famous wrongdoers were among their numbers!

The idlers about the street-corners and those out for a respectable evening walk invariably followed the procession to the field. Though there would be no brass band tonight, there were going to be baptisms in the pool.

The Corinthians called the pool in Hopkins's field The Waters of Bethesda. Hitherto this shallow pool had been known chiefly as a place where small boys could catch tadpoles. But tonight greater things were to come out of it.

'Come and be saved in The Waters of Bethesda,' a Corinthian would shout from the procession.

'Wash yourself in the sacred waters and be clean again.'

'Yes, yes, they shall cleanse all bad stains away.'

Reuben Daniels, Bible in hand, silent and meditative as though he trod in a mystic vision, walked behind the red banner – so young, with such lucent calm within his face, that he evoked admiration everywhere. The people thought: Surely God is with this young man who has glory on his brows like a heavenly peace and words noble as Holy Writ within his tongue.

Following him came the crowd of bawling converts, preceded by the officials of the sect, notable among them Catherine Pritchards in a dress of orange-coloured silk and a blue hat (she had prepared for these meetings).

The field was thronged. The lawful chapel people were there in great numbers, with their umbrellas and distant, bigoted faces, and the people who haunted public-houses too, the people who assumed airs and wore collars and ties or feather boas, the people who lounged and spat about the Valley, young women with heavy glistening faces, and long-faced young men with restless, religious eyes, and staid older folk remembering the stimulations of a former revival, and the scraggy looking rabble who are too poor to venture into the comfort of the chapels but who have, too, in their ill-kept bodies the mysterious religious fire of the Welsh. A revival belongs to everybody, like the sea at the seaside on Bank Holiday.

The refreshment stall was doing a busy trade, but many people who had come from the far parts of the Valley or over the hills from the mountain villages had brought food with them, and these picnicked about the hedges while waiting for the service to begin. And though trade was brisk at the stall, the eye of Mrs Bangor Davies, who was responsible for it this evening, roved over these picnickers with some indignation; she loudly denounced one woman who came to her and asked for the loan of a tumbler.

When the procession arrived in the field, there was a rush towards the pool, and Morgans the Bakehouse had to appeal to the crowd to move back a little so that a space could be obtained for those who were to lead the service.

A hymn was sung and re-sung; then many prayers followed. The power began to work again and it was not long before subdued moans, wails, and fervent cries were to be heard coming from the crowd. Reuben began speaking in a sudden quiet that was very flattering.

Tonight he spoke of the Pool of Bethesda that was at Jerusalem:

'There were gathered the sick and the weakly. Their hearts were withered in their suffering and to them there was no dawn that brought singing and no night that gave peace. But to the water came an angel from God, everlasting healing in his touch. Then the water held forever the message of heaven, and he who watched for it the most faithfully stepped in and was healed. How beautiful is the tale, brothers and sisters! Think, all about us there is water of Bethesda, if we will look with the eyes of faith. Ailment might be far from your body, but who is there here that has no sickness in his soul?' He paused, and in answer to his question a suitable groan rose from the attentive crowd. The complaint seemed a common one. 'And the pain that is in your soul is harder to bear than the pain of the flesh. But there is healing. Oh, there is healing in abundance, healing for those who will open their souls

197

to God. The angel waits at the door of heaven and again a pool will be stirred by his holy touch. Call to the angel to come to us, call with your soul that is weary of its burden, and he will spread his gleaming wings and be with us. He will touch the water and there will be healing within it. Only have faith...'

He soon roused their already expectant souls. Though there was a sincere simplicity in his words, his voice was as a fiercely burning torch. When he had finished, the sighing murmurs that at intervals had floated over the crowd burst into passionate cries to the Almighty. People lifted their arms and searched the sky for signs of an angel. 'Send him down to us, dear Lord. Waiting we are for him.' 'Be good to your little people now and send a white angel to us.' No angel made himself visible, and the people turned their attention to the pool. Strangely, a slight breeze was gently stirring its surface just then. The loud cry of a female, 'Look, look you, the angel is upon the water,' brought a dangerous rush to the edge, and the miracle was observed amid awed exclamations.

Then there was a sudden hush; it was as though everyone felt the presence of the sacred visitor. The ripple passed from the pond, and the voice of Catherine Pritchards lifted itself in chastened and subdued clarity:

> *'I heard the voice of Jesus say,*
> *Come unto me and rest;*
> *Lay down, thou weary one, lay down*
> *Thy head upon My Breast...'*

She earned back her respectability in those moments. Out of the hush her voice came like quivering cello notes, and she sang as though the angel had gently bade her, pellucid and tremolo, her hands clasped mystically on her breast.

Softly the people took up the hymn, then louder and louder as the ecstasy of the moment worked within them. Many fell on their knees and prayed with contortions of their bodies. Soon the din of worship was loud enough to please the most avaricious of Gods. Louder and louder the hymning voices swam up exultingly to the sky, eagerly and agonizingly women and men prayed for attention to their individual needs. Reuben and the officials took their stand at the edge of the pool. Reuben cried out:

'Let the hand of God be within this water.'

He waded into the pool and standing in the centre, continued:

'Those who would be baptized into a new life follow me.'

His eyelids were scarlet over the gleaming darkness of his eyes, his face was lifted up in rhapsodical vehemence. He was as a god, calling in his choric primordial voice; his gestures were authoritative of a divine sanction.

The first to follow him were three Corinthians – two men and a youngish woman who was afflicted with a wen on her neck. A hymn was begun and the people craned forward to watch the dipping.

They sat in the shallow water and Reuben grasped their shoulders and immersed them for a moment. Beautiful symbol! The cleansing of which all stand in need! There was supreme magic in this performance of it. The people

199

flocked to it, singing joyfully, their faces gleaming with obsessed desire.

Sweat began to exude on Reuben's forehead, though the water chilled his legs. He had to keep a firm grasp on some of the young women, for directly their faces were immersed they wriggled with sudden strength; others panted and snorted and made bubbles, some were very heavy. Women were in the majority.

After the immersion they trailed off dripping to the tents reserved for them, where they changed into their dry clothes. Those who had brought no clothes hurried home. Their mien expressed pride in their state, even though their wet clothes hung on them disagreeably.

And the crowd passed from hymn to hymn as they watched the fifty-seven baptisms that evening. Another sensation was caused when a man who had a stiffened leg cautiously entered the water and after immersion hopped out hurriedly and, reaching the bank, ran a few steps, then cried excitedly: 'Jesus Christ be praised, my old leg is healed of its badness!' And indeed he hopped away with much more energy than he usually displayed. He was Dai Rees, a steady and faithful Corinthian.

Others were healed afterwards – a woman of temporary deafness, another of sore joints; many with medically certified complaints experienced instant relief after immersion.

> *'Glory to Jesus, who now has taught us*
> *How meet is the touch of his loving hand,*
> *How good are the gifts that Calv'ry bought us – '*

Reuben at last waded out of the pool. He passed through the murmuring crowd and entered the little tent kept apart for the private use of the officials. He was alone. And immediately he fell on his knees and prayed, his voice heavy with passion.

'Clear my eyes, O Lord, and let me not judge others in vanity and bigotry. If it is thy will that I see in the behaviour of thy people that which is unworthy, let my eyes be not dimmed by it. Does not thy light shine behind the dark walls of the flesh? Keep it visible to me, O Father of Jesus Christ, who knew all the woes of men, keep it visible to me...'

He fell prostrate in the intensity of his praying; and when he rose up his face was strained and haggard, though the dark glow in his eyes was not diminished.

After changing into dry garments he went back to the crowd. Morgans the Bakehouse was addressing a section of it, his voice pealing out in denunciatory phrases as though he were a proper college-trained preacher. In another part a group of people were on their knees praying with sighing pleasure. A woman rolled on the grass in sacred frenzy. About her were her companions, kneeling and singing encouragingly. Reuben went among them, knelt beside the woman, who was uttering short, bitten cries like an animal in pain, and held her head in his hands. She suddenly shot up, stretched her neck, and screeched, 'And the carcase of Jezebel shall be as dung upon the face of the field.' A moment afterwards the inspiration left her, and she joined her companions, calm and satisfied.

He observed the holiday crowd in the field. About the

thicker hedges youths and maidens idly ogled each other, with the rolling leer of the eye that is adopted in chapel on Sunday. At the refreshment stall Mrs Bangor Davies was wiping dishes and crying excitedly to a friend, 'Every cake sold, Mrs Evans, and every drop of small beer. But some peppermint-lumps I have...' And here and there were two or three women gathered together in active conclave and deaf to the work of the Lord about them. And all seemed to enjoy themselves.

He stood alone for a moment. He was conscious of words within him: What is this earth? What secret lies within this garment of flesh? What sleeps in the heart of the world?

Someone touched him. He turned his head and gazed at the woman who stood before him.

'Mr Daniels bach,' she said in a half whining, half demanding voice, 'excuse me now disturbing your thinking, but I am one of those who gave testimony, last night – '

'Yes, I remember you.'

She wore poor and slatternly garments, and in the brownish unwashed pallor of her face her eyes protruded, livid and disordered. She was one of those who uttered their testimony in long unintelligible phrases full of noise and a tangled history of their past.

He looked at her searchingly. Her worn thin lips and fleshless face made his heart ache dully. Labour and stony acceptance of her lot had destroyed all but the bare lineaments of her features. But to her too Christ had come and was visible in her livid eyes.

'Ever since, I have been with Jesus,' she went on, 'and when I went home last night did I not take his light with me! Bad with an old cancer is my man and he lies crying on the couch in the kitchen all day. But did I not make him peaceful last night with the beautiful prayers and hymns I sang! Told him I did about you too and he said: "Ask Mr Daniels to come here and pray with me. Nearly finished is my life on the earth and I am sore tried in faith." But I said, "Busy is Mr Daniels with the meetings – "

'I will go with you now,' Reuben said.

They went from the field together. Near the refuse-tip of the colliery is a collection of old, black cottages, where live the very poor. They entered one of these smelly dwellings.

In the living-room a man lay on a couch that was draped with old coats, cloths and ragged pillows – anything to make it soft. He looked bloated and ill. Five children lifted soiled and staring faces from some game with rags on the stone floor, and two others in a corner played, aloof and unconcerned, with a wire cage containing a live rat.

'John, John, see I have brought Mr Daniels to see you,' cried the woman, throwing her hat under the table.

John turned his head. His voice was a hoarse groan.

'Son of Hugh Daniels who married Martha Howells late in life you are?'

'Yes.'

'Well, well, religious loins have you come from. Remember I can how your father came out of a pub one night and knelt down in the middle of a meeting that the Baptists had in the street. A queer one he was for mixing the beer with his worship.'

'Never does he go to the pub now though,' Reuben said softly.

'Tut, tut,' the woman cried, 'there's talk! Not for this has Mr Daniels come here. Is he not going to pray with us! Is he not going to ask Jesus Christ to be with you?'

'Aye, I need him,' groaned the man. 'Jesus Christ I need if he can make me forget this old cancer.'

The woman was already on her knees. She clasped her hands and moaned beseechingly:

'Pray we must that he will come to cleanse your soul before you go. Are there not many things of which you are ashamed? Pure you must go out. Repent you, John, and confess. Was not our eldest, Mattie, conceived before we were married!' For a moment her lids dropped in shame over her livid eyes. 'And have we not used the Sabbath in wrong pleasure sometimes?'

'Hush, woman,' John muttered. 'But pray you for me, Reuben Daniels bach.'

Reuben knelt before the couch. The children stared at him vacantly.

'Take away, O God, the pain that is in the spirit of our brother here. Our voices are as voices crying in the wilderness and everywhere we turn there is the desert where the flesh hungers and thirsts as it lives. But within us, pure and gleaming like the sun at day-break, is the sacred image of thee. The flesh is torn with the labour and travail of the earth, the blood that flows in our veins has the savour of dust. Yet shall we not let the sun of thy image shine forth on those bruises and purify our corrupted blood in its healing rays? Thou art within us, O God, thou art within us...'

The sick man raised himself a little. He listened closely, nodding his head in approval. No other race can enjoy sermons with the discernment of the Welsh. A sermon will triumph over all disaster and melancholy.

Reuben went on for some time. The children withdrew their attention and resumed their cutting of the rags on the floor. The two who had been playing with the rat-trap had disappeared. His voice was clear and resonant as a bell.

'Amen,' John echoed as Reuben finished.

'Yes, indeed, Amen,' echoed his wife. And she began to sing in a high-pitched febrile voice:

> *'We are but little children weak,*
> *Nor born in any high estate:*
> *What can we do for Jesus' sake – '*

'Sober now, Maggie,' her husband interrupted, 'rusty is your voice I am always telling you. And look you at those two messy brats.'

The rat-trap had been abandoned for the little pantry under the stairs. The two children emerged eating slices of bread thickly covered with condensed milk. Patches of that viscous liquid were stuck on the coat of the boy.

The woman uttered a scream and leapt towards them. The boy dropped the bread and turned to flee, but his mother pounced on him with furious agility. She beat his bare legs in a passion of anger. The little girl looked on with strange interest, chewing her bread and quite unalarmed, though the five in the middle of the room rose and huddled themselves in the furthest corner.

'Wicked thief,' the mother screamed violently, 'wicked thief, stealing your father's milk.'

Reuben stared at them. The woman seemed mad.

He noticed, too, the heavy, vacuous face of the little girl. And he shuddered. The room seemed suddenly dark and evil to him, like some sunken chamber with rotting walls and an aroma of death. The dirty rags, the catafalque draped with them, and the unclean man upon it, the rat-cage, the peeling distemper of the walls, the bellowing raucous woman, the chamber-pot under the couch – he was suddenly nauseated and sick. His lips moved soundlessly:

'Jesus, Jesus, leave me not alone.'

The mother dragged the boy to him.

'Thieving the milk I keep for his father he's been,' she almost wept. 'Dear it is, and extra washing I have to do so that I can buy it. Speak to him, Mr Daniels, tell him how angry God is towards a thief.'

'Wrong it is to steal the milk,' Reuben said gently.

The boy looked at him tearfully: he had eyes blue as cornflowers, and long delicate brows. His lips were pouted out like a rose. But he suddenly cried viciously, 'I don't care if God is angry, I don't care if he will kill me and I go to hell – '

His mother's face became white and awful in anger. Reuben laid his hand on her arm and muttered: 'Leave him alone. He does not know what he is saying.'

He bent to the boy, whose lips were now stretched snarlingly, and laughed into his face:

'Shut up now. Ugly as an old goat you are when you are crying like that. Look, this is how you are.' He contracted his face into a jibe, so that all the children burst into laughter.

The mother felt that such levity was not suitable to Reuben Daniels, and she sniffed.

'A little thief he is always,' she protested.

'Maggie,' her husband groaned, 'bad I'm feeling.'

She ran to minister to him. His peevish eyes looked out cunningly from the grey dough of his puffed-out flesh. He nodded towards Reuben.

'Mr Daniels, come you soon again,' the woman said oilily. 'Too poor we are to offer you supper.'

A last shaft of dim evening light came through the window. It lay in dusty splendour on the patched remnants of clothing that draped the couch and on the white claw-like hand of the sick man. The children, now there was nothing to fear from their calmed mother, came from the corner and stood looking at Reuben with waiting eyes.

He left them with all the money that was in his pocket; about twelve shillings.

Slowly he went back to the field. And he felt that he had failed in his mission to that cottage.

Had he left behind him the Peace of God?

There was something in the souls of those people with whom he came into intimate contact that was dark and impenetrable as death. They might be moved to fervent confessions of faith, to demonstrations of inner ecstasy, but buried deep in them, dark and stony as death, was a mystery he could not penetrate, but remained firm and impregnable. And that mystery seemed evil and terrible to him.

Was it the fatal knowledge of death, the secret mortal recognition that one day the blood will flow no more from the cold heart and the flesh would be the worm that crawls blindly through the triumphant earth? The ruinous knowledge that then all must cease and we are forever lost?

He could not tell. Only he knew that, however eagerly he tried to pierce into the emotion of the human consciousness, however ardently he yearned to suffer and sweat in martyrdom for those who were torn and bruised, there remained beyond his vision a dark fatal terror that was as an evil canker in the happiness of man.

It was nearly dark when he reached the field. A service was in progress in the marquee: the lusty noise of it reached him and seemed to cast contempt on his melancholy thoughts. Here was faith in abundance, here was joyful crying in the certainty of divine life. Everyone would be an angel.

Outside, in the field, the mood of the young people became sportive as the darkness fell. Some, scorning the amorous joys that were most in evidence, played leap-frog. A group of youths sat together and from their coarse guffaws and secret faces one could tell that low stories were being circulated.

He looked about the field with desolation in his face.

A day must dawn for him, a day must dawn when his mind would stumble upon the secret of his life and he would go forth in a morning that did not hurt or mock him. A sword of clear light would cleave his soul and he would walk no more in the cruelty of despair.

The chanting voices of the people reached him. He stood and listened. And again love for them flowed up in him, a fountain of strength. Labour, there was labour for him. They looked to him for inspiration, they drew from him a vision of eternal life, they saw in him a symbol of the purity of life.

He went to the tent, his face purged of tribulation.

Chapter V

They went on from triumph to triumph that week. There were hundreds of converts – all ages and creeds. Already the public-houses were suffering, trade in tobacco was diminishing, the cinema was half empty, and obscene words were dropping out of use. Other sects started competitive meetings – in every village of the Valley there were services of joy, though, of course, they were minor affairs compared to the magnificent triumphs in Hopkins's field, and without a star attraction like Reuben Daniels.

The Welsh newspapers passed on the torch. Soon Reuben was receiving offers from various parts of Wales.

A greater campaign was arranged. Morgans the Bakehouse had hired a man to look after the bake-house, and, his nostrils quivering with delight, organised this campaign with rhetorical importance. There were many committee meetings, sometimes lasting far into the night.

And well they might. Was not the spiritual welfare of a nation at stake? All agreed that the religion of Wales, its chief ancient glory, was becoming stale and weak-jointed because of the shocking inactivity of the lawful ministers. And the Lord had chosen an outlaw sect to restore the lustre to the worship of his little people in Wales. It was a great task for them, but triumph would be theirs.

They possessed an inspired young man, a being who received the Word direct from God, for how else could he, who had no earthly education, speak such marvellous eloquence?

He was cherished and guarded like some precious flower by the officials of the sect, and already legends were told about him. It was said that in his lonely walks on the mountains angels spoke to him and that he often left his body and travelled himself (that is, with the spiritual reflection of his body) to Heaven. God had ordained he should work in the pit, so that he might know the hard labour of man and mix with them. One night he had opened his eyes to find Satan staring at him from his bedside; the Evil One had promised him property and quick advancement to the job of managing a pit if he would abandon religion, but Reuben had opened his Bible and read the Sermon on the Mount aloud, so Satan disappeared in anger.

Reuben ignored this fame and when he was not occupied with meetings, spent the hours in lonely meditations. He could always enjoy a tranquil peace alone on the hills. But Morgans the Bakehouse came up to his home in the mornings now, to discuss the campaign they were to start beyond the Valley.

Eager, and in his Sunday frock coat, he would sit in the bleak parlour and spread many papers on the table, from which Martha had removed her precious damask cloth.

Morgans looked at Martha with ill-concealed distaste. She was the one blot on the fame of her son. Did not the Valley know that while Reuben was occupied in delivering God's Word, his mother sat with drunken characters in the dark passage of some pub! Ach, it was not seemly.

The old man and the young man sat in consultation for a couple of hours. Morgans watched with keen glances the shifting expressions on Reuben's face. He was not quite at peace concerning Reuben.

'Happy you are in this labour?' he asked anxiously, his fierce denunciatory eyes softened in these moments.

Reuben always protested he was quite happy and proud of his task.

Though in the mornings, with the dusty sunlight of the Valley over the hills and the disturbing presence of Martha in the house, he would have preferred to go alone to the mountain and lose himself in the distances of sky and upland. He knew that when again he stood on the platform in the marquee, before the crowd of singing people, the fountain of inspiration within him would not fail and he would be moved to splendid exaltations and passionate desire to chant the poetry of divine love.

'Well,' Morgans resumed, rubbing his hands, 'Important your labour will become. Look you at the pile of enquiries for you!'

He outlined the campaign. Three or four of the officials would travel with Reuben: they would visit the villages in the week-days, working up to a grand Sunday crescendo in the various towns of South Wales. There were enough villages and towns to keep them busy for four months, then perhaps they might tackle the remote and savage villages of North Wales – though, as a cultured South Welshman, Morgans was doubtful that any good religion could ever exist in North Wales. They would be the honoured guests of the towns, live in comfort, see the land, travelling, all expenses paid by the chapels, from one fresh place to another and 'sowing heavenly seeds everywhere'. He was going to demand a substantial fee too – or else a fair percentage of collections that would certainly be large; he was not yet quite decided which to demand. What did Reuben think?

Reuben listened vaguely, his hands clasped between his knees, the heavy lids dropped over his faintly smiling eyes. A deep tinge of morning colour made the pale mask of his face like rose-glowing marble – for thus, vague and dreaming, his face had a certain marmoreal repose.

He told Morgans to do as he thought best.

Morgans observed that Reuben was possessed of one of his mystic reveries and did not stay long.

Reuben had been thinking of his mother. That morning she had looked at him with a strange haunting fear in her eyes. Subtly he knew that her venomous hatred of his religious life was breaking and dwindling before his triumphant fame. In her too, though dimmed and warped in her associations, dwelt the old fear of the sacred mysteries – her blood was pure Welsh.

He went out to her now. She was in the kitchen, just

lifting a glass of pale ale to her drooping mouth.

'Say if you want me to do a job for you,' he said gently.

She drank the ale and put down the glass jauntily.

'Too holy are your hands for vulgar tasks about the house,' she said with sour sarcasm. 'How would the Corinthians look if they saw their angel emptying slops or cleaning the frying-pan?'

He looked at her with a gleam of dim humour, but, singing in an exaggeratedly indifferent voice, she began to take the brass candlesticks from the mantelpiece.

The laborious daily polishing of these twelve candlesticks was an obsession and a religion with her. They were heirlooms of the family, and in her childhood her mother had asked on her dying day if they had been polished that morning. 'Do you the candlesticks every morning and a good woman you will keep,' she had muttered to her young daughter. 'A beautiful set they are and put your mind thinking on bright matters they do.'

'Let me polish the candlesticks?' he asked.

She shook her head. Her nose begin to twitch as her fingers polished the cherished brass. Lately her nose had developed that habit to an alarming extent and the sight of it always made him go hot in a kind of angry dismay. He thought it was a sign of her fading faculties.

His passionate eyes looked at her heavily. She suddenly met this gaze and immediately tossed her head with an odd, almost girlish, movement.

'Why don't you go out!' she said angrily.

A faint caressive smile was upon his lips.

'Fool!' she cried. 'If your mind was proper in your head

214

sure I'd be that those candlesticks would go down in the family. But a crazy-headed bachelor you'll be, I can see, and live your old age like a crotchety parrot in a cage. Why don't you show yourself natural and go out to find a female? There's strange ways you are going into. Ach, the heart in your breast has got strange blood in it.'

It was as though she forced the invisible hands of her soul against him. But he was aware too of the fear hidden in her plangent voice.

'You know what you said about Eirwen Vaughan,' he said.

'Better it would be if you married her than this old religion.'

'It's not too late – ' he said subtly.

'Ha, so you haven't heard about her?'

His brow contracted.

'What?' he asked with cold indifference.

'Marrying young Lewis of the Cauliflower she is in a week or two.'

He stared at her silently.

In the activities of the past days he had not thought of Eirwen. After his last visit to her he had forced her out of his consciousness – thought of her was too disturbing an element in these exalted days. He had not believed for a moment that she would marry that fellow of the Cauliflower. She was altogether too lovely a being for the brutal clutches of the ruffian.

'She would not be so blind,' he said slowly.

'He,' cried Martha, 'a suitable match it is, I think.'

At last he turned and left her. Ten minutes later he was slowly walking to Bryn Farm. Once he paused as though to

215

turn back, but he went on, his face shut and pale once more.

Mrs Vaughan greeted him with respect and warmth, and she put him in the parlour, looking at him in admiration.

'Heard you we have,' she said excitedly. 'There's fire! There's great words! There's a preacher! Shifted into heaven I was.'

He sat in the chair she obsequiously thrust forward. And she insisted on a drink of small-beer. Then he asked her about Eirwen.

'True it is,' she said mournfully. 'Used my tongue all I could against it I have, but obstinate as our old cow Phyllis she is.'

'Live with him in that pub she will?' he asked in wide-eyed horror.

'No, thank the dear Lord. Taken a cottage for her he has.'

'She won't go to serve in the bar?'

Mrs Vaughan rocked in her chair.

'Perverse she is. When I told her, "Be stern and do not put your feet behind those vulgar counters," laughed she did and said, "A public life it would be and that is what I like." Ach, lost I am to think from where comes her savage ideas.'

Eirwen, who was moving about upstairs at the morning work, began to sing, and her voice, rich and careless, floated down to the melancholy parlour.

'I will send her down to you,' Mrs Vaughan said, 'and speak you to her seriously, Reuben bach.'

She went out and Reuben stared broodingly through the window. The blood beat swiftly in his wrists, and his hands were clenched. The landscape beyond the window seemed

216

stern, and, and stonily desolate, as though the sunlight was suddenly lifted from it.

Eirwen came in.

She made a low and mocking obeisance before Reuben, holding the edges of her skirt and, as she bowed, lifting her duskily golden face in a derisive grimace.

'Mr Daniels,' she breathed, 'proud of this visit I am.'

'Get up, fool!' he said angrily.

She sat opposite him and looked with eyes of satiric amusement at his grave face.

'So you are going to be married,' he said.

'Yes, at last.'

'At last!' he exclaimed. 'And you only twenty.'

'I want to be married. It's no good thinking anymore about my voice and becoming a singer. Poorer than ever we are. So I want to be married and begin a new life.'

She filled the bleak parlour with the warmth of her arrogant youth. Her awakened face with its derisive scarlet lips was poised in the vindictive vanity of desirous youth, all the sleek and supple contours of her body were exquisite with youth. She sat in her chair proud, exultant in the dazzling gleam of that beauty. Reuben looked at her, his lips parted, his eyes full of a cold glint.

'Do you love him?' he asked.

She smiled and her gaze dropped languorously. All her desire for beauty and the long ardours of her caresses were in her smile. There was a silence. She lifted her face, and the soft, eager movement of her throat seemed to be expressive of her vulnerable soul.

The sudden silence in the room was like a dark spell on

their minds. Each trembled and was afraid to speak.

'You only want him because – ' he began with muttering difficulty, and stopped.

' – Because of what?' she asked curiously, her eyes naked and full upon him.

'Ah,' he cried, 'how can I tell! But there is no love in you for this man. No love. Not the love that will make you happy for ever.'

She leaned back her head and said softly and subtly, 'I like his mouth and the way – '

'Stop!' he cried angrily, his brows drawn with wrath. He went on furiously, 'That is all you want, the pleasures of the flesh, and he who can give it to you in better quantity than another is your lover.'

'And when you can have quantity *and* quality together,' she said, 'one is lucky.'

Reuben thought of Eirwen's lover – one of the bloods of the Valley, a young man aggressive and filled with physical well-being and a kind of vulgar handsomeness.

'Quality!' he echoed in contempt.

'And, besides,' she said, 'I'll be able to serve in the bar of his father's public-house!' She laughed. 'When I feel like it.'

He made a sharp sound of disgust, but she laughed the louder.

'Why don't you wait...' he said at last.

'Why should I wait? Watcyn is very anxious for me to marry him at once. He is not slow and full of dreams.'

Suddenly his blood seemed to run in a flood through his body. He wanted to clasp this supple girl and bear her away with him into some night of endless passion, where he would hold her mouth against his hour after hour, press the cool gold of her flesh triumphantly against his own flaming body. His limbs stretched tense and hard as, in the absolute strength of his desire, he watched her.

She looked back at him, her eyes kindled too. But now she did not make the slightest physical effort to enslave him. She sat back in her chair and looked at him long and cruelly.

He was muttering, his body stretched forward, his voice like a chant: 'If you would wait for me, if you would wait, I would give you such love, Eirwen, such love – ' But as suddenly the flood of hot blood seemed to recoil back into his heart, and, his face pale with hostility, he said:

'Marry him then, if you would be a fool. I cannot ask you to wait for me. I have other things to do...' His face darkened as her lips began to smile. 'And you would turn me from that labour.'

'You would be happier with me,' she said.

He shook his head.

'Ah,' she said, with ironic certainty, 'I know.'

But he saw himself as a martyr. The pleasures of the sensual world were not for him. Far up among frozen mountains, built in the soundless heights of that desolate region, there was a stony temple open to the sky. He saw it in a vision: the lonely frozen temple amid desolate snow. To that temple he must go, climb, his feet torn, his flesh as a garment of sackcloth upon his sacrificial soul. For there, upon those shining walls and within the pure sky above, were the symbols of eternal life.

He stood up.

'No, no,' he cried, 'never again will I think of you.'

'Go on,' she said, 'only human you are, like the rest of us.'

He went out, and in his ears, then and often afterwards, the sound of her laughter was like the echo of all the careless pleasures enacted in the flesh.

He went to the hills.

The vision of the icy temple on its snow-covered pinnacle was still bright in his mind. It made his soul quicken with a piercing bliss. Far up, far up, inaccessible to all but those who would sacrifice every earthly joy to reach it, was the temple, where the martyr, prostrate at last upon its frozen floor, would learn the final secret of life, listening to the clear harmony of God's universe.

Ah, he would reach it.

That evening he preached of his vision. The people listened attentively, open-mouthed, but his sermon did not have quite the success of the others. It was as though his description of the frozen heights had a chilling effect on his listeners. The stony and jagged path, that led to the holy temple, was not very inviting, either. No, they preferred something with fire in it.

But nevertheless there were numbers of converts again that night. It was heartening for Morgans the Bakehouse. He had listened to Reuben's address with aesthetic appreciation of its imagery, but, ever watchful and vigilant, he saw that it was not what the people liked most.

After the service, when, as Reuben leaned tired and brooding against the platform, he spoke gently:

'Beautiful was your sermon.'

'But too cold – ' Reuben said swiftly.

Morgans laughed.

'Hard is the path you spoke of, too. An easier way to the truth do people like.'

'They want to be comforted,' said Reuben with quick vehemence. 'That's what they want – comfort, and assurance that they will sit in Heaven.'

Morgans said apprehensively:

'Don't you lose faith in them now. Faulty and patchy in their minds are most of them I know, and too greedy to tell their woes in public are some, especially the females, but very frail and liable to blemishes is the human flesh and overlook a lot we must. Better it is to keep our eyes fixed on the little lamp of God that is hanging in the darkness of each of us...'

Catherine Pritchards approached.

'Now you are both together – ' she began.

'Want to come with us on our travels she does,' Morgans said. 'Drat me, I don't know what to do with her. Say what you think, Reuben.'

'You know how my singing has helped the services, Mr Daniels,' she pleaded. 'And anxious to do all I can for the Lord I am.'

'Very soulful indeed your singing has been,' Morgans admitted.

Yes, she had enjoyed quite a success, standing on the platform and letting loose all the vocal power of her excessive strength. She had trampled her old reputation beneath her newly pious feet and now stood chaste and cleansed in the eyes of the people.

'Long have I watched for this opportunity to work for

Jesus Christ,' she went on ardently. 'Let me come with you, Mr Daniels. Let me help in this great work.'

'I am willing for anyone to come,' Reuben said, 'but the business of the committee it is.'

Morgans meditatively stroked his beard. He looked out of the corner of his eye at the ornately arrayed Catherine, whose firm bosom, encased in red velvet tonight, was lifted up pantingly as she spoke to Reuben.

'Set my will on coming I have,' she said, turning to Morgans and archly shaking a finger at him.

'Then,' he answered, 'come you must.'

'A woman there ought to be in the party, to look after you,' she said, smiling with sweet lusciousness. Joy shone from her.

She turned back to Reuben.

'There's moving your sermon was tonight, dear Mr Daniels. Often now shall I see a chapel on top of the mountains, when there is snow. Power was in your words. Felt I did, when you were speaking, as though I was buried in the snow – all my flesh went like ice and my blood seemed to be frozen. Very powerful you were.'

He walked home in acute melancholy that night. Dark and ragged clouds were drifting wearily over the hills: the dry weather was breaking. All the world seemed to him exhausted and dark within itself. Why, why was he so tired and melancholy each night after the service, when he should have been filled with joy and rapture because of the manifest faith he roused in the people? The fierce joy that had been his when he left Eirwen, the martyred eyes of his soul lifted to the vision of the lonely temple, seemed utterly to have left him now.

Darkly, like sad and weary ghosts, the clouds wandered about the hill-tops. Far before him, the Valley was shut in by a huge faint shoulder of earth. Below, the pale lights of the colliery burned dimly, and the houses were huddled together like a flock of grey sheep.

CHAPTER VI

He did not expect Martha to give way so soon. It happened on the last evening of that triumphant week.

Notable indeed was the last evening. Hopkins's field was a mass of excited faces. The sides of the marquee bulged dangerously from the crowd inside and several times the whole structure swayed in a most ominous fashion. But the people who had failed to push themselves into the tent were not to be denied their pleasure. Several impromptu speakers arose from the crowd and conducted little meetings all over the field: and the various hymns swept up and mingled in a grand paean to the sky. Great was the spectacle.

On a bench a good distance from the platform sat Martha, a black-spotted veil drawn over her face. She had set out early without a word as to her destination and now she sat tightly wedged among strangers in a meeting that never, never had she thought she would ever attend. But she was there, in her black-spotted veil, her face calm and her voice silent. Her neighbour on the bench, a visitor from another district, had nudged her violently in the ribs and cried, 'Sing, dear sister in Christ, sing. Is not glory with you?' But Martha remained silent and joyless throughout the meeting.

Reuben saw her very soon after he had taken his stand on the platform. It was the yellow bird with spread wings on her best black hat that he recognised. He trembled and she shifted with difficulty in her seat. He saw her eyes close behind the veil. His sermon that night was a prayer of passionate sadness. He was like a young John coming from the desert with wild and beautiful words in his hungry mouth. He spoke of the suffering that turns the heart to salt bitterness and of the invisible tears that drop in the soul like sullen rain... He spoke of children who cannot utter the love that trembles on their lips and of men whose harsh violences become as stinging thongs upon their flesh. Of these things and others he spoke with passion and knowledge, so that women began to weep and then bowed their heads in shame.

'Amen, Amen,' they sighed at frequent intervals. And they dried their eyes and hung their heads and thought how sad, sad was the world, with all its errors and misunderstandings and unnecessary hatreds.

His voice was like a music, his face and gestures a symphony of controlled emotions. He concluded with a description of the Kingdom of God upon earth. Of that he spoke in such a glowing but simple language that the crowd

225

took comfort and began to brighten and utter little noises of satisfaction. If only the people knew not greed or hatred, if love were the only sap in the roots of life...

The meeting lasted into the late night. Dozens of hymns were sung; there was no counting of converts, for they swarmed in such abundance to the front of the tent that their individual confessions became one great chorus of repentance. Several notable sinners of the Valley confessed Jesus: and, as usual, after their acknowledgment their faces beamed in the satisfaction of knowing themselves respectable once more.

'O Jesus, I have promised
To serve Thee to the end – '

One incident caused scandal for a little while. A young married woman, who had been wailing and praying since the end of the sermon, at last succeeded in pushing her way to the front. Her face shone with sweat and her eyes glared menacingly. She stood in front of Reuben and began to scream: 'I have suffered well for Jesus Christ. No more will I do sin with my body. Look you how I can prove it.' With a sudden gesture she tore her flimsy garment from her shoulders, and in a moment her breasts were exposed. 'Look you at the bruise that my husband has left on my clean flesh,' she cried madly, her voice rising to a screech. 'God told me in a little vision that disgusting is the old filth – '

Reuben stood as though turned to stone. It was Morgans the Bakehouse who went hurriedly to the woman and led her, still screeching, away to the curtained space behind the platform.

The crowd had become silent, except for much whispering. Bangor Davies, however, began a hymn with a flourish that roused everybody. Quickly the meeting resumed its rejoicing way.

And all the time Reuben was deeply conscious of his mother's presence. That consciousness had made his sermon more impassioned, his prayers more exulting. She was there, she was there listening to him. He knew, with the profound certainty of his instinct, that at last she had come to him.

The meeting did not finish in Hopkins's field. It was continued into the main-street and in the Square about the rusty old fountain. There the people, singing with unabated strength, gathered for final prayers. Various persons obliged, each eager to excel the last in fervour. Then Reuben, using the fountain as a platform, stood up, and a proud shout arose.

With a voice that became the chant of a bard, he spoke to them of the heritage that was their richest possession. Always the country of Wales had been the country that was nearest Paradise. They were sacred people – in them God had found his most faithful children. Was not their life a continual psalm of praise to God! He invoked the ancient spirits of the hills to keep continual guard over the Welsh people: and in words of simple beauty he appealed to the rapt crowds to keep the society of their souls intact from the jeers of foreign lands. Wales would be forever pleasant in the sight of the Lord.

He climbed down from the fountain at last. His eyes were like smoky lamps in the yellowish pallor of his face. What were these words he had been saying, up there, exalted before this multitude that was pressing on him like a nightmare crowd? He could hardly remember. Vaguely he passed his hand over his dazed eyes. Then suddenly it was as though a stream of glittering light was poured into him, the blood ran like a silent cry through his body. A gentle smile upon his dreaming face, he made his way through the admiring mob.

He went towards his home. Everywhere he could hear singing – the whole Valley seemed to echo with hymns. He looked up. A pale sheet of grey light hung behind enormous billows of cloud, and the hills were like cliffs of dark stone.

But in his own being was a solemn joy that was as the nude vitality in the very core of the soul. He felt that he must pierce through to the quivering source of life, where he would pass into an ultimate consummation of all that had hurt and exalted him.

He said softly: 'The womb of life.'

He would scale the stony altitude of suffering and in a final crucifixion of his purity ascend, a white flame of rapture, to the gleaming breasts of the eternal mother.

His lips murmured softly in their anguish of joy: 'Rocks and blood, water and the proud sun in the sky, shall pass away, and through her, the eternal mother, I shall endure.'

Stumbling, his head swooning with visions, he went alone. His flesh was heavy and trembling about the rich tissue of his dazzled soul, his veins were like branches pliant with warm sap, his thighs were tense in a wild, lithe flood of power. Broken phrases came to his lips: he wanted to open his arms and call softly, beseechingly, to the beings who veiled their shining beauty beyond the perception of his flesh. Call to them to witness his triumph.

Trembling he climbed to his home. The two rows of aged cottages set in the jaw of the hillside curved round like the dirty teeth in the head of a ram. Reuben gazed at the cottages and his heart burned up within his quivering flesh.

She was there.

She would look at him as he entered the house. Her brows would not be sullen, and her voice would be secret and sad. She would say to him, 'I heard you tonight.'

Martha and Hugh were in the living-room. Hugh sat in his chair, grey and silent. Lately his face had become a little dim. Since in his age he had quite forsaken the joy of his evenings at the public-house, his soul seemed to retire into a dim seclusion – as though it demanded no more of life and waited in patience for the final release.

Not even the remarkable happening of that night stirred him very much. Martha had come in, but without her customary tipsiness, and he had continued to read the Bible. She took off her hat and veil and went immediately into the kitchen. He heard a cork drawn.

Then she had come back and sat on the edge of a chair near him.

'Hugh Daniels!' she said loudly.

He looked up. Strands of her iron-grey hair were wild about her brows, her loose mouth drooped. Her face was strange to him.

229

'Well?' he said, and he coughed uneasily.

'I have just had my last glass,' she said.

'Your last, Mrs Daniels?' he murmured doubtfully, hardly understanding her.

'The last,' she repeated loudly, 'the last.' For a moment or two she seemed occupied with some profound thought. Then the sagging flesh on her face took on a new ardour and her pale eyes began to sparkle. 'Yes, tomorrow shall I begin a fresh life.'

'How – how is this?' he asked.

She said, darkly, 'I have been to see our Reuben.'

He shifted uneasily in his chair. He could find no word to utter. His head bowed upon his chest, he gazed dimly at his bruised collier's hands.

She cried in a shrill voice, 'Silent you are. And you that was always bumptious in your holy complaint about me.'

He lifted his head and said sadly, 'Late you are, Martha.'

His eyes shone, but not with the joy she expected. She gazed at him and her face became aggressive. 'Late I might be, but does not the Bible that you have just shut say, More joy is there in Heaven over one sinner that repenteth – '

'Thinking I was of all the years you have wasted,' he said in gentle reproach.

'Happy I've been,' she answered, with a toss of her head.

'Selfish was your happiness. And now that frightened you are getting since you are young no more, offer to the Lord only what is left you do.'

'Better that than nothing at all,' she said with rising anger. 'A peevish old man you are getting, Hugh Daniels.'

He stared at her. She was beyond the capacity of his mind now. He thought of all her jeers at religion, her insults and venom. He shook his head. 'Strange are your ways,' he muttered.

She cried suddenly, 'There's emotion I had, listening to Reuben tonight! Noble he was.'

He sighed. 'Afraid for him I am. Better it would have been if we had worked to give him schooling and make him a proper minister.'

'Then like all the others he would have become,' she said spitefully.

Reuben came in. She did not turn round to look at him, but she sat, her hand at her throat, gazing into the fire.

'I saw you in the meeting,' he said.

'Yes,' she answered, 'and enjoyed it I did.'

Hugh lifted his dim eyes and stared searchingly at his son.

'Happy you are, Reuben?' he asked.

'I am happy tonight.'

He went to the chair where his mother sat and squatted down beside it. He took her hand and murmured proudly, 'You were there and I was so glad.'

She drew her hand away: but she said, 'I was too.'

'I saw you at once,' he said.

'Always looking at me you were,' she answered in a soft, yielding voice that was utterly strange to her own ears.

Hugh gazed at them in veiled astonishment, and he said, 'A victory you have had, Reuben bach. Strong your sermon must have been.'

Martha began to weep. Softly, with a strange working of

her brows, she wept, the tears rolling thinly down her brown-tinged yielding face, and her loose mouth drooping pitiably.

Hugh murmured inaudibly, 'Well you might weep.'

Her son cried out, 'That is finished now, and there is nothing else but peace. Think how happy we will be together! Always we will be together! Hugh, say you how glad you are.'

'Oh, very glad I am,' Hugh said fervently enough.

Martha's tears ceased, and she said, her new voice breaking like sweet music on Reuben's ears:

'When I was a girl I used to go to Saron and sit with my mother in our own pew. Very religious I was and closely I listened to the sermons. The name of Jesus Christ was in my heart then. Always I prayed to him and comfort I found in his name. How is it that I wandered from his hands into the paths of error?'

'Yes, indeed, how?' Hugh sighed.

'Weak my will was,' she moaned. 'Well I remember the first drop of liquor that went into my mouth.' Remembering, she shook her head, woe upon her face. 'In chapel, a young man used to wink at me from the gallery and when we went to the seaside for the Sunday-school excursion, took me away from the others he did, and we walked into the country. Happy I was with him – ' She glanced for a moment at Hugh, upon whose face displeasure was written, 'for there's strict my mother was with me at home. Full of jokes was the young man and lovely was the day. We came to a little inn where they had geraniums on the window-sills and a big red parrot that could say a bad word in Welsh. There it was that I tasted spirits first.' Her head dropped and she added in a far-away voice. 'Liked the feeling it gave me I did and there's happy I was...'

Hugh moved his spectacles up from the end of his nose. 'Who was that young man, then, Mrs Daniels?' he asked in a casual manner.

She lifted her head and gazed at him.

'I forget,' she said, 'and he went to Australia.'

'Ah,' Hugh murmured, 'a lot of young men used to go there.'

Dreamily Reuben listened to them. He was tasting of a perfect peace. Now tranquillity reigned in this room. Serene, he gazed, still squatting by Martha's chair, at his father's face, that now was gentle and dim again. The old wooden clock seemed to tick-tock with a comfortable tranquillity too, and the tabby cat in the hearth yawned and stretched out a paw in satisfaction. And for a while each sat in silence, while the night advanced towards Martha's new day...

The next morning Morgans the Bakehouse arrived with the usual sheaf of papers under his arm.

'Arranged everything is,' he said, drawing up a chair to the table in the parlour. 'Start in Pontypridd we do, staying there three days and then we will work round to Maesteg.'

Reuben sat on the sofa and said almost shyly:

'My mother is converted at last.'

'Praise to God!' Morgans announced warmly, bringing his fist down on the table. 'A good piece of work that is.'

'She was in the meeting last night,' Reuben said.

233

'Praise to God!' Morgans repeated.

'This morning she said to me, "Peace is in my heart," and better she looks already.'

'Amen. May she always have that peace now,' Morgans said quickly.

'A pity it is that I'm leaving home so soon after her conversion,' said Reuben, a sudden doubt entering him.

'Trust in God to keep her firm,' Morgans advised. 'Now, Reuben bach, look you at this list.'

They bent over the papers.

Later Reuben asked about the young married woman who had made such an exhibition of herself in the meeting of last night.

'Doubtful of such people I am,' he added.

Morgans shook his head dismally.

'Strange it is,' he said, 'how a revival gathers people like that to it. But put up with them we must, for we cannot stand at the door and question everyone regarding their intentions. The young woman is a bit lost in the head. One of those who ought never to marry she is. Horror of her husband is within her. Spiritual is her mind and not much did it take to upset her.'

A dark shadow seemed to cast itself on Reuben's mind. Somewhere in his consciousness a hateful knowledge brooded, like an evil fume over the bright pastures of his soul. He remembered how sometimes in his most exalted visions a certain flame of desire leapt with searing and blinding force within him, and he would see within stretches of dark night the naked white bodies of women.

'Ignore such people we must,' Morgans continued, 'and

234

bring to the Lord those who are balanced in the head.'

He announced that the seven days' mission had been a marvellous success and handed Reuben a packet containing fifteen sovereigns. Also the Committee had decided to raise their young pastor's salary to four pounds a week. And a big chapel was to be built for him.

'So you must stay with us for a while, Mr Daniels,' he added, assuming a business air for the moment, 'and shut your ears to tempting offers that you will have from our rivals.'

Reuben promised to stay with them.

'Indeed, I do not want to wander from the Valley,' he said. 'My father and mother are getting older, and where they are content, I shall be also.'

After Morgans' departure, he went into the kitchen, where Martha was peeling potatoes, and laid the fifteen coins on the table before her.

'Buy yourself some present with them,' he said.

She counted them.

'Fifteen!' she said. 'Good payment for a week.'

'The money is nothing to me,' he said.

'I don't want them,' she said, slowly pushing the coins away.

'Yes,' he said firmly, 'Buy yourself clothes or anything that you want. Heard you complain I have about your shabby garments.'

'No right to complain have I,' she muttered, 'for on drink I spent my money.'

'Now!' he warned her, 'forget all that we must.'

'Ha, not so easy is it.'

He laid his arm across her shoulders. Pain in his voice, he whispered in her ear. 'You will not go back, Mam fach? Stay with me now. I want you. I am going through Wales to work for Christ and successful I will be if I know that you are still faithful to me. Say that you will be faithful to me!'

'Ach,' she said, with something of her old arrogance, moving away from his clasp, 'I can be faithful to religion as I have been faithful to drink.'

And with that promise he had to be content.

CHAPTER VII

Eirwen Vaughan married her public-house lover before Reuben left the Valley for his evangelistic tour.

He saw her once, in the main-street, where she was occupied in buying eatables for the wedding-day.

'Alone you leave us now,' she complained, smiling ironically into his white face, from which every drop of colour had fled when she stopped him in his walk. 'But, of course, much too busy to visit old friends you are.'

'You know why I didn't come,' he said austerely.

'No,' she said.

Though her lips smiled and a pale golden tint was still on her pastel-like skin, there were dim shadows about her eyes, and behind them, too, there seemed to be a lurking shadow. Yet she had a jaunty air, as though she were about to begin a long-awaited holiday.

He looked at her, he gazed through her eyes, and the

smile on her lips faded and she stared back at him in silence, a kind of shame upon her face.

'You do not love him,' he said with sudden passion.

'Oh, love...' she said, moving away from him slightly, '...you are always worrying about love.'

'I want to think you are happy,' he persisted.

'I can content myself with many things,' she said.

'Money you mean,' he said sternly.

'That,' she answered, 'and other things.'

She lifted her delicately-shaded face to him, her eyes that were strangely haunted with shadows. And her beauty went like a sword into his soul and he realized what he had lost.

The colliers returning from the day-shift were beginning to tramp into the street. She murmured:

'I must be going.'

'You will forget me now,' he said in a dull voice.

'No,' she answered swiftly, 'never. I... I...' But she stopped and looked at him, smiling a little coldly. 'There has been something that has kept us apart. I don't understand it. You know how I have wanted you and how harsh you were with me.'

'Perhaps if you had waited – ' he said painfully.

She looked away at the passing colliers, the young men swinging past her, hard and dark from their underworld. Vaguely she shook her head.

'When you worked among them,' she said, indicating the miners, 'I liked you.'

And she left him with that.

He continued his walk. So be it. He must cast her out of

238

his memory. Her white-gold hyacinth face must never be within his mind, her mockingly caressing voice he must hear no more. Quickly he walked on. And presently the ache in his breast ceased. He was thinking of some passages he had read in the Bible that morning. They came from Lamentations, and he repeated them silently, his being echoing them with a deep and melancholy pleasure:

How is the gold become dim! how is the most fine gold changed! the stones of the sanctuary are poured out in the top of every street.

The precious sons of Zion, comparable to fine gold, how are they esteemed as earthen pitchers, the work of the hands of the potter!

They that did feed delicately are desolate in the streets: they that were brought up in scarlet embrace dunghills.

For the punishment of the iniquity of the daughter of my people is greater than the punishment of the sin of Sodom, that was overthrown as in a moment, and no hands stayed on her.

Her Nazarites were purer than snow, they were whiter than milk, they were more ruddy in body than rubies, their polishing was of sapphire.

These verses gave him an aesthetic emotion. Again and again he repeated them, until, walking on to their rhythm, the image of Eirwen became subtly mingled in the words. Gold and scarlet, earth and desolation, snow and rubies, yea, and dunghills too – her image was in those words.

Quickly, anger gathering in him, he went on. And his

will triumphed. His mind was soon filled with elevated thoughts.

But the next day he spoke to Martha about Eirwen.

'I want to give her a wedding-present,' he said. 'What do you think will be suitable?'

Martha spoke her mind. She had never liked the girl.

'A big bottle of perfume, I should think, to keep the smell of beer off her.' She felt she had a right to say that now.

Reuben was shocked.

'Ah,' he said, 'she won't go to work in the bar. And they are going to live in those new little houses upon the side of the mountain. Speak sensible now. What shall it be?'

They decided on a clock, and they went out together that afternoon to buy it.

Reuben had confidence in his mother's taste. She chose a handsome clock set in pink china and decorated each side with pretty white babies climbing to tear little roses off the main structure. It cost thirty-five shillings, but it looked worth all that.

He asked Martha to take it to Bryn Farm. And Martha, who had been persuaded to buy new clothes with the money he had given her, consented. She went through the streets with quite a new pride now.

She basked in the reflected glory of her son's fame with rightful satisfaction. Her known arrogance was justified. Not many women could give birth to a glorious natural preacher like Reuben. Her face, that lately had a scarred look now acquired an almost genteel air. Straightening her back, she felt that however numerous her errors, she would at least die in an odour of respectability.

Hugh's bitter melancholy since her conversion made her very indignant. He, with the Bible always on his knees and a Baptist face even on week-days, he should have cried aloud in proud joy to the Lord.

'Sour you are because now you will have nothing to complain about?' she asked him sarcastically.

'Miserable is your repentance now,' he replied. 'Past sixty I am and before long I will be in my coffin.'

'Tut, tut,' she said, her voice rising in fear, 'how do you think that way?'

'My mind goes always to these matters now. So empty to me seems your change. How was it that you didn't take warning years ago, when I was young, and little trips we could have had together, and the money that has been wasted would be safe in the walls of houses!'

She took her apron off and pulled up a stocking, preparing to go to a service in the Corinthians' chapel.

'Ah,' she said, 'why didn't you behave like a man of power in those days? Strength like a whip you ought to have had in your hand, and the sting of serpents in your tongue.'

'Ach,' he said then, his nostrils pinched and quivering, 'no man has there been who could make a black pig white.'

She laughed and arranged her hair in the mirror behind the brass candlesticks on the mantelpiece.

'Not for Reuben have you changed,' he added. 'No, because you are afraid it is – that is why. Fear is in your soul. Have you not felt that your feet are made of damp clay, has not your heart been like a lump of earth within you?' He stared at her with cold resentment. 'To satisfy yourself you have changed, but even so, no faith in you I have.'

241

'Hugh Daniels,' she answered, 'squint-eyed your mind is getting.'

Already, in the gratification of her surrender, she seemed to have taken on a new lease of energetic life. She went with a sprightly set of shoulders to the parlour, to fetch her new and fashionable hat. And Hugh gave a deep sigh, wrinkled his nose in contempt, and opened his Bible at the pages of Job.

The fervour of the meetings in the chapel had not diminished. There were no fresh converts, however– everyone in the Valley who was addicted to this class of worship – and there were few who did not take advantage of it – had entered into bliss during the special meetings; and now they contented themselves with declaiming flowery prayers and singing, with untiring heat, dozens of Welsh and English hymns.

But people were healed of many bodily complaints – recent and longstanding ills disappeared with a clean, finished rapidity, leaving such a fresh and glowing interior behind them.

Miss Mattie Matthews, a spinster, who consumed, for her gastric complaint, eighty bottles of medicine a year, announced that in a vision she had been told to 'trust in God's best medicine his love' – so she had taken no earthly medicine – for a fortnight now, and never had she felt so well: she could even eat veal and pork, and of God's lovely fruit, apples and pears.

Lumbago, rheumatism, varicose veins, anaemia, stones in the bladder too – all miraculously vanished in ratio to the fervour of the convert. Even a floating kidney was fixed in its rightful place again. The panacea worked best in visions.

A lurid happiness flowed through the Valley. The lawful chapels profited by the accelerated zeal: special services were called and there were no empty seats if it was announced that converts would give testimony. The ministers added extra fire to their sermons.

Only the publicans, the cinema-proprietors, and the tobacconists, denounced the revival. Drink, of course, was damnable in God's sight, the public-house was a temple of carnal delight; and tobacco was an evil, unexplained, but an evil, though chewing sweets in chapel, if done in a subdued fashion, could be overlooked.

Yes, the Valley was rapidly becoming a Heaven upon earth.

Reuben Daniels fulfilled all expectations. His orations could loosen tears, whip the blood to a terrible heat, calm the soul, refresh the weary; his prayers were poetry better than any heard in the great eisteddfodau.

Really, his greatest asset was his simplicity. To see him advance to the front of a platform, a pale light upon his grave face, eyes dark with austere love, chastity gleaming upon his visionary brow, was to be moved to an expectant interest, even before he began to speak. Then his voice, that had in full measure the sweet burden of the Celtic melancholy, was finer than harp music and purer than the note of a Church organ.

He spoke to the human heart – as though to one simple human heart, thus speaking to all.

But nearly always, after the meetings he would flee to a

lonely place – some hollow in the silent hills or among the rocks that litter one part of the Valley – and, lying on the earth, yield up his soul to the passing clouds, the drifting sky – he seemed to attain a flawless peace thus, his soul stretched within the sky, his body empty of emotion and thought. After the meetings, he needed this peace so much.

BOOK FOUR

CHAPTER I

Soon all Wales was filled with the desire to purify itself again. In every county the meetings and services in the chapels began to burn with a new ardour, and everywhere people spoke of their hunger for fresh spiritual joys.

The newspapers were crowded with faithful reports of the more remarkable of the meetings – the ordinary worldly news faded in importance before this spiritual revival that was sweeping so furiously through the country. One newspaper, indeed, printed a Revival Supplement every Saturday – six sheets containing prayers, a sermon, reports of conversions, details concerning Reuben Daniels, a short story or fable with a powerful moral, and photographs of chapels and the leading revivalists. One photograph showed the group that had set out from the Valley – Reuben Daniels, Morgans the Bakehouse, Bangor Davies and Catherine Pritchards – and very impressive and pleasing the group looked – with youth, maturity and venerable age represented so admirably in it.

The four were received with acclamations wherever they went. Large posters announced their coming, and the biggest hall or chapel in the town was reserved for them. But the biggest building was never big enough. Morgans talked vaguely of borrowing money to buy a large marquee and charging a fee to the officials of the towns they visited, for its use each night. But the fuss of having it constantly packed, unpacked, and travelling with them, dismayed him.

This tour of the larger domains of Wales had begun in Pontypridd, the fussy little market town that is at the mouth of the Valley. There everything had been a triumph. One meeting had lasted until two o'clock in the morning – over three hundred converts had declared themselves that night – and even after the meeting, some prolonged their declarations in the streets, kneeling in little groups on the pavement.

Always when Reuben appeared in the pulpit a hush went over the singing crowd. The people gazed at him with a curious awe, and instantly they became receptive and eager for his words.

He got to know their needs. Ah, they loved words that were as whips on the soft fear of their souls, and they loved, too, words that placed them consciously in that holy of holies where God was very aware of each of them. If he spoke of God's pain because of the apathy and evil of the world, they writhed in contrite sensations, and if he chanted of that splendid love and understanding that unites the people to Christ, their faces exuded a soft balmy

246

satisfaction. But best of all they liked the rolling phrase that thundered as from a new Revelation, and the style that casts a lurid light over the last pages of the Bible was the most successful. As the tour progressed and the meetings became more numerous, Reuben often read those pages before a service and came from them laden and refreshed.

Inspiration never failed him. The eager and excited emotions that flowed up from that mass of gazing figures gathered beneath him always roused in him a power that seemed to make his being swell to superhuman proportions. Then his voice came forth as though it were the voice of a greater being than he. His ears heard the words, but he was hardly aware of their formation in his mind.

But he was always conscious of those faces beneath. And sometimes a sick wave of nausea surged up through their consciousness, and the faces seemed to congeal into one solid mass of greasy white flesh, flesh animated by a thousand watching eyes: and then a violent disgust would pass through him. But still, swelling triumphant over these emotions of his lower orgasm, his soul issued lofty and divine words to the hungering creatures of earth gathered there, so simply eager for joy.

'...Then the world will be like the eternal green meadows of Paradise. The rose of love will bloom in the soul and not fall with the passing of time. We shall dwell in those white courts of the mind where there is always a deep and faithful peace. Is not that state worth the attainment?...'

Such picturesque dreaming moved them to sighing affirmations of similar ideals. But sometimes he cried like a prophetic bard:

247

'The scorpions of woe shall sting them into death. They shall go out to the pit of darkness and expiate their sins in awful loneliness. Bitter as wormwood shall be the water they shall drink, and the food of their miserable days shall be as dust in their mouths – '

And then they would sweat in satisfied pleasure. (He was speaking of the despots, the tyrants, and the evil livers in the world.)

Lately he preferred not to take a very active part in the welcoming of converts after his oration. He did not want to grasp their hands and, through their eyes, peer religiously into their souls. So now he usually stood in the pulpit or at the edge of the platform and now and again uttered invocations or prayers.

Morgans the Bakehouse did not mind. Enough that the young man spoke his wonderful words with such passion – his work was done then. And done exceedingly well, for immediately after the hymn following his oration, the converts arose in such plenitude that Morgans and the other officials were rather overworked taking count of the declarations and issuing a kind of absolution.

Whenever it was possible, special baptismal meetings were held. Pools and rivers in the various districts were utilised for that popular feature of the revival. Reuben fulfilled his obligations in these meetings with a strange and solemn composure. He stood for an hour up to his knees in water and immersed with austere care each of the converts.

They went on from village to town with undiminished success and by the end of August the newspapers calculated that fifty thousand people had entered upon a new spiritual life. But there were many more thousands still waiting for the visit of the evangelist...

The four enjoyed their travels. They saw the country and, when they stayed a few days in a town, lived sometimes in luxury. They were flattered and feasted with unctuous gravity in many an opulent ministerial home. Were they not going to bring thousands back to the chapels?

They passed on from the mining districts of Glamorgan to the farming lands of Pembroke. There Reuben spoke in Welsh. The language came easily to his tongue and it seemed that his Welsh orations struck still deeper into the soul. For the music of religious words blows in a piercing and majestic wind through the Welsh language...

Reuben loved the land he saw. The soft green pastures of Carmarthen were full of a fresh and virgin richness. The air was cool and sweet. After the stark hills of the Valley he loved the halcyon meadows, with their cows that looked at him with a deprecating gaze, and the supple virginal curves of the little hills beyond. The day skies were a tranquil blue and the night skies a pale green: and a moon hung orange and full during his stay in Carmarthen town.

In his customary lonely walks after a meeting his mind would bathe in the quiet beauty of this countryside that had no eruptions of coal-mines, no sullen and weary acceptance of man's labour, as the Valley landscapes...

Before, not often had he gone beyond those sombre walls of earth that rose like a doom about his childhood. Sunday-school excursions had taken him to the seaside – always one of the noisy resorts by the muddy Glamorgan sea. There he ate beef sandwiches and drank mineral waters until it was

249

time to go back to a train crowded with bawling and smudgy children. He had always been miserable in that, his annual and only holiday.

Now his heart was filled with a strange half melancholy joy when he saw the clean and simple charm of this well-tempered scenery. Something was awakened in him; and he would gaze, a beseeching stare in his eyes, at the moonlit country.

A vague gold flower was in the sky; the dim pastures were asleep in the faint blue air. He leaned against a low wall of loose grey stones. The old leafy trees were still and only the thin branches of a curved sapling near him swayed a little, its leaves delicately shaking through the silent breeze. The dark gold flower was open in the pale sky. Nowhere the sound of man, nor beast, nor bird... His head drooped, his hands moved over one of the old cold stones. And the calm beauty of the night slowly entered him as a vision of earth that would be with him forever.

He turned back to the town – he had walked about three miles out – and all his tired acceptance of the happenings in the meeting that evening had gone from him. In the world there were valleys that had kept their pristine enchantment; quiet hollows of shadowy green and lucid purity. Grass, ferin, greystone, tree, thin brook of water – their roots, colours, silence, and flowing, were in him and gave him of their purified calm.

A desire to cast off his clothes and go down to the stream that was flowing between the roots of the great trees came to him. He would go over the soft grass, through the wild shadows of that thicket, and in the pure water his body, again become an elemental thing of the earth, would be at peace. His body would be rich with all the enchantment about him.

He went along the white road, shaking his head. But his eyes were bright from the sudden wild flight of his mind, and his face was flushed with a handsome vitality, as though he had become a young man who found life and love exceedingly beautiful...

Back in the town, he hurried through the silent streets, for it was past one o'clock and everybody seemed to be in bed. The four were guests in the house of Isaiah Jenkins, a Congregational minister, and Reuben had left them after the meeting without a word.

He need not have hurried back. Morgans, Catherine and Bangor were enjoying themselves with Isaiah Jenkins and his housekeeper Margaret Ann Hopkins. They were having a little party.

Reuben went into the parlour and apologised for his late arrival.

Catherine cried loudly, in a thick and excited voice, 'Where have you been to, so late, Reuben?'

'A walk in the country,' he said abruptly.

'By yourself?' she asked, and her lips leered.

He stared at her. Four large bottles stood on the table and glasses, and a dish containing a few sandwiches.

The housekeeper stood up.

'Kept these sandwiches for you we have, Mr Daniels. And something to drink.'

Isaiah Jenkins, stout and ruddy of countenance, said in his bullying voice, 'Only elderberry wine it is. A respectable drink, taken in moderation.'

Margaret Hopkins gave Reuben a plate of sandwiches and a glass of wine.

'Another glass to keep him company we must have,' Isaiah said. 'Fetch you another bottle, Margaret.'

'Indeed now,' Catherine began to protest, her face shining with pleasure, 'enough I've had, I think.'

'Go on,' Isaiah sniggered, 'elderberry wine, taken in moderation, is harmless as cow's milk.' His blue lips protruded from the ruddy flesh of his fat face. 'Good it has done you, I can see.'

'A splendid wine it is,' Bangor Davies sang. 'Like a strong tonic it has gone into my old blood.'

Morgans looked, a little dimly, at Reuben. Sometimes he was doubtful of him. Lately a strange glint had come into Reuben's eyes. And vaguely Morgans was afraid for him. Tonight he had had several glasses of elderberry.

'Laugh and be joyful, Reuben,' he cried, raising his arms. 'Let the souls of the Lord's prophets be joyful in their success. Let them take their pleasure after their labour among the wicked and the slothful people of this old world. Yea, pleasure in this good wine, taken in moderation, as Mr Isaiah Jenkins tells us, and pleasure in telling jest, story, and history like this together.'

'Telling us was Mr Isaiah Jenkins just before you came in,' Catherine said to Reuben in her excited voice, 'how it was he found his housekeeper.' Margaret Hopkins had not yet returned with the bottle. 'A widow she is, and he found her in the market at Cardigan selling bottles of home-made wine. She it was who made this elderberry. And they say her first husband died from too much drinking of his wife's brew – '

'Darro me,' Isaiah broke in, laughing loudly, 'why say you 'her first husband'. Only one she has had.'

Catherine echoed his laughter.

'Well, well,' she screamed, 'there's a funny mistake I made!'

Bangor added, 'Tut, tut, Catherine, too much imagination you always had.'

Reuben drank a mouthful of the wine. He did not like it. He looked about him with discomfort. He did not want to stay in this room: he felt himself alien to these high-spirited manifestations of his colleagues. Margaret Hopkins, a comely woman of forty with little lively blue eyes and a firmly corseted figure, came back carrying a bottle and began to fill the glasses. And he wished he was back again amid the silent fields and trees.

'Mrs Hopkins fach,' Morgans pronounced gravely, 'A masterpiece is this brew. Gifted by heaven you are.'

Isaiah leaned forward and whispered, 'A hundred and sixty bottles of it she made.'

Catherine uttered a little shriek. 'Ach, industrious as an old black she is. Go into business you ought to, Mr Isaiah Jenkins. A fortune you would make between you.'

Mrs Hopkins broke into loud laughter herself.

'Well,' she cried, 'I always said that in the wine trade Mr Isaiah ought to be. The looks and the talent for it he has.'

Catherine's shriek was a little louder. She kept on glancing from the widow to the minister. Her eyes were vivid and wicked, her nose seemed to twitch with perception. 'Coax him you should, Mrs Hopkins. A place for a business like that there is our way. Turn your gifts to account you ought to. Natty you two would look in a little shop. And more money is there in a business like that than in the ministry.'

'Ho,' the other answered, still laughing, 'foolish you talk. Only a servant to Mr Jenkins I am.'

'A very good servant, I can see,' Catherine added.

Mr Isaiah Jenkins opened his waistcoat, sighing deeply. The veins in his hairy neck were like thick worms, his mouth hung open as he breathed, as though in difficulty, through it. He was like a Silenus who dare not be drunk. Now and again his eyelids shot up and he would glance swiftly at Reuben.

Reuben pushed away his plate and passed his hand over his eyes.

'I am sleepy,' he said.

'Drink you the wine and it will wake you up,' boomed the minister. 'A tonic you need after your labour. Your sermon tonight was splendid. There's passion you put in your words! A holiday it was for me to listen to you. So drink up the wine and you will get back the strength you have spent.'

Reuben smiled. But he was faintly nauseated.

'I do not like its taste,' he said gently.

'Ho,' cried Mr Isaiah, 'rare is its flavour.'

'I have no tongue for wine, I think,' Reuben said.

Catherine's voice and face became excessively maternal. 'Quiet he wants, that's all,' she said softly. 'Ever since we left the Valley I have watched him and seen how it is with him after a service. Understand it I do. A terrible amount of strength he gives in the meetings.' She looked at Reuben

254

and smiled, drawing back her lips and showing her false teeth, wells of solicitude in her eyes. 'A great sacrifice he is making for Jesus Christ. How many at his age are occupied in giving their strength to enjoyable earthly matters!'

'Ah,' said Morgans piously, 'eternal glory shall be his. Is he not as a young saint already!'

'The Lord God knows of this work that is being done in Wales,' Mr Isaiah announced. 'His blessing is upon us.'

'Amen,' said Bangor Davies.

'Amen. Glory to his name,' said Morgans the Bakehouse.

'Amen. Jesus Christ be with us always,' Catherine sang out intensely.

Reuben stood up to go.

'Well,' Morgans said, 'perhaps Miss Catherine Pritchards will finish the little gathering with a suitable solo. One from the *Messiah* perhaps.'

But Mr Isaiah Jenkins held up his hand.

'Too late,' he said. 'Hear her the neighbours would. We must not disturb their rest.'

'And who knows what they might say!' Mrs Hopkins said as she gathered the glasses and bottles together. 'Especially Mrs Lloyd-Jones who lives this side.'

The four guests went upstairs. Each had a room. It was a large house for a minister: and it was furnished in a richly ponderous fashion. Reuben's bed was a huge four-poster affair hung with heavy curtains. The single candle in the room lit dimly the shadowy spaces.

He had just shut his door when a gentle tap sounded upon it. Then it was opened and Catherine Pritchards came in, carrying her candle.

255

'Neglected to put matches in my room has Mrs Hopkins,' she said. 'Give me a light and one or two matches, Reuben bach.'

Reuben took the candle and as he set it to his own, she looked about the room. There was a strange tension about her.

'Dear me,' she cried, not too loudly, 'there's a bed! Enough room for a dozen there is in there.'

'A good rest I get in it,' he said, handing the candlestick over.

She held the candle. Over its flame her face gleamed with a strange ardour. She murmured:

'Reuben, there's happy I am to be with you in these travels!'

'Yes?' he said. He had turned to the dressing-table, waiting for her to go.

But she moved a step towards him. She drew a deep and sighing breath and added, 'Yes, the happiest time I have ever had or will have – except for one thing.'

He looked at her curiously, but did not speak.

She went on, in a whisper, 'Except for one thing... But don't you look at me like that, Reuben. When you look at me like that I am ashamed. And there is no shame about this thing that is within me.' Her eyes seemed to sink into the hollows beneath her brow; her mouth was twisted into a smile that was both sad and fearful.

'What thing?' he asked at last, nervously taking up a hair-brush.

Her whispering voice was hardly articulate. He bent his head to hear it.

256

'I love you,' she said.

He drew back quickly; he was acutely embarrassed and averted his eyes.

'I love you,' she repeated, strength gathering in her voice. 'Ah, say how could I help it, when I am made as I am, loving the Scriptures and always taking delight in sacred things! No religious woman is there who could help loving you, if she was always with you, as I have been lately – '

He made a warning gesture and she stopped.

'Hush,' he said, 'do not say those things.' He moved away from her. 'Go back to your room, and forget what you have said. I shall too.' His voice was coldly gentle.

She stared at him. A pale fire burned in her blue eyes. She laid the candlestick on the table and followed him, caught his arm and pressed her cheek upon it, just below the shoulder. He stood quite still, afraid of this. They were guests in a minister's house. There must be no scene.

'I have been as Eve,' she began in a kind of rhythmic canticle, 'I have listened to the serpent in the garden of my dream, I have eaten of the blessed fruit, my soul has taken delight in its sin. I have longed for your flesh, my fair one, I have longed for the beauty of your shining flesh. David took pleasure in the wife of Uriah, and the rose of Sharon desired the body of her lover.' She lifted her head and stretched her throat. 'I sat down under his shadow with great delight, and his fruit was sweet to my taste – his head is as the most fine gold, his locks are bushy, and black as a raven – ' Here she lifted her hand languidly to his hair. He remained quite still, as though entranced. 'His cheeks are as a bed of spices, as sweet flowers: his lips like lilies, dropping sweet smelling myrrh.' Tremblingly she passed a finger over his lips. 'His hands are as gold rings set with the beryl: his belly is as bright ivory overlaid with sapphires – ' She turned and put her arms about him, pressing her breasts upon his chest.

He put his hands on her shoulders and with an iron strength thrust her away.

'You are mad,' he cried. 'Go from this room at once, or I will leave it.'

Her head drooped.

'Reuben,' she said, in a low agonized whisper, 'I love you, I love you. Take pleasure in me, or I die. Ah, I will give you such love... And none will know.'

He pointed to the door, his face so wrathful that she began to shudder. Slowly, her head bent, she moved towards it. Then she stopped, hesitated, came back to him and fell on her knees.

Tears choked her voice. She grovelled at his feet, she shuddered and writhed, suppressing the cries that rose to her lips. He took hold of her and lifted her. Her face was ugly in its grimace of weeping. He muttered:

'Be quiet now and we will forget it all.'

Her head dropped. She tried to speak and failed. Finally she drew herself from his grasp and, almost tottering, took her candle from the table, and without another glance, went out.

He lay in bed, shocked and bewildered. Then, as he thought of Catherine, he saw how since he had first come into contact with her, she had been subtly casting the net of her piety upon him. Time after time she had tried to force herself into the inner fastnesses of his soul – by confession and avowals of solicitude – maternal and sisterly. He had always felt that within her was a fierce jet of passionate life that longed for some fulfilment. And when she had craved to accompany him and the others on their travels, he thought of her as a woman who had found disappointment in her existence and longed to use that passionate strength of hers in service for Jesus Christ.

She had been the aesthetic relief in the evangelistic programme. Her repertoire consisted of those arias and hymns from the sacred cantatas that the Welsh people so love. He had wished she would dress in a more subdued style – her wearing of purple, yellow and red garments did not seem suitable to their solemn task of kindling God's light in Wales. But she had been useful, often filling a pause in the conversion meetings by suddenly rising into impassioned song: and her voice was thick with a rich and rousing influence that certainly affected the people – particularly, it seemed, the men.

He turned restlessly in the bed. What was to be done with her! He dreaded meeting her in the morning. He was ashamed for her. Strange, how strange the workings of the mind. He knew that she had sincere worship of God in her soul, and a love for the beauty of the Scriptures. Then he remembered something Philip had said – 'In some natures the impulse of religious worship is mingled inextricably with the sexual impulse – especially in women. The desire to yield oneself to the ecstatic power of God is but a sublimation of the desire of the flesh to achieve

259

consummation in the flesh of another who stirs our worship.' He had not paid much heed to Philip's words then, but now they came back into the dark bewilderment of his mind. And again, 'The wilder that impulse of worship becomes, the more violently it is reflected in that baser part of us which is, alas, the fundamental and necessary reason for our existence. Thus, the atmosphere of a revival meeting is electric with those lovely tremblings of the flesh that intense love or worship so naturally provokes – '

Of course, Philip's mind was hopeless because of his tragical life and in his way he was as bigoted as any old-fashioned Methodist minister. But nevertheless, his words persisted in Reuben's mind – came back, indeed, with a mocking insistence – and he turned over and over in the bed, thinking of them.

He had noticed himself, amongst the converts, expressions on their faces that repelled him – sometimes, if the convert was of a repulsive appearance, sending an active wave of nausea through his stomach. And he had witnessed peculiar rapt states of the mind during which the convert uttered strange sighs of gratification and pleasure that were almost revolting.

But what of that! The flesh is deceitful and thick with snares; and the flesh is also weak and smitten with decay. But within it is the enduring spark of the soul, that in the withering husk of the shell rises in loosened splendour to the immortal Flame from whence it came. To that spark he must reach, that spark he must fan with the power of his words. So that from it the rare glow of peace would emanate – the Peace of God.

At last he slept. But in the light of the dawn his countenance was troubled.

CHAPTER II

In September they worked through Cardiganshire and into mid-Wales; and by this time the four had acquired a celebrity that assured an absolute victory in any place they chose to honour. Often a town, impatient for their visit and fired by the displays of zeal reported in the newspapers, organised prior campaigns for the Lord, so that by the time the four arrived they had the gratifying pleasure of beholding a righteous community prepared and adorned with grace, like the wise virgins whose lamps were so bright and shining for the bridegroom.

It was decreed that there should be little rain in September, so many open-air meetings were held – in field and meadow, on common and village green. It was observed, however, by Morgans the Bakehouse, that open-air meetings were not so successful in conversions as those held under a roof. Some atmosphere, it seemed to him, was

262

missing in the open air. The people sang and the prayers were as numerous, but their vitality, instead of remaining over their heads, as in a building, was dispersed to the clouds. That vitality was too valuable to lose – Morgans knew its importance in securing converts – so he began to look upon the open-air gatherings with disfavour. Baptisms were the only really satisfactory open-air performances.

He spoke to Reuben about it: 'Do you notice, Reuben, that people are staider in the meetings we hold in the open?'

'Yes, cooler they are,' Reuben agreed, shutting an old edition of *The Pilgrim's Progress* that he had picked up in his travels. They were sitting in the garden of a minister's house.

'Peculiar it is. Hang back do the converts.'

'I think,' Reuben said, 'I like the open-air meetings. An awful atmosphere there is sometimes in a chapel that is crowded too much. Unhealthy to the mind and the body it seems to me. But the atmosphere over a meeting in the open is pure and calm, and the people keep saner.'

Morgans stroked his nose uneasily.

'Critical you are getting, Reuben bach, and a dangerous habit to get into that is. No good will it do such as you.'

'Why?'

Morgans sighed and shook his head dismally. 'A bag of strange contents is a human being. Odd things lie in him, like mysterious shaped parcels. Better it is not to examine these parcels.'

Reuben was silent. Then he said slowly: 'I have had a suspicion, sometimes when we have been at the meetings, that the people attend as they would at a circus where they'll be able to perform themselves.'

Morgans held up his hand in horror.

'Do not think things like that! If you will go on thinking in that manner your inspiration will surely leave you. *Ach y fi*, don't you say that the people are hypocrites and come to religous meetings to while away an evening, like the old English do.'

'Oh,' Reuben agreed, knitting his brows, 'I don't doubt now that they believe what they say in our meetings. But when they stand up and say they have been converted, how much does it really mean?'

'They lead fresh lives! Do not those who were drunkards give up the drink and those who smoked cast away their dirty old pipes. And think you of that youth who came to you and privately confessed of his secret weakness, that the Lord cured afterwards!'

'They might be cured of little failings of the flesh, they might not drink and smoke any more, perhaps; but trivial seem those things to me. I want to be sure that their lives have taken on a new glory and all the suffering of their souls is destroyed.' He stopped and his brow became dark. Had the suffering in his own soul been destroyed? For all his ecstatic visions and raptures, his certainty of the existence of a Being beyond terrestrial life, had the brooding ache of desolation and loneliness gone from him? Ah, more than ever his soul was lonely and desolate within him. Still he strained in anguish towards an imperishable joy that still was as far away.

'Forever the people will fail the Lord,' said Morgans, with sudden gloom. 'Impossible it is to make earthly flesh shine with the purity of even the worst angel in Heaven.'

Reuben dropped *The Pilgrim's Progress* and stood up, young and despairing anger on his face. 'Then why are we spending our time at this task! "Forever the people will fail the Lord." True that is. I have seen it. I have looked for a wonderful thing in the souls of the people. I have looked and seen only greed. Greed of the soul for pleasure in the flesh. They cry "I have been saved", and through them goes a thrill as though they possessed the whole of Heaven for themselves. The soul sticks fast in the flesh. A gluttonous pleasure I see upon the faces of the converted.' He stared obsessively at Morgans, and went on, 'I can't understand. I am driven to the people and I want to take their blood into my veins. But there is no answer in them when I look for the beautiful thing I seek. Pieces of heavy dough they seem to me then.'

'Ah,' Morgans the Bakehouse exclaimed smartly, 'there it is your labour comes in. The heat to make that dough into crisp and well-risen bread you must be. Patience, patience, Reuben. Too much you expect of poor human beings.'

Reuben sat down again. He said in a slow, tranced voice:

'There is an evil heritage in man. It comes out of the earth into his flesh: it is in the darkness of the womb. That it is which urges him to slay and lust and maim, so that he is as the snake, the leopard, the wildcat, the sharp, the swine. Deep, deep in man is that heritage, and its shadow is upon his mind continually. Is it within the power of a man to root out this thing? Can a man forget the earth that is his flesh?'

Morgans ran his hand nervously through his beard, glancing at Reuben. Was the boy going crazy? From his long contact with religion he knew the effect of it on some young minds – Reuben had thrown back his head and was gazing into the sky. Slowly, in his tranced and mystic intonation, he continued:

'A kingdom is in my mind. There live creatures whose souls are white with endless beauty, whose bodies are purged of the sins of hate and greed. Their faces are not as our faces, for they live in ages which are yet to come. They have risen out of the deceit and vanity of our darkness, as sometimes a perfect flower rises from a heap of stale dung. There, in clear golden light I see them, and their language is a rich music, their movements proud and solemn with beauty.'

Morgans listened as though he was occupied in judging a poem at an eisteddfod, moving his head up and down slowly, and somewhat doubtfully –

'Splendid is your talk, Reuben bach. The habit of the young it is, to dream like that. But profitless such dreams are. The world went a wrong way somewhere and wandered down a dark lane and got lost. Since then, trying to make the best of a bad job we've been. Never shall we see the state you dream of.'

Reuben's face, abstracted in thought, was tender and sad. His hands clasped his knee as he sat, bending a little forward, his firm body relaxed. He seemed to be waiting, lonely and recoiled into the sad places of his soul, vaguely waiting for some realization that would fill him with a naked joy. Morgans' old and worn eyes watched him with an austere scrutiny, and presently he said:

'Reuben bach, great it is to devote one's whole soul to

spreading Christ's Word. But a man is not made only for that, not even one who has it within him to become a great saint. Sincere I am, and out of deep regard I say this. The blood in your veins is not cold and your body is rich with life. One to share that richness you should find. Then quiet and contented your heart would become, and out of your contentment a clear vision would flow!'

Reuben got up, his face averted from Morgans. The old man's words seemed like the soft touching of cool fingers upon the tissue of his hot soul. He walked a yard or two away and gazed nervously at a sunflower whose vigorous stem had climbed carelessly and victoriously from the tangled and withering bushes about it.

'I have thought,' he said, 'that more I could do by being alone and quite free – '

'Alone!' Morgans repeated slowly. 'A terrible thing that is. Especially when you are old.' He paused, thinking of his own state. A shrewish and quick-tongued woman was Mrs Morgans, but she possessed him as she did one of her much-bewailed and precious ailments, and though their mutual esteem was bright with the acid of complete understanding, life could not be imagined without either of them. 'No, not alone must you be, Reuben. Listen you to me and take upon yourself the natural pleasure of man.'

Reuben muttered, 'There is no one now – '

And in his mind, white-gold and ironic, the face of Eirwen gleamed, its mouth parted a little in a carnal smile. Yet, he should not regret *her*. A clear spiritual mission would certainly not flow from marriage with *her*, he thought, a dim grimace of laughter on his face. He shook his head and

267

added, 'I want to work out this business we are occupied with now, first. Then I will think of marriage.'

Morgans exclaimed. 'Work out this business first! Mean you that you might leave the Faith?'

'I don't know,' Reuben said quickly, 'but there is something within me that disturbs me. It is like a conflict. Sometimes I feel that I would use all my blood and strength in labour for that Faith you call Christ's Word. Then at other times my heart is black with a miserable hatred.'

'Your faith is not abiding!' Morgans cried in anxious sorrow. 'Ah, how is it you are going astray like this? As I have said, too much you demand of poor human flesh. Thick with blemishes we are, I know, but those blemishes fade in the light of eternity and go back into the dust with the flesh, while the white wings of the pure soul rise, no dirt upon them.' He raised his hand and his voice became sing-song. 'Yea,the flesh is evil with tares and poisons, and peculiar can its antics be. But can you not find it within you to smile at those antics and fix your eyes upon the immortal soul?'

Reuben said uncertainly, 'Often I have laughed at them. I have laughed and then my laughter has turned to contempt. Think you of that woman in Aberystwyth who wouldn't pay her rent – ' The woman, one of the most violently raucous of the converted, had obtained a vision in which God had told her that she was not to pay rent for her house, because landlords were wicked thieves. Acting upon that, she locked her door upon the landlord when he called one morning. His continued knocking brought her to the window above and she told him with fury of God's declaration. The earth was the Lord's and the fullness thereof. The landlord's blasphemous abuse – he was of the unsaved – angered her, and she had quickly emptied upon him a pail of slops. – 'Am I to laugh at that woman or despise her?'

'Exceptional is her case,' said Morgans, 'I have said before that strange-minded persons come to our meetings and behave foolishly – '

'I cannot always laugh at them,' Reuben cried with passion. 'For in laughing at them we ignore them.' He paused and then added slowly, 'And in despising them we lay up for ourselves a burden of cruel hatred.'

Morgans shook his head with doleful despair.

'Ach,' he muttered, 'I can see that within yourself you must fight out this thing. Tonight I will pray for a long time that your faith will endure. No more can I do, it seems.' He looked sadly at Reuben. 'But for our sakes, keep you with us. The people look to you for inspiration, and a symbol of the glory of Wales you have become.'

Reuben thought of the old man. Did his soul really burn with spiritual love for the people and with desire to exalt them to greater consciousness of Christ's teaching? Or was he one of those Welsh fanatics obsessed with a lust for religious notoriety, who, lacking the lawful power of the ordained ministers, strive to gratify their lust by performing any rhetorical tasks connected with the chapels? He had worked with flourishing zeal since they had started on the tour, and the delight he experienced in standing on the various platforms – and in the sacred pulpits – was obvious and artless; and Reuben had seen his nostrils quivering with excitement when he read the newspaper reports of their success. And Morgans' care and daily anxious scrutiny made Reuben feel that he was not unlike an eccentric star performer in a play, or a temperamental opera singer, who needs constant nursing to the right mood... Yes, it was in the actual performances of their religious power that Morgans took pleasure. Then his gratification was deep and satisfying.

All that morning Reuben meditated, his brows drawn and a dark glisten in his eyes. Yet out of his brooding a certain sombre inspiration sprang, thoughts of wild poetry and words that glowed like rubies, so that he was impatient for the evening meeting and he longed to be again amid the people – the people that he had loved with such consuming desire.

He wandered about the garden and the house in preoccupied silence, his mood respected by the others, especially his host, a bachelor minister who looked at him with a kind of mournful admiration.

He happened to go into the study, wondering if he could find an interesting book. Catherine Pritchards was there, peering round the shelves, a look of heavy boredom on her face. Seeing Reuben, she immediately turned away, as though in shame.

Lately they had treated each other with careful consideration – not a word had since been mentioned concerning her confession of amorous inclinations that night. But Reuben was often aware of her fixed gaze upon him, and sometimes when their eyes met, her features would contract and then harden into immobility. And she seemed now to put even more power into her singing; when she stood, queenly and almost menacing, at the edge of a platform and let her voice issue like a scorching flame from the volcanic well of her taut bosom, one could feel the community gathered beneath tremble, like the earth shaking beneath an elemental storm in the heavens... Morgans said that she had become very useful. And the musical conductor, Bangor Davies, observed admiringly that she ought to be on the stage, singing great operas. But in his heart Reuben disliked her vehement singing; and at times he thought he detected beneath it a terrible and unworthy force, a savagery.

'I want a book – ' he said tentatively.

'Looking for one I am too,' she said. 'But a dry collection is in this room; only history and old Welsh poetry, it seems.'

'Welsh poetry! That will suit me.' He went to the shelves.

'Do *you* write poetry?' she asked, her voice subdued.

'No. I should like to, but I have not the talent.'

She said, 'When I was a young girl I used to try to write hymns.'

He turned to her with interest. 'Did you! Perhaps if you have still got them, you will let me see them?'

Her lip quivered. She would not look at him, and in the silence that followed she seemed to be struggling with acute emotions. He turned away hastily, but after a moment or two her voice came, subdued and heavy:

'No, I have not got them now. In a little note-book I had them all, and I gave it to that minister – you remember I told you – who was the father of my child – ' Her voice lifted itself from its subdued murmuring like a heavy snake lifting itself to strike. 'He used to say that not trashy were they, like a lot of hymns in the hymn-books. I remember, wrote a lot of them I did after – ' her voice became almost brutal – 'after he had taken me – '

Reuben stood gazing at her in pained surprise. Then quickly he looked away again: her face seemed to numb him. Uneasily he made a step towards the door. But her voice came writhing towards him:

'I used to write them in those nights when we could not be together. Ah, Reuben, then I was happy. No sin did there seem in the thing I did. His was the sin, for when he had taken his pleasure, he passed on. He promised me marriage, and by night I used to steal out of my home and go to him. But it was he, it was he who was the real sinner. Say it was he was the sinner, Reuben Daniels!' She went to him and clutched his arm, stared madly into his face. 'For this thing is upon my mind. Well you might think, why is it I say these things to you. But they are in me like a burden, and I must speak of them to you, for then the burden will not be heavy. Say it was he was the real sinner!'

He made no movement, and she continued to cling to his arm with a frenzied clutch that seemed to burn to his bone. To calm her, he said quietly, 'You must not ask me such a question, Catherine. Why do you worry about something that is past and dead! Why do you rake up this old thing now. People have forgotten it and they are not interested in it any more.'

'People!' she repeated with venom. 'Know too well I do that they do not forget. They remember, in the Valley.'

He shook his head.

'Exaggerate you do,' he said in an attempt to soothe her,

and gently moving his arm away. 'Silly you are to brood on these things.'

She dropped into a chair, and as he hastily looked over the shelves again, watched him intently. Upon her face now there was a look of appeasement, and her brow, for the moment, was clear. But she watched Reuben with eyes that were still disordered...

Selecting a book of poetry, he turned to the door. 'You are better now?' he asked awkwardly, glancing at her.

She smiled, a cold and painful smile, and looked at him humbly. 'You make me want to confess all that is bad in me,' she whispered.

He opened the door. 'Catherine,' he urged, 'you must control yourself.'

But if he had gone back he would have seen her crouched on the floor, her shoulders writhing and her head buried in a cushion, from which came strange broken sounds that would not be suppressed...

He went up hurriedly to his bedroom and for some time stood gazing out of the window. And his heart was sick.

What was this woman who continually tried to waylay his soul? His body was fearful of her and shrank in a kind of active terror when her body came near. And he was aware, too, of her soul straining for contact with his. It filled him with nausea.

Ah, how mysterious was the human being! Must he accept the evil, bow his head, close his eyes to that dark shadow upon man? His own words came back to him despairingly. 'There is an evil heritage in man. It comes up out of the earth into his flesh: it is in the darkness of the womb. That it is which urges him to cruelty and lust and gluttony – '

He threw himself on the bed and opened the book of Welsh verse: and he forced himself to read of flowers and winds and birds and fair women, until he was called to tea.

He was glad when it was time to go to the meeting. He knew that in the big Congregational chapel he would forget his own woes for a time.

And that evening his address was mighty. He appealed to that force which is in man like the image of God to arise and scatter those other forces that are the creatures of Satan. The evil forces in man were numerous, but like a great white column of light God's strength should endure above them all. He used thunderous words and soon the people felt themselves lifted to the stature of mighty and divine beings. Ah, yes, they would conquer, like angelic soldiers, those sinister beings of the world who represented its evil, they would drive them away with the thongs of their divine strength, or slay them utterly with their gleaming swords. Their eyes became bright in the lust for this heavenly battle.

The chapel was crowded to the doors and again converts swarmed everywhere, crying their repentance, needs, and woes. Catherine Pritchards sang again and again: at every opportunity she whispered to the organist the most rousing items from her repertoire and sang them with a conquering power, standing like a Boadicea in the pulpit.

Long before the meeting ended, Reuben was utterly wearied of this clamorous worship. But he persisted in faithful labour to the end, giving wonderful prayers in alternation with Catherine's songs. Morgans received converts with a fervour that never diminished, and Bangor Davies, bristling with energy, led the congregation in singing, almost unaware of his sweat-dripping face.

When finally Reuben crawled into bed he was limp with exhaustion. He had been too tired to go for his lonely after-meeting walk. Morgans, a little worn out too, but still proudly exulting, said:

'Ah, properly roused they were. Quite wild they became. Massacred tonight were all the forces of evil in this town.' He glanced with a smile at Reuben, who was trudging along silently.

'Let us hope they will not rise again,' Catherine observed in a strangely bitter tone.

'Yes,' Morgans sighed with surpassing pessimism, 'very apt they are to rise in triumph again.'

They were all suffering from physical and mental exhaustion. Each had given of his psychic strength to the last, and each crawled into bed and was soon in deep slumber. None could say the four did not earn their fame.

The next morning Reuben had a letter from Martha:

'DEAR REUBEN, well how are you now and I hope that all the meetings are not breaking you up, as it has been so hot and I have read in the newspapers of the crowds you are having and what good is being done. I have been to the meetings here but since you are gone something missing there is, so I didn't go last Sunday but stayed home and your father read one chapter out loud and I read another. From Saint Mark. Your father's sight is going bad though and he grumbles if I tell him to get new spectacles. Very stiff necked in some things he is. He wants me to go with him to his chapel but I will not go because Mr Hughes-Williams said one or two things about me in the past. Your father behaves strange sometimes and has gone into a habit of talking to himself, but I can't hear what he is saying. We are thinking of the time when you are coming back. Eirwen is having a bad time, her husband has run away now with over 200 pounds belonging to his father, the talk of the place it is. I met her yesterday, she told me she doesn't care though she looks very upset and she asked me a lot about you. A funny girl she is. What will you do now I asked her, serve in the bar I suppose, but she said no, she would teach the piano to children and earn enough for food that way, as she doesn't pay rent of course on that little cottage her rascal of a husband bought for her. What a ruffian he is, though good looking and that it is what deceived her. I expect she is sorry she would not wait for you now, though I don't think she is the sort of woman you ought to marry. Your father and myself have been thinking have you met anyone on your travels, all the ministers' houses you have been staying at, surely some of them have nice daughters. Fine it would be if you married into a minister's family, and some of them are very rich, but there, I know you don't think of things like that...'

Martha wrote ten pages in her large sprawling writing and he read every word with the closest attention. He went out into the garden and read the letter again, lingering over the passages devoted to Eirwen.

Poor Eirwen, he thought, she did not deserve such treatment. And yet, he knew that she would look upon this

276

disaster of her married life with an amused and philosophic contempt. She would await the next thing that life brought her, languid and indifferent, yet eager for its experience when it came.

And then he became aware that his heart was glad within him.

CHAPTER III

The rain and dismal chilliness of October did not affect the progress of the revival. Town and village in mid-Wales flared up faithfully into rapture during the stay of the new evangelist; the next town was not to be outdone by the last, and each strained to surpass in piety those already visited.

Morgans the Bakehouse, with a gentle sadness, appealed to Reuben to forget his gloomy criticism of the people's behaviour in the meetings, saying that he no longer belonged to himself but, in a glorious martyrdom, to a noble Cause. For he saw that Reuben's brow was becoming darker and the style of his sermons stern and sombre.

Yet, he saw also that those sermons were quite as successful as the others – the poetic and psalm-like orations Reuben delivered with such effective artistry. The congregations seemed to enjoy his frequent denunciations of those elements in human nature that now seemed to obsess him – meanness, avarice, gluttony, the lust for possessions, and other lusts. But Morgans feared the ultimate consequence of this obsession in Reuben.

Then a painful accident occurred one evening in a town they were to leave the next morning. As it was the last meeting, a big crowd had stormed the doors of the chapel, which, as everybody knew, would hold but a third of the determined mob. A girl of ten, who was accompanied by her already converted mother, was trampled to death a second after the doors were opened. She died silently, but the shrill screams of the mother filled the air with piercing lamentations. Reuben heard her as he sat with the officials of the chapel in the vestry at the back, and a few minutes later he was told of the tragedy. His face became white and fearful and, watched by the dismayed Morgans, he asked to be taken to the mother.

When he stood in the clean and poor cottage of that woman, listening in dread to her cries and gazing numbly at the muddy little corpse lying upon a bed, his heart beat in great hammer strokes of terror within his icy flesh. Ah, the young girl could not be dead. It was too terrible a thing to happen. She must not go forth from the earth in cruelty like this.

'Holding my hand she was,' sobbed the mother, 'holding my hand, and then I lost her. Then I saw her hat under their feet – ' She glared round the whispering people huddled about the room. 'When is the doctor coming! Oh, run, people, and fetch him quickly.' Her voice was frantic with fear and hope: and yet her heart knew the child was dead.

Reuben shrank back as the doctor entered: and, his head

bowed, went back with unconscious steps to the chapel. Morgans, troubled and silent, was waiting for him outside. The people were still being turned away in droves from the doors, and they crowded about the pavement discussing the tragedy.

But within the chapel the mob sang a hymn, waiting for the service to begin: they crowded each pew and stood about the aisles and at the back – a packed mass of people congratulating themselves on their luck in getting into the chapel at all.

'I cannot speak to them tonight,' Reuben muttered to Morgans, in the vestry.

Morgans took his arm and peered sorrowfully into his eyes. 'You must, Reuben bach. No preparation has been made for anybody else to speak, and no one can depend on his inspiration like you. Think how the people will be disappointed! The last meeting here, and the finishing touch to your labour in the town. Owe a sermon to these people you do, for converts have flocked to us in big numbers and the collections have been heavy.'

Reuben cried in sudden wrath: 'Why has that child been killed!'

'Reuben, Reuben, an accident. A grievous accident, but every day such accidents happen – ' Morgans tugged at his beard in distress. The people were singing with loud patience. 'Come, they wait for you.'

'If we hadn't come to this town, that child would be living,' cried Reuben. 'Oh, don't ask me to go into that pulpit. I want to go to the mother of that girl and tell her how sorry I am.'

'Afterwards!' Morgans began to be stern. 'Your duty you must do here now.' He drew Reuben to the door leading to the chapel.

Reuben submitted to the old man's desperate entreaties and he climbed the pulpit as the hymn was finishing in a great hosanna. As usual, his appearance caused the sea of faces to tilt upwards in a pale heavy mass of staring flesh.

He sat in the square-cushioned seat at the back of the pulpit, and while Morgans spoke, watched from beneath lowered lids those faces beneath him.

And a cold flash of loathing went through him. The unsubdued pleasure on those faces shone as a film of bright grease upon their flesh. Old, terribly old in the baser living of the flesh, were some of the faces, and some were as though moulded in wax, a fixed bright grimace upon them, and some were sickly in adolescent rawness, and some stared up in crafty and primitive crudity. Yet all the faces shone in expectant pleasure. They knew how later they would be in the midst of a stirring performance of the emotions: and all would feel God within them.

No stern grief was visible, no head bowed in shame because of the life that had been trampled out by their savage feet. But they sighed with a kind of thick oily pleasure as Morgans began to drop mellifluous phrases in a Biblical manner.

'Big Jesus Christ, I can see you here with us,' a woman cried out impatiently in Welsh. Morgans always spoke too long.

Another followed: 'I see his head crowned with thorns over the pulpit. Welcome, Jesus Christ.'

They were getting impatient to loosen their cries in a hymn.

Reuben, still and deathly, gazed at them from his mask-like face. But his heart wailed in anguish. Why was he there, in this pulpit, what had driven him there, to stand like a figure on the stage of a peep-show, about to perform for the gratification of a vulgar mob who would cry out their approbation if he performed well enough! A creature of mechanical devices – angelic gestures of 'Come to me, oh, ye weary' invitation, a voice issuing forth with inexplicable words from the formations of his despised body, the lightning glare of a divine disorder flashing through his glassy eyes... And he felt that the exalted emotion which sent such a flow of burning words to his lips would shrink, crumble, and fall if he dared stand in the front of the pulpit tonight. He would see himself as a mechanical doll, lifting one arm in suitable gesture, then the other, while, forcing himself to go on, his voice sang out brokenly until the glittering machine in him ran down. And all the time the rapt staring faces before him would exude a sweat of gratified pleasure and their bodies would pant and their breasts heave as that pleasure sank into their very bowels.

A sick ache surged through him. To be away and seek some lonely and silent hollow hidden amid high mountains. To be away and fall into a cool sleep, to awaken in clear air and solitude, his mind cleansed into primary enchantment again. To live in the morning solitudes of the world, undisturbed of man.

Morgans was sitting down, glory still in his faded eyes.

Then Bangor Davies got up to announce and lead the hymn. Reuben watched him strut importantly to the rostrum, heard the whining notes of the old organ begin a familiar tune that suddenly seemed to him maddening and stale. He bent over to Morgans.

'I am going,' he whispered. 'Tell them I am ill.'

And immediately he got up and went quickly into the vestry. Hurrying, for he wanted to escape Morgans' troubled and mournful eyes, he went out of the vestry into the side-street and turned towards the country beyond the town.

A dull ochre stain drifted across the west, and upon the isolated country a pale brownish light was deepening into blue, blurring the trees and the meadows and revealing the virgin and sterile glitter of Venus. Reuben, looking back almost furtively now and again, went on into the deserted country, stumbling on, only aware of a desire to be alone in some secluded tree-shaded silence.

But his heart cowered in dark misery; beneath the keen instinct of this flight a dim emotion of fear and shame gathered. He had abandoned his faithful disciples because of these miserable and futile woes that he had not the strength to cast out of him, he had fled from his moral responsibilities, like some wretched coward, thinking only of his own disordered dreams. – He stopped for a moment or two, biting his knuckles, a faint moan escaping his lips. Then, with an almost angry toss of his head, he went on.

He went on over the silky grass, towards the trees.

He came to a little vale where the low sound of a stream murmured amid the silence of the thick trees. And he stood and listened, his head stretched forward, as though he searched for some shy and mocking lover fleeing through the blue gloom.

And the desire to identify himself in closer rapture with the primordial nature about him came to him again. He came to a place where the soft stream widened into a pool fringed by leaning great trees, and with quick eager haste he cast off his clothes, smiling vaguely in delight.

He crept into the pool and, gently immersing himself, lay down on the fine gravel of its bed. And the water crept over him like the smooth embraces of a quiet lover, passing softly and caressively over his relaxed thighs, his belly, his throbbing breast, his vaguely smiling face. The softly flowing water cooled the heat of his flesh, passed in chastity over his supple body, lay upon his eyelids like the touch of delicate lips.

But it was not enough. The thick jet of desire sprang unappeased within the inner walls of his being. He got out of the water and shook himself like an animal, crawled up among the trees, lifting himself on their outstretched branches, and standing upon the bank at last, he flung his arms about the trunk of an elm tree and pressed his naked flesh against it. The rough bark seemed to yield into soft and sleek tissue against his body. He drew away from the elm and wandered into the grey-blue gloom. Then he came to a sapling, a young silver-birch, rising graceful and fragile amid the complete vigour of the other trees. A slim branch drifted down a little. And he caught it in his mouth and fixed his teeth into the wood.

With a low and baffled sound he loosened the branch, drew away his mouth, bitter with the strange taste of the wood; then, in a sudden access of keener passion, again fastened his teeth deep into the slim branch.

He sank to the ground, his teeth deeper in the wood, tearing the branch from the young trunk, until at last it was broken away from the tree and he lay panting on the earth.

He lay there, the tide of his blood as though receded forever into the dark peace of his heart, his body become cold, the torn branch, that he no longer clasped, lying discarded upon him. One arm was flung across his eyes and his lips were drawn back sensually from his strong gleaming teeth.

Then later he entered the pool again, shuddering in its cold, and after immersing himself fully, lay on the bank until he was dry. Afterwards he put on his clothes.

Tall, refreshed, straight, and gleaming, he began to walk back to the town. His mind was clear and chastened, his body relaxed and cool. The knowledge of his flight from the meeting suddenly rushed back on him, but he was neither alarmed nor ashamed now.

Only, he thought then of that young mother filling the air with her terrible cries as her child lay trampled beneath the savage feet of the obsessed mob... And a black fury rushed over him like annihilation and as quickly ebbed away, leaving his mind hard and bitter, his heart heavy with grief for the young mother.

He got to the little house, one of the long cemented row, drab and monotonous, and knocked at the door. It was opened by an old woman, who peered at him mistrustfully, sucking in her underlip.

'Can I come in?' he asked gently.

She shook her head. Then she burst forth in a cracked screech, 'How many more! Ach, how many more want to push their noses in here. Hundreds of people coming to the house, then when I have sent them away, beginning again it is. What do you want? No one can see the corpse – '

'I have come to see the little girl's mother,' he said painfully. 'I am Reuben Daniels – '

'Mam, Mam,' a voice called from within, 'let you Mr Daniels in.'

The old woman made an obsequious obeisance, her face dropping in surprised alarm.

'Dear me, dear me,' she quavered, opening the door wide, 'a blind old cow I am behaving. Come you in, Mr Daniels, and do you excuse me.'

In the living-room the young mother sat beside the fire, her face vacant, her hands clasped limply on her lap. She gazed round when Reuben entered. There was another young woman in the room, who obscured her shrinking body in a dark corner, covering her face with her hand. A cheap oil-lamp gave a wan light. And the young mother sat exhausted and vacant, lifting her heavy eyes dispassionately to Reuben, as he took the chair the old woman brought forward.

And he scarcely knew what to say to this woman who stared at him from her numbed soul, who seemed to be altogether beyond the hearing of those trite words of sorrow that left his lips.

'No fault of yours is it,' she whispered at last. She was talking to the religious Reuben Daniels, the great evangelist, and she added with a false strength: 'And with Jesus Christ is my daughter now. In his bosom she sleeps – ' But the falsity of her voice could not continue and suddenly her face contracted into tearless sobs. 'What will my husband say when he knows?' she wailed. 'What will he say when he knows that little Olwen is dead!'

'Where is he then?' Reuben asked the old woman.

She flung up her hands.

'Ach, on the booze he has been for two days now and went away this morning with his mate.'

Her daughter cried out in sudden heat, 'Don't you believe her, Mr Daniels. Only a little rest my husband is taking. Not a drunkard he is.' Then her voice sank to a moan again. 'Worshipped his little Olwen he did. Oh, what shall he say when he comes back!'

And Reuben gazed round the room with a vague desolation in his soul. He became acutely aware of the terrible irrevocability of death, the power that utterly destroys, the disaster that slays in a blind and cruel force, moving over the fair earth like a searing blight, destroying into oblivion one who a moment before lived as though forever in our consciousness. He gazed helplessly at the young mother. Death, death, death. He saw as in a vision the figure of the little girl withering into a heap of dust that the wind blew carelessly away. What need to lament her? Useless and vain were lamentations for that little heap of blown dust.

'Say a prayer for her – ' the young mother asked, gazing at him stonily. 'Perhaps you will say a little prayer for my Olwen?'

And then he wanted to cry despairingly, 'Do you think *my* prayer will be of any use! Why do you ask me to pray?

If I prayed all night and used every sacred word in the language, it will not alter the fact of your Olwen's death, it would not bring a shred of lasting comfort to your mourning soul. Deceit, vanity and deceit. Your child is dead, and if I prayed it would be only for *you*, prayer for the strength that would force memory of your child out of your mind.'

But he looked at her in silence for a while, got up, still staring at her with his eyes of despair, and took her cold hands.

'Do not ask me to pray,' he muttered. 'Not now. When I am alone I will pray for *you* – ' He looked at her quietly for a moment or two. 'What can I say to you! I cannot find any words that will tell you of my sorrow. The death of your little girl will be always in my soul. If I said to you "Forget her" you will think of me as a heartless fool, but in forgetting is the only comfort, it seems to me. So do not ask me to pray for her. My words now would be empty.'

He went out. And he was glad to be out of that house again. His steps faltered as he went down the street. It seemed to him that sheaths of worn and stale deceits were falling from his soul, dank and decrepit cerements falling from the awakening consciousness of his soul.

But his feet dragged and faltered as he went towards the house where he was staying, his mind seemed to be tottering on the edge of darkness. And his stomach was craving for food.

He could not get a reply at the house. So they had not returned from the meeting, though it was half-past ten. He thought ironically that the meeting must be lasting very well without him – while there was a crowd, plenty of hymn-singing and praying, it was not likely that the people would go home because of the absence of that star-phenomenon of Welsh youth, Reuben Daniels. He went to the back of the house and entered through an unlocked door.

And he drank two tumblers of milk and diminished a large fruit-cake and a tin of biscuits with almost mindless enjoyment. Then he went up to his bedroom, taking with him a volume from the bookcase – Landor's *Pericles and Aspasia*, which he had selected at random.

Weary but strangely contented, he lay in the bed and by the light of the candle turned over the pages of the book, reading here and there carelessly, waiting for the arrival of Morgans and the others.

He lingered over one or two passages:

'*Tears, O Aspasia, do not dwell long upon the cheeks of youth. Rain drops easily from the bud, rests on the bosom of the maturer flower, and breaks down that one only which hath lived its day.*

'*Weep, and perform the offices of friendship. The season of life, leading you by the hand, will not permit you to linger at the tomb of the departed; and Xeniades, when your tear first fell upon it, entered into the number of the blessed.*'

He repeated :

'The season of life, leading you by the hand, will not permit you to linger at the tomb of the departed – '

Ah, he had stayed too long amid the tombs of life, in this stale and arid churchyard of religion, his young and vital body occupied in the fanatical obsessions of a death-worshipping people. There was something far greater in life than this miserable wailing before God, who suddenly appeared before him as an image of Death, an emaciated visage wasted into a skull. There was a glory flung over the highways of the world and over the great cities and across the mighty oceans that he knew not; there was a final flame of pure life in the core of the world that he had not pierced to yet.

He heard them come in downstairs. And he lay in a bright tranquillity, waiting for Morgans, who he knew would come up immediately.

Morgans the Bakehouse did. He knocked at the door and entered uncertainly. He did not know whether to denounce Reuben or use forbearance and overlook these temperamental outbursts in the young man. He gazed for a moment at the uplifted face of Reuben.

His natural wisdom prevailed and he asked gently, 'How are you now, dear Reuben?'

'Very well,' Reuben said promptly. 'How did the meeting go?'

Morgans shook his head.

'Hard work it was to beat them up to the usual fire. Tonight I was made aware how precious you are and how the people look to you in adoration. I made the sermon, but' – he averted his face in sad resignation – 'you know how it is when I speak. Glorious very often are my words, but if I speak too long the people begin to behave mockingly – not like you can I put beauty into my voice.'

'But the meeting went well though?' Reuben insisted.

'Many converts there were,' Morgans admitted unwillingly. 'Sing many hymns we did. Bangor says that we sang thirty-six.'

'I thought that,' Reuben cried, his voice breaking into

sudden laughter as he gazed at Morgans' grave face.

Morgans was disturbed. Was Reuben mocking him too? But still his wisdom prevailed and he kept his temper even.

'Reuben,' he said sadly but firmly, 'forget this nonsense you must.'

Reuben's face also became grave and for some moments he did not speak.

'Wearying it is to go over the same ground again,' Morgans continued, 'but again I must tell you of your sacred duty to the people. They wait for you – '

'They wait for us,' Reuben said, 'as they wait for the circus – '

Morgans' face became pinched in anguish.

'Oh, Reuben bach,' he exclaimed, 'do not continue to say those things. An affliction has come to your vision.'

The old man's face was so distraught that a great pity welled up in Reuben. He muttered slowly:

'Morgans, be calm. I will try not to fail you,' – Catherine Pritchards was coming up the stairs, crying out something in a bright and plangent voice – 'though my heart is going sick of this business.'

Catherine, after knocking loudly, asked if she could come in. Reuben was about to refuse, but Morgans had already opened the door and Catherine, glittering and splendid in a white satin dress, swept in.

'My word,' Reuben in admiration, 'that's a new one, Catherine. A change it is to see you in white.'

Catherine beamed for a moment.

'Morgans said I look like one of those big marble angels on expensive tombs.'

'Yes, like their robes your dress is,' Reuben agreed. 'Simple and flowing, with a girdle round the waist.'

But Catherine's face took on an expression of active concern.

'How is it with you, Reuben bach? Very ill you looked in the chapel and I was going to follow you when you went out, but Morgans stopped me.' She came nearer to the bed. 'A holiday is what you want. Overworked you've been. Send him away on a holiday, Morgans, a fortnight's holiday. Manage easily we can. To the seaside he should go.'

Morgans asked, 'How about that, Reuben?'

Catherine continued in her maternal voice, her gaze drooping down solicitously on Reuben, in bed with his white young throat and chest showing – 'Wonders a fortnight by the sea will do him. You go, Reuben. Go to Tenby. There's a homely place for you! Quiet and respectable and pious. Very blue is the sea there.' She sighed and for a moment turned her gaze reminiscently inward. 'A fortnight I spent there once. A splendid minister they had in the chapel I went to... Send him to Tenby, Morgans. A holiday he ought to have.'

'Leave it to him I will,' Morgans said. 'Go he can if he wants to.' And as Catherine did not seem disposed to leave the room, he went to the door, opened it, and stood waiting for her.

'Come on, Catherine,' he called at last, for the woman was reluctant to curtail her solicitous advice, standing by the bed in her long and billowing white gown.

Left alone, Reuben blew out the light, stretched himself tiredly in the feathery warmth of the bed, and, his mind closing softly over its brooding, drifted into a satisfied sleep.

292

In the morning he rose with a quick serenity flowing over him. A clear perception of his duty, as Morgans called it, was in his mind. He would fulfil his obligations for a certain definite period, and when that period ended he would insist on complete isolation from the sect for another period, during which he would decide his return or not.

He told Morgans this.

But the old man looked at him gloomily – the morning did not bring him such serenity as Reuben possessed – and complained that Reuben was treating his 'sacred task as though he was an insurance-agent or an auctioneer.' But he said he would think about it, though again warning Reuben that if he allowed his mind to occupy itself with such brooding, God would surely withdraw his gift of inspiration. That afternoon they moved on to a village, travelling in a gig kindly offered by the local doctor, a Baptist, and assured by everyone that the bereaved young mother would be well looked after, the four contributing generously to the fund opened for her.

And Reuben, that evening in the village hall that had been taken for their meeting, was made aware of the truth in Morgans' warning. He began his own oration with a few well-chosen words, but, speaking them, no flame of inspiration began to rear its glow within him. He went on in a flat conversational tone more suited to a curate of the Church of England than the famous evangelist Reuben Daniels. He did succeed, after much straining, in issuing words shining with a little glow, and helped by continual exclamations of fervour from Morgans, Catherine, and Bangor Davies, the meeting was not wholly a failure.

But it was not a success. Only ten people were induced to confess their new possession of salvation. After the meeting Reuben sat, quiet and meditative, in the parlour of the house that was sheltering them for that night, and listened with scarcely a word to the others.

Catherine insisted it was a holiday he stood in need of – a fortnight in Tenby... But Morgans could not rid himself of his hopeless gloom, and Bangor Davies fussed about and made bird-like exclamations of futile advice – he thought Reuben was suffering from delusions consequent upon absorption in the declarations of converts, and advised him to cultivate a sense of humour.

Reuben listened and made no contribution to the discussion. He seemed to be chiefly occupied with some inner problem of his own. Finally he got up, saying he would do better in the next meeting, and went to bed.

He was almost utterly weary of the whole problem. He seemed to be waiting for something to happen, something extraneous to himself, that would lift him out of the weary enigma of his position. He seemed to be waiting for some sign, aware that it would come, from the depths of his own being possibly, but more likely from the vague future that hung as a shining sword over his head.

Something *did* happen, two days later.

They were now in the town of Llandrindod, and the morning after their arrival a telegram came for Reuben.

'COME HOME AT ONCE MOTHER'

Immediately he knew something had happened to Hugh.

Death. The word trembled on his tongue. There had been the gloom of death about him of late: there had been death in his own soul, and his eyes had seen death too, silent in the trampled corpse of a child. His brow darkened, his muscles became taut, he seemed to be gathering all his strength to resist the icy touch of the enemy. And he knew with absolute certainty that his father was dead, and as that knowledge sank into him, a wild grief possessed him, destroying all other emotions.

They saw him off at the station, Morgans' face looking a little thwarted, Catherine pale and subdued. And all through the journey he sat as though turned to stone, gazing vacantly through the window, his hands clenched in his pockets. As the train at last crawled between the sombre walls of the Valley, he relaxed a little and could have wept, seeing those ugly and desolate hills again, the hills that brought back to him all the dreaming of his childhood.

Evening had fallen when he reached the house. There was a little commotion as he arrived; the house seemed full of people, prominent among them Mrs Williams, Martha's old companion in liquor. Mrs Williams drew him into the parlour.

'Your father – ' she began, her large face stern and forbidding.

'Where is my mother?' Reuben demanded excitedly.

'Your father,' Mrs Williams finished, 'was killed in the pit this morning.'

'I know,' Reuben cried. 'Where is my mother?'

'Trying to offer their comfort are the people in there,' Mrs Williams said sternly, as though he needed a firm hand. 'Thought I did that it would be better for you to see her in here, away from them.'

He knew the ritual that followed on a death, the procession of neighbours to sympathise, and view the corpse.

'Let them go away,' he cried.

'I will fetch Martha in,' Mrs Williams said.

And Martha came in, bowed and tired, lifting her worn, tear-scarred face to him, her pale lips trying to smile a little in welcome. All her strength seemed to be gone. She was breaking. Ah, with an agonized flash of intuition, he saw death in her too.

CHAPTER IV

He lifted the candle and gazed long at his father's face.

They had laid Hugh on the bed and covered his broken body with a white sheet. The sheet was gathered up to his chin, but his face, untouched by the fall of rock that had killed him, lay revealed upon the pillow as though dreaming in the sweet air of deep slumber, remote and inaccessible.

But the repose upon the brow, the gently fixed expression of the lips, all the eternal peace that had fallen upon that face, gave Reuben's grief no ease.

'That he should end like this,' he muttered, 'in that damned pit, that had cracked his soul with its labour and sweated all joy out of him, so that he became dry and cold as a stone – '

What fine pleasure had there been in this dead man's life? Born under the gloom of these hills, nurtured in the barren wastes of this desolate Valley, from his twelfth year a labourer in those sunken galleries of the earth scooped out by the frantic lust of others, his running sweat earning him that pittance which gave him the right to thank the Lord for all his gifts and bought him a little bread and a miserable dwelling in a street fetid with poverty – what had he known of the extravagant and sensuous pleasures that make youth a glamour and old age tranquil in memories?

His son's eyes were heavy with grief. A dull grief for his father and for himself, who, too, had trod the same bleak path through the wastes of the Valley. For, after his travels, he saw the life of the Valley as an existence apart, his eyes, that had gazed on fine and comfortable towns and people who knew nothing of foul underground life, saw as in a projected vision this sordid mining region in all its distorted nakedness, the imprisoned community dwelling in sullen acceptance of their existence, gathered about the black sprawling filth of the mines, so that the very souls of the people seemed to blacken and life was an arid wilderness where toil and the animal processes fulfilled the years...

Long, long, standing alone by that bed, he gazed at the grey and peaceful face of his father. Once he called softly, the familiar name breathed out in a sigh: 'Hugh, Hugh! You are dead. Oh, Hugh, you are gone forever, and there is so much I wanted to tell you, there is so much in the world I wanted to show you – '

Yes, there was so much. He and his father, born in the slavery of a constricting heritage, here in this mine-torn Valley, they were become deathly in the tomb of existence. And now all that was left of weary life in Hugh had been crushed out, cruelly and in agony, by that earth which had given him so little. They had told Reuben of his death – they had carried him, as he moaned from his crushed breast, out of the pit and for an hour he had lingered with eyes staring into death. Once he had whispered his son's name, pain blurring the pride of that murmur, and they had bent to catch the message, but he had died before his tongue could utter it.

Reuben thought in anguish of those hours they had spent together, those hours of his childhood when Hugh, in his grave compassionate voice, would read out of the New Testament or take his son for long silent walks over the hills. A crystal-clear happiness had seemed to glow over those periods. But now thought of them pierced him with anguish and it was as though he knocked wildly at the stony door of a tomb, shuddering in the consciousness of a bliss irrevocably lost.

And then slowly his soul became still, as he continued to gaze upon the immovably calm face of his father, became still and seemed to harden into a shell-like impregnability, seemed to withdraw itself into a secure eyrie of bitter loneliness, sheathed about with the darkness of this present grief.

He sat down by the little table and laid his head on his arm. And his eyes were loosened of their sombre mourning.

Martha came in.

'At last, – ' she muttered, 'they have all gone – '

He lifted his head, his face suddenly eager.

'We are alone now? Oh, I was sick of that crowd downstairs.'

'Only me and you now,' she said slowly, gazing as though in fear at the figure on the bed, ' – and poor Hugh, who is dead.'

And over her old worn face a sinister shadow fell, the grim shadow of that ancient fascination death evokes in the Welsh. She drew up a chair and sat at the bedside. 'Gone away from me as queerly as he lived,' she cried, ' – shutting himself up in death like this, so suddenly, and not a word of good-bye. Ach, he was a man to shut himself up always.' She rocked herself in acute grief, fixing her gaze disconsolately on the corpse. 'The words of the Bible were more to him than the words of my mouth. He shut himself away from me, dwelling in Jerusalem, and if I spoke to him of the little matters of life, look down his nose at me he would and mutter to himself holy phrases.' Her gaze moved quickly to Reuben. 'A pious and respected man he had become, I know, and well I know, too, that Jesus Christ in the soul is worth a hundred times more than earthly ease.' The prompt last sentence seemed to be uttered as an afterthought.

Reuben answered, 'He did not think enough of the earth. He looked to Heaven for happiness, and there should have been joy for him here.'

Martha meditated. But she decided it was not necessary to tell Reuben of his father's drunken bouts that had alternated with his religious moods, years ago. But it seemed to her that Hugh too had snatched from life some joy – in those frequent festivities, enjoyed in that which was, to her, the only palace of earthly pleasure – the public-house.

'In his own way he took his pleasure, I suppose,' she sighed – 'like us all – '

And the dead face seemed to smile. The gentle expression of the chaste lips seemed to mock softly at their distressed pity for his sake, and the repose of the brow was final and eternal.

'What pain he must have suffered, before he died,' Reuben muttered, his eyes hardened again in anguish. 'They told me he had his senses after the fall – '

She bent her head and her voice shuddered as she said, 'Yes, and he spoke once or twice. "Calvary", he said, and just before he went, "Reuben". It was Christ and you were in his mind at the end, it seems.'

Reuben got up. His mother looked at him almost humbly.

'Taller you seem to have got, Reuben, And older, oh, so older, Reuben bach. Stronger your face is looking, but there's darkness about your eyes!' And she herself seemed to be so broken and old, as she sat there, her face, that had been so proud, become flabby, as though crumbling into a slothful indifference. 'Is there peace in you, Reuben? Have you been happy in your great work?'

He did not answer. Only he fell on his knees before her and laid his head in her hands.

But the cold dry touch of those ageing hands made him shudder; it was as though he pressed his face against a heap of dead wrinkled leaves. And he got up again, shaking his head with a gentle smile, looking at her. She, too, tried to smile in answer, but what was there to smile at? – with Hugh lying there broken forever in death, and the strange terror hidden in her son's eyes, that she was dimly conscious of and did not understand! So her worn lips broke into a grimace that was both a smile of love and the expression of a hopeless resignation to the cruelty of life, and the terror she did not understand.

He left her, carrying with him the memory of that grimace, and went into his own room.

And he felt that he was on the verge of a reality that would utterly destroy the past conceptions of his mind. Death had rung in his consciousness like the iron clangour of a mocking bell, and his soul had lifted itself from its vain dreaming, tense and ringing in that ominous echo.

And the next few days passed for him like days of a vague and symbolic ritual. He moved about the house in a silent abstraction, his face betraying neither grief nor interest in the funeral details. He seemed to be unaware of the daily reception of ghouls in the house – the continual procession of friends, acquaintances, neighbours, unheard-of relations – who climbed up to the house from the various ramifications of the Valley, immovable condolences on their observant faces.

One night he told Martha he did not think he would go back to his evangelistic labour. Martha was shocked.

'Reuben, Reuben, mad you talk. Queer your mind is going, surely! Rising so well, and a chapel they say is going to be built for you. Prosperous you will get. And if only you will find a nice quiet young woman from the country, fit to take her place by your side, a happy life waits for you. Say you are speaking idly. Go on with you, turn tail on the others you will! Upset is your mind, I can see.'

He did not remind her of her former denunciations of his religious inclinations. That would bring back all her past inebriated life; and nothing was mentioned of that now, though he noticed that her friendship with her old companion, Mrs Williams, was still intimate.

He paced up and down the room.

'I cannot think what to do,' he cried. 'If I leave this work, shall I go back to the pit? Sometimes I have thought that would be better! And we could live together, we should be alone, and I would have no troubling of my mind.'

'Rubbish you talk,' she said sharply. 'And a fool you are to let your mind be troubled. A comfortable life yours could be, no getting up in the middle of the night and no washing thick dirt off your body every evening – ' She seemed to search for other gratifications of the religious life – 'Mix with the best people in the land you will, too. And no better earthly task is there than being a labourer for Jesus Christ.'

'If,' he said, 'my heart were pure enough for that labour!'

She cried, almost shrilly, 'And is it not pure enough! What sin have you done, I should like to know? A cleaner heart no one of your sex ever had. Know you too well I do. Not in you is it to do any sin.'

He shook his head.

'You don't understand me.'

She had to accept that.

Her face drooped, began to sag, and she passed a hand over her eyes with a hopeless gesture. Then she cried out:

'Want to see you settled I do, before I die. How can I go in peace if I know your mind is wandering about like a lost sheep? No health is there in your soul, I think. A chance to settle down in luxury you have, a large chapel behind you, and a big flock of faithful worshippers to keep you busy for ever. But your talk of going back to that old pit, making yourself into a sweating slave again! Oh, queer is your mind. From where does it come? Odd your father was in his quiet ways, but control he had on his mind. And no queer ones were there on my side – only my old grand-father, perhaps, who used to have a craving for climbing to the roofs of houses and spitting on the people who passed underneath.'

Reuben smiled. 'I expect,' he said, 'his tastes have come down to me.'

Martha became suddenly threatening.

'Don't you behave foolishly now! Go you back and finish your travels, then come and take your position in the Valley. If you behave madly, finish with you I will. Have I not given up pleasure for your sake – '

His eyes burned. 'Yes, I shall never forget that.'

'Well, be thankful then and take you my advice. In you I have placed my hope. Do not fail me now – '

But he would not say a word.

His face white, his eyes full of a kind of smoky burning, he went about silently, as though he waited for some message, some expected communication that would seal up his destiny. He went out a little, gazing at the life of the Valley, his brows knit, his lips sometimes trembling. And though he attended no meeting in the chapel, he noticed that the faces of those people he remembered as converts had lost the shining bliss which had lit them in that memorable week. And the public-houses were full again, the cinema-queues restored to their normal length. Though

Martha and others assured him that the chapel still overflowed with zealous worshippers, and it only needed his return for the whole Valley to be stirred again to holiness.

Then on the evening before the day on which Hugh was to be buried, Eirwen came.

He heard her voice as he was sitting in the window of his room, and immediately his heart began to throb nervously.

Quickly he got up and went downstairs, entering the parlour, which was deserted. Eirwen was in the living-room, among the other people gathered there in final condolences for the widow. He knew Eirwen would hear him go down and enter the parlour, and he knew too that the people thought his conduct strange – for he would not appear if he could avoid it, unable to bear their curious glances and exclamations at his changed visage. And it was not long before Eirwen came to him. She gazed at him without a greeting, her eyes intent and considering and, a strangely shy modesty in her bearing, sat in the chair that was farthest from him.

'Well,' he said, a painful smile that was almost sickly on his face, 'aren't you going to say, "There's older you look!" '

'Yes,' she said, 'older and more attractive.'

'You,' he said with a rudeness strange to him, 'look more meek.'

'Yes,' she continued, 'I'm expected to look that now.'

But, ah, her beauty still wavered flame-like about her still proudly sensuous face; the long thin brows drooped so calmly, the heavy flower of her mouth still with its subtle leer. He looked at her face for a moment and, his eyes lowered, fixed his inscrutable gaze upon the lithe thickness of her white throat.

'Mother wrote to me about you – ' he said.

She began to laugh, softly and satirically, her mouth distorted... 'Do you think I ought to be bowed in sorrow?' she asked. 'Do you think I ought to drop a tear at every step I take in the street?'

'You look much quieter than you used to,' he persisted mockingly.

She looked at him with a long, cruel glance, a look in which was gathered all her female sapience, potent and destroying, as she sat there with the flame of her beauty immeshed in her power.

'I thought,' she said calmly, 'to see you a proper little preacher, black as a crow, and with a thin nose and watery eyes – '

He sat still, troubled by her voice, in which she seemed to be wielding a coldly gleaming blade.

'Pleasure you take in mocking at preachers,' he said. 'A common pleasure it is.'

'But instead,' she continued, ignoring his interruption, 'you've come back a man – ' She paused and added softly, 'for something.'

And he looked at her now with a sombre austerity that drove the cruel derision from her eyes. Her lids dropped, she laid her hand upon her throat, and her breasts seemed to swell with a gentle movement as she leaned back from his immovable gaze.

His limbs tightened, his heart was harder than a rock, his blood thickened and corroded in a calculating hesitancy that made him clench his hands until the nails penetrated his sweating skin.

But her voice came over to him coldly, remotely:

'We must have a long talk before you go back to your work, Reuben.'

His body relaxed.

'Yes – if I go back. But – ' he hesitated awkwardly, 'can I come to see you sometime?'

She laughed.

'Quite proper would it be, Reuben, for you to visit an old sweetheart whose husband has run away from her? What would they say in the chapel?'

'Can I come to see you sometime?' he repeated, almost brutally, as she rose from her chair.

'I go to my mother's a lot,' she said, 'but I still keep on at my cottage – a nice little place it is, Reuben, furnished with taste, for my husband could be quite refined when he liked – '

At this mention of her husband, Reuben's face became as a mask again. She watched him subtly. And the heavy flower of her mouth seemed to bend back its petals and quiver in a kind of naked delight.

'I ought to have waited for you – ' she said suddenly, with a subdued laugh, leaving him to return to the other room.

And he grasped the arms of his chair as though he would break them violently away. His face stretched out in a sort of convulsion, he could have cried aloud his agony of desire.

Later, subdued and abstract again, he went to look for the last time at his father's face. And, alone in the room, he fell at the bedside and tried to pray. But the words that rose to his lips were stale and lifeless, barren of any meaning.

The talent of prayer seemed to have withered within him, that talent he had possessed so abundantly.

And the day of the funeral, his hardened immobility of countenance had not relaxed. This was disappointing for the people who had gathered about the house for the ceremony. He might have given them, at least, the pleasure of looking upon a face stricken in a manner worthy of an evangelist. Many hoped, too, that he would deliver a funeral oration.

But, instead, there was something in his face that caused them to cease their whisperings, a glint in his eyes that was like the silent laughter of a sinister joy.

Mr Hughes-Williams conducted the ceremony. There was a little service in the parlour before the coffin was carried out, and the minister's recital of the deceased man's value in the sight of God and man was delivered in the usual groaning voice.

A great crowd had gathered outside. When the coffin appeared, they started to sing, the procession of men, which precedes the hearse, beginning to form down the street.

Martha, leaning on her son, walked to the first carriage in almost an hysterical state. The long, exacting preparations for the funeral and the meat tea that was to follow, the arrayal for the actual ceremony (her new Leghorn hat, though expensive, did not suit her), Mr Hughes-Williams' protracted groaning of Hugh's virtues, and, more disturbing than anything else, Reuben's cold behaviour, as though he wasn't really concerned in his father's funeral – Martha felt that it was going to be the worst day she had ever known. No wonder her Leghorn hat, which was in the new big brim fashion, became all askew as she got through the carriage door.

Then the people, peering and staring into the carriage with remorseless eyes that would not miss a thing, suddenly annoyed her into a burst of temper.

'Haven't they seen a funeral before then?' she demanded of the relations squeezing into the carriage. 'Staring in here like a lot of nanny-goats.'

'A funny funeral it would be without a crowd,' said Hugh's oldest sister, frigidly.

Martha's temper, however, cooled during the long soft ride to the cemetery, and by the time she got out of the carriage acute grief had swum up in her again and was evident in her flowing tears. Heading the procession which made its way to the grave, she leaned distressfully against her tall son, whose inhuman aloofness of mien was afterwards discussed, to his detriment, by the crowd.

His mind seemed far away, the vision of his widened eyes impenetrable.

'Man that is born of a woman hath but a short time to live, and is full of misery. He cometh up, and is cut down, like a flower; he fleeth as it were a shadow, and never continueth in one stay – '

He heard the sing-song voice of Mr Hughes-Williams rising and falling in the chilly air, to the accompaniment of women's sobs that could not be restrained. *'Man that is born of a woman hath but a short time to live,'* his mind

309

dully repeated, his eyes fixed upon the lumps of mould heaped by the side of the grave.

The earth was of a pale brown colour and was wet from a recent shower. He noticed that the coffin, which had been laid on the heaped-up earth, sank into the moistened mould with a slight movement, and this movement fascinated and gave him a peculiar feeling of dread.

Martha's hand clutched desperately at his arm. They were lowering the coffin into the grave.

But in the depths of Reuben's soul a dark laughter echoed: a mysterious, abandoned laughter that seemed to penetrate into the foundations of his being.

They sang a mournful hymn as the relations of Hugh stumbled in couples to the side of the grave and peered in.

Back in the carriage, he whispered to Martha, whose funeral grief was now manifest merely in accepting sighs, that he would not appear at tea.

A spot of colour appeared in Martha's cheek.

'How is it,' she suddenly began to wail, 'that in my grief my son behaves as though he is a stranger!'

The others in the carriage gazed at Reuben with a scrutinising disapproval.

'Yes,' Hugh's eldest sister declared in an outspoken manner, 'no help in this funeral has he been.'

'Do you mean,' Reuben asked calmly, 'that I haven't made it enjoyable for you?'

A shocked silence followed that. Martha wept a little, and the others ignored him with resentful though inquisitive faces. Reuben Daniels, the evangelist, was allowed his idiosyncrasies.

He slipped out of the house during the busy fuss of the tea, and made for the hills.

Evening would not be long in coming – already there was a faint darkening far away at the opening of the Valley, where the tawny hills were thrust out, like the paws of gigantic beasts. He climbed in haste as though eager to escape something down there in the Valley, and as he climbed, his soul seemed to laugh at his every step, and his limbs were flooded with a strength that made him want to leap swiftly up the steep hill-side.

The great pure sky of approaching evening opened out like a yellow rose, and, softly curving before him, the uplands stretched away far into the faint dusk under the distant horizon.

A night was coming. Soon it would close on him like a doom. And there was something to be done in his soul, there was a constricted violence awaiting release. In silence within the stony darkness of his soul, a slumbering violence on the verge of awakening.

He wandered on the hill-top, he lay on the grass, watching the changing sky, examining the long sinuous formation of his fingers, or, closing his eyes, he let his mind sink into the dark consciousness of his soul, and felt therein the slow shudder of his being.

Night came. Now he had wandered to a certain hill-top from which he could see the dim shapes of a few cottages below. He kept his gaze fixed on one of these.

Suddenly a light gleamed in a window of that cottage; and as it appeared, the watcher on the hill-top moved as though in extreme relief. Reuben slowly descended the hill.

311

He knocked at Eirwen's door. When she appeared, he looked at her with a strained smile and said gravely:

'I've come to you at last, Eirwen.'

She let him in, a trembling smile in her face as they went into the living-room. But when, in the light of the oil-lamp, she saw his face, that was suddenly vulnerable in a kind of fearful pain, her eyes became as softly burning stars, and her voice was thick with a caressive pity, when she said:

'Poor Reuben, did the funeral try you?'

He shook his head:

'I wasn't there, really – not my mind. But I had to go because of my mother. I couldn't stand the tea afterwards, with all those people there, so I've been on the mountains since, waiting for the night.'

She looked at him doubtfully.

'Do you mind?' he asked, his brows gathered. 'I don't think anyone saw me come here.'

'You must go,' she said, 'in the morning, before people are about.'

His voice quivered. 'If I want you to come and live with me always,' he said, 'you will come?'

She did not answer.

'You will?' he repeated.

'I cannot say – now,' she said vaguely. She stood up, her eyes looking away from him. 'I will get you some supper.' She laughed rather forcedly. 'Hungry you must be after that funeral and all the time you spent on the mountains.'

She made coffee.

He could not take his eyes off her. She complained of this, with a laugh, and he laughed, too, guiltily, a deep flush upon his face.

312

'Don't be too long,' he implored, as she gathered the supper things to take them into the scullery.

Then she went upstairs, saying she wanted to prepare the room. But before she had gone she had gazed at him with a long tranquil look that destroyed his impatience, so that his being was heavy with peace as he awaited her call.

Two candles were lit on the little mantelshelf of her bedroom. She was clad in a long soft cream garment, sitting before the dressing-table, brushing her hair. She did not turn as he entered the room.

A sleeping-suit was placed on a chair for him; and the thought that it belonged to her husband flashed ironically through his mind...

'I knew,' she said in an even voice, 'that you would come to me like this some day.'

He did not answer: but he threw off his clothes with hastening gestures that she watched, through the mirror, with a vague expression of pleasure.

She got up from the chair and, standing in a languorous attitude, almost of indifference, looked at him as he stood in the trousers of his sleeping-suit, his white chest and shoulders bare.

'How white and smooth you are!' she said wonderingly, mentally comparing him to her hairy and brown husband.

And intuitively he knew her thought and moved to her with an angry gesture.

'You are mine tonight,' he said.

And his voice, coming deep from his chest, was brutal. A sensitive expression came to her face; and she stood for a moment as though frightened. And immediately he fell on

313

his knees before her and, clasping her thighs in a fierce embrace, cried:

'You belong to me. For ages you have belonged to me. The touch of your body is so familiar and I know your eyes and your smile as though I knew them from the beginning of the world – '

Her fingers went through his hair with a gentle touch of pity. Then she laid her hands tentatively on his naked shoulders.

He got up and looked at her with fixed eyes that seemed blind in their intent purpose.

'Your beautiful body – ' he breathed.

Then when at last he saw her, his eyes were as a flare of madness in the avid intensity of his flushed face. She smiled, a little smile of pride in her own flowered beauty, and, sitting dreamily upon the chair, wound a fine black rope of her hair about her throat.

His voice was glad. 'Why do you do that?' he asked, only aware that he must say some trivial thing.

She did not speak, but the downward smile of her contented lips deepened, and, near her, he stretched out a hand and slowly, delicately, moved his trembling fingers over her still-reluctant breasts.

The sombre robe of his brooding fell away from his soul, and the chaste constrictions of his mind broke like crashing glass. God's shining face shrank in mist, prayer left no last wisp of grief, knees hardened into iron, all the past characters of his life withered into vapour. He squatted before her, and already the flare in his eyes was dying before the grave purpose of his mind.

'Go into bed,' he said, in a new voice.

'Am I beautiful?' she asked, and, bending, touched his hair with her lips.

'I could not imagine such beauty,' he whispered. Later, his mouth sought hers and clasped it, in a kind of blind pain that was as a silent cry of all the lonely agony his soul had endured.

But here was peace. He held her body as though he held in his hands an eternal flower of the world, a white eternal flower burning out of the primordial creation, in the shifting oblivion of time a static symbol of the undying desire of man.

Deep, deep, he fell into the chasm of sleep, fell with a relaxed body become exquisite in tranquillity. No dream penetrated his consciousness, no images of the outer world haunted with ghostly lineaments his fulfilled rest.

A touch awakened him.

In proud desire she received him again. But now no terrible beauty sprang through him like a flame that had given him the stature of a god. This was a dark ecstasy, secretive and nocturnal, the almost playful embraces of a goddess weary of the epic grandeur of her god's lust. They lay gently in each other's arms, prolonging the sweet emotion of their tenderness...

Dawn came. And even with the first faint gleams of light he woke.

'Eirwen,' he called.

She woke with a start, opening her eyes as though in quick fear, and, seeing him, they looked as though she did not recognise him.

'Eirwen!' he said softly.

But she did not return his tortured smile, only looked at him with a foreboding that dulled his heart.

'What are we to do now!' she cried suddenly.

He saw that she was still in the daze of half-awakened slumber. She shook her head despairingly and lay back again on the pillow. But he whispered:

'It is better that I go now, Eirwen, isn't it?'

'Yes, go,' she murmured, almost bitterly, 'go.'

Acute depression descended on him. The bedroom was cold and grey in the dim light. He drew the curtain and looked out: the sky was ragged with dismal clouds.

Yet, in his soul there was a white-burning frenzy, a newly-born consciousness.

'I am going downstairs,' he whispered to Eirwen, who had turned over in the bed.

She did not answer, but her shoulders shook beneath the clothes.

He went downstairs. He found a little oil-stove and placed the kettle on it. It was a long wait. But just as he poured the water in the teapot, Eirwen entered the living-room. He took in the tea and some biscuits he had found and looked at her intently.

She sat in a chair. Her face was very pale and her eyes seemed to have sunk deeper into her face.

'Are you glad you came?' she asked in a remote voice.

'Yes,' he answered, his hands moving spasmodically over the tea things.

'I am not,' she cried suddenly. And then she was weeping.

'Why?' he asked almost inaudibly.

She wept into her hands. He went to her and touched her, but she drew away from him. With a feeling of shame he went into the scullery, hardly aware of his movements. A deathly coldness came over him.

Her voice came to him:

'I had a letter from my husband last week. No one knows I have heard from him. People think he's gone abroad – '

Reuben went back to the living-room. 'Well,' he said, 'why are you so strange about it?'

The anguish in his voice seemed to whip her into raving.

'He loves me,' she cried loudly, 'still he loves me. Such love is in his letter! All day after I had it I cried. Oh, he loves me, and I have done this to him – '

'I thought,' he said coldly, 'that you were disgusted at his conduct.'

'All the time I have loved him,' she went on, 'all the time. So wonderful he could be – ' She paused, looked at Reuben wildly and then continued, 'My own darling wife,' he began in his letter. Reuben, he struck me one night, struck me several times, so that my shoulders were covered with bruises. But afterwards, so wonderful he was, and I forgave him. Can't you see that I love him!'

'Why,' asked Reuben painfully, 'did you allow me to come here?'

She looked at him and did not answer.

'Lust!' he muttered brutally. 'You were always the same with me.'

He took his cap and left the cottage.

And again he climbed the hills. Blindly he went on, up those slopes, over the uplands, then, farther on, he climbed another hill, walking south, towards the sea. Over the hills, down into the vales, past clusters of houses he went, blindly and numbly, walking on in his oblivious frenzy, only conscious of his desire to be utterly away from the Valley, from all the misery it had held for him.

A fine rain began to fall. He was hardly aware of it. But later the craving of his stomach asserted itself and he descended to a village. Looking in his pocket, he found he possessed three shillings. He bought a loaf of bread, drank a glass of milk in the shop, and set out over the hills again.

'Dear me, where is your overcoat?' the old woman in the shop had asked. 'Wet you will get.' But he had shaken his head and left her without a word.

He ate the bread as he climbed, tearing the loaf with his hands. It got wet in the rain, that now was falling in a more persistent way, but still he went on.

His head was full of a strange glamorous light, his limbs felt full and lithe with a nervous strength. Once he muttered – 'I am going away from the Valley, I am going among new people, I am going to work and begin anew.'

The journey from the Valley to Cardiff is twenty miles. Walking over the hills, it is a long wearying task. But Reuben seemed not to feel it. He was not aware, either, that his body was shuddering in its rain-soaked garments. The longer he walked, the fiercer burned the piercing flame in his head.

CHAPTER V

At last, dim in the mists of rain, he saw the city stretched in the distance, straggling before a pale line of sea.

There he would hide. Vaguely he formed plans: he would find some lodging for the night and tomorrow he would go to the docks district and search for work. Any kind of work. He would take another name and live in some mean quarter where, possibly, the world of religion was unknown. And never would he go back to the Corinthians, never would he go back to the Valley. He thought of Martha. Perhaps, later, if he became prosperous enough, he would be able to persuade her to leave the Valley, and then they would live together, in peace...

He began to laugh softly and then he wondered why he was laughing. At every step he took, a shudder ran up through his being. And he wished the sharp convolutions of white light would go away from his head – their continuous twists and stabs almost blinded him, so that he stumbled and lurched several times. He would stop for a few moments and lean against a tree or a rail, and suddenly his head would become clear and cool, and he trudged on with a new energy, looking ruefully at his rain-sodden clothes. Then as suddenly, revolving, twisting and stabbing, again the keen flames of white light pierced into his brain, and he had to force his limbs to go on, or he would have tottered to the ground and laid his head in the wet grass – and some instinct warned him that if he once lay on the ground he would not be able to get up again. Now he was descending the last hill and he looked over the flat land, where groups of pretty red-tiled suburban villas stood like bunches of marigolds thrown on the green plain. Here he would like to live, quietly with his mother, in one of those pretty houses encircled by a bushy garden. Oh, he would work hard at his new labour in the city, so that he might live here in the contentment of evening, undisturbed. The thought of it made him push on with new eagerness. Tomorrow he would begin.

A faint roaring sound was in his ears – he looked about, as though searching for its source. A shaft of yellow light came aslant from the sky to the city, and over the distant horizon a thick greenish cloud hung, sickly-looking, like the vomit of some god. Pale and dark, a rainy grey, the taller buildings of the city loomed up in the early evening dimness, some lost in the shaft of yellow light, that seemed to glare in his own eyes too. His thighs were icy and his belly seemed to contract and expand with a strange unknown movement that almost made him burst into laughter again.

And still the faint roaring sound was with him, and continuously the wheel of white flame revolved in his brain.

At the first opportunity he would have something hot to drink – steaming hot broth he thought vaguely – and after that he would be well. Then he would find a bed in some lodging-house, and tomorrow he would begin his new life...

The road stretched away; presently there was a row of houses each side of it. He noticed that the few ghostly people he passed looked at him strangely, and he tried to hurry on, fearful that they would stop him and attempt to interfere with his plans. The street was endless; the rows of houses were like oblongs of grey cardboard, the heavily shrouded windows betrayed no life within: it became a nightmare street of the dead. Now and again, when a person passed him, peering at him through the rain, he recoiled as though he met a ghost, and, averting his face fearfully, he went on.

Faces. He hated them. Faces pressing about him with fixed malevolent stares, peering into his eyes, vindictively searching into his soul, avariciously forcing their attention upon him. He hated people. His being suddenly flared into hatred. He hated their mean, lustful souls, the deceit of their faces, the secret ugliness of their animal minds. And most of all, he hated Eirwen...

With a slow, drunken motion of his head, he looked about. He had come to a square in some poor quarter of dismal shops and tenements that blinked with dim gas lights. He wandered about and found a kind of eating-house, a shop divided with partitions, a table and benches in each division.

A man came forward, wiping his whiskers with his white apron. There was no one else in the shop.

'Have you got some broth?' Reuben asked.

The man shook his head. His voice seemed to come from a remote distance:

'Too late for broth.'

Reuben, holding a table, sank to the bench.

'Something hot – ' he whispered.

'Beef tea,' the man said faintly, 'or a nice 'ot coffee.'

'Beef tea.' And Reuben looked at him in astonishment. The man's face was receding backwards without his body.

'What's up?' the voice came faintly.

Reuben sat up with a great effort.

'Your face – ' he mumbled.

'My face!' the man repeated. 'Oh, indeed, and what's wrong with my face then?'

'It was going away from you – '

It seemed to Reuben that they stared at each other for an age. Then the man hurried away and brought back a bottle and glass.

'This is what you want, my lad.'

Reuben drank the whisky obediently, too weary to ask what the liquid was. But he was glad to have it inside him. He suddenly felt warm and clear.

'Bring me something to eat and drink,' he asked presently, lifting his head.

'Better sit by the fire and warm yer clothes,' the man said, indicating a stove in a corner. 'Where 'ave you been, to get so wet?'

'Oh, walking about,' Reuben said vaguely.

The man glanced at him queerly and went away.

Reuben took off his coat and waistcoat and laid them over the top of the stove. Then he sat down. He wanted to sleep, but he forced the drowsiness from him, shuddering in the warmth of the stove.

Waves of heat and cold sprang up alternately within him. Then he became aware of his heart thudding with extraordinary loudness. He wished the man would hurry, so that he could get away and look for a lodging for the night. He wanted to be up early in the morning, to look for work.

A large cup containing a dark steaming liquid was thrust before him.

' – 'ere, wake up.'

The beef tea burned his throat. Already he felt better. He asked for something to eat, and bread and cheese were brought to him.

'Where yer going to?'

Reuben averted his face. He knew a search would be made for him.

'London,' he said.

He ate the food hastily, anxious to get away now. But, in the street again, he looked uncertainly at the thick rain. He wanted to reach the docks district tonight: he would be quite hidden there. Once he had found a lodging he would go straight to bed, and he would recover his normal strength by the morning. So he set off at a run, buttoning up his jacket over his throat.

It was not long before he stopped, a sharp pain shooting through his head. He had come to some lamp-lit gardens where great white buildings stood, austere and ghostly among the trees. He dropped on a seat and held his head between his hands. His brain was bathed in flame.

'Hello.'

He saw a woman's face. It was red as blood, except where the mouth was distended in a smile, displaying a white glitter.

'Wet, isn't it!' the voice went on. 'I didn't expect to see anyone out tonight.'

He stared vacantly at her bloody face.

'Lost your voice, dear?'

'There is blood on your face!' he cried, not knowing he shrieked.

'Here, don't shout, damn you.' She moved away in alarm.

Now he saw crimson everywhere. The trees were red, and blood-red shadows were about the white buildings. Strange! He must get away to the streets. 'Hell!' his lips moved silently, 'blood-red as hell shall the cities be – ' And he got up and went on, through the rain and the red shadows, until he came to a bright street, where great lamps swung like angry moons in the hissing rain.

He had never seen such a street. The buildings sloped away from each other crazily – some soared up in curves to the black sea of the moving skies. A church that stood alone, as though in mid-air, was shuddering like a ship – he stopped, waiting for it to swerve over and fall. But after a moment it was still, and he crept on, fearfully staring up.

A window was raised and a woman with bared breasts leaned out and nodded to him. The people on the crimson pavements were stiff and straight, made of gleaming metal, moving their limbs like wound-up dolls. And stranger than all were the dead white faces lying in the crimson glow of the pavements, faces no one dared tread upon, that lay, pale and terrible, in that bloody glow of the stones.

He crossed the road with exaggerated care. Docks, docks, docks. The word sounded in his head like the ticking of a clock.

'Oh, Jesus, help me!'

His face strained up to the sky, he whispered the prayer. And immediately memory of it went out completely from his mind.

' – if Morgans knew, if Morgans knew, if he knew, standing up for Jesus – and Catherine Pritchards weeping, the old man dying of cancer: Philip rotting in disease: a blue bruise on the nipple of a breast: and women who let any man go into them, dead faces of children, bloody corpses in the pit... oh, the womb of life... a bloody hell.'

And he trudged on, muttering sternly under his breath, 'A bloody hell, a bloody hell.' The words seemed to give him relief.

He was quite used to the crazy buildings now. No line was straight, no window parallel with the next. A bottle crashing on the pavement shattered into a thousand blue and yellow fragments in his mind. The wind threw the white lamps spinning down the street. A tramcar sped along like a pale green rat. Crossing the angular bridge over the canal, the water had the stale odour of death.

There were other smells now. He had entered the slum district. His steps dragging, he went out, past the odours of garlic, fish, onions, beer, filthy urinals. Where could he look for a lodging? Here was a house whose wet walls blistered in yellow patches, with little secretive windows high up. He climbed the three steps carefully and knocked. A man in shirt and trousers appeared.

'Have you a bed for the night?'

'No.'

The door was violently slammed.

Wearily he turned to the street. His legs seemed to be turning into a soft boneless substance. Slowly, with infinite caution, he went on. Once the pavement rose up to meet him, but quickly he jerked himself away from it, his hand clasping a rain-pipe.

The crimson shadows darkened and now the lamps hung still in the drizzling rain. A sudden sharp clarity had come to his mind, a single shaft of clear vision. He realized there was something wrong with him, that he was ill. He must find someone who would take him to a lodging and fetch him a doctor. He gazed intently through the rain.

He had come to the sea. That was the sighing he heard. Faint, a pale spume of spray, it washed over the wharves, which were stuck out like black tongues licking up the water. The quay on which he stood was deserted, but across the way low buildings squatted, the dimly lit windows gleaming.

If he could get across to them, he must go no further, but drop there, anywhere under a roof, and lie down to sleep, for ever. For ever. Oh, he did not want to wake again. Only eternal sleep could ease his head and limbs.

He put one leg forward carefully, then the other, forcing strength down into them. At each step a flash of searing pain went through his body. His face was dripping with sweat...

He pushed open a door and fell on the wet sawdust. Feminine voices shrieked. He felt himself picked up and laid on a bench. His heart was bursting and he looked wildly at the faces suspended in the air above him.

Such faces! They were painted with hot shining colours – red, blue, green, gold. The mouths leered thickly over him, the noses were stretched forward like the snouts of swine, the eyes shone as lit glass. One with a flaming scarf about its throat was like a corpse arisen with the green slime of earth still upon its flesh.

They chattered like excited parrots over him. Then one came nearer to him and gazed at him closely. Dimly, his mind reeling away, he gazed at her and faintly, an emotion of gladness within him, he recognised her.

'Ann Roberts,' he whispered.

He lay in delirium for two weeks. Then slowly, wearily, his faculties returning in gradual strength, he began to notice the room he lay in, the woman who came to the bedside and looked down at him with a bright, grave scrutiny.

'Where am I?' he asked hopelessly.

The bright face above him seemed to leer with a sort of secret laughter.

'Don't you know me yet?'

He stared at her, his protuberant eyes lost and piteous.

'Crikey!' the woman exclaimed, 'we must do something to fatten you up, now you've decided to stay down on this earth, that you cursed so much in the last fortnight. Your face has gone three-cornered as the mug of a sheep.'

'Ann Roberts!' he said suddenly.

'Ah!' she grinned. 'The very same Ann Roberts who pulled your nose because such a serious little boy you were always.' She went on in a more strident voice: 'And the very same Ann Roberts that you followed to the river when my father drove me from my home. Do you remember? Eighteen shillings you gave me, to get back to Cardiff.' She grinned again. 'I got back all right.'

His dilated eyes stared at her, as his mind began to open into memory.

'How long have I been here?' he asked painfully.

'Past a fortnight.'

His mouth dropped open in surprise.

'Is this your house?' he asked, breathing with difficulty.

'God, no. I rent two rooms of it from an old slut who lives on the top. Now be quiet, and don't bother yourself or me with questions. You're not in a fit state to begin thinking. Take things as they are for a bit.'

'I am,' he insisted with sudden strength. A little flush had come to his face. 'Who has been paying for me to live here?'

'No one.'

'*You* have,' he insisted, his voice thin and trembling. He glanced at the various bottles that stood on the little table by the bedside. 'I must have cost you a great deal.' His eyes were full of pain. 'Why didn't you let them take me away?'

'That pub you fell into is quite near here, and when I recognised you I thought I'd look after you for a day or two. Then you started to shout to me, "Don't let them find me. Hide me. They'll take me away again", so I thought you must have done something wrong, and I told everyone you were an old friend of mine who was out of work.

'I can't remember anything after I fell,' he muttered.

'Ha, you didn't half scream some things when you were ill. My word, I didn't think such things were in you, knowing you as a boy. Horrible nightmares you had, too – You were always shouting that you was lying in the mud and a pack of swine and goats was coming to trample over you. It was a hard job to soothe you sometimes. I had to hold you down in the bed more than once.'

He closed his eyes, the lids quivering.

'There!' she cried. 'You'll be having them again. Shut up and don't make me talk.'

'But haven't they made a search for me?' he asked. 'Oh, there was something in the papers about you,' she said carelessly. 'But as you were so strong in shouting not to let them take you away, I thought best to keep quiet until you were well enough to do as you liked. And besides,' she said, with a sudden half-leering smile, 'what a scandal it would have been for you, for them to have found you here! Reuben Daniels, the great young evangelist!'

He was silent. Ann Roberts went out of the room, leaving the door open. He could see into the other room – a tiny place almost filled with a couch that had been roughly made into a temporary bed. So he occupied the bed of the prostitute. His young face twitched. And he could have wept in his weary hopeless despair. To what pass had he come!

The next day, after Ann had gone out, he tried to get up. He must gather his strength as soon as possible and go away from this house, where he lived on a harlot's pity. But

329

he failed to stand on his legs and he crawled back shivering into the bed.

It was late evening when Ann arrived back.

'Where have you been?' he asked almost peevishly.

'Oh, doing a little job.'

He looked at her with suspicion. Her thin carelessly rouged face had the glitter of a mocking devil. A purple silk scarf was tied ornately at her neck and from her bright hat a single orange feather floated jauntily. He sank deeper into the bed, watching her unwrap the parcel she had brought in. It was a large jar of calf's-foot jelly.

'This will do you good,' she said.

He did not answer. Shame was upon his countenance.

'For shockingly bony you have got,' she went on vaguely, reading the label on the jar.

'You must not buy me these things,' he said in a dreary voice.

'Oh!' she said slowly, 'you'll pay me back some day.'

But he shuddered in the bed. His mind saw her emerging from her trade and, the payment in her hand, entering a shop thinking of him.

Later, anger on her face, she forced him to eat the delicacy.

'I'm much stronger,' he protested, 'you mustn't buy me anymore.'

The doctor came. He was an old bleary man with a hanging coarsely red face – he smacked Ann playfully on the back, boozily opening his tiny red eyes, and, after examining Reuben, offered her a drop of whisky from a flask he took sighingly from his pocket.

'He's a story,' Ann said when he had gone. 'Did something or other in his young days, and now he does his doctoring business on the quiet for us – us people.'

'Has it cost a lot, him coming here for me?' Reuben asked painfully.

'There you go again. Don't worry about the cost. When you are working once more and got some brass, you can pay me something if you like.'

He looked round the sordid bedroom. Oh, he could not stay there any longer. Here, in this very bed, she conducted her accursed trade. Its squalor was in the room like an evil odour. And now, since he was there, did she conduct it in some other convenient place, earning the money to pay for his illness?

Raising himself, he looked at her wildly.

'I think I can get up now,' he cried.

'Try!' she said, the hateful leer coming on her face.

'If you will go into the other room – ' he muttered.

'Ho!' she cried, laughing loudly, 'after nursing you for a fortnight. You needn't be shy of getting out of bed in front of me. Besides, I shall have to help you back.'

He looked at her helplessly.

'I want to get up and put on my clothes,' he groaned.

'And what are you going to do then Reuben bach?'

He did not answer.

'If you went out now,' she said, 'you'd die. It's very cold out.'

Tiredly he lapsed deeper into his mood of dreary hopelessness. Then the thought of death rose up like a solemn music in his being. Death. A destruction of the iron

331

ribs that chafed the soaring soul, a breaking of the filthy integuments that stained her. Loosened of his miseries, he would enter that quiet kingdom and perhaps, farther on, find a lovely dawn-world where, in the enchantments of a new vesture, he would toil amid landscapes shaped like softly-coloured flowers....

'Here,' Ann said ' – I'm going out for a bit to see someone – a girl I know. I'll send up a friend who lives underneath to keep you company. You've been alone enough today – I can see you've been having a broody time – '

'I'd rather be alone,' he said dreamily, occupied with his vision.

'I'll ask her to read something to you,' Ann went on, 'for you might not have anything in common to talk about – ' She adjusted her orange-feathered hat. 'You needn't be shy of her; she saw enough of you when you were delirious.' She tied the purple scarf dexterously at her throat. 'Now, Reuben bach, behave yourself and bear your cross like a man.'

There seemed to be nothing left for him on earth. Sick at heart, he had fled from his labour, from a sacred task, despising the people he had longed to serve. What devilish mood had forced him to flee? He seemed to have lived in a horrible nightmare – he remembered writhing bodies, fanatical faces, clamouring voices, and his own being, pitched as though on a pinnacle of whirling space, burning in exalted frenzy. Oh, something had gone wrong. He had set out from his youth, the white peace of austere meditation in his soul, longing to speak of that calm beauty to weary humanity. The people had flamed about him like a conflagration and he had taken fire from their zeal, and then the still harmony of his

332

youth had seemed to be destroyed. He remembered it all now as a lurid dream, etched in harsh and brutal contours in his mind. And, too, the knowledge that he had miserably failed brooded like a darkness over his consciousness.

Ann had gone. He suddenly leapt out of bed with one spring and immediately fell to the floor. Oh, how cowardly his behaviour had been! Lying on the floor, he bit his knuckles and groaned. He had left Morgans, like any coward fleeing from a battle, with no explanation, no attempt to excuse his conduct. How had the revival progressed? he wondered. Morgans had warned him that it was he whom the people looked to for inspiration. 'Yet,' he groaned, 'the revival seemed wrong to me. All that frenzy – But I have been a coward. I should have stayed and tried to tell them it was all wrong, and that no harmony could come from such frenzy.' But he had followed his own despair and fury and behaved miserably – horribly, he thought, as memory of Eirwen was added to his woe.

Clinging to the bed, he got up and laboriously, trembling from head to foot, crawled back into the bed, realizing it was no good attempting to escape yet. But, as soon as strength came back to him, he must get up and go back to the Valley, go back and face the criticism of the people he had abandoned. He would tell them as simply as he could of that selfish despair and weariness that had driven him away. And he would go back to the pit to work, begin again –

There was a knock at the door, and a girl entered.

'Ann sent me up,' she said. 'To read to you.'

She carried a novelette, a woman's publication, and, sitting down, immediately opened it.

333

'Don't read that to me,' he asked peevishly.

She was a small flimsy creature, with big plain eyes and a childish mouth.

'It's a good book,' she said, with some indignation.

'I don't want anything read to me,' he said.

He looked at her feverishly.

'Are you a friend of Ann Roberts?' he asked.

'We go out together sometimes,' she answered, cautiously, her doll's face lifted up.

'Can you tell me why Ann has kept me here, then?'

'Don't ask me,' she said; 'all us girls, her friends, have wondered why. She made us promise not to tell who you are, when it was in the newspapers about you disappearing. And she has behaved in a funny way since she's been taking care of you. She's even taken a job on – I mean a real job.'

'A job!' he repeated wonderingly.

'Yes,' the girl said, almost in a voice of complaint, 'a job in a blouse place. She sits in front of a machine for hours and works hard.'

'Oh!' he said faintly.

'Yes, God knows why! When she has her regular boys!'

He looked at her with a dark fixed gaze.

'Once or twice,' she continued, 'us girls have thought she was keeping you here on the quiet because she had a spite against religion. She used to tell us about her father, who was cruel and a big bug in his chapel!'

'Do you mean,' he asked quietly, 'you think that later she would let it be known that *she* had taken care of me, here, in this place?'

334

'Oh, no. We thought that she wanted to lead that religious lot a dance, keeping you hidden here. But, of course, we were wrong. I don't know why I am telling you these things. Only you look so lost! And now I'm sure Ann is looking after you just because she lived near you when she was a kid, and she said something about you helping her when her father turned her out.'

'Oh, God!' he cried. And all his face was piteous with anguish.

'What's the matter?' the girl cried, jumping up. 'They're not coming on again?'

He shook his head despairingly.

'I wish you'd go back to your room,' he whispered. 'I want to be alone.'

'I don't think I ought to,' she said doubtfully.

'Oh, I'm all right. But I want to be alone.'

She left him. And when she had gone he broke completely into tears. Ah, he was unworthy. He was unworthy of the regard of Ann Roberts. She had done something noble for him – she, whom he had despised and recoiled from, sick at the thought that he lay in her bed of sin. He had sickened away from the delicate foods she brought in, thinking them bought with evil earnings, he had imagined her in those terrible contacts, richened to bear the cost of his illness –

More than ever it was necessary to get well, to earn money, repay this great debt. He must get back and work, work. And he would rescue Ann from this life; he would tell everybody of her noble act. She would not nurse him on the proceeds of evil! How fine that was. Money would never repay her. But he must get back to work, so that he could send her enough to keep her away from her former traffic. He had given Martha, before the funeral, a sum of money, his earnings in the tour, and if there was any left he would send it to Ann immediately. But he must get well soon.

Already, in the exhilaration of his thoughts, he felt better. He would try and get up again, to become accustomed to standing on his legs. So he got out of bed and, holding the bed-post until the sick waves that the effort sent through him had gone, he slowly, carefully, searched for his clothes, finding them in a drawer of the dressing-table.

He succeeded in dressing. But his head was so painful – a heavy ache numbing his brows, and, behind his eyes, sharp flashes of pain. He sat wearily in a chair before the little fire, and for a little while he dozed in a kind of aching trance.

Dimly he heard the door open, then an exclamation. He opened his eyes slowly, as though drugged.

'Reuben Daniels!' Ann cried angrily – 'a fool you are, and a bitch that girl is to have left you.' Slowly he got to his feet. She was advancing to him, and dimly he saw her face, pale, with the bright red upon her cheeks.

'I know,' he whispered, 'how you have cared for me!'

'Back to bed!' she cried furiously.

His soft-burning eyes were dilated, like stars in the thin pallor of his face.

'Your soul is lovely as the dawn!' he whispered.

And he fell at her feet, down to the floor, dropping his head in submission and worship before her, ashamed and yet proud, a penitent at her feet.

CHAPTER VI

And one morning he escaped.

For days he had talked of going back to the Valley. But Ann had laughed and said he would have to rest for another three weeks at least, before thinking of going into the November open air. He had indignantly protested, knowing his normal strength had returned to him, and when she persisted in laughing at him he decided he would have to go secretly. Ann was foolish; and latterly she had begun to look at him with a bright dreamy regard that he disliked, and she would touch him gently and lingeringly – a touch that he could not bear, in spite of his intense regard for her.

So one morning, after she had left for her work, he dressed, and in half an hour was ready to begin his journey back. He would have to walk – there was not a penny in his pocket. He cut some slices of bread and butter, wrapped them up; then he found an old woollen scarf, which he tied around his neck. It was a clear morning, there was no sign of rain in the winter sky, and he felt that he could walk forty miles – double the distance to the Valley. Strange how light and airy he felt – a lithe power in his limbs, an ethereal clearness in his head. What nonsense to say he was not recovered! His body felt as though it were made of an aerial substance that would leap lightly over a thousand hills.

Hastily, afraid Ann might suddenly return, he gave one glance round the room and went out. How good to be in fresh air again! There was a wind blowing from the sea, and he shivered a little. But, hurrying on, soon a pleasant glow coursed through his body. He sped on over the bridge, into the city, vaguely remembering his previous passage through these streets, when all the buildings had seemed to swoon drunkenly and there was a lurid light everywhere.

Two hours, and he was climbing the first ridge of hills, the last suburb behind him.

And as he climbed it was as though a wound opened in his soul. He was going back to the Valley. He saw the dark weary hills again, the squat rows of dwellings, the harsh eruptions of the mines, the grey people. He was going back, to labour there, to people who would look at him with laughter and disdain, point to him as the young man Reuben Daniels, who fled ignobly from his sacred task, who had abandoned those who placed their faith in him.

'But I must go – I must go back,' he muttered. 'I will endure all their jeers and their just criticism.'

Yet his heart was becoming dark with dread: and even as it became heavier within him, he repeated more sternly: 'I must go back.'

Up, and still higher, the ridges piled squatly above each other, he climbed. It was now midday and he was a little hungry. He rested for a while against a stone, eating the bread and butter, his gaze on the distant sky before him. There was a grey darkness there he did not like, a gathering of sullen clouds, high and remote, that might mean snow. It was cold enough, he noticed now, resting by the rock. But if he hurried he might escape it and reach the Valley before dark.

So he went on quickly, but his breathing was not so rhythmic as it had been, and he was compelled to slacken his steps.

'Ah, the life of man is not easy,' he suddenly burst out, inexplicably. 'It is a journey over stony hills and through barren valleys.' His voice was helpless and strange, echoing over the silent upland. 'And what are we seeking, enduring, the anguish of this journey, what is there for us at the last?' A feverish flush had begun to burn in his face. He gazed round as though in mute appeal, but there was nothing but the cold spaces over the uplands, the remote air, and the iron grey hills in the distance. 'I have sunk,' he resumed, almost in a whisper, 'to depths blacker than hell contains, depths in my own soul deeper than words can tell, where the images of eternity mock at my torture and there is no succour for my breaking mind. And I have cast away my faith, torn love from my being, and derided those who looked on me as the earthly mouthpiece of God.'

And it seemed that he listened to his own words with an ironic detachment, smiling a little. Then, as the last word left his mouth, he shuddered in a sudden convulsion. Was he getting light headed, he asked himself fearfully. And then he became aware of the sweat on his body.

Oh, he must not think; he must press on, concentrating on the journey, force his legs to carry him swiftly to the Valley. He must arrive before dark or he would be lost, and he looked again at the distant sky – the heavy clouds had not moved.

Another ridge, then a swift descent to a vale, where houses were clustered a mile or so away. But he passed on, climbing the farther hill with a mechanical precision, his will concentrated on the process. He had to rest when he got to the top, and he sighed with a great panting movement of his chest, his limbs hot as a fire.

The sky was darker and nearer: it was like a lowering mass of grey wool, here. He would have to force his legs into swifter strides – there were more hills yet. And now for a while he went on at a great pace, his breathing a little easier. But when he had covered that ridge and saw again another, a still higher ridge beyond the sunken vale, he could have wept. He was so tired, his belly so empty, his head so strange.

Yet he went on with unabated steps, his eyes staring fixedly before him, a deathly look of vacancy on his face. Now he did not notice the sky, was unaware, too, that the world had become darker, that the air seemed to hold itself in a tense and waiting hush.

When he reached the brow of the other hill, the snow had begun to fall.

'O Lord, if I spat upon thy worshipping people, if I fled in

contemptible cowardice, a craven fool, from the labour
thou gavest me, do not look upon me with anger now! For
I have seen the error of my behaviour and I return to bear
the burden of my miserable conduct.'

He had fallen on his knees in the snow and lifted his face
through the drift of flakes eddying about him. Then he got
up, slowly, a sob in his throat, and stumbled on. Someone
was walking behind him – some presence was there,
noiselessly following through the snow, someone shrouded
in a white garment, menacing his progress, coming nearer
and nearer – oh, nearer, through the white air, a dread –
He screamed and turned, stumbling to his knees, his arms
lifted as though in protection, his mouth gaping. But there
was nothing.

He lay panting on the ground until he could feel the
dampness of the snow penetrate his garments, then he
dragged himself to his feet again.

On, on, his body lurching forward, covered with snow.
An unearthly light gleamed softly through the falling silver
flakes, a faint bluish-rose light in the distance. But all over
the world white snow, deep, deep snow, snow that would
never cease to fall, covering all that was dark and filthy, all
the evil stains on the earth, all the sorrows, the miseries –

And then a white face, a shadowy body rising out of the
depths through the silver veil of the snow, the sunken eyes
gazing at him, from the dead.

'Philip!' his lips moved soundlessly.

And he listened to a voice that was softer than the noise
of the falling flakes touching the fallen drift:

'Shall I keep countenance with the living dead! There is

a kingdom unknown of men. Rocks and forever rocks in a sunless light with never a pool of water. There are no roots, for there is no soil; there is no touch, for there is no flesh; there is no horror, for we are dead. Think, Reuben. Just then you desired to die. But the blood in your veins is dyed with rose, the shield of your breast is not tarnished. See, beyond the hills, a crucifixion! The blood in the snow is black. A carrion bird, created by God, hovers about the cross.'

And then there was only the snow and the silence. Had he seen anything, had he heard a voice? Philip! He peered through the wavering veil of snow, still plunging on, his feet sinking in the depth.

Were those stars, those points of gold light, far above! Was it night, then? Oh, no! It was much too early, and this bluish-rose gleaming in the distance – it was the light of late afternoon, and he would be home by evening. Home! He stumbled on more hurriedly in a sudden access of strength at the thought of it.

But now there was an iron band pressing round his head. Someone was pressing it on... He shook his head violently, crying aloud, 'No, no; I don't want to die now! Let me go, I beg you, let me go.'

He fell, and lay in terror, hearing his heart beat with a dull dread that was like the prelude of death.

'Reuben! Reuben!'

Again a soft, almost noiseless voice! And without moving his head he saw his father before him. Ah, with what sad and mournful eyes Hugh gazed at him! And Reuben uttered a cry of joy.

'Arise, Reuben, and go to your mother.'

'Stay with me!' Reuben breathed.

But all the sadness of man was in his father's eyes. A pale radiance was on his brows, and through the dusk his thin and tired hands shone too.

'Stay with me,' Reuben repeated. And even as he looked, again there was no shape of man before him.

He leapt up. A blinding flash had gone through him, an exalted energy possessed him. And he sprang through the snow like a superhuman creature.

Then quietly, like a final benediction, the last flakes fell, and Reuben, looking about, was astonished at the beauty of the world.

Ridge after ridge of pure white, pale shoulders of snow resting tranquil in a primeval solitude, and, higher up, beyond, stretching dim under the evening sky, banks of pale gold snow, and higher still, ridges of pale blue – softly coloured snow almost in the sky. Astonished, he stopped. And immediately he stopped something seemed to wake within him.

A dead weariness was in his limbs, a dry choking sensation in his throat. Water, he was choking for water. Then he dropped on his knees, and picking up some snow in his hands, he sucked it into his mouth.

That was better. Now, if he could force his lungs to go on he would soon be home. There was the Valley, he knew, that dip in the distance. And he began again.

It was night when he descended the last slope. By that time normal consciousness had almost left him – the only thing he was clearly aware of was thought of his mother. There would be peace at last.

343

The back of the Row faced the slope he descended. There would be no need to go through the street. Dimly he searched for light in the window of his home. He could not see any gleam.

He groped at the gate and crept drunkenly up the path of the little back garden. How terrible the silence! The world seemed to be slipping away from him. But a few moments more and all would be well! Martha was surely at home.

He lifted the latch and entered. No light, not a sound anywhere. There was a fire in the living-room, and immediately he began shuddering, with great convulsive violence. Swaying, he found the jar of paper spills, thrust one in the fire and managed to light the lamp.

'Martha!' he called in a whisper.

His clothes were very wet. He must get them off. He crawled upstairs, found fresh things, and carefully descended again.

And he wanted to sink down before the fire and give himself utterly to darkness. But no, he must change and wait patiently for Martha. She must be visiting someone. Ah, how lovely it would be to see her again! And, thinking of it, tears began to fall, without his knowing it, over his cheeks.

Laboriously he cast off his clothes and dressed in the others. And then he sat in the armchair and forced his eyes open. Only a few moments, only to look at his mother, touch her, and then he would give himself to the darkness rising so slowly up to him.

'Who is here?' he heard her voice strangely. She had seen the light.

She came in. And his lips had tried to stretch themselves in a smile.

She lurched into the room, blinking her eyes in tipsy surprise at the light. Her hat was askew, her mouth hung open; and she stood, holding the edge of the table, and stared at her son, her head wobbling forward.

'Reuben!' she exclaimed doubtfully, as though she was not quite sure.

And he, too, lurched forward to her, and then, a strange cry within his throat, he recoiled and fell, knocking his head against the table.

Two days, and he was dead.

Martha sat, her face yellow with fear, by the bed on which he lay. Only when people came to look at him, she waved them away, her words angry and grievous.

And yet he looked so content – she should have been comforted. His face was beautiful with a peace it had never possessed in life. A faint, incredibly delicate smile, touched his lips. The brows were chaste and untroubled as the brow of a gently sleeping child. It was the face of one for whom life had not yet begun.

Foreword by Lewis Davies

Lewis Davies is a writer and publisher. His work includes novels, plays, poetry and essays. He won the Rhys Davies short story award for his story *Mr Roopratna's Chocolate*. His play *Sex and Power at the Beau Rivage* about the meeting of Rhys Davies and D. H. Lawrence in the French Mediterranean town of Bandol was produced by Theatr Y Byd and toured nationally.

Cover Painting: *The Pilgrim* by Tony Goble

Tony Goble was born in 1943 in Newtown. He studied art from 1961 to 1964 at the Wrexham School of Art and was a leading member of the Welsh Group, exhibiting at the Royal Academy, the Royal College of Art and the National Portrait Gallery in London. He was Artist in Residence and Gallery Director at Llanover Hall Cardiff from 1979 to 2007. He exhibited widely in the UK and internationally, winning numerous awards and his work is held in many private and public collections. He died in 2007.

For more information www.welshartsarchive.org.uk

LIBRARY OF WALES

The Library of Wales is a Welsh Assembly Government project designed to ensure that all of the rich and extensive literature of Wales which has been written in English will now be made available to readers in and beyond Wales. Sustaining this wider literary heritage is understood by the Welsh Assembly Government to be a key component in creating and disseminating an ongoing sense of modern Welsh culture and history for the future Wales which is now emerging from contemporary society. Through these texts, until now unavailable or out-of-print or merely forgotten, the Library of Wales will bring back into play the voices and actions of the human experience that has made us, in all our complexity, a Welsh people.

The Library of Wales will include prose as well as poetry, essays as well as fiction, anthologies as well as memoirs, drama as well as journalism. It will complement the names and texts that are already in the public domain and seek to include the best of Welsh writing in English, as well as to showcase what has been unjustly neglected. No boundaries will limit the ambition of the Library of Wales to open up the borders that have denied some of our best writers a presence in a future Wales. The Library of Wales has been created with that Wales in mind: a young country not afraid to remember what it might yet become.

Dai Smith
Raymond Williams Chair in the Cultural History of Wales,
University of Wales, Swansea

LIBRARY OF WALES
FUNDED BY

Llywodraeth Cynulliad Cymru
Welsh Assembly Government

**CYNGOR LLYFRAU CYMRU
WELSH BOOKS COUNCIL**

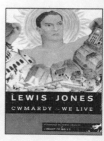
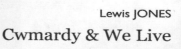

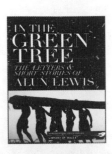
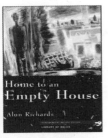
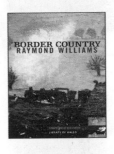
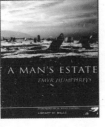
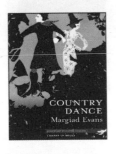